I broke cover and scrambled into the darkness. Reaching the mounds, I slithered on my belly like a lizard, groping, hoping to touch the softness of cotton. Nothing! Reaching the peak, I slid like a toboggan down the other side. Pushing snow first one way then the other with outstretched fingers, as if I were swimming the breast-stroke, I feared that my blind search was doomed to failure. Then . . . there it was! My hand closed around the soft bundle and I drew it to within inches of my face. I could feel the pills inside, hard as dried peas. I wanted to cry out at my success but instead rolled over and began to climb up the slope.

Someone grabbed hold of my left leg. I twisted round and duly received a poke in the stomach from a rifle barrel. I looked up and in the grey dimness saw the face of a young German soldier bearing down on me . . .

RESISTANCE

CRAIG SIMPSON

CORGI BOOKS

RESISTANCE

A CORGI BOOK 978 0 552 55571 5

Published in Great Britain by Corgi Books,
an imprint of Random House Children's Books

This edition published 2007

3 5 7 9 10 8 6 4

Copyright © Craig Simpson, 2007
Maps designed by James Fraser

Resistance is a work of fiction. Any resemblance of characters
to persons living or dead is purely coincidental.

Set in 12½/15pt Bembo

Corgi Books are published by Random House Children's Books
61-63 Uxbridge Road, London W5 5SA
a division of The Random House Group Ltd

Addresses for companies within The Random House Group Limited
can be found at:
www.randomhouse.co.uk/offices.htm

THE RANDOM HOUSE GROUP Limited Reg. No. 954009
www.kidsatrandomhouse.co.uk

The Random House Group Limited makes every effort to ensure that the
papers used in its books are made from trees that have been legally
sourced from well-managed and credibly certified forests. Our paper
procurement policy can be found at: www.randomhouse.co.uk/paper.htm.

Mixed Sources
Product group from well-managed
forests and other controlled sources
www.fsc.org Cert no. TT-COC-2139
© 1996 Forest Stewardship Council
FSC

A CIP catalogue record for this book is available from the British Library.

Printed and bound in Great Britain by
Cox & Wyman Ltd, Reading, Berkshire

To Elaine and Alec

ACKNOWLEDGEMENTS

Many thanks to Carolyn Whitaker,
Charlie Sheppard and Shannon Park for
all their effort and support.

An old Norwegian saying:

A man who is a man
goes on till he can do no more,
and then he goes twice as far

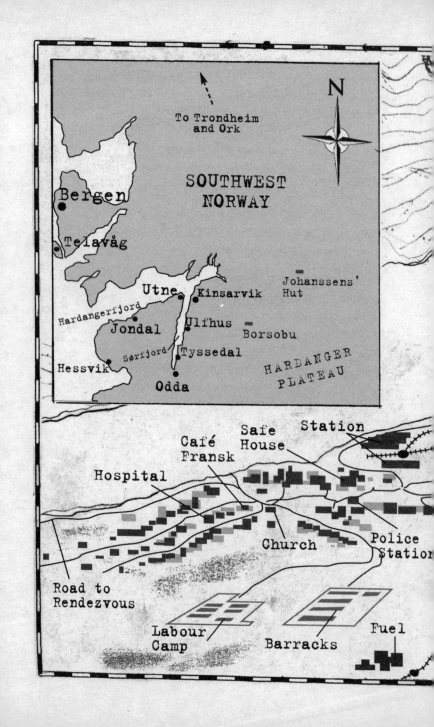

To Trondheim
and Ork

N

SOUTHWEST
NORWAY

Bergen

Telavåg

Utne Kinsarvik

Johanssens'
Hut

Hardangerfjord

Jondal Ulfhus

Borsobu

Sørfjord Tyssedal

Hessvik

HARDANGER
PLATEAU

Odda

Station

Safe
House

Café
Fransk

Hospital

Church

Police
Station

Road to
Rendezvous

Labour
Camp

Barracks

Fuel

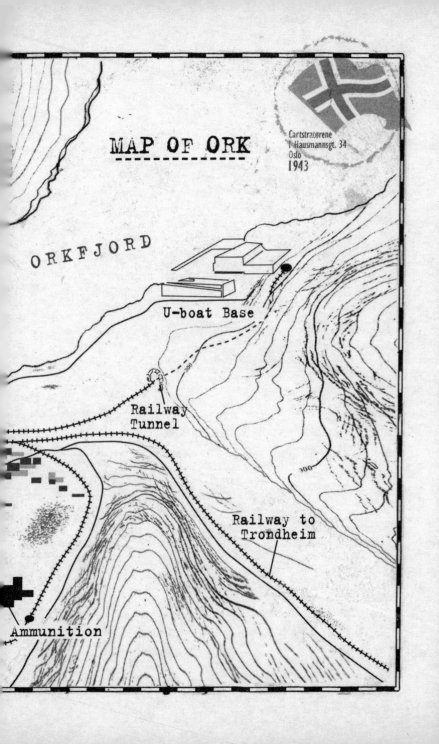

Chapter One

September 1943

Her dying cry echoed across the Hardanger plateau. She slumped onto her haunches, twisted awkwardly and fell heavily onto the soft snow.

My brother, Olaf, reloaded his rifle, took careful aim and fired again. She jerked and then lay silent.

'Still think we didn't need to shoot her,' I said.

He turned and stared at me coldly. 'Marek, look around you.'

I did, completing my circular gaze with an exaggerated shrug.

'I despair of you,' he muttered. Rising to his feet, he brushed the snow off his anorak and casually slung his rifle over his shoulder. 'You just don't get what all this is about, do you?'

Actually, I did. In the midst of the great wilderness, pitting our wits against nature, we needed to seize on any opportunity in order to survive. At least that's what Olaf wanted to believe. That's what made it exciting for him. The reality differed. We were hardly close to starvation.

Fixing on his skis, he thrust his poles into the snow

and leaped over the crest of the ridge, gliding effortlessly down the slope, knees slightly bent, poles tucked firmly into his ribs. I followed in his tracks.

For three days we had ventured from our hut early each morning and scanned the whiteness for telltale tracks. And until today we had seen nothing.

At first I thought my watery eyes had deceived me. Although I was wearing goggles, I had to continually blink away the stabbing pains in my eyeballs. It felt as if someone had thrown sand in my face and much of it had stuck. Convinced I was just one step away from snow blindness, I complained bitterly to Olaf. In a huff, he peered beneath my goggles and cursed. 'You're fine, so stop whining.'

The cluster of distant dots turned out to be a herd of reindeer heading southwest, and not spots before my eyes. My brother's excitement bordered on the maniacal and, briefly, he became a man possessed solely by the uncompromising, deep-rooted instincts of the hunter. Luckily the sweeping ridge provided cover, enabling us to approach the herd downwind and without their knowing. Had they seen or smelled us, they'd have bolted and my brother would have proven inconsolable.

I caught him up beside our kill. Even in death she looked magnificent, her thick brown coat shining and her hoofs broad. She had not yet shed her antlers; they were about three feet long – I had seen larger but nevertheless her velvet felt wonderful to the touch. The thought that she'd survived the hell of the Hardanger for years only to be felled by a young man desperate to prove himself saddened me. Olaf wasted no time in reaching for his hunting knife, checking its blade held a sharp edge by running a finger along its full length. He intended me to receive a lesson – a harsh lesson but one that might save a man's life. That was Olaf through and through, always taking it upon himself to teach me everything he knew, whether I was interested or not.

Unfastening the straps of his rucksack, he lifted the flap and removed two small tin mugs. Then, carving into the poor beast's throat, he positioned one beneath her dripping blood until it brimmed. He held it out towards me. 'Well, go on then, Marek,' he said. Her thick red juices steamed, as did our breaths. 'Quickly, before it freezes.'

Reluctantly I took the mug and held it close to my lips. The sharp, metallic smell sickened me. I didn't feel that hungry. Olaf filled his mug and thrust it above his head, intent on celebrating his first kill. In the past it had always been Father who squeezed the trigger. Howling like a rabid wolf, Olaf cheered loudly enough for the gods to hear him, and then adopted a rather stern expression, one in which his square jaw sharpened and jutted out, and his blond eyebrows lifted to reveal the full blueness of his eyes.

'Here's to us, Marek. And may we live to see a free Norway. May we Jøssings one day liberate our great country.'

I gazed into my mug. Not to drink to such a toast

would be tantamount to treason and so I reluctantly pressed it to my lips, tilted back my head and swallowed the warm, sticky juice with pride, desperately trying to forget what it was that was slipping down my throat. Even so, I nearly puked and the silvery taste lingered long after I'd emptied my mug.

My brother appeared delighted that I'd participated in his ritual without my usual complaints. I had done so only because I did indeed consider myself a Jøssing, a 'true Norwegian'.

He slapped me heartily on the back. Then, like a man consumed with the heady euphoria of altitude sickness, he gulped madly from his mug, refilling it twice, not caring a jot that he spilled a little down his anorak. 'Ah, Marek,' he said, smacking his lips contentedly. 'Here, we are truly free.' I believed him.

The Hardanger was vast, mile after mile of virtually uninhabitable wasteland freckled with lakes and meandering rivers and streams that for much of the year remained frozen to a depth that would support the weight of man, sledge and beast. Although not far from Oslo to the east or Stavanger to the west, and despite being south of the Arctic Circle, to tread on this place was akin to a trip to the North Pole. At least that's what Father said. And its landscape deceived. Although there were no great mountainous peaks, the plateau lay more than three thousand feet above sea level and so the air was thin and could alter a man. And once on it, you were truly exposed, truly naked before nature. The

Hardanger knew no mercy and could kill a man in hours with its howling breath of ice wind. Unless, that is, you showed it respect and did not attempt to tame it. For it could not be tamed.

Olaf and I grew up in Ulfhus, a village on the shores of the Sørfjord, close to where the narrow finger of water joins the much broader Hardangerfjord and a good few miles from Odda to the south. Father, a local schoolmaster, gave his blessing to our expedition despite Mother's protestations and tears. In truth, I'd been quite shocked when he agreed to it, as it broke so many of the rules: no travel without proper documents; must stay within thirty miles of home; no hunting allowed; no guns to be carried. Normally Father's a stickler for rules, saying they give order to our lives and make many things between men possible that otherwise would not be. Perhaps the fact that the rules being broken were not our rules, not Norwegian rules, but rather rules imposed by the Germans, led to his uncharacteristic display of defiance. Father liked being defiant when it came to tyranny. And so did Olaf. And so did I, despite the risks. Like many others, we wore paperclips on our lapels, a tiny symbol of our resistance. Trivial, perhaps, but it was an open gesture and strangely unifying for a people whose national flag had been torn down and replaced by Nazi swastikas.

My brother began skinning and butchering the deer, slicing right down her belly and peeling back the flesh. Once he'd cut through her membranes, much of what lay coiled inside her slithered out and began to melt the snow. 'Marek,' he said, 'we'll have a grand feast tonight.'

I shared in his delight at the thought of a memorable stew. We had some dried fruit, a couple of potatoes and other bits and pieces back at our hut, enough to fill the pot twice over. Located close to a sparse and rare glade of birch trees providing ample firewood, our hut, the Borsobu, originally belonged to our grandfather. He'd built it after falling in love with the small, gently sloping Borso valley as a boy. Now it belonged to Father. Reaching for my knife, I knelt down next to Olaf and began carving the bloody flesh.

He paused from his toil and punched my shoulder lightly. 'See, Marek, isn't this just a perfect moment? Two brothers working alongside each other, doing what men have to, to survive.'

'Still don't think we needed to shoot her. We've got enough food already,' I complained.

He looked hurt, perhaps even a little angry. I think I'd shattered his dream because he didn't speak again for several minutes, apart from occasionally cursing to himself as he tore meat from bone and sinew. We'd brought plenty of cloth to wrap up our kill and to prevent the blood from staining our rucksacks. As Olaf stuffed her meat into his bag, I recalled that the soft bone marrow contained much-needed sustenance. Using all my weight I managed to snap one of her leg bones and extracted some of the pale mush with my knife. It would add richness to the stew. While I scraped and prodded, my brother set to work trimming fat from the hide.

Olaf's first shot, the one that had brought down the reindeer, had stampeded the rest of the herd, and I'd watched them race, spring and lollop until out of view. In the eerie, frozen quiet that remained I realized for the first time just how alone we were. The nearest village, Kinsarvik, lay at least a day's hard skiing west, followed by a slippery descent from the plateau into the wooded Husedalen valley. And unless itinerant hunters wandered our way, no one would hear us shout, even though such calls carried miles over the snow and ice. And yet, curiously, it wasn't totally silent. Not all the time. Now and again the earth spoke. From beneath our boots cracks reverberated, each startling me, for each lacked a warning. It was the sound of the earth freezing – the sound of winter.

'What shall we do with this?' Cupped in both hands, my brother held up the beast's steaming stomach.

'That's *disgusting*. Throw it away,' I cried. I caught a whiff of the awful smell of her innards and it led to an involuntary, clenching spasm in my own belly. I placed a gloved hand over my nose and mouth and refused to breathe.

'No, we'll take it. And do you know why?'

I stared at him blankly and he shook his head at me.

'Man cannot survive on meat and fat alone, Marek. Least, not for long, and if you want to avoid getting sick. Here, wrap it up as well. The moss inside it will boil up nicely. It's a good source of complex sugars and goodness.' He smiled triumphantly. Another lesson for *little brother*. Appalled, I cringed as I pressed it deep into my rucksack.

Not for the first time during our trip, I wished I were Lars Andersson. Lars should have come with us. He's Olaf's best friend: they're generally inseparable and, with both being eighteen and six feet tall, crowned by blond locks and prone to dressing alike, some mistook them for brothers, twins even. But just days before we set out, Lars had been struck down by *omgangssykdom*, with the usual diarrhoea, vomiting and feeling of snakes wriggling inside his belly. Having drunk his *kull*, a horrid black liquid charcoal, he retired to bed and told the world to keep well away. Just the thought of Lars tucked up snugly beneath his quilt filled me with envy in spite of his discomfort. I suppose we should have taken it as a sign. After all, those prone to the sickness usually come down with it at around the time one season changes to another. Like a barometer, Lars's green complexion should have alerted us to the imminent onset of winter – real winter, hard and uncompromising, with wrestling winds and cold that sapped life from every being. Not that Olaf would have changed his plans. Ever since finishing high school in the summer he'd spoken of little else than his 'expedition'. For him it was all part of his rites of passage to manhood, as important as the *russ*, a celebration that always takes place immediately after graduation. Endless partying and creating mayhem at ungodly hours are the order of the day. For the one and only time in our lives, such behaviour is tolerated by our parents without fuss or complaint. It's as if they're saying, 'Go on, be stupid. Do it now and get it out of your system.' Naturally Olaf made the most of it. He partied as hard as anyone and drank more beer than I thought humanly possible without requiring hospitalization. His memory of it all remains vague, or so he insists, and he looked quite shocked when reminded of the improper suggestions he made to Mrs Tørstig, a rather large lady who embarrasses easily. Luckily Mr Tørstig saw the funny side and didn't floor him with a clenched fist.

We had made quite a mess. Though our rucksacks bulged, together they held but a small fraction of the reindeer's considerable mass. The carcass and intestines lay untidily around a large red smudge in an otherwise white world. I thought the foxes would appreciate the plentiful scraps.

Olaf hauled his stuffed rucksack onto his shoulders and tightened the straps. 'Come on, Marek, race you back to the Borsobu.' He hurriedly attached his boots to his skis and pulled his poles from where he'd stabbed them into the drift.

In any race on snow or ice, Olaf would receive the gold medal and I the silver. Past school champion at both downhill and cross-country disciplines, he's built for Norway's outdoors and had mastered the telemark technique by the time his friends had learned to crawl. Knowing this, and being a full four years younger, and weaker, I decided a race would achieve nothing other than to confirm his prowess and render me depressed. So I followed some distance behind him, taking pleasure in making good use of the compressed snow in his tracks.

Our hut lay just a few hundred yards ahead when I heard the noise. Initially faint, the hum grew into the characteristic whine of propeller blades. Olaf heard it too and came to an abrupt stop. Shielding our eyes, we searched the sky.

Flying exceptionally low, the aircraft seemed invisible until it suddenly appeared above a ridge at one end of the Borso valley. It roared and spluttered over our heads and then banked into a tight right-hand turn, climbing slightly in the manoeuvre. The howling anger of its engine faded as it flew away and then slowly grew again as it broke out of its turn and headed back for a second pass.

I wanted to hide. But in the bleakness of the Hardanger we were totally exposed and at the mercy of any sharp-eyed hunter with the benefit of a bird's-eye view. My heart drummed at the sight of the black crosses of the Luftwaffe painted on the wings and tail. I felt a sharp prickle at the nape of my neck and shuddered as it worked its way down my back.

'Probably thinks we're the Resistance,' shouted Olaf.

Rumours abounded that the Resistance Movement, the MILORG, was growing every day. These brave men and women often took refuge in the wilderness when their cover had been blown or they feared reprisals for their violent acts of sabotage.

Norway provides many places to hide. In deepest winter the Hardanger is the most perfect place to bide your time – remote, treacherous and blanketed by almost continuous darkness. Fiercely inhospitable, its ferocious winds and blizzards can force a man to his knees, make him crawl – bury him even. Alas, true winter was only just knocking at our door. It wasn't yet the most perfect place to hide. Thankfully Olaf did not seem unduly concerned. I took heart from his lack of fear.

The aircraft made its swooping second pass. I glimpsed the pilot staring from his cockpit. Hell, I almost waved to him. Perhaps I should have. The plane continued into the distance.

'Bastards!' my brother shouted.

'He'll report our position,' I said. My head filled with a vision of hundreds of crack Nazi troops descending on the Borsobu, or of the hut being bombed while we slept.

'So what?' My brother waved his ski poles in a 'couldn't give a damn' gesture.

I loved his healthy disregard for authority and wished I had his confidence. When it came to the Germans, he delighted in following them down the street and spitting at the back of their heads. And he relished every opportunity to annoy and inconvenience them – always being painfully slow to produce his papers, giving wrong directions should they ask, letting down their tyres and peeing into their petrol and diesel tanks. Often he talked about joining the Norwegian army and ridding our country of 'vermin'. Of course, I pointed out to him that unfortunately we no longer had an army as such, but details like this made little difference to him. In his head, he was a soldier.

'One day, Marek,' he'd say to me, 'one day we'll kick the bastards back to Berlin.'

Naturally I prayed it all turned out to be true and I dreamed of taking part in the 'kicking', but reckoned it was best not to hold my breath in anticipation, as the outlook for Europe seemed bleak. Olaf slid on down towards our hut in a series of tight, effortless turns on his skis.

I heard the faint whine of the aircraft again and called out, 'He's coming back.'

My brother had a favourite saying – 'If you've got an annoying itch, scratch it.' I saw him swing his rifle from his shoulder, slide open the breech and reach into his pocket for a bullet.

'Are you mad?'

Ignoring me, Olaf loaded his weapon. Turning towards the plane, he pressed the rifle butt hard into his shoulder and peered along the barrel.

I panicked. Shrugging off my rucksack, I set off towards him as fast as I could, flinging one ski in front of the other. 'You'll never do it. You're insane.'

The plane skimmed the ice at an altitude I guessed to be no more than fifty feet. A distant speck like an insect, it grew larger as it bore down on us, its course unwavering. 'Put your rifle down, Olaf!' I cried, but to no avail.

I think he pulled the trigger at the same moment as the pilot opened fire: I saw the recoil of his rifle but heard not a single shot – only the plane's *rat-a-tat-tat*. As the bullets forged two parallel lines in the snow, each shell ripping and sending up a spray of ice, I raced towards him and made no attempt to brake. I threw myself forward, intent on bowling him over. It was all I could think of. As my shoulder sank into his ribs, I felt us tumble and our skis tear from their bindings. The aircraft's fire ripped past us.

We lay still. I held my breath. The plane roared into the distance. Only when I was certain it wasn't coming back did I dare move a muscle.

Olaf sat up and gazed angrily towards the horizon. 'Bastard!' he yelled.

I frowned at him. 'You idiot! That's the stupidest thing you've ever done,' I cried. 'You almost got us both killed.'

He reached for his rifle and said calmly, 'But he missed. We're both fine. Just one more shot, Marek, that's all I needed.'

It was only later, inside our hut, that I saw the two bullet holes in Olaf's rucksack. The blood drained from my face.

Chapter Two

Our meal that evening should have been eaten amid high spirits. After all, the stove crackled and radiated much-needed warmth, and the stewing pot's lid rattled as its contents simmered, each belch of steam filling the hut with the wonderful aroma of succulent venison and rich gravy. But Olaf seemed unusually quiet. He sat in a corner cleaning his rifle. Somehow I knew the incident that afternoon had brought the truth about the war into sharp focus. It had suddenly become very, very personal. For sure, we had all been inconvenienced by the occupation, but until today neither of us had been truly touched by it, neither of us had been *shot at*.

Built on solid stone foundations, the Borsobu had been constructed some fifty years ago out of pine brought by dog sledge from our village. Made of vertical timbers under a gently sloping roof, remarkably it had withstood the worst the Hardanger could throw at it, only requiring occasional minor repairs. Dozens of reindeer hides liberated by generations of huntsmen plastered the walls and back of the door. They did a fine job of keeping in the warmth and covering the tiny gaps through which the ice wind whistled and howled. And they gave the air a slightly musky but undeniably pleasant odour that always seemed so very welcoming to a weary traveller. Though quite large – about twenty-five feet by twelve – the hut was pretty basic inside. A few pine stools, a couple of cupboards for emergency food supplies, racks and hooks bearing the weight of cooking utensils, plates, bowls and mugs, and, of course, a stove. The stove was the focal point, the heart of the place.

I thought of Father and the many times he'd reminded me of the simplicity of the Borsobu, stressing that despite its sparseness it contained all that a man really needed. Usually such reminders fell at about the same time as my birthday and again at Christmas, when I let slip my desire for a brand-new something or other. 'Quite unnecessary, Marek,' he'd say brusquely. 'Got more than you need already.' Sadly it was hard to argue against such truths.

While I stirred the pot, Olaf examined the holes in his rucksack.

'Well, Marek, guess you saved my life.'

I looked up from the stove and saw his fingers poking through the two perfectly round holes in the canvas. He wiggled them and laughed, a laugh that sounded forced, as if out of politeness at a friend's joke that simply wasn't funny.

'Maybe,' I replied. 'Reckon you should thank that reindeer too. If it weren't for your rucksack being stuffed with it—'

'Yes,' he interrupted, 'but you shoved me out of the

line of fire at considerable risk to yourself. Wait till I tell Father. He'll be so proud.'

I couldn't help but smile. Just the thought of Father being proud of *me*. I had saved his first born, his favourite. I almost couldn't wait to get home and for Olaf to tell the tale. I ladled some stew into a pair of bowls and we sat close to the stove and ate. The meat was tender and the potatoes had softened to a mush you could suck through your teeth. It would have slipped down a treat had the flavour not been so overpowering, so velvety rich and with a horrid metallic edge. I reckoned the sharpness came from the handful of moss my brother insisted on shoving into the pot. I wished he hadn't.

'We'll set off first thing tomorrow,' Olaf announced once he'd finished noisily scraping his bowl.

'But I thought you wanted to stay another couple of days.'

'I did. But you're probably right about that pilot. He will report our position and, who knows, maybe they'll send out a patrol. Could prove difficult if they catch us. I mean, we're not supposed to be here.'

'True. And we're not allowed to carry guns or hunt reindeer either,' I added sharply.

He grinned. 'Is there any more stew?'

As our bellies expanded and a warm contentment grew within us, we talked of the future. Olaf had been accepted at the University of Oslo to study medicine. In just a few weeks he would set off from our home on the

Sørfjord to begin his new life. Through a family friend, Father had arranged lodgings in the centre of Oslo, and Olaf looked forward to a new independence and freedom to get drunk as often as he could afford. It sounded exciting. I knew he couldn't wait to be rid of the constraints of family life. He often spoke of a yearning to seek out his own destiny, saying he longed to test life's winds and tides for himself. But his travel papers had not yet come through and he feared the Germans would prevent him from going. Recklessly he said he'd go whatever, his defiance shining as brightly as the midsummer sun.

Looking at him, strong as an ox, fire in his eyes, hatred in his voice, I couldn't help thinking that trouble lay ahead for my big brother. He wore his national pride on his sleeve, and that, I thought, might prove his undoing. I tried to hide my fears, disguising my fretting with murmurs of agreement and frequent nods. 'I think there's some coffee left,' I said when he finally paused for breath.

He put down his bowl and clapped his hands. 'Can do better than coffee, Marek. I have a little something rather special tucked away.' He rose from his stool and began ferreting about in a bag in which he'd brought a spare set of clothing. He emerged from his foraging looking exceptionally pleased with himself and clutching a bottle of transparent liquid. I instantly knew what it was – *aquavit*, potato whisky!

'Where did you get that?'

'Ask no questions and I'll tell no lies. Here, give us your mug.' He poured large shots of the colourless, potentially lethal brew. 'Here's to a successful hunting trip, to saving my life, and to Fritz getting his arse kicked. *Skål!*'

'*Skål!*' I cried. We downed our drinks in one, our eyes locked together in brotherly competition. Needless to say, I choked first. As my throat burned, I gasped for breath and wondered if my eyes had actually popped out of their sockets because they certainly felt like they had. Tears blurred my vision.

'Wonderful!' he said, smacking his lips. He sounded just like Father. 'Can you taste the caraway, Marek?'

I couldn't. It felt as if my tongue had dissolved. Hearing the chink of bottle against tin, I realized he was refilling our mugs. I wiped my eyes and braced myself. After our sixth or seventh '*Skål!*' the world seemed a much nicer, cosier place.

'So, Marek, what are you going to do with your life?'

By now, with the bottle nearly empty, we lay on our mattresses of reindeer hides, staring at the roof of the hut, which, curiously, had begun to rotate slowly clockwise.

'No idea,' I replied with a distinct slur. And I spoke the truth. I had absolutely no idea what I would do when I left school. It was just another way in which I differed from Olaf. He had decided years ago that he would become a doctor and from that moment on everything seemed set, mapped out, understood. I lacked such ambition. Mostly my brain was preoccupied with thoughts of Olga Radervit, by far the prettiest girl for miles. Briefly I recalled her bright, hazel eyes and thought them like deep wells. My heart whirled and my pulse raced. Olaf reached into his rucksack and took out a cigarette.

'Where the hell did you get that?'

He ignored me. Using a small piece of kindling drawn from the stove, he lit it and drew deeply, exhaling with immense satisfaction. 'Nothing like Virginia tobacco, Marek. Here, try it.' He passed it to me and I pressed it to my lips. Inhaling made me cough, of course, but the mellow sweetness was wonderfully exotic and a perfect accompaniment to the lingering aftertaste of the *aquavit*.

'These English brands are definitely the finest,' Olaf declared authoritatively.

A flash of dizzying panic fizzed through me, as if I were traversing a deep crevasse on a tightrope. I gawped at him.

'Don't worry, Marek. Nobody's watching.'

Not for the first time I realized that my big brother, for all his stature, learning and ability, could be more foolish than a blind elk trying to cross a busy street. If he was caught in possession of an English cigarette, the Germans would suppose that he had contacts with the MILORG or, worse, that he was a Resistance fighter himself. That would mean arrest, interrogation by the

Gestapo, followed by execution. All for a few puffs of tobacco. I couldn't credit such stupidity.

Although I desperately wanted to know from whom he'd got the cigarettes, I knew he wouldn't tell me. At least not beyond saying that it was from a friend of a friend of a friend, and someone I'd never met. I reckoned many of his acquisitions came from our flourishing black market. For the right money or favours you could acquire just about anything, no questions asked. But I think my brother believed that such activity under the noses of the Germans brought him closer to the Resistance. He enjoyed the thrill and revelled in the danger.

I stared at him as he lay on his back blowing smoke rings, each drifting and curling upwards before finally dissipating beneath the roof. The more I thought about it, the more I realized that his recklessness was a vital part of his being. Of course, the stakes were high, but to have courage to look danger in the eye, to stand tall and not show fear or cowardice, were traits that made Olaf Olaf, and also made him a Jøssing. If our country was full of such men and women, then surely there had to be hope, no matter how bad things got. And I had shared his English cigarette. I had given Fritz the two-fingered gesture too, and I suddenly felt stronger for having done so.

'You're good at fixing cars and stuff, Marek. You should think about becoming an engineer or a mechanic.' He turned to look at me, his eyes wide with encouragement.

'Not quite what Father had in mind,' I replied. Father rather liked the idea of my becoming a lawyer or a dentist. Neither occupation appealed.

'*Stuff* what he thinks. Do what you want to do, Marek, and screw everyone else. Do what brings you happiness, not what makes someone else happy.'

I liked his logic and couldn't help but grin at his open display of disrespect towards Father. It reminded me of their many arguments, usually over insignificant trifles. Father might say, 'Chop up some wood, Olaf.' He'd reply, 'Do it yourself, you old fart, you need the exercise.' And from then on it was downhill until, inevitably, they faced each other like two prizefighters. Occasionally they might wrestle a bit, but always without real aggression or malice. Mother says that Olaf is reaching that difficult age, that the time is nearing for him to fly the nest. And she says Father cannot cope with it. She says Father's difficult *whatever* his age.

I mulled over what Olaf had said and decided he might well be right. Marek Olsen, engineer, had a certain ring to it. It *was* what I excelled at. After all, for years I'd spent much of my spare time tinkering with broken cars, motorcycles – basically anything mechanical that needed fixing. I loved dismantling and rebuilding things and had a vast collection of manuals whose pages had grown soiled, dog-eared and loose from their bindings.

Before turning in, I spent a while gazing through the Borsobu's small window. The landscape shimmered and glowed under a crescent moon and countless stars. Now and again I thought I saw the distant flicker of the northern lights and imagined that somewhere far to the north a great battle was being waged, our Thor defending us good Norwegians once more against the demons. I prayed he'd win such an epic battle. Eventually I lay back down, closed my eyes and dreamed of becoming Norway's greatest engineer, building the world's fastest car or the fastest aircraft. Warmed to the bone by the whisky, I drifted to sleep amid a contented haze. I felt safe. In fact, I decided, it had been a perfect day. Our near-miss already seemed a distant memory, almost as if it had never really happened, as if I'd simply imagined the aircraft swooping in low, as if those bullets weren't real at all.

I awoke to see Olaf already up and busily packing for our journey. My head throbbed, my brain felt shrivelled and my tongue like chewed leather. My complaints and groans were met with pitiless laughter and gruffly spoken orders to rouse myself. I think he felt as hungover as I did.

It had snowed during the night, about a foot at a guess. But the temperature had risen and that meant the snow would be wet and make skiing all the more arduous. It remained overcast and I suspected more snow was on the way. The wind had picked up too, and snapped about my ears when I poked my head out of the hut. I retreated inside and felt glad to be going home. We had a small breakfast of dried meats and biscuits washed down with a little weak coffee, and then set off, having made sure the Borsobu was tidy and welcoming in case anyone should pass by, unlikely though that was until next spring.

By the following afternoon we'd covered nearly thirty miles and my limbs felt hellishly sore. We paused to rest at the edge of a pine forest lining one side of a gently sweeping valley. We were very close to the edge of the plateau now. Soon we would begin our slippery descent towards the village of Kinsarvik. Desperate to rub the cramp from my calves, I shed my skis and found a boulder to sit on. Although I knew Olaf wanted to keep going, he did not complain about my frailty, instead suggesting we build a small fire and boil up some snow for a hot drink. He set about the task while I rubbed, squeezed, stretched and cursed at my lack of fitness. When it came to stamina, I took after Mother. She too grew breathless at times. Father and Olaf, however, were as strong as bears and possessed the stamina of an elk.

'There you are, Marek. Drink it slowly.' The mug of coffee warmed my gloves and the steam felt refreshing against my face.

Our wariness of stumbling across German patrols grew as we came closer to home. As far as we knew, they didn't usually bother venturing more than half a day's trek from their warm beds, and so until now we hadn't been too concerned. But increasingly we spent more and more time gazing across the landscape, squinting to detect tracks or figures moving against the white backdrop. We also strained our ears listening out for aircraft, and Olaf swore that if he got another chance, he wouldn't miss again. Good shot though he was, I doubted him but said nothing. The Germans had threatened to shoot anyone caught hunting deer. But then again, the Germans threatened a good many things. Barely a week passed without some new threat or edict being plastered onto church notice boards or stuck onto lampposts. I didn't really believe for a minute that they'd shoot two boys just for having a little fun. Olaf seemed convinced they would. And strangely that added to his enjoyment.

The wind gradually changed direction as I sipped from my mug, the mild westerly giving way to the breath from the north. The weather could, and often did, change in a blink. A northerly meant an abrupt fall in temperature, maybe to minus ten degrees, perhaps even lower. Thinking of home, I swigged down my coffee, packed away our mugs and set about extinguishing our fire by kicking snow onto the glowing embers. Without warning, Olaf suddenly dropped to the ground.

'Keep still, Marek. Don't move a muscle.'

Naturally I froze. He rolled in the snow towards me and, once beside me, pointed across the valley. 'There are three of them,' he announced.

I could only see a white blur. But my eyes gradually adjusted and then I saw them, three stooping figures skiing slowly in single file about two hundred yards away. Worryingly, they were heading towards us. Olaf seized his rifle, rested it on the snow in front of him and pointed it in their direction.

'Are they Germans?' I whispered.

He stared with great concentration and then shook his head. 'Don't think so. Hard to tell. They might be.'

My heart quickened. I recalled the various lies we'd concocted before setting out on our trip to explain why we were there – an aunt was sick and we were on our way to visit her; we were lost; we were driving to Odda when our car broke down and we were taking a short cut – all utterly useless reasons, of course, all lacking an ounce of credibility. And then there was Olaf's rifle. I wanted to shout to him to bury it before they spotted it. But I said nothing.

'Damn,' he said. 'Probably saw smoke from our fire. I thought those branches were too damp.' He tutted. 'Listen, Marek, if they speak to us, leave the talking to me. If it's a German patrol, I'll make our excuses. And if they're Norwegian, possibly MILORG even, then for God's sake don't ask them any questions.'

I looked at my brother quizzically. It seemed odd that, even if they were friendly faces, I still had to remain the dumb brother. But his expression appeared more serious than I'd seen it for a long time. I decided it was best to behave as instructed.

The leading skier suddenly stopped and looked straight towards us. He pulled off his anorak hood and lifted his goggles onto his forehead. Only about fifty yards now separated us and I guessed we'd been spotted. Sure enough, he waved and gestured for us to approach. His two comrades stopped beside him. Although I could see a rifle slung across his shoulder, the others did not appear to be armed.

'Nothing for it, Marek,' said Olaf. He stood up, waved and shouted, 'Hello!' He turned and said to me grimly, 'Stay here and look after the rifle. Only come if I call you.' He fixed on his skis and slid off towards them. I had never felt so scared, not even on the afternoon the Germans first drove through our village in a convoy of trucks. I shall never forget their faces – wretched, soulless expressions amid a threatening sea of grey uniforms.

As Olaf reached the group, their leader skied a few yards forward to greet him. The other two remained behind, leaning on their poles. I watched a while as they spoke, and blew a huge sigh of relief when, finally, they shook hands. Olaf turned and gestured for me to join them. I grabbed my rucksack and his rifle and hurried down the slope.

'This is my brother,' said Olaf. The man nodded a greeting to me. His blond curly hair lay matted with sweat, and a week's growth on his chin indicated to me that he'd been living rough. He looked weary, his skin scorched sore by the sun, wind and altitude. I did not recognize him. To my relief, though, he was Norwegian and spoke with an accent I placed much further north, possibly as far as Narvik or Tromsø. Out of politeness I might normally have asked. But I remembered what Olaf had told me. So I asked nothing.

'We have just spent a few days at our hut,' said Olaf. 'It's in the Borso valley. It's not marked on any map. If the weather turns harsh you're welcome to use it.' From his anorak pocket he took out his map and showed the man its location. The man seemed grateful. As he squinted at where Olaf's gloved finger pointed, I looked at his comrades and smiled. They did not smile back. They had remained several yards behind, had kept their hoods raised and their goggles over their eyes. One maintained a vigil of scanning the surroundings while the other simply stared at me. They were clad in white, with white canvas rucksacks, and at first I did not notice their machine guns because they too were white. They looked like they had been painted. They hung at their sides at waist level on white straps running up and over their shoulders – virtually invisible at a distance. I could not help but stare and wondered what mischief they'd been up to or were planning.

'Come across anyone else?' asked the man. Olaf shook his head. 'Good.'

'There was an aircraft,' I blurted. The man's eyes darted sideways and his glare cut into me. 'Made several low passes and opened fire on us,' I added. Something about him led me to think he didn't believe me. 'Show him the bullet holes, Olaf.'

Looking apologetic, my brother twisted round at the waist to reveal his rucksack with its two round bullet holes. 'I didn't think it worth mentioning. It didn't hang around long. With the weather closing in, I'm sure they won't bother sending a patrol,' he explained.

The man nodded, looked at me again and said, 'Takk.' He shook both our hands.

'Good hunting,' said Olaf with a grin.

The man waved to his men and they set off towards the pine forest behind us. None of them looked back.

'Come on, Marek. We must press on while it's still light. Don't want to be camping out here. I can smell snow in the air.'

'They were MILORG, weren't they?'

'Best not to ask,' he replied. 'What you don't know can't harm you.'

'They were, weren't they?'

Reluctantly he nodded.

'Thought so. Did you see their machine guns? They'd painted them white.'

'I think the other two were British commandos,' he said.

'*Commandos.*' I stopped and looked back to the distant tree line but saw nothing except their tracks. 'Really?'

'Think so. That's why they hung back. Just in case.' He paused and rested his weight on his ski poles. 'Well done for not asking any questions. You listened to me for once.'

'Of course,' I said sarcastically.

'No joke, Marek. If even for a moment they had

thought us Quislings, we'd be done for.'

'Collaborators. Us? *Impossible*. We're good Norwegians.'

'Yes, Marek, and be grateful they thought so. You do know, don't you, that their orders are to shoot Quislings?'

I gulped and nodded like I knew, but in truth I didn't until that moment. Norway suddenly seemed a very dangerous place. Not only was there the risk of being shot by Germans, there seemed to be an equal risk of being shot by our fellow countrymen. We pressed on, and as I slid one ski in front of the other, a thought struck me. 'Olaf, how did they know we were really just returning from a hunting trip?'

'Blood, Marek. He saw the blood on my anorak. That persuaded him.'

With our skis resting yoke-like across our shoulders, we traipsed down the steep forested Husedalen valley, past the thundering waterfalls and towards Kinsarvik. With dusk upon us, the cluster of lights below beckoned us on. Across the narrow, glistening mouth of the Sørfjord I caught glimpses of the tiny hamlets of Utne and Grimo on the far shore and heard the engines of the Kvanndal ferry. A small town on a glacier-forged ridge at the mouth of the Kinso river, Kinsarvik was once an important Viking marketplace. Spring meltwater from high up on the Hardanger plateau tumbles through the valley, roars past the town and into the fjord. We headed through the side streets and turned left towards home. It would have been easier to go by the road overlooking the fjord but Olaf insisted we took a higher, parallel path to avoid the attentions of any patrols. I wasn't about to argue. Away from the Hardanger the snow lay as a thin, threadbare rug, mostly far too slushy to ski. Passing through leafless orchards, through copses and narrow fields, we could see our village just ahead. We finally decided it was safe to join the road.

Our village, Ulfhus, clung to the shore of the fjord, creeping up the steep slope of granite as far as the road to Odda. Beyond, a few scattered farmhouses lay at the end of winding tracks. I've often wondered why it's there at all, as there seems little point to the place. Its fragile existence reminded me of small alpine plants and lichens that grip precariously to exposed rocks. You look at them and marvel at their achievement while at the same time feeling sorry that they ended up in such a miserable location. From windows lights glowed.

'Poor Lars missed a fine expedition,' declared Olaf. 'I'll visit him later to see if he's recovered.'

And, no doubt, to give him a blow-by-blow account of your first kill, not to mention being shot at, I thought. Now there's an evening's worth of tales. We strolled down towards the small harbour. Our house lay one street up from the shore. Most houses are alike in Ulfhus, at least outwardly. Timber clad and painted a dull reddish brown, they form rows like troops advancing as far as the rugged terrain will allow. I saw the outline of the church silhouetted against the shimmering surface of the fjord. Mother and Father had stopped attending soon after the invasion and I wasn't sure why at first. Father struggled to explain. He said that it wasn't that he'd lost his faith in God, rather he needed time to reassess the Lutheran doctrine. I had absolutely no idea what the hell he was talking about, but guessed it had something to do with the fact that Martin Luther had been German. So I stayed away as well.

Unusually the streets were deserted. We saw no one as we trudged down the road. Then Olaf stopped. 'Something's going on,' he said.

'What?'

'Don't know. What's that truck doing there?'

He pointed to where the road curved sharply left beside the harbour. Partially blocking the road and teetering on the edge of the quay, the truck appeared empty, its grey canvas awning tied back. Olaf rested his skis against a wall and removed his rucksack and rifle. 'Come on, let's take a closer look.' We crept forward, keeping to the gloom hugging the side of the buildings.

An army truck meant soldiers. But why? Why in our village? I couldn't fathom it. The place held little significance to the Germans and merited just a handful of servants of the Reich being stationed here. These were mostly middle-aged and elderly low-ranking troops who desperately missed home and their families and wanted to see an end to the war as much as we did.

We made our way along the street until the harbour

came into view. We crouched beside a small red *rorbuer*, one of several tiny huts used by visiting fishermen. I scanned the handful of bars and shops that lined the quayside. Outside a large guesthouse belonging to the Johanssens, two German guards stood to attention while somehow managing to look bored and miserable.

'What's going on?' I whispered.

'Trouble.'

My brother's reply did nothing to quell my anxiety. It occurred to me that our illegal hunting trip might have been the reason for the troops. Were they here on a *razzia*, searching for us? Were we to be rounded up and questioned? Locked up even? Sent to the camps? I broke into a cold sweat.

The door to the guesthouse flew open. An officer stepped out, placed his cap on his head and fastened the top buttons of his grey trench coat. I could not see his rank from such a distance but he held himself straight, almost rigid, in the way senior officers of the Wehrmacht always did on those propaganda newsreels shown at the cinema in Odda and everywhere else. He turned and peered into the glow from the hallway as if waiting for someone. Two men soon emerged, black leather coats draped about their shoulders. Neither bore uniforms. One of them was tall, the other short.

'Jesus,' exclaimed Olaf. '*Gestapo*.'

I wanted to gulp with fear but my mouth was suddenly bone dry. I felt angry with myself too, for trembling. I watched as the short man fed his fingers into tightly fitting black gloves. All three hovered on the street amid their steamy breaths. Then it happened. Two soldiers emerged. Next Mr Tørstig came out, his hands tied behind his back. After him Mr Johanssen, a tubby man in his late fifties, emerged, followed by his wife. And then – then came *Father*.

About to cry out, I found a hand cupped across my face. Olaf's palm pressed against my lips and his fingers dug firmly into my cheeks. His other arm swung round me and held me tightly, restraining me to the point where I could barely breathe. 'Keep still, Marek,' he whispered. His breath felt warm against my ear. 'Don't shout out.'

The truck spluttered into life and drove round, stopping in front of the guesthouse. Father and the others were loaded into the back accompanied by the soldiers. The canvas awning was lowered and tied. A car appeared from a side street and the officer and the two Gestapo men climbed in. The car's horn tooted and the convoy set off up the hill towards the main road to Odda. One German remained standing outside the guesthouse. Especially plump in his heavy coat, he was familiar to me: Tauber, the oldest of the men stationed in our village. The light from the hallway bathed his rugged face. He looked troubled.

We ran. We grabbed our rucksacks and skis and darted down a back street and kept on running until we reached the rear door to our house. Olaf tried the handle but it was locked. He hammered on the door.

Bent double with a stitch and a rasping breathlessness, I wanted to cry out but couldn't. Mother slid the bolt and yanked the door open. A frightened, weepy face greeted our homecoming.

Chapter Three

Seeing Mother on the point of collapse, Olaf seized her and sat her down at the kitchen table. Hurriedly he reached for a glass and a bottle of brandy. Oddly pallid, as if the life had been sucked from her, she appeared worryingly frail. She had never looked frail before.

'We saw Father being taken away with the Johanssens and Mr Tørstig,' I said. 'What's happened?'

Her moist, puffy eyes stared at me and then at Olaf. 'They came this afternoon,' she said. About to continue, she paused, her stream of tears replaced by considerable alarm. '*Taken?* What do you mean taken? They were just questioning them at the guesthouse.'

Olaf gently explained what we'd just witnessed and Mother's head and shoulders sagged. She seemed dumb-struck, and from the concerned look on Olaf's face, I think he feared she was slipping into shock.

My head ached and thumped from the horror of it all. What could they possibly want with Father? Of course, he hated the Nazis, but surely that wasn't enough, was it? OK, so he complained bitterly when they told him what he could teach and what he couldn't. Was that it? Was complaining enough? Like many teachers, Father spoke out against our 'minister president', Mr Vidkun Quisling, and his fascist Nasjonal Samling Party, the NS. But so did many members of the church and organizations like the trade unions. Father was hardly unique in that regard. I often thought of him like a tree in a strong gale, bending and straining to conform to Nazi edicts that went against the grain. I could think of nothing special he'd done to warrant arrest. That is, unless they knew about his trips to the city.

'Where have they taken them?' Mother asked.

'Here, drink this,' said Olaf, placing a brandy in her hand. 'I don't know, but I'll find out.'

She wiped her eyes and looked up. 'Remember those men who came a few weeks ago? Said they were from Oslo. They stayed at the Johanssens' guest house.'

We nodded.

'They told everyone they were here to survey the fjord.'

Olaf sat back in his chair and frowned.

'Well, that wasn't all they were up to,' she added. 'They were looking for signs of the Resistance and people speaking out against Vidkun Quisling.'

'But they were Norwegians,' I said both naively and without thinking. Olaf's frown deepened. 'Anyway, why Father?' I shouted.

Mother managed a weak smile, barely more than a hairline crack between her chapped and unpainted lips. 'It's all a big misunderstanding,' she said. She reached across the table, seized my hand and gripped it tightly. I saw her trying to appear strong and failing miserably to do so. 'It'll all sort itself out,' she added, squeezing my fingers.

Not for one minute did I believe her.

'You must be hungry,' she said. 'There's some bread and a little cheese.' She rose unsteadily from her chair. 'How was your trip?'

The last bloody thing I wanted to talk about was our trip. I wanted to know where they'd taken Father. What was going to happen to him? When would we see him again?

Mother took just three steps towards the pine dresser before collapsing.

Olaf leaped round the table and knelt beside her, lifting her head into his lap. 'Quick, go and fetch Doctor Haskveld,' he barked.

My world had fallen apart. I ran blindly from the house, down the street, round the corner and did not stop until reaching Dr Haskveld's front door. I hammered on it and shouted his name.

The elderly doctor appeared wearing a thick brown roll-neck sweater, clutching a heavy novel and with his spectacles two-thirds of the way down his bulbous nose. Over the thick lenses he peered at me enquiringly. I blurted out our crisis in a series of breathless sentences and felt angry that he didn't immediately panic in the way I had. I suppose as a doctor he was used to such outbursts. I guess many evenings had been similarly interrupted by knocks at his door: *Come quick, the baby's coming! His heart's stopped! She's stopped breathing! There's been a crash!*

'Calm down, young Marek,' he said in his professional, unflustered tone. 'I'll fetch my bag and coat. You run home now. I'll be right behind you.' He smiled reassuringly. 'Probably just fainted, that's all.'

He closed the door on me.

I began running, but a tightening stitch in my chest and cramp in my left calf forced me to slow. Perhaps I needed attention from Dr Haskveld too. In agony, I eventually had to stop. I stood on the corner and looked towards the fishing boats moored in the harbour. Their rigging jangled and clanged in the breeze but otherwise the scene was one of peace and calm. That just didn't seem right. Where was the raging tempest?

I spotted Hans Tauber standing by the edge of the harbour, rocking on his heels, his mind probably preoccupied with a favourite tune. He was smoking and staring out across the fjord towards the imposing greyness of the Folgefonn mountains and the Torsnut peak. I'd spoken to him on several occasions, and one thing in particular had always struck me. Despite the fact that we all hated him – he was a German soldier after all – underneath his crumpled, ill-fitting uniform I thought lay a rather ordinary, harmless soul, bordering on the likeable. He once told me that he came from a small town called Remsheid and that he had been a teacher like Father. He produced the obligatory family photograph, tatty and faded. I recalled seeing moistness in his eyes and a longing to be home radiating from within. I think he wished the war to be over even more than we did. He also hated the cold and thought Norway the coldest place on Earth. I strode up to him.

'Herr Tauber, sir, what have they done with my father?'

My presence startled him. Nearly dropping his cigarette, he spun round and squinted. He rubbed the wiry grey bristles in the folds of his chin, and his left cheek twitched. 'Marek Olsen.' He glanced down towards his feet. 'I'm sorry. There was nothing I could do.' He seemed almost embarrassed, almost apologetic.

'Why did they take him?'

He shrugged. 'The Gestapo tell us nothing.' He stared back towards the mountains as if ignoring me.

'It's insane,' I added.

He laughed without looking round. 'I think you're right, young man. But the whole world's insane.' He flashed me a glance. 'But don't tell anyone I said so, or else I'll be heading for the Russian front.' He chuckled to himself.

'Father's a good man. He's not done anything wrong,' I protested.

He puffed thoughtfully on his cigarette and eventually threw the butt to the ground, extinguishing it with his right foot. 'If that's true, then he has nothing to fear. But after the fuel dump at Skånevik was sabotaged last week, the orders are clear – crush the insurgents.' He looked me in the eye. 'That's the sort of order the Gestapo relish.'

'You mean reprisals?'

He nodded. 'Perhaps. If nobody talks.'

'But Father knows nothing. He's just a teacher. Like you!'

He sighed heavily. 'Teacher, soldier ... soldier, teacher.' He looked at me searchingly, his stare drilling into my brain. 'And your father? Just a teacher?'

Frowning at his implication, I felt a flush of bravado. 'Yes, you idiot, just a bloody teacher.' I wanted to punch him.

'Actually,' he added, 'I understand that the saboteurs were probably British and not the Resistance. Apparently they fled leaving behind bits of equipment that identified them. If that's true, then, although they probably received help from the Resistance, I doubt there'll be reprisals.'

I remembered the men we'd met on the plateau and supposed they'd been responsible. I felt proud of them but kept it well hidden. But I also recalled what had happened to Telavåg, a fishing village, in the spring of 1942. Men of the Resistance had shot two members of the Gestapo. German retribution was swift and uncompromising. The village, close to Bergen, was stripped of its inhabitants. Rumours hinted that the men had all been shipped to camps. The women and children were interned. In fact, we knew the story to be true because the elderly women had been locked up in a nearby school in Hardanger. The Germans then levelled the entire village. They say smoke could be seen for miles. And Fritz made no attempt to hide his heinous deed. He wanted us Norwegians to understand the *new order*. A chill swept through me. 'But why Father? Why the Johanssens? Why Mr Tørstig?' I cried.

Tauber did not offer an answer but appeared thoughtful. 'And where were you this afternoon?' he asked. 'And where was that big oaf of a brother of yours?' His eyes narrowed. 'Come to think of it, I haven't seen either of you for several days.' His right eyebrow climbed his forehead menacingly.

'Been about. Here and there.'

'I see,' he said slowly. 'Thought perhaps you might have gone fishing.'

Tauber knew full well we weren't fishermen. Was he trying to catch me out? 'Hardly,' I said. 'Get seasick just looking at the waves.' OK, so I lied. But I did so while looking him straight in the eye.

'Me too. Perhaps you went skiing. Up to the Hardanger.'

Now it was Tauber who was fishing. 'Bad weather's setting in,' I replied, shaking my head vehemently. I decided our conversation was heading towards difficulties like a rudderless ship heading for the rocks, and so I made my excuses and headed off.

He called out after me. 'Marek Olsen, they've taken your father to Odda, to the central police station. If I hear anything, I'll let you know.'

Dr Haskveld stood in the kitchen washing his hands at the sink when I burst through the door. Olaf hovered by the pine table. 'Where's Mother?' I shouted.

'*Shush.*' Olaf held a finger to his lips. 'She's resting upstairs.'

Dr Haskveld wiped his hands on a towel and folded down his sleeves, fastening the cuffs. 'Let her rest and if she has trouble sleeping, give her one of those powders in a little water. Not more than three a day, though,' he said to my brother. 'Make sure she eats plenty, although I doubt if she'll have much appetite. I'll call in tomorrow just to see how she is.' He fastened his bag and reached for his blue anorak. 'Don't look so frightened, Marek. She'll be fine.'

I hadn't realized that I looked frightened and for someone to mention it made me think it had to be true. My legs suddenly gave way and I crumpled onto a chair.

Olaf saw the doctor to the door and they exchanged meaningful looks as well as handshakes. I supposed they'd talked about more than just Mother and I desperately wanted to know what. I interrogated Olaf but he resisted.

'Never you mind, Marek,' he said. 'Nothing to concern you.'

God, there's nothing more irritating than being excluded. So what if I was the youngest? Hell, I was only four years younger than him. I felt close to boiling over inside.

Olaf ferreted in the cupboards for some bread. 'Want some?'

I shook my head. 'What do you think it's all about?' I asked.

He shrugged. 'Father's hardly NS. Perhaps his protests against Quisling are the reason.'

No, I thought, it had to be more than that. 'What are we going to do?'

Olaf slumped onto a chair at one end of the table and held his cheese knife threateningly. 'Find out where they've taken him, and why, and then see what we can do.' He slammed the knife angrily into the wood. It stuck.

'They've taken him to Odda,' I said.

He stared at me and ceased chewing.

'To the central police station.'

'How on earth—?'

'Tauber told me.'

'That fat pig!'

'He's not so bad.'

A knock on the door heralded the arrival of Lars. Cured of his *omgangssykdom*, he looked well, if perhaps a few pounds lighter. His thick woollen jumper appeared a size too big about his midriff. Olaf filled him in and Lars responded with sentences littered with swear words and much exaggerated gawping. When Olaf finished, Lars simply said, 'The bastards!' I thought he'd summed it up perfectly.

That evening we received a stream of visitors, our neighbours all needing to personally deliver their good wishes in a gesture of Norwegian solidarity. Several insisted on paying Mother brief visits upstairs. I suspected that Mrs Tørstig got an equal number of knocks on her door. After all, no one from our village had ever been carted off before.

Lars made himself comfortable and didn't think Father would mind if he drank some of his beer. Olaf joined him and when, finally, we were alone, we began planning our course of action.

'We need to get to Odda,' said Olaf.

'How? Do you know anyone with spare petrol?'

Lars had a point. Fuel was scarce and guarded like precious metal.

'Damn it.' My brother hammered his fist on the table. 'Father's car still needs fixing too.' He glared at me.

So it was my fault now! I hadn't finished tinkering with her Solex carburettor and got her running sweetly again. A picture of the oilcloth lying on the floor of our garage, the components of the carburettor neatly set out on it, filled my head. 'I could fix it,' I offered.

My brother sneered at me disdainfully.

'No, really, I could.'

Lars's face lit up. 'There you are, Olaf. One problem solved.'

My God, I thought. I'd actually convinced someone that I could do it. 'If I work through the night, I could have her running by dawn.' I hoped my bravado hadn't got the better of me.

'He's been fixing that car all damn summer,' Olaf

grunted. He folded his arms on the table and buried his head.

'Anyway, her tank's almost empty,' I added, recalling the reason why I'd not rushed to mend the blasted thing. 'Barely enough to get us out of the village.'

A rare moment followed in which none of us spoke. I knew – at least I'd persuaded myself – that I really could fix Father's car. After all, I'd studied the manual until I was almost blind and had figured out that all it really needed was a good clean and for the idling jet to be adjusted with a few turns of a screwdriver. At least I thought that was all it needed.

Lars rocked precariously back and forth in his chair. 'You know who's got plenty of petrol.'

I looked at him, my mind blank.

'Old Tauber.'

Great! We all knew that. The Germans had plenty of everything, including our bloody country.

My brother lifted his head. 'Do you think we can get some?'

There followed a brief analysis of the best method for extracting petrol from Tauber's car. Lars, being a farmer's son, said he could lay his hands on a length of tubing ideal for siphoning and thought a milk churn would be perfect for carrying the load. He was all for fetching them immediately.

Billeted in a requisitioned house – the finest house in the village, of course – the Germans parked their vehicles right outside. It meant much stealth and tiptoeing about would be needed if they weren't to be disturbed from their sleep. And a keen eye had to be kept open, as they patrolled the village and shoreline of the fjord day and night, albeit half-heartedly. We banked on the fact that they would exhibit their usual laziness and slope off for forty winks at the earliest opportunity.

'Right then,' declared Olaf. He smacked the palm of his left hand on the table. 'Marek, time to get your hands dirty.'

I pulled on my oldest, grubbiest dark sweater and grabbed a torch from a drawer. Lars headed off to fetch his gear. My brother chewed his nails. Grasping the door handle, I had just one question for him. 'What are we going to do when we get to Odda?'

He shrugged.

Chapter Four

The secret with Josephine was to smooth-talk her, to cosset her and treat her like a real lady. I've only resorted to striking her with a hammer once, and that was out of pure frustration at her refusal to start. She was French, and Mother had long since accepted the fact that Father had a mistress. And, being the only French girl in town, she'd drawn quite a few stares the day Father drove her to her new home. Now it was my job to piece her back together and coax her into life. I shone my torch at the oilcloth and realized I had a lot to do. I lifted her bonnet and twisted the manual so that Diagram 4F bore some passing resemblance to her engine. Setting to work, cleaning each part thoroughly before reassembling it, I paused to hunt through Father's workbench drawers in search of some fine wire to clean out the tiny hole that was the idling jet. The best I could find was an old wire brush and I removed a couple of bristles with pliers. They did a fine job. All the while I listened out, half expecting to hear the shouts, possibly even gun-shots, aimed at Lars and my brother at the moment of their discovery. But I heard only the wind and the grainy sound of dry snow being driven against the garage door.

By two o'clock in the morning I reckoned the task

was complete. Or rather I presumed I'd fixed Josephine because everything I'd removed from her had been replaced and, unlike previous occasions, I had no parts left over. Of course, proof of the pudding would only come when we tried to start her, and that had to wait.

The garage door creaked open.

Lars appeared first, then my brother, and slung between them the milk churn looked heavy. From their sniggers and broad grins I knew the Germans were missing a considerable volume of petrol. The churn made quite a thud as they put it down and the sweetness of petroleum fumes quickly filled the garage. Lars and Olaf shook hands in victory.

'Well, Marek?' My brother peered under the bonnet with the torch.

'It's all done,' I replied.

'And she'll start OK?'

'Of course!'

'First time of asking?'

'Hope so.'

'Got a funnel?' asked Lars.

As the petrol gushed and gurgled into the tank, I figured we had enough for several return trips to Odda. 'Didn't need to steal quite so much,' I remarked.

'Stop complaining,' said Olaf.

'I'm not – it's just that surely they'll realize some has gone missing. And they might work out who's responsible when they see us driving off in the morning.'

Lars burst out laughing.

'What? What's so funny?'

'Their fuel gauge will indicate that nothing's wrong,' my brother replied.

'But they won't be going anywhere,' added Lars, still amid a fit of giggles.

I did not need to ask. I knew both had relieved themselves into the tank and probably added some snow for good measure. 'Hope you didn't leave any tracks.' I imagined a disgruntled Tauber stomping his way to our garage door.

'What do you take us for? Actually, we did.'

'What?'

'All the way to the front door of Mr Jensen.'

'You what?'

'Figured it was about time the old goat got into trouble.'

That's inspired, I thought. Jensen was a Quisling, or so Father reckoned. The man was our local government representative and seemed to have done well for himself since Fritz parachuted in. And come to think of it, he had spent time in the company of the men from Oslo Mother had spoken of. I supposed, given what had transpired, it might prove beneficial to Mr Jensen's health if he left town sooner rather than later.

We decided to get some sleep and rise early. The quicker we got to Odda, the quicker we'd learn about Father. Returning to the house, we crept upstairs, but Mother was still awake and fretting. Olaf waved to me at the top of the stairs. 'Go to bed, Marek. I'll talk to Mother.'

My bedclothes felt welcoming and snug, a far cry from the reindeer skins and hard floor of the Borsobu. Once on my back, I felt exhaustion lap over me as a series of dizzying waves. But I couldn't sleep. Whether I pressed my eyes tightly shut or stared towards the pine-clad ceiling, all I could think about was rescuing Father. I imagined us marching into the police station in Odda and demanding his immediate release. I imagined us having to threaten them, or being forced to fight our way out.

I was still awake when the floorboards creaked, indicating Olaf was finally turning in. He had spent a good hour with Mother. I wondered what they had talked about and worried that events were more serious than I could possibly imagine. I tried to imagine the worst. I thought of never seeing Father again, of him being driven to a lonely spot with the Johanssens and Mr Tørstig, of them being blindfolded and marched into the woods. I imagined hearing gunshots and I cried.

Olaf's hammering on my bedroom door startled me from my dreams. For a moment, hung in that semi-consciousness of waking, I had forgotten everything. Then reality returned with an uncompromising thud. I leaped from my bed, hauled on my trousers and hurriedly buttoned my shirt.

Downstairs, Mother stood close to the front door,

dressed ready to go in her knee-length charcoal winter coat. A silver brooch in the form of a lovers' knot was pinned to a lapel. Father had given it to her the day they got engaged. She only wore it on special occasions. It was her favourite. She looked smart, with painted lips and a little rouge on her cheeks. Her finest black felt hat crumpled her mass of brown curls and was tilted slightly in the way fashion demanded. Last time she'd made that kind of effort, we'd been burying Edith Ladveld. I prayed it wasn't an omen. Oddly, in all my dreaming I had not thought of Mother coming as well. I suppose I thought her too fragile for what might await us. But this morning, with the low sun streaming through the hall window and bathing her cheeks, I witnessed gritty determination, resilience and a renewed stoicism in her face. It gave me strength.

'Let's hope you've done a good job, Marek,' said Olaf. He appeared from Father's study carrying a revolver, busily inserting bullets into each empty chamber. I thought it might have been wiser not to be armed on such a venture, as we would surely pass checkpoints and might be subjected to a thorough search. If the gun were discovered, we would be joining Father in the cells. But I said nothing for now, and reminded myself to make sure he hid the gun well.

Lars arrived. 'Thought I'd come for moral support.' He looked at Mother. 'If that's all right?' She said nothing but gave a fleeting nod.

'Good,' said Olaf, pulling on his gloves.

The moment of truth had arrived. Opening the garage doors, I stood to one side next to Lars and Mother while Olaf climbed into Josephine. Peering from behind the dusty windscreen, he waved, smiled and then turned the ignition key.

Come on! I willed her to start. Her engine turned, spluttered, clanged and coughed. 'Don't press the accelerator,' I shouted. 'You'll flood her.'

He continued cranking the engine, and Mother grew anxious at the thought of waking everyone in the village. The grin on Olaf's face drained away like a leaky oil sump. He stopped, waited a few moments and then tried again. Eventually she fired up, only to stall. Repeating the exercise three times, he grew increasingly impatient.

'Wait!' I shouted. I ran and grabbed a screwdriver. Lifting the bonnet, I tweaked the idling jet a quarter turn and shouted at Olaf to try again. It was better but not perfect so I gave it another quarter turn. Now she purred.

I was saved.

Driving up through the village towards the main road, we met Tauber walking the opposite way. 'Don't stop,' said Lars. We didn't. Olaf reached into his pocket. I knew he had a firm hold of Father's gun. I'd forgotten to tell him to hide it somewhere safe but it was too late now. If luck was on our side, the corporal wouldn't bother interrupting our journey.

Tauber's eyes tracked us suspiciously as we passed him, and for some unfathomable reason I waved to him. In what must have been a vulnerable moment, he waved back, quickly stopping the gesture and wiping his hand on his coat as if it were soiled. I laughed to myself. The old fool. Strangely, I quite liked the old man, hopeless though he was.

Olaf might be a skier without equal in Ulfhus but I reckon even a stray dog would prove a better driver. He seemed curiously unco-ordinated, able to concentrate on only one thing at a time, like steering through the slush, braking or changing gear. Mother said nothing, Lars frequently covered his eyes, while I shouted, 'Try double-declutching, you twit,' every time the gears ground. Fumbling for the mustard-spoon-shaped gear lever poking from the dash, he ignored me.

Few things on Josephine had ever worked properly, including the rudimentary heater. What blew from it barely kept the windscreen from misting over and felt as cold as the air outside. I nevertheless sensed sweat trickling down the inside of my shirt, and it grew worse the closer we got to Odda.

The main road tracked the course of the fjord, and brilliant sunshine lit the landscape to its full glory: crystal clear waters, craggy snow-capped mountains and ever-green forests weighed down with icicles. I never tired of the majestic panorama. Gazing out of the side window, I let my focus drift across the place we called home. For mile after mile nobody spoke. Passing through the village of Tyssedal, I knew we were getting close to our destination and to where Father languished.

Olaf suddenly let his foot off the accelerator and seemed uncertain what to do next. I peered over his shoulder and saw the checkpoint ahead. He looked round at Mother and said, 'Get your papers ready and remember what we agreed.'

What? I hadn't agreed anything. I soon realized I'd been ignored yet again. Had the opportunity arisen, I'd have kicked my brother viciously in the shins. He slowed and pulled in at the side of the road.

We had chosen a bad time because the Germans were in the process of changing the guards at the post. So instead of being confronted with half a dozen, we found twice as many. And they all looked bored, cold and intent on inconveniencing the locals. A young, spotty private approached the car, blowing his misty breath into cupped hands while shivering, his shoulders scrunched. Olaf wound down his window.

'Papers.'

The order had become frighteningly familiar although it never stopped making me shudder. Olaf passed our identity cards through the window. Awkwardly, with blue, bloodless fingers, the young man flicked through them. 'Where are you heading?'

'Just into Odda,' replied Olaf.

The soldier glanced up the road. I reckoned he was thinking, Why on earth would anyone choose to go there? He stooped and glanced into the car, peering at each of us in turn. 'What's in the back?'

'Nothing.'

'Why are you going to Odda?'

'To collect someone from the police station.'

'You have no travel permit.'

'Don't need one. You can see we're only from Ulfhus. It says so on our identity cards.'

'I want to see in the back.'

'There's nothing in the boot.'

'Get out of the car.'

The soldier stepped away from Josephine and took hold of the rifle slung over his shoulder. Olaf got out and opened the boot. There really was nothing in it.

Another face appeared at the side window, a face bearing a broad smile upon which was mounted a ridiculously bushy moustache. '*Bonjour! Citroën Sept!*' he declared.

I looked at Lars and frowned.

The soldier stepped back three feet and held his arms out. '*C'est magnifique!*'

I felt rather confused. 'That's French, isn't it?' I said.

Ignoring me, the man set about running his fingers along the line of the black bonnet and appeared to be admiring Josephine from every angle. Having inspected the white-painted Pilote wheels, he stopped directly in front of the car and, hands on hips, gazed longingly at the chevron grille.

There followed a discussion between him and the

spotty youth, which, although my grasp of German remains pretty poor, I thought had something to do with the merits of French automobiles versus German models. It seemed that Herr Moustache had an eye for the curvaceous, just like Father, rating it above the relentless reliability but dull design of vehicles from the Fatherland. Herr Spotty disagreed strongly, waving his arms dismissively and sneering at Josephine's unique front-wheel drive and monocoque body shell. As baffled as the rest of us, Olaf gawped.

Eventually Herr Moustache dismissed his comrade and approached Olaf. 'You're going into Odda?'

'Yes.'

'Good, then you can give me a lift.'

My heart tripped and missed a beat.

'Better still, I'll drive.' He handed his rifle to Lars in the passenger seat and climbed behind the steering wheel. I opened the rear door to allow a rather bemused Olaf to climb into the back. We headed into town, a German soldier at the wheel.

'He's a better driver than you, Olaf,' I said. Needless to say I got thumped in the ribs.

The German introduced himself as Hartwig Lauder from Bremen. 'My father buys and sells cars,' he informed us proudly. 'At least he did before the war. He always said French cars were the most beautiful albeit least reliable. Like the best women!' He turned and smiled sweetly at Mother and she scowled back. As we trundled on in silence, I stared at the back of his head, wondering what it would take to strangle him, garrotte him or plunge a knife into his back. Then again, I thought, he seems quite reasonable. Lars sat clutching the rifle between his knees and, judging by the strange flush to his face, appeared petrified.

The benefit of our strange encounter showed itself as soon as we reached the next checkpoint. No need to show our papers here. No one wanted to look in the boot. Just a few cheery words out of the window from Hartwig and the barrier was lifted and we were on our way. Bloody marvellous.

Odda loomed ahead of us, tucked away on the flat plain on the southernmost tip of the Sørfjord. The sun picked out the brilliant white spire of the church, pinpointing the centre of town; an industrial town producing zinc and smelting iron. It was the sort of place you visited only when you had to. Because of its importance to the Germans and the machinery of their intended world domination, I wasn't surprised to see the place crawling with troops. Once in the centre of town, Hartwig pulled over. He squeezed the steering wheel lovingly. 'Will you take two hundred Reichsmarks?'

'She's not for sale,' replied Olaf.

'Three hundred. My final offer.'

'Sorry.'

Hartwig sighed and opened the door. Lars handed him his rifle. 'A most pleasing example. And you're sure she's not for sale?'

'I'm sure,' replied Olaf.

Hartwig shook my brother's hand and smiled at Mother. 'The central police station is half a mile further on.' He pointed. 'You can't miss it.' He wandered off along the street.

'Jesus!' exclaimed Lars, his head slumping forward in anguished relief. 'Thought we were done for.'

'I wouldn't have shot him unless it was really necessary.'

I stared at my brother. Given the pleasant nature of our escort, I thought his words were ridiculous, but then again, I suppose it might have all turned out differently. We parked close to the police station and made our way towards an entrance ominously flanked by smart German guards. A pair of swastikas dangled from poles above their heads.

Once inside the bland foyer filled with the odour of wax polish, Mother went to an enquiries desk while we loitered just beyond the door. She quickly returned and spoke anxiously. 'They said we have to wait. It may take hours.'

So we waited and waited along with numerous other fear-ridden faces. It seemed the Gestapo had been busy. Now and again we struck up conversation with our fellow hopefuls, only to be shushed into an uneasy silence by the guards. Mother's hard exterior varnish of resilience she'd begun the day with now started to crack and peel. She paced back and forth, arms either folded tightly or nails gripped between her teeth. Lars sat patiently next to me. Olaf followed on Mother's heels like a devoted hound.

Four hours later a dumpy suited man with thinning hair and round wire-framed spectacles wandered out through a door clutching a piece of paper. His sharp, officious face looked around the gathering and enquired, 'Mrs Olsen?'

'*Yes.*' Mother sprang to her feet and raised a hand.

'Right. Come with me please.'

She took two steps and then turned to Olaf. He got up and grasped her arm. 'Lars, wait here with Marek. I'll go with Mother.'

They disappeared through a door. *Ignored again.* I wanted to scream. Instead I sat back down next to Lars and waited.

After an hour he nudged me. 'Did a fine job with Josephine, Marek. Your father will be very proud of you.'

Hah, I thought. Proud! Twice in just a few days. I knew he was only trying to be supportive but he sounded as if he were talking to a child to stop it fretting. It really irritated me. I got up under the pretext of stretching cramp from my legs but inside I felt the overwhelming urge to do something. I couldn't think what, though. 'I need some water. And the toilet. Can I get you anything?'

He shook his head.

Wandering through a set of double doors and along a corridor, I passed endless unmarked doors. A tall lanky woman appeared and challenged me. I asked where the lavatories were. She smiled and directed me up a flight of stairs and told me to turn left. So I did and found myself in a large room decorated with grubby white tiles, a room stinking of pee. A long metal urinal confronted me. The room's atmosphere reminded me of some horror film or other I'd seen years ago. It sent a chill through me and even the ticking sound of dripping taps could not make me relax enough to relieve myself. Instead I went to a basin and cupped water into my mouth from the spurting tap. The pipes clonked and rattled noisily. I heard a lavatory flush and the lock on a door click but thought nothing of it. When I'd finished, I straightened up and looked into the cracked mirror. I almost died of fright.

Chapter Five

'What are you doing here?'

Via the mirror, my eyes were locked together with those of the Gestapo. The shorter of the two thugs I'd seen the previous night outside the Johanssens' guesthouse in Ulfhus stood but a couple of feet behind me.

'Just getting a drink of water.'

'You shouldn't be here.'

'Sorry.'

'What's your name?'

I wanted to lie but thought better of it. 'Marek Olsen, sir.'

'Olsen . . . Olsen,' he repeated. I could see his brain ticking over. 'Related to Bernd Olsen from Ulfhus?'

'My father.'

Surprise settled on his face and he seemed pleased. 'Surely you're not here alone.'

'Mother is with someone right now. Trying to find out what you bastards have done with my father.' I cowered slightly over the basin, expecting punishment for my outburst. But all I detected was a glint in his eye and, strangely, I found that even more threatening.

'I see. Tell you what, Marek, why don't we have a chat and see if we can sort all this out? My office is just along the corridor.' He held out a hand. 'Come, no need to be frightened. I'm not going to harm you.' His voice was like oil, his tone slippery, his manner friendly yet, I reckoned, utterly untrustworthy.

Of course, I had little choice and soon found myself in his office and settled into a large leather chair opposite his desk. Feeling panicky inside, I wished Olaf or Mother were with me. It did not feel like a good moment to be alone with the Gestapo. Yet although scared, I was also angry. *This is our country, damn it. How dare he order me about?* I suddenly felt strong. A picture of the Führer hung on the wall and I wanted to spit at it.

Having rifled through a filing cabinet, he placed a thin pile of folders on his desk and reached for his cigarette box. He lit up, leaned back in his chair and plonked his feet on the desk. I studied him closely. He did not look particularly evil, at least not obviously so. In fact, he struck me as being rather an inadequate man. Perhaps that was it. Perhaps a career in the Gestapo was perfect for such men, for it offered the opportunity for power and for them to wreak revenge for whatever chips lay heavily on their puny shoulders.

'Now, Marek, I'm Wolfgang Stretter,' he announced, 'and it is my job to make sure everything runs smoothly in this sector of Norway. I am sorry that we had to arrest your father yesterday but we needed to bring him here in order to ask him more questions.'

'About what?'

'A number of things,' he replied.

'He knows nothing.'

'About what?'

'About anything.'

He laughed and licked his twisted lips. 'I like you, Marek Olsen. You have spirit.' He drew long and hard on his cigarette and then removed his feet from his desk. Leaning forward, he continued, 'Listen, you may well be right. It may all just be a mistake. And if so, the quicker we clear up any misunderstandings, the quicker you may be reunited with your father. That's presumably what you want, isn't it?'

'Of course.'

'Then will you help me sort all this out?'

'How?'

He settled back in his chair again and swayed gently to and fro. 'We understand your father travels regularly to Bergen.' He flicked up the cover of a file and peered at its contents. 'About once a month, I believe.' He closed the file.

'So?'

'Do you know why he goes there?'

'Yes, to visit Uncle Knut.' I pictured Uncle Knut and his odd collection of fossils that filled every shelf and display cabinet in his home on the Nygårdsgaten, a short stroll from the bus station.

Stretter nodded. 'Good. That's very helpful, Marek. And tell me, does your father ever travel to Oslo?'

This question gave me a problem. The answer was yes, although his trips were very occasional and at short notice. He would be gone for a week or so at a time, sometimes longer. Curiously he'd always say he was going to Bergen even though I'd seen train and boat tickets that suggested otherwise. Even after he knew that I knew, he still kept referring to Bergen, as if it were some sort of code. Mother once let slip that in Oslo Father met with others of like minds to rally against the NS Party. The fruits of their labours were articles and newsletters in opposition to Quisling. I had absolutely no intention of confiding in Herr Stretter on this topic. And, of course, while the Gestapo's reputation for barbaric cruelty and causing unbearable pain was indisputable, I knew that the friendly, soft, coaxing interrogation technique could also be used. I suspected that's what I was being subjected to.

'Oslo?' I repeated thoughtfully. I shook my head and pursed my lips. 'Don't think he's been there for years.' I hoped I appeared convincing. 'What on earth made you think he had?' I added for good measure.

Herr Stretter looked disappointed. He wrung his hands, a gesture that reminded me that he'd not washed them before leaving the lavatory. 'We do know that he's been to Oslo,' he said.

'Really? When was that?'

He bristled and his face sharpened. 'Don't play games, Marek Olsen. This is not the time or the place. Your father's future is in the balance.' He paused to collect his thoughts. 'Now, do you know who he visits in Oslo?'

'No.' That reply required no acting on my part for it was truthful. 'Why does it matter anyway?'

He sighed wearily. 'Let's go back to Bergen. He visits your uncle, you say – Knut Olsen. What does he do there?' Breaking eye contact, he sifted through his files, locating one with my uncle's name on it: 'Knut Olsen, Bergen, number two-two-three-two-two.'

I managed to swallow my shock. Did he have a file on me as well? 'He lectures at the college. He's a geologist,' I replied. 'But you already know that, don't you? You probably know all about him, down to his shoe size and nervous tic.'

Stretter smarted at my impudence. He cleared his throat and then said, 'But why does he go there?'

'They're brothers. Don't brothers normally get together now and again?' Wanting him to know that I thought it was a ridiculous question, I pulled a face. Stretter was unmoved. 'And they're the best of friends,' I added. 'They do a little fishing. Drink a few beers. Talk about rocks, fossils and women.'

'Fishing?' His unblinking gaze fixed on my face again and his pupils flicked from side to side as he focused on each of my eyeballs in turn.

'Yes, Uncle has a boat.'

He scribbled a note without looking down. 'Would you say they are good sailors?'

I shrugged. Well, what's a good sailor? I thought. They never ventured far out to sea. Father always liked to be able to see land. Uncle Knut, however, would happily point his boat out to sea and go as far as the wind and currents would take him. He possessed much more spirit of adventure than Father.

Stretter replaced the cap over the nib of his pen. 'It is a pity that you can't assist us regarding his visits to Oslo,' he said. 'That's what we really need to clarify. I mean, before we can release him.'

Hell, he's turning the screw, I thought. The emotional screw. Searching my brain, I wondered if there was anything I could say to help Father's cause but knew saying anything truthful would mean trouble – trouble for him and for others, maybe including myself. So if I were to say anything, it had to be a lie, and a credible lie too. But having had the merits of honesty drummed into me since birth by the very person I was now trying to help, I felt divided over the urge to spin Herr Stretter a yarn. I had to be careful. One slip-up, one lie too many, one fact contradicted by others and the consequences were too horrible to imagine. I wanted inspiration. I needed to say *something*; I had to feed the vulture sitting before me.

A knock at the door heralded the arrival of a uniformed man bearing papers requiring Herr Stretter's signature. The young corporal seemed surprised at my presence and peered at me as if I were some sort of fairground curiosity. The papers were probably trivial but, as Stretter scrawled his mark and stamped each page, I couldn't help wondering if I was witnessing the signing of death warrants. 'How did you know your father was here in Odda?' he asked.

'One of the soldiers in Ulfhus told me.'

He flashed me a glance. 'Who?'

'Corporal Hans Tauber.'

He jotted down the name and I realized I had put the harmless fat German in jeopardy. Somehow that seemed wrong. 'He's a good soldier,' I said. There was no reaction from Stretter. 'He's firm and takes no nonsense,' I added. Still no reaction. 'But he has that knack of winning people's trust.' Stretter looked up with curiosity, as if he wasn't quite sure what I meant. 'I think Herr Tauber takes the long-term view. He knows that you're all here for good and so thinks that we Norwegians need to be treated firmly but fairly. Only by appearing a good role model does he believe we shall see the greatness of Germany. I reckon that's important if you want to reduce the amount of sabotage and stop people joining the Resistance.'

Stretter laughed. 'This Corporal Tauber sounds a remarkable soldier.'

'He is,' I replied. 'I'm amazed he hasn't been promoted to General.'

I think Herr Stretter had rumbled me because he laughed again, very loudly.

'OK, you can go,' he said.

The announcement took me by surprise.

'Well, go on, off you go.'

'And Father?'

'We'll see.'

I left with a strange feeling inside. Had Stretter simply given up on me? Did he have more important business to attend to? Could I read any optimism into his part-ing words?

In the corridor Lars spotted me and jogged up with a look of desperate angst. 'Where the hell were you? I've been worried sick.'

'Sorry.'

'Your mother and Olaf have finished their meeting. They're waiting in the entrance hall.'

My hopes were quickly dashed for neither Mother nor my brother displayed the slightest ray of hope in their weary faces. And Mother looked ill, unsteady on her feet, her eyes hollow. Olaf looked ready and willing to kill.

We returned to Ulfhus defeated. Much of the time they'd spent in the plump little administrator's office had been taken up with Mother completing forms, which probed just about every aspect of our lives. Officialdom clearly needed to know as much about us as we did. Finally she and Olaf learned that an early release of Father was nothing short of a preposterous dream. We all knew that meant the outlook was bleak but no one said as much. Father might not be released for months – years even. In fact, we might never see him again. I just didn't want to think about it.

As we drove home, I spoke of my meeting with Stretter, and Olaf tore into me for being foolish enough to dare speaking to him alone.

'You should have called for me,' he snapped angrily.

As if I had any choice! My brother vowed to cut his

balls off should the opportunity ever arise. I thanked him and offered to hold the little bastard down.

The following few days proved the strangest of my life so far. Father's absence created a void in everything. Most of the time Mother remained admirably stalwart. Without warning, however, her fortitude would crack, resulting in tears. This happened when she stood by the sink, baked bread, ironed and cleaned – in fact, at any moment she found herself with time to think. At night I listened to her sobbing and felt wretched and so completely helpless. I think that's the worst part, not being able to do anything, not being able to make everything all right. I swore to the Norse gods Odin and Thor that I would stop at nothing to ensure Father's safe return home, but knew, of course, such a promise to be an empty gesture. I was but one boy against the might of the Third Reich. Now, if I possessed Odin's great spear, Gungnir, or Thor's great hammer, Mjollnir, such a contest would be even or possibly tilted in my favour. I lay in the darkness and dreamed of great battles.

Our fellow villagers displayed endless kindness but quickly the benefits wore thin. And my friends still came to see me, and I visited them, but our previously carefree chatter had been replaced by a curious caution in their conversation. They always greeted me with overly sincere enquiries as to how I was bearing up, but they never, ever mentioned Father. I think their parents had told them to avoid the subject. That annoyed me the most because such reticence often accompanies a death in the family. I wanted to scream at them, 'He's not dead!' but I didn't, not wanting to tempt fate.

Without warning, Hans Tauber left our village a week after our trip to Odda. Rumours hinted that he was heading for the Russian front. I prayed for him as much out of guilt as from kindness.

Tauber's replacement arrived shortly after his departure. Unfortunately for us twenty-five-year-old Lieutenant Klaus Wold differed from Tauber in every respect. Young and ambitious and intent on making our lives hell, he soon whipped the rabble that served beneath him into a small band of intolerants. And, not content with bringing a whole new meaning to re-pression, he set about tasting the delights of the young women of Ulfhus and neighbouring villages with unnatural zest.

Everything seemed to be changing and I liked none of it. Worst of all, I realized for the first time that my parents, on whom I'd relied to solve every problem and make everything OK, simply couldn't. It hit me hard. My safety net had gone and the real world looked frightening.

One evening Olaf returned from visiting his long-term girlfriend, Agnete Hilting, and made an announcement. 'I've decided now isn't the time to be going to Oslo,' he said. 'I shall write and ask that my place at the university be deferred a year or two.'

Mother hugged him.

'Will they do that for you?' I asked.

'Yes, I hope so. I'll write to Uncle Knut and ask him to put in a good word.'

The slight tremble to Olaf's lips as he spoke revealed the first hint of vulnerability I'd ever seen in him. I guessed it was possible that his place might not be deferred and that he might be sacrificing his future for Mother and me. Clearly he saw himself as a surrogate head of the household until Father returned. Although sorry for him, I confess I felt happy that evening and slept much more soundly. Olaf said he would get a job and that meant an income and food on our table. I offered to do my bit whenever possible and argued a case for my premature departure from school in order to work too. Unfortunately neither Mother nor Olaf bought into my reasoning.

The days grew shorter, the snow deeper, and the ice wind began to blow from the north almost daily. I returned to school all wrapped up and slipped into the winter routine that was so familiar: lessons, more lessons, and evenings poring over books and my manuals. Olaf got a junior teaching job at the school but our paths rarely crossed during lessons. Every day I made a point of wearing two paperclips, one on each lapel of my jacket. One was for Father. It made me feel closer to him somehow. And I wanted the world to know he wasn't forgotten. I would have willingly worn a thousand of them.

On 23 October Mr Tørstig returned to Ulfhus. It had

been almost a month since his arrest. He had lost weight and wanted to say little about his ordeal. It appeared that he had finally convinced the Gestapo that he was innocent. Following questioning in Odda, he'd been taken to a camp outside Oslo. The place sounded grim, with little food, cramped huts and nothing to occupy the prisoners' minds other than their thoughts. Father had been taken there too. Mother was ecstatic to hear that he was alive and well, apart from a nasty chest infection from which Mr Tørstig assured her he was recovering. I thought that the camp sounded like purgatory and that Father would regret having been so quick to abandon his churchgoing. Like Mother, I thought that by now he would have returned to daily prayer for salvation. That night I prayed that he'd be strong and unwavering and that, like all of us, he'd not abandoned hope. Worryingly, Mr Tørstig had seen nothing of the Johanssens but had heard rumours that the Gestapo had found a radio transmitter hidden in a suitcase at the guesthouse. He feared that the Johanssens had been executed. I had trouble believing it. Surely Mr Tørstig was mistaken, I thought. But, if it were true, what would happen to Father? Would they execute him too?

With winter came a big increase in the activities of the MILORG. Almost daily news filtered through of some act of sabotage or other. Olaf and I celebrated with a small glass of *aquavit* and the occasional English cigarette. Pretty risky, of course, but we were determined to remain defiant. The Germans responded to the troubles by pouring more troops into the area. A dozen joined those already stationed in Ulfhus, taking over the Johanssens' guesthouse by the harbour. Lieutenant Wold wasted no time in putting them to work making our lives a misery. He took to mounting random searches of our homes, to stopping people in the street and refusing almost all travel requests. Oh, how I missed Hans Tauber.

When we came to celebrate Agnete's seventeenth birthday on the last day of October, I think we all hoped for a rare evening of cheer and celebration. With her parents running one of the village bars, they decided to put on a party and most were invited. As we huddled in a convivial fug amid pipe smoke and beer glasses, many attempted the foxtrot on a cramped makeshift dance floor to songs played on Agnete's father's gramophone player, its volume stretched almost to the point of distortion. And Agnete's father took turns with Dr Haskveld on the upright piano in unique and uplifting Norwegian songs. For the first time in months I saw people smile and heard laughter. Of course, it couldn't last.

The door to the bar swung open and the tall figure of Lieutenant Wold stepped into where he wasn't welcome. The buttons on his uniform gleamed. However much we hated him, we had to admit that he did dress well. The music and laughter died away to a fretful hush as everyone became aware of his presence.

'Ah! A party. And what are we celebrating?' he asked.

Agnete's father approached him. 'Please, this is a family celebration. A private affair.'

Wold looked put out. 'Is that so? Well, most of Ulfhus appears to be here. Does that mean you're all interbred like wild dogs?'

Mr Hilting got the message. 'No. Please, Lieutenant, you're welcome to stay for a drink.' He grabbed a glass of wine and offered it to him.

Wold took it. 'Thank you. And what is it that I should be toasting?'

'My daughter's birthday.'

'Indeed. Well, where is she?'

Agnete stepped reluctantly forward, forcing herself free of Olaf's restraining grip on her arm. I must say she did look spectacular in her home-made ruby-red velvet party frock, her long blonde hair layered, folded and pinned into a perfect frame for her freckled face. She looked almost as pretty as Olga Radervit, whom I'd been trying my best to impress all evening with my extensive knowledge of the internal combustion engine. Olaf said to me that I had a unique way with women: I had the ability to send them into a catatonic state. I made a mental note to look up 'catatonic' in the dictionary but thought it must mean something similar to a swoon.

Wold eyed Agnete lasciviously and the corner of his mouth curled upwards. 'Ah, what a delight,' he said. He clacked his heels together and bowed in that well-mannered but ridiculous way German officers always did to impress on others their superior breeding. He held out his hand to her. 'Come, don't be shy.'

Agnete gave him a fearful, hesitant look, as if she'd seen a rat. Of course, she had! Olaf stepped forward between them. 'You're not welcome here, Wold. So drink your wine and leave us alone.'

The lieutenant did not bat an eyelid. 'Olaf Olsen, you really must learn some manners. I merely wish to toast this young lady and wish her luck. Would you deny me such a simple, well-meaning gesture?'

'Make your toast then, and get out.'

What was he doing? I watched my brother heap trouble onto his broad shoulders. I guessed the beer, the occasion and his hatred had all mixed together to fuel his outburst. Of course, we all knew Wold's reputation with the women, and I didn't blame Olaf for defending his territory but I knew he'd picked the wrong time and the wrong place.

The lieutenant raised his glass. 'To you, young lady,' he said, downing the wine in one go. He placed the empty glass on the bar. 'Thank you.' He smiled at her. 'Another time perhaps.' He turned and glared at Olaf before leaving.

A murmur of relief swept through the bar. Many of Olaf's friends slapped him on the back for standing up to Wold in a way no others had ever dared. I, on the other hand, feared for my brother's safety.

Chapter Six

When daylight manages only a brief appearance, bathing the land with a sickly pale, watery light, we Norwegians can be prone to depression. Add to our woes a temperature measured only in minus degrees centigrade and the vindictiveness of Wold and his men, and we relish doing little other than complain and mope. I knew it would be a hard winter. Everything was in short supply – except potatoes. So we ate a lot of them.

Each evening we spoke and prayed together for Father's safe return. Mother appeared to be bearing up well and I could see she appreciated Olaf sticking around. Likewise, Agnete seemed happy that the boy she'd been going out with for years had not fled to Oslo to begin a new life at the university. She hung around more than ever, sticking to him like a limpet, but he didn't seem to mind. I figured she knew this might be her last chance to snare him permanently. Agnete Olsen had a certain ring to it. It slipped off the tongue with ease.

One night at about nine o'clock I'd just finished my trigonometry homework and had begun thinking about the overdue essay on the lifestyle and customs of the Laps when I heard a commotion downstairs. I needed little excuse to abandon my schoolwork.

Lars and Agnete stood in the hallway, my brother draped between them. His arms rested outstretched on their shoulders, his head bowed, and he appeared bloodied. He looked like Christ on the cross. I ran to assist them. Mother screamed.

'Wold's men have given him a good kicking,' said Lars.

We sat Olaf down in the kitchen. 'What happened?' asked Mother. She looked to Agnete but my brother's girlfriend was struck dumb and appeared close to tears. Mother fetched some cloths and moistened them at the sink.

Lifting his head, Olaf said, 'Wold came to the bar.' His voice was slurred and he looked dazed. 'Insisted Agnete accompany him on a stroll by the harbour. Wouldn't take no for an answer.'

Mother began dabbing the blood from Olaf's swollen jaw and seeping cuts on his brow. 'Shall I fetch Doctor Haskveld?' I fretted. No one took any notice of me.

Agnete sobbed, 'What could I do? I had to go.'

'No you didn't,' snapped Olaf angrily, wincing at Mother's every touch.

At first I couldn't decide from their fragmented story whether Wold had simply been trying his luck or whether he'd planned an ambush for my brother, or both. Slowly the full horror emerged.

'At first we walked,' said Agnete in little more than a whisper. 'But halfway around the harbour I said I was freezing to death. He said, "Then let us find some

77

shelter," and he led me towards one of the *rorbuers*. I knew something was wrong and said I wanted to go back, but he gripped my arm and dragged me into the hut.' She turned away and hid her face in her hands.

Until that moment I hadn't noticed the tears in her thin sweater and the marks on her neck – scratches and bluish bruising. I suppose I'd simply been transfixed by Olaf's wounds and his generally beaten appearance.

'I followed them,' spat my brother.

Mother's lips trembled. I think she knew what was coming next – probably that female intuition of hers at work. She put down her cloth and took Agnete in her arms. Agnete crumbled.

'The bastard,' hissed Lars, his spittle showering my cheek.

'It was awful,' Agnete wailed.

'I tried to get to her but Wold's men blocked the way,' said Olaf. 'They told me to go home and forget about her. Of course, I couldn't do that.' He reached out, clutched her hand and squeezed it tightly. 'But there were too many of them.'

It took a week for my brother to lick his wounds and regain his strength. Dr Haskveld thought he'd bruised several ribs, which accounted for his considerable discomfort. Luckily the cuts and bruises were superficial. I wish the same could be said for Agnete. Outwardly her injuries appeared trivial, but beneath her skin the trauma was deep and lasting. You could see it in her face, a strange look as if she were lost.

Olaf had only one thing on his mind – Wold had to pay dearly. He spoke to Lars and his other friends, trying to drum up support to gang up on Wold, to drag him into an alleyway and bash the hell out of him. However, his friends' enthusiasm failed to match his. They thought it would only bring more trouble, with reprisals against everyone. Lars gripped my brother tightly and told him to back off. Looking him in the eye, Lars uttered the fearful words '*Nacht und Nebel*', words that sent a shiver down our spines. 'Night and Fog' – we all knew what it meant. Fritz used it whenever he ordered that someone be dragged off and made to *disappear*.

Of course, Agnete's parents filed a formal complaint against the lieutenant but the apathy with which the matter was dealt with added to their despair. Apparently no charges were to be brought. I think that proved the last straw for Olaf. I saw his growing thirst for revenge, and sensed the hunter's instinct taking him over like an aggressive cancer. One evening he came to a decision, leaped from his bed and knocked on my door.

'I need your help, Marek.'

As it was late, I didn't reply, but he barged in, closed the door and settled on the edge of a bookcase crammed with textbooks. 'I've had an idea.'

I stopped what I was doing at my desk and gave him my undivided attention.

'I've got a plan to deal with Wold.'

'Go on.'

'Figure the world would be better off without him! You know that stretch of road before you get to Kinsarvik, the wooded bit?'

'Yes.'

'Good place for an ambush. Ideal spot to blow him and his wretched Mercedes to hell.'

I mulled it over. Was he being serious? Initially I couldn't decide. But the wildness in his eyes told me his plan had been brewing in his head for some time. 'I like it,' I announced finally, thinking it was the only answer of interest to him. He grinned. 'Just one thing,' I added.

'What?'

'Where are you going to get the explosives and detonators from?'

'The same people who sold me those English cigarettes.'

'You're joking!' I quickly realized he wasn't. 'What about Lars? Is he part of your plan?'

'No. He knows nothing. I figured if he wasn't up to giving Wold a good hiding, he certainly won't want anything to do with this. Well, Marek, are you in?'

I nodded.

'Good! I do believe you have the makings of a true Jøssing.'

A compliment, no doubt, but I already considered myself one. We discussed the details well into the night, pausing only to raid the kitchen for some bread and cheese. Olaf hogged most of the ultra-sharp stinky

Gamalost – local to the Hardanger – and left me with a chunk of reddish Gudbrandsdal. The stench filled my bedroom as if all the soiled socks in Ulfhus had been collected up and dumped beneath my bed.

The following afternoon I hurried home from school and set to work. Several years ago I had helped Father rewire the house and remembered we had a reel of cable left over. In the garage I hunted for it and finally came across the dusty thing hidden behind his workbench. Mother always complained that Father never threw things away, that he hoarded them 'just in case', and for once I was grateful for his irritating habit. I suppose we are all creatures of habit to some extent. Now it formed one vital element of our plan. Wold had taken to visiting Kinsarvik every Thursday evening. I didn't know why but supposed it had something to do with a wider choice of female company there. Kinsarvik was twice the size of Ulfhus. Anyway, without fail, between seven and eight o'clock in the evening, Wold would climb into his car and set off, often not returning until the following morning. In a village like Ulfhus people noticed these things.

Unravelling the cable, I measured it and considered sixty feet to be marginal but about right. It felt stiff and difficult to bend and in parts the rubber sheath had begun to perish. It was heavy too, not exactly ideal for its intended purpose, but it was all I had. Next on my shopping list was a decent battery. Unfortunately Father had been remiss and not hung onto anything more powerful than a couple of leaky torch batteries that barely fizzed on the tongue. And the torch I'd used when fixing Josephine was dead. I sat on the bench and racked my brain. Such everyday items were hard to come by in the village during wartime and neighbours would not willingly lend them, cherishing them as prized possessions since they powered their radio sets during power cuts. And being able to listen to the outside world while in darkness was important to all of us. Of course, the Germans tried to stop such simple pleasures, demanding that everyone handed in their radio sets. And did we? Well, some did, but like us most refused despite the threats of internment.

I stared at Josephine and spoke to her of my problem. And in doing so, I realized that beneath her bonnet lay just what I needed. I disconnected her battery and lifted it out. God, it was heavy: too heavy. I needed something portable, pocket-sized. I dropped it onto the bench and studied it. Just half its acid cells would probably suffice but I couldn't figure out a way to divide it.

Olaf slipped in through the door. 'How's it going?'

'Got the cable but it's in a poor state. And we need a decent battery. The only one I can find that comes close is Josephine's but it's much too heavy.'

My brother inspected the cable, cursed in disgust and threw it to the floor. Rubbing his chin, he then clawed at the back of his neck thoughtfully. 'This is all too complicated, Marek. There must be an easier way,' he said.

'Let me think a minute.' I watched him pace back and forth, scratching his head and muttering and cursing to himself. 'Ah!' he suddenly declared. Grabbing a scrap of paper and a pencil, he began drawing. I peered over his stooped shoulder. His design looked ingenious. He then began rummaging feverishly in a box at the back of the garage, eventually returning with a reel of strong fishing line. 'Now,' he said, 'for this to work we need a grenade. If we fix it and attach the wire to the pin, then—'

I could almost hear the resulting *bang*. 'Can you get hold of one?' I asked.

'I think so. In fact, I'll try to get several. That way, the explosion will be powerful enough to make sure the job's done properly.'

'Just who is it you know?'

'I can't tell you that.'

I desperately wanted to share his secret but he wasn't stupid enough to let it slip. 'How long will it take to get them?' I asked.

'A couple of days.'

He drew me a picture of the sort of grenade he reckoned on being able to source. It differed greatly from those the Germans carried around, being sort of fruit-like in shape, about palm sized and curved. I started making a small shallow wooden box in which the grenades could be arranged with one fixed firmly to the side. Drilling a small hole for the fishing line, I applied a little grease to the rim to make sure it wouldn't snag. Once that was done, I burned Olaf's drawing, having committed the simple mechanism to memory. I feared an unannounced visit from Wold and his men. Such a diagram would not be easily explained, particularly as Olaf had crudely scrawled a figure being blown to smithereens and bearing the name 'Wold'!

The wait was almost unbearable but, to my delight, two days later my brother gave me the nod. I followed him into the garage and held my breath in anticipation as he lifted the wooden boards covering the inspection pit on the floor of the garage beneath Josephine. He reached down into the darkness like a polar bear fishing through a hole in the ice, and rose clutching a canvas sack. 'I managed to get four,' he said proudly. 'Sadly that's all they'd let me have. Wrong time of year. They're still waiting for new supplies to be shipped from England. Due in soon but I decided not to wait.'

He unfastened the sack and handed me a grenade. I felt all sweaty and feared it exploding in my hand. Recognizing my trepidation, he laughed. 'It's safe,' he said. 'So long as the pin remains fixed.'

I made damn sure the pin remained fixed!

That Thursday the thermometer next to our front door showed a miserable minus fifteen degrees and the wind added a further ten of chill. The snow had compacted and hardened into little more than sheets of ice. I waxed my skis, taking particular care with the edges, knowing it might prove important. I prepared my rucksack. The grenades fitted neatly into the box but I added a little straw packing to ensure a snug fit. I fed the fishing line through the hole and left the end ready for tying to the pin. I thought it was better to leave that final task until we set our trap, fearing the pin might get pulled accidentally in transit.

Olaf entered the garage carrying his rifle. 'You'd better take this,' he said, handing me Father's revolver. 'It's loaded, so be careful.'

It felt heavy but comforting in my grip. I slipped it into my anorak pocket. Handling it brought home to me the reality of what we were about to do. I suppose it's natural to have second thoughts, and I did, but said nothing. It was too late to turn back.

We headed out of the village along a string-thin path that clung to the edge of the fjord. We chose our route to minimize the risk of being spotted. We knew the path well but had walked it only a handful of times in the darkness and frost of winter. Olaf had reconnoitred the route and seemed confident in his steps. To me it felt slippery and I feared stumbling and damaging the contents of my rucksack. I trod cautiously and, irritated by my hesitancy, Olaf kept whispering at me loudly and impatiently to get a move on.

The road lay above us and occasionally we heard the odd car whine past, the headlights bouncing and reflecting off the snow. They created strange moving shadows that at one moment looked like trees, the next like mythical giants sneaking and creeping. My heart thumped. Olaf struck out ahead with purposeful strides.

I pleaded with him to slow down but he'd turned deaf.

Moonlight bathed the mountains on the far shore of the fjord and glistened on the surface of the water. Together they created a clandestine twilight that allowed us to get our bearings and work out where we needed to deviate from the path and begin our ascent to the road. Olaf had brought some rope and a couple of ice axes in case the going got tough.

'I think that's the place,' he said, pointing.

I peered up the slope of pristine, undisturbed snow peppered with jutting fangs of granite. 'A little further on,' I replied. 'To where the trees begin.'

He nodded. I looked at my watch and felt grateful to Father for parting with a few extra kroner before the war to buy me the one with a green luminescent dial. Having captured the light of the day, it glowed six-thirty. 'Time's getting on. We'd better hurry.'

In finalizing our plan we'd taken into account the terrain and road conditions and chosen the precise location based on three factors. One, a short stretch of pine trees lined both sides of the road. Two, the road was at its narrowest. And three, its surface was poor owing to heavy use, repeated snow ploughing and lack of repair.

Olaf stopped, removed his skis and drew an ice axe from his rucksack. We decided to carry our skis on our backs rather than leave them at the bottom of the slope and so helped each other to make sure they were firmly tied on. Olaf turned and looked up. Taking a deep breath, he sank his left boot into the slope. Kicking at the surface, he forged a foothold and pushed himself up, thrusting his pick into the snow above his head to aid his climb. Repeating the process, he made quick progress towards the road. I followed in his footholds. With fifty feet to climb, I first detected his rasping breath and effort-laden grunts about midway. I suggested he pause a moment but he ignored me. I sensed an intensity about him, a determination that knew no stopping.

Reaching the road, we crouched in the trees and listened. Nothing! Olaf lifted the box carefully from my rucksack and unwound the line. I pointed to a suitable pothole in the road, a place where the asphalt surface had been grazed away, forming a pothole deep enough to house the box. There was enough ice and gritty slush around to cover the box and conceal it.

'Which trees?' he asked.

That proved a tricky question. On paper it all looked so simple. Ideally we needed two trees, both sturdy and unbending, and each positioned just right. Unfortunately the trees hadn't grown quite where we'd pictured them in our minds. So we made do with two sited on either side of the road and roughly opposite each other, and a good forty feet from the pothole – forty feet in the direction of Ulfhus. Simplicity itself, the idea was that if we stretched the line across the road, Wold's car would drive into it. By attaching the line firmly to one tree and passing it around the trunk of the opposite tree, the effect of Wold striking it would be to yank the line and in doing so pull out the grenade's pin attached to the other end. A few seconds later Wold would be history. But we had a problem. Several actually. Did we have enough line? The reel contained only about sixty feet. Of course, it depended how fast Wold was travelling and the precise delay in the grenade's detonation. I tried to do the maths in my head but simply muddled myself.

Olaf shouted, 'Never mind that. It'll work. Don't worry.'

Then there was the trifling matter of tension, I realized. Too much and the pin could pop out at any time. Too little and the line might not snag properly on his car. He would simply drive over it. The original plan of remote electronic detonation directly under Wold's car now seemed far superior. If only Father had kept a suitable battery.

'Come on!' my brother shouted.

I crept into the middle of the road and placed the box in the pothole. I tugged some slack in the line and began tying it firmly to the grenade's circular pin. I put the lid on and covered it as best I could. It would do. It had to.

Olaf crouched at the other end of the line, behind the tree. 'Everything set?'

I knelt beside him and nodded. He passed the line around the trunk at a height of about two feet and began tightening it. 'Wait!' I shouted. 'Not too much or the pin will come out.' He loosened it.

I considered our options. 'Listen, we'll have to wait here until we see him. We'll pull it at the last minute.

Either he'll trigger it or we'll do it. Either way, he'll be heading towards hell.'

We sat on the cold ground and waited.

'After tonight, we must never speak of this,' said Olaf. 'Not to anyone. At least not until after the war, assuming we win. You must promise me, Marek. Our lives depend on it.'

'I promise.'

'Not even to Mother.'

'I said *I promise*.'

'Good.'

My fingers began to go numb and my nose soon felt as if it were no longer part of me. The cold sapped my energy. 'Does Agnete know we're doing this?' I asked.

He shook his head. 'What she doesn't know can't harm her.'

I didn't believe him but knew it was best to keep my mouth shut. I supposed she would be mighty glad to hear of Wold's demise. And she'd suspect Olaf had had a hand in it. After all, he'd made no secret of his hatred. Yet he was not alone. There were plenty of others in Ulfhus the Germans could point an accusing finger at.

'And if they question us, Marek, say nothing,' Olaf added.

'Of course.'

'But . . .' My brother grabbed my anorak tightly. 'But if they interrogate you, and you have to speak, then say it was me and me acting alone.'

'I couldn't do that, Olaf.'

He shook me. 'You must. This is my fight, not yours. It is something I'm willing to die for. You will have your share of causes.'

'But—'

'No buts, Marek. That's my final word. Promise me.'

'All right.'

'Good.'

We didn't say another word.

At just after seven o'clock we saw headlights. An annoying lump settled in my throat. Olaf picked up the line. 'Remember, Marek, as soon as he passes us, lie flat on the ground, close your eyes and cover your ears.'

I had every intention of doing just that.

The headlamps drew closer and I began to sweat. 'What if it's not his car?' I whispered.

'Shush.'

'No – really, what if it's someone else?'

'Shut up.'

Squinting, I tried concentrating on the approaching vehicle to make sure I had the earliest opportunity to identify it. Its lights, however, were blinding and I couldn't see. Olaf got ready with the fishing line. I heard him count backwards from five under his breath.

'Three . . . two—'

'No!' I shouted. I snatched the line from him. 'Jesus.' The car rattled past. 'It's Doctor Haskveld.' I'd caught a glimpse of the car's shape and recognized it.

My brother's face drained to match the colour of the snow. I knew he would be unable to forgive himself should a true Norwegian prove to be the victim of our scheme. And true Norwegians would never forgive us!

I heard another vehicle. For a moment we did not move, as if we'd abandoned our mission. Olaf simply stared at the snow at his feet.

'Come on,' I said. 'Concentrate. Listen to that engine. It sounds much more like Wold's Mercedes to me. We just have to be careful, that's all.' He looked up and into my eyes. 'Right?' I said. He nodded.

The car sped along far too quickly for the road conditions, its tyres slicing and sliding through the slush and making a loud *shushing* sound. Its engine growled and complained as it climbed through its gears. Olaf spat into each palm of his gloves, rubbed them together and then seized the fishing line gently, as if it had the fragility of rice paper.

'It's him!' I shouted. 'It's his Mercedes. I can see the sloping bonnet.'

Olaf hauled and screamed as the car flashed past, falling heavily onto his back. For a second I thought the line had snapped but then realized our plan had borne fruit. I threw myself into the snow face first and covered my ears. Two . . . three . . . I counted. I got to six and, about to fret, I then heard the explosion and felt the ground tremble. Debris smattered onto the back of my anorak but felt so light I assumed it was only snow and dirt. I turned over and looked up the road. What I saw wasn't quite what I'd anticipated.

Forty feet proved a slight underestimate. Nevertheless

the explosion had sent Wold's car careering into a tree. I got to my feet. Olaf seized his rifle and released the safety catch. Taking his cue, I felt in my pocket for Father's revolver. 'Let's make sure,' he spat uncompromisingly. Cautiously we approached the vehicle. I couldn't see inside but I hoped all was still. I heard a hiss and saw steam billowing from the crumpled grille wrapped around the tree. I sniffed for leaking petrol but detected none. I felt a surge of elation. We had done it. My God, we'd actually done it. Us!

My celebration proved premature.

The driver's door swung open and Wold, somewhat dazed, fell out onto his knees. He looked up and stared towards us, bewildered. He frowned and blinked repeatedly but said nothing. Olaf strode towards him, lifting his rifle to his shoulder. He stopped barely six feet from the German. 'You bastard,' he spat. The lieutenant frowned and then began to cough. 'You thought you'd got away with it, didn't you?' my brother continued.

Wold slowly came to his senses. Then, rather unexpectedly, he laughed. '*Olsen!*' he cried. 'Should have guessed.' He struggled to his feet.

'Yes, it's Olaf Olsen,' my brother shouted. 'Your judge, jury and executioner. For attacking Agnete Hilting, I sentence you to death!'

Wold shook his head violently. 'Don't be stupid. Think about it. There will be reprisals if you shoot me. Think of your family. Think of your neighbours.'

Of course, the lieutenant had a point. It was one I'd

pushed right to the back of my mind. I'd not wanted to think about it. But hearing him say it, I felt a chill sweep through me as I recalled the events at Telavåg and imagined the same awful fate falling on Ulfhus.

'Too late for that,' barked my brother. 'Can't let you go now. You'd see to it that we suffered and no doubt carry out the reprisals anyway. Just for the hell of it.'

'No, no, no,' pleaded Wold. He straightened up. 'We can do a deal.'

'Hah! Do you really think we'd trust you?'

Wold feigned a shrug and then moved as if intent on diving towards the cover of the trees, his right hand slipping towards his pistol's holster. Olaf fired and I saw the bullet thump into Wold's chest. The shot echoed through the Sørfjord. The lieutenant slumped and lay still. I don't know why but I thought of the reindeer my brother had shot up on the Hardanger. I recalled the pity I'd felt for its demise. Towards Wold I felt nothing, despite him being a fellow human being. I suppose he represented to me all the evil of the Nazis. And some-how that rid me of guilt or shame. My brother checked for a pulse and then kicked Wold in the belly, twice, something he would never have done to that deer. I understood his pain but thought it was unnecessary.

'What now?' I asked.

'Here, give me a hand. Let's throw him down the slope and into the water. That'll buy some time. It'll take them a while to figure out exactly what's happened.'

Wold proved surprisingly heavy. Finally we got him

to the edge and spun him over. He slid all the way, bouncing over the rocks. We heard the splash. 'Come on, Marek, let's get out of here.'

'He's right, though,' I said. 'There will be reprisals, won't there?'

'Probably. Unless—' He stopped. 'If we set fire to his car and push it over the edge, then maybe, just maybe, they'll figure it's an accident. That's if they don't find his body.'

Approaching Wold's car, I spotted tracks – tracks that led down the road towards Ulfhus. My blood ran cold. 'Olaf, see these?' I pointed. Then I focused into the distance and saw someone running with a slight limp into the darkness. It never occurred to me that Wold might have had company on his trip to Kinsarvik. Neither of us had bothered to examine the car closely. Somebody had been sitting in the back, out of view. 'We're done for,' I shouted. Panic-stricken, I thought of revenge and of Mother. Oh God, what had we done?

Chapter Seven

My brother ran down the road towards Ulfhus in pursuit of the shadow. Raising his rifle, he fired into the darkness and I heard a pinging ricochet. I don't think he struck anything other than a rock. Hurriedly I started fixing on my skis and then heard a vehicle heading down the road from the direction of Kinsarvik. I called out to Olaf, and we just managed to conceal ourselves by the time the car reached us. With Wold's Mercedes still hissing and steaming, the car drew to a stop and the robust figure of Dr Haskveld climbed out. I watched as he first checked inside Wold's car for casualties and then began looking around, somewhat perplexed. He called out to the icy landscape, 'Anybody hurt?'

To my shock, my brother shouted to him. Why on earth would we reveal ourselves?

'Doctor Haskveld, Wold's dead.'

We broke cover and approached him.

'Olaf? Marek?' He peered through the gloom into our faces and sighed heavily. 'You fools, this will only bring more trouble.'

'We had to do something,' my brother replied.

'Yes, but this wasn't the way.' Dr Haskveld raked the

back of his head with his fingers anxiously. 'What did you do with him?'

'He's gone swimming,' I said. 'But we have a problem. He had a passenger and he's escaped.'

'Does he know it was you?'

'He might,' said my brother reticently. He hesitated then added, 'Actually, Wold called out my name.'

'Oh, dear God.' Dr Haskveld's shoulders sagged. 'Well, if that's the case, you can't return to Ulfhus. You'd be arrested before the night's out.'

Can't return to Ulfhus! The words crushed me. What the hell were we going to do? I looked to my brother for inspiration but received none.

'Right,' said the doctor forcefully. 'We must act fast. You need a safe house. You need to lie low. And you've placed your mother in great peril. They will arrest and interrogate her unless we reach her first.'

My worst fears had become reality. 'Come on then,' I shouted. 'Let's get back to her.' I made for Dr Haskveld's car.

'No, Marek, leave her to me. I'll see to it. You must not waste a second in getting away. You need to put distance between you and Ulfhus.'

'But where can we go?' I started to panic.

'That's up to you but don't tell me. If I don't know, then I can't betray you.' He climbed into his car and started its engine. 'Try to send word to me when you're safe. I'll pass on any messages to your mother.'

'Where will she go?' I asked.

'Leave that to me. For now it's best to ask no more questions. I strongly suggest you get a move on because within hours this place will be crawling with troops and every road will be blocked.' He stared at Olaf through his window. 'People will thank you for what you've done, and they'll bear the terrible consequences as all good Norwegians have to. But think about this, Olaf: there will be others to fill Wold's shoes. They'll just keep on coming.'

'And we'll keep on fighting them,' said my brother defiantly.

Dr Haskveld shook his head. 'I know. That's how it has to be.'

'Now what?' I blurted as the doctor drove away.

'We're just a few miles from Kinsarvik,' my brother replied. 'I know a place we can hide tonight. I go there sometimes with Agnete. First thing tomorrow we'll head up the Hardanger and make for the Johanssens' hut. It's too risky to use the Borsobu. Come on, follow me.'

He slung his rifle over his shoulder, patted me on the back and set off along the road, quickly breaking right onto a path that took us into the woods and away from the fjord.

The Hardanger. The thought simultaneously thrilled me and scared the life from me. We would be heading for where no sensible man would dream of venturing during winter so ill prepared. Like those men and women of the MILORG, we were desperate, we were fugitives.

Again, the thought was both exciting and terrifying.

The lights of Kinsarvik twinkled between the branches of the trees. My brother stopped. 'There's a small shed hidden away behind the church. Not very comfortable but there's some old hay so we'll keep warm.' He set off again.

On the outskirts of town we removed our skis and tightened the cords of our hoods so that little of our faces showed. We both knew many people in Kinsarvik and they knew us. I prayed everyone had stayed at home. We stopped on a corner, the church directly opposite. The street in between lay empty, but I could hear music coming from several bars and felt that at any moment someone would burst out from a door, spot us and shout a greeting. Olaf seized my arm and stepped forward. I snatched him back. Two German soldiers had just appeared some fifty yards down the road. We slunk back into the shadows and watched them. They ambled slowly past in deep conversation. I saw their moist breaths fill the air and listened with bated breath to the crunching of their boots in the snow.

Eventually, the coast clear, we plucked up courage to risk all and strolled innocently across the street, down the side of the church, round the back and into the trees, to where the shed lay hidden. 'Shed', it turned out, was a case of exaggeration on my brother's part. Somewhat ramshackle, it had countless holes in its wooden walls through which the wind whistled a tune, and I could see stars in the heavens from inside. At least Olaf got the bit about the hay right. It smelled damp and mouldy though, and as I sat down on it I could not help thinking we were sharing our bed with various rodents.

At first we sat silently amid our own thoughts. Despite our predicament, all I could think about was Olaf and Agnete romping in this godforsaken den of iniquity. I began to snigger uncontrollably. My brother thumped me when I whispered my thoughts. I think he felt embarrassed.

My mind drifted towards Mother and Dr Haskveld. I prayed that he had reached her in good time and that she would be safe. I missed her already. And I realized I was lucky. I had Olaf beside me. She had no one now. I wiped a tear from my cheek and repeatedly told myself that I needed to be strong. *Be strong, Marek*, I chanted inside.

My brother remained quiet and I didn't like the silence. 'Doctor Haskveld's a member of the Resistance, isn't he?' I whispered. 'That's why you were quick to reveal us to him, wasn't it? You were certain of his reaction.'

'Yes.'

'Will he do what he said? Will he take Mother to safety?'

'He will certainly do his best, Marek. Don't worry, she's in good hands. In fact, we were damn lucky he returned when he did.'

'Thank God. And we'll see her soon, won't we?'

'One day, Marek. We'll see her again one day. Be sure of that.'

I tried desperately not to cry but the more I tried to

stop the tears, the more they came. My brother hugged me. 'What have we done?' I asked.

'The right thing, Marek, the right thing. This is war and we are part of it.'

I plumped up the hay as best I could to fashion a bed and packed some around me for insulation. But I couldn't stop shivering. 'What do we do when we get to the Johanssens' hut?' I asked.

'We wait until it's safe.'

'How long will that be?'

'A month perhaps. Maybe longer.'

'Then what?'

'I don't know.' My brother sounded angry. 'I don't have all the answers.'

'Perhaps we could go to Bergen, to Uncle Knut's.'

'You said the Gestapo had a file on him, Marek. That'll mean they're watching him. It wouldn't be safe. Anyway, we'd need false papers to travel on the ferry and train.'

'We could try to make it to Sweden,' I said enthusiastically. As a neutral country, it would be safe for us. And although the border controls were tight on all the roads, in the hills and mountains the border could be crossed undetected at will. But it was a hell of a long way away.

'That's a possibility, Marek. They might consider us refugees because of what's happened. Then again, not all escaping Norwegians are given sanctuary. It all depends.'

'What about the Resistance? You're always boasting about your contacts.'

'Impossible!'

I saw a look of anguish on his face. I suspected he'd already thought of my idea. And then it dawned on me that I was the reason he dismissed the option out of hand. I was only fourteen and he felt responsible for me. God, it all seemed so utterly hopeless.

My brother periodically crept to the door of the shed and peered through the slats. He listened and looked for signs of heightened activity from the Germans. It would only be a question of time, he told me. With any luck their initial focus would be on Ulfhus as that was Wold's patch. When they found nothing, we guessed they would gradually widen their search.

I tried to get some sleep but achieved nothing better than the occasional doze. The freezing cold gradually embraced me and I kept checking my zips and toggles to ensure my anorak was still done up. I thought about our trek to the Hardanger. Only once had we ventured there in deepest winter. And that had been with Father, Uncle Knut, Mr Johanssen and several other men and boys from the village. We carried plentiful supplies on small toboggans and stayed just a week during fine, settled weather. An adventure for sure and one I remember for happy days tracking deer in air touching minus thirty degrees, so cold it hurt to breathe. Somehow I didn't think this trip would prove quite so easy.

The hours passed painfully slowly and I stiffened to the point where I doubted I could stand up straight. In the darkness I kept glancing at my watch as, gradually, the glow of the dial faded, its captured sunlight escaping into the night.

Olaf nudged me. 'It might be wise to set off early. If we can get halfway up the Husedalen valley by dawn, we'll be safer.'

We set off at four o'clock and my brother insisted we avoided the main paths. That meant working our way through trees laden with snow. The going proved horrendous. Unable to ski, we climbed by foot, our boots sinking into snow up to our knees, occasionally our waists. Only by clutching at trunks and branches could I maintain my balance. And as I did so, piles of snow slid from the branches and covered me. In the forest, the darkness seemed more intense, more menacing. But we kept on going.

The Johanssens' hut lay deeper into the Hardanger than our Borsobu. I kept trying to convince myself that our hut would be just as safe as the other one but Olaf would hear none of it.

In places the trees thinned and the terrain became an obstacle course of granite boulders, deep drifts and slopes that were not for the faint hearted. Eventually I heard the sound of water and knew that one of the waterfalls lay ahead. It wasn't flowing as fast as it did during the spring thaw. Even so, it roared as water slammed against water, and in the quarter light of the moon the spray glistened and sparkled like a million diamonds. Jagged ice spears hung from every outcrop and the freezing flow hammered down over rocks cased in ice.

Olaf paused. 'Hear that?'

'What?'

'We chose wisely not to hang around in Kinsarvik.'

I listened and heard dogs barking in the distance. 'You think . . . ?'

'Yes. They've arrived.'

'They'll track our scent.'

'Perhaps. We better press on.'

Overcome with anxiety, I froze. I hurt like hell and knew that in any chase I'd be no better than a sick elk – easy pickings for a hunter. I felt done for, and the emotion of it welled up inside like a volcanic eruption. I jabbered fearfully, making little sense. I knew the Germans would be tireless in their search. They'd stop at nothing to gain revenge. Growing tearful, I ordered myself to grit my teeth. My brother saw my weakness and patted me on my back encouragingly. I detected moistness in his eyes and knew I wasn't the only one hurting.

'Come on, Marek,' he said calmly. 'We can make it. Old Fritz will probably waste the morning searching the town. By the time they figure out that we might have headed up here, it'll be growing dark again and they'll not bother.'

I believed him. I had to. Otherwise hope had gone and that meant the beginning of the end.

The feeble light of dawn glowed from behind the hillside. There would be only a few hours of light and we had to make the most of them. I took a deep breath and stomped past my brother: time for me to take the lead.

We saw no one all day. I suppose I should have been happy, but my sense of isolation and abandonment grew with every passing hour. Spasms in my belly reminded me of my hunger. Oh, what I'd give for the crispness of a thin *lefse*, my favourite flat bread, topped with lightly salted butter and cinnamon sugar, or even some salt herring, or, dare I say it, even some stinking Gamalost. God, I must have been hungry! But we had no *lefse*, let alone any tasty toppings.

Olaf paused, surveyed the scene and announced that we'd reached a good spot to make camp. We were already well up the valley and the Hardanger lay ahead, almost in touching distance, the forest giving way to the infinite sweep of white, of occasional rocky outcrops exposed by the wind, of frozen rivers and streams. There would be little shelter for us there until we reached the hut. We took off our rucksacks and I sat on a fallen log and rubbed my calves. My boots were soaked through, as were my outer clothes. No sooner had I stopped and cooled from the heat of exertion than I felt the damp seep into me.

'I could do with a hot drink and something to eat,' I complained. 'Don't suppose there's a café nearby, is there? One serving pancakes and chocolate sauce.'

My brother laughed. 'A bowl of *lapskaus* would slip down a treat.'

I thought of sliced root vegetables, sausage and left-over meat boiled into a soupy stew, and my mouth watered. It was also the time of year for *lutefisk*, cod soaked in soda solution until softened, rinsed for several days to get rid of the lye, and then poached. I loved it but my brother loathed its mushy texture. I shook my head. My thoughts were pure torture.

Our camp lay some fifty yards from the floor of the valley and at the edge of a particularly dense cluster of pines. Choosing a deep triangular fissure in the hillside carved during the last ice age, we hid out of sight of anyone trekking through the bottom of the valley. We dug a large hollow in a bank of snow and compacted its sides. We remembered to make sure the opening pointed south, away from the prevailing wind. I searched for some dry wood suitable for making a friction device for creating fire. With a block held firmly under my boots, I spun a twig back and forth between my palms, the end drilling against the surface of the block. I think I had chosen the wrong sort of wood, or wood that was too damp, because it simply didn't work. All I achieved for my labours was blisters.

Olaf looked on in amusement. Only once I'd got angry and chucked the stick and block as far as I could in frustration did he produce his box of matches. 'Always be prepared,' he said cheerfully. I wanted to thump him.

We waited until dark before lighting a small fire in a shallow pit opposite the opening to our snow house. That way, no one would see the smoke rise and, as it was out of sight of the valley, we thought it unlikely anyone could see the faint glow. My brother proved to be a magician. From his rucksack he took two small mugs, a tin and a small bag of ground coffee. He melted some snow and brewed us a welcome drink on the fire. Then he produced some dried meat, oat biscuits and a couple of apples. A feast!

'Father always said you should never leave home in winter without taking sufficient provisions to keep you going in case of an emergency,' he explained. 'So I always carry the essentials.'

I took a peek into his rucksack and was heartened to see enough provisions to last several days if eked out carefully. I sat back and sipped my coffee. The fire crackled and Olaf continually added branches to keep the flames going. What we had been taught on school trips and by our father about building shelters appeared to be true. Although the fire lay outside, its warmth seemed to collect inside our home for the night and I was more comfortable than I'd been in the shed in Kinsarvik.

Olaf fell into one of his quiet, reflective spells. 'Thinking of Mother?' I asked.

He nodded but I doubted him. 'Of Agnete?' He nodded again. I believed him. 'When this is all over, will you marry her?'

He threw me a glance, his face uncertain. 'Maybe.'

'Do you love her?'

'Kind of.'

'What sort of answer is that?'

'Well, I do, but I'm not sure if I do enough to marry her. You know, having kids and all that. Just the thought scares the hell out of me. *And* our world's changing so fast, Marek. Right now we don't know how it's all going to end. Now is not the time to be thinking of such things.'

'Will you go to Oslo to study medicine? I mean, once Father returns.'

He dwelled on my question at length. 'We'll see,' he said. He looked rather glum.

'What's the matter?'

'Nothing.'

'Come on, it's Marek, tell me.'

He stared at me, his lips quivering. 'About Father,' he began. 'Don't expect him to be home too soon. I think they'll keep him at the camp for a long time.'

'Why?' I shouted. 'What's he done?'

'Father's been involved with men united against the NS and Mr Quisling.'

'I know. Mother let it slip.'

'And . . .' My brother hesitated. 'Can you keep a secret, Marek?'

'Of course.'

'Father is a messenger for the Resistance.'

My heart leaped with pride and joy and the excitement was almost overwhelming. 'You sure?'

'Yes, Marek. I'm sure. He told me.'

'That's great. I feel so proud of him.'

'It's not so great, Marek. Old Fritz suspects something, and should he gather even a shred of evidence, none of us will ever see Father again!'

He'd stunned me into silence. It took a while for it to sink in. 'And the Johanssens?'

'Resistance as well.'

'Does Mother know?'

'Yes, but none of the details. That's how Father wanted it.'

I suddenly felt angry that everyone knew about this except me.

'Father thought you were too young to know. But I reckon you've proven yourself. You're a man now, Marek, whether you like it or not. And with manhood comes responsibility.'

Instantly I felt older and wiser. 'Don't suppose you've got any English cigarettes hidden in that rucksack of yours, have you?'

'Might have.'

'I think we should share one.'

'That's a grand idea, Marek.'

We took turns puffing on the cigarette and our house of Norwegian ice filled with sweet fumes. 'If only,' said my brother.

'If only what?'

He sucked hard, puckered his lips and blew out a stream of thick grey smoke. 'If only we could do something to help him.'

Having no meaningful reply, I said nothing. Instead I

pictured Herr Stretter of the Gestapo and thought that persuading that horrid, evil little beast to release Father would be harder than enticing a snow hare into a cooking pot. We sat in silence.

Eventually my brother's posture slumped and he dozed off, snoring loudly, his head tilted too far forwards. I stared into the darkness and then up towards the stars and moon. I thought of the old Norse myth about time – the sun and moon racing across the sky in celestial chariots pursued by the huge wolves Hati and Skoll snapping at their heels, trying to devour them. Olaf and I were the sun and the moon, and the wolves weren't far behind. I wondered what was to become of us. It is said that in Åsgard, a fortress built by the gods, live three Norns, three goddesses of destiny, Urd, Verdande and Skuld. They would know the answer. They knew the destiny of every living being. I wondered if they wept for us.

Our fire grew weak and so I piled on a few more broken branches and used my elbows to scrape and shape the snow beneath my back. *Sleep, Marek*, said a voice inside me. *Sleep now, for tomorrow shall prove a hard day*.

I awoke, startled by a noise. Olaf was dreaming, a nightmare that crept into the real world as groans and muttering that spoke of turmoil in his soul. He twisted and writhed. I nudged him. It seemed to help his escape from the dark shapes that skulked in the shadows of his mind. He lay still. My watch glowed dimly. I could barely make out the time – five-thirty. The wind had picked up and sang through the trees. The stars and moon had gone, replaced by a rug of cloud that hugged the mountains. Our fire had given up and I felt chilled to the core. My brother began snoring again. What the hell were we doing up here? It all felt crazy. They'd miss me at school. What would they think? And even if we held up at the hut for a month, maybe two, maybe the whole winter, what then? The future looked not so much bleak as simply blank. I just couldn't picture it. Surely our escape spoke of our guilt, and so Dr Haskveld was right, we couldn't return to Ulfhus, maybe ever. What would Father think? As a member of the Resistance, perhaps he'd understand what we'd done and forgive us.

I looked at my brother and wondered whether killing Wold had really restored the balance of the scales of justice. It had seemed right until the deed was done. How strange was that? The desire for revenge had been fed, our anger satiated, but it changed things, cast a different light, a light in which everything appeared different. Oh God, we'd killed a man! Had we become as evil as those who brought tyranny to our land? Had we become infected? I tried to shake the thought from my mind, for it did me no good, merely making me anxious and forcing me to endure a deep sense of guilt. OK, so I'd not pulled the trigger. But I had been a willing part of it. That was surely enough.

It began to snow.

Chapter Eight

In the morning I asked Olaf about his nightmares but he could remember nothing. How lucky, I thought.

With it snowing heavily, we did our best to destroy our camp, burying the embers of the fire and making it look as if no one had been there. Our final climb onto the Hardanger proper would take a couple of hours – that's if we could find our way since visibility had deteriorated. Olaf produced a tiny compass from his anorak pocket. We set off and spoke little as we ascended, scaling the rocks in a zigzag, taking great care that each step was balanced and gained a firm hold. I began with my goggles on to stop the driving snow from stinging my eyes but soon removed them to ensure I could see which rocks were slippery and which were loose. Now was not the time to risk a fall and injury. The muscles in my legs quickly began to burn and I puffed hard to feed them oxygen.

As we left the forest behind, the landscape opened up and became one of rock, boulders, fissures and snow. It was awesome, even to someone like me who'd lived in the shadow of mountains all his life. It's what makes us Norwegians different. Whenever we get above ourselves, we only need to look up or down to feel humbled and utterly insignificant.

At last we reached the point at which skiing became possible. It gave us a new lease of life and we hurriedly attached our boots to our skis.

'Stay close, Marek. Keep in my tracks,' my brother instructed. He held his compass aloft until the needle settled. He pointed east and took a deep breath.

'Don't go too fast – you know I have trouble keeping up,' I said.

He nodded, flipped a ski a half turn and headed off, his poles pushing hard into the snow. Although we knew the way, given that I couldn't make out the landscape beyond a hundred yards, I felt happy to rely on Olaf as navigator. For hours we slid along, our pace steady, our skis perfectly parallel. What had been little more than a gusty breeze in the Husedalen valley turned into a fierce gale across the endless white sweep of the plateau. The wind howled incessantly like a pack of starving wolves and whipped up the powdery snow into a swirling panic. As for the cold, it tore through our anoraks and bit our cheeks. At times I found it difficult to breathe, snowflakes filling my mouth, making me cough and splutter. The Johanssens' hut still seemed a long way away. My brother slid to a halt and turned to check I remained on his tail.

'You OK?' he shouted.

I nodded, unable to speak between gasps.

'Bit rough, isn't it? Still, look on the bright side. At least old Fritz won't bother. And it would make little sense for them to send out a reconnaissance plane. And'

– he shook his poles – 'and our tracks are quickly getting covered. So, all in all, it's pretty perfect.'

'Perfect' was not the word I'd have chosen but I understood what he meant. 'How far to the hut?'

He grimaced. 'Far enough.'

'You know where we are?'

'Roughly.'

His vague reply did little to bolster my confidence. 'Roughly where?'

He pointed to his left. 'As long as we keep parallel to that distant ridge, we'll be fine.'

I couldn't see a ridge. I tore my goggles off and squinted. 'What ridge?'

'Over there, stupid,' he said irritably.

'Oh, right.' I prayed he could see something I couldn't. 'You absolutely sure?'

'Of course. Don't worry. Do you want to take the lead?'

'No thanks.' That was the last thing I wanted to do. 'Thanks for asking anyway.'

We continued on. The wind turned from a howl to a whistling scream. I could barely stand, let alone ski. In fact, I reckoned I could have leaned into the angry breath of the gods and its strength would have held me upright. Worryingly my hurting limbs no longer felt sore. I couldn't feel them at all! I tried shouting to my brother but my words were snatched from my mouth. I tried catching him up but struggled. Slowly I lost sight of him in a growing veil of whiteness. All I could do was look down and make sure my skis followed in his tracks. That would keep us together, so long as he didn't put too much distance between us.

Was this our punishment? Would the storm blow until all life was extinguished from our mortal bodies? Desperation overwhelmed me. I knew there would be no respite.

Still staring downwards, I bumped into Olaf, who'd paused to let me catch up. 'Whoa, Marek. Jesus, you should look where you're going.'

'This is hell.'

'Hell on the Hardanger, Marek. Isn't nature glorious?'

I began to think my brother was quite mad.

'Can we stop a while? I'm knackered.'

'Just long enough to catch your breath. Any longer and we'll get too cold. Don't want us seizing up. We're making good progress. It'll be dark soon, so I'll keep an eye out for somewhere to make camp.'

Camp! Oh God, I'd pushed to the back of my mind the fact that no way could we reach the Johanssens' hut in one day's skiing – at least not in these conditions. And a night on the plateau, exposed, wilted my flagging legs. I leaned on my poles and cursed.

With the last remnants of daylight, Olaf stopped close to a low ridge of granite that offered a little shelter. He removed his rucksack. 'Get those skis off, Marek. We're going to have to dig and build ourselves another snow house.'

The effort needed to dig a hole big enough for the

both of us and then pile and compact the snow into something resembling a shelter nearly finished me off. Only the prospect of getting out of the wind drove me on. The whole process seemed to take an age, and when it was complete, I collapsed inside and yelled in a mixture of agony and anguish. We hadn't eaten all day and I'd passed well beyond hunger pangs. I felt so sick and weak I didn't think I had the energy to chew, let alone swallow. The worst thing, though, was the knowledge that we couldn't build a fire; there weren't any trees in this part of the Hardanger. So I couldn't even look forward to a hot drink. I couldn't even muster the energy to cry.

'Pass me your rucksack, Marek.'

I dragged it next to my brother.

'Coffee?'

Surely that's a cruel dream, I thought. But then my brother unfastened the straps and removed some kindling and fir branches from my rucksack. 'How did that get in there?' I asked.

'Be prepared, Marek. Remember my motto? Figured something like this might happen so I took the opportunity to gather some wood this morning.'

'But that's my rucksack!'

'I've got the food in mine. Thought you'd not mind lugging your share.' He stared out of our shelter and looked thoughtful. 'Think we'll have to build it just inside or it'll get blown out.' Whistling cheerfully, he set about lighting a fire.

I realized that had I been alone, I'd not survive. Olaf

had remembered the compass, the matches and the food. He had thought ahead. Just like Father always did. The four years separating us suddenly felt like forty.

I had never tasted a better cup of coffee. Each gulp revived me as if I were drinking at the fountain of life. As I thawed, feeling returned to my sore limbs and they complained bitterly. My brother forced me to eat something.

The storm showed no signs of abating, and now and again we kicked the accumulating snow from the entrance to our shelter, fearing that otherwise we might awake to find ourselves entombed.

My brother pulled the cord of his hood tight and blew into his hands.

'God, this place is like the plain of Vigrid,' I said.

'The what?'

'You know, the old story. Of how the world is supposed to end – the final battle between gods and men, giants and monsters.'

'Tell me, Marek, I've forgotten.'

I settled back onto my elbows. 'It's the time of Ragnarok, the "twilight of the gods", the day of doom. Three years of harsh winter are followed by the appearance of the sky-wolves who devour the sun and moon. You remember, don't you? Uncle Knut used to tell us the story.'

'Go on, Marek, remind me. It seems a perfect night for such a tale. What happens?'

'Mountains crash and crumble and the Fenris Wolf

storms around the world with its jaw scraping the earth while fire burns in its eyes and flames shoot from its snout.'

'That's right, I remember now. And isn't Loki, the god of strife and spirit of evil, finally freed from being shackled to a rock? And doesn't he sail from the north in command of Hel's sons?'

'Yes, and the giant, Hrym, sails his ship, *Naglfar*, a ship forged from dead men's nails, with ragged sails and a crew of rotting corpses.'

'I can picture it,' said my brother enthusiastically. 'Go on.'

'Then the Midgard Serpent comes ashore and slithers over our fields and meadows. The heavens get torn apart—'

My brother interrupted me. 'And from Muspellsheim, the land of fire, storm mighty horsemen in shining armour bearing swords of fire.'

'Yes, and everything in their path catches light.'

'And the final bloody battle takes place on the vast plain of Vigrid.'

'That's right.'

My brother frowned. 'But how exactly does it end?'

'The Fenris Wolf devours Odin. The Midgard Serpent battles with Thor and they slay one another, as do Loki and Heimdall, the great watchman of the gods. And the whole world burns until it is nothing more than a smoking ruin. And what remains slips beneath the sea.'

'Ah, what an end!' my brother exclaimed.

'The end? Far from it, it's merely the beginning.'

'How's that?'

'From the sea is born a new earth, washed clean of evil, and the new land provides a bountiful supply of food. New life may begin, with an existence free from hunger and cold.'

'Aha!' My brother nodded happily. 'So there's hope then?'

'There's always hope,' I replied.

We settled onto our backs, each entertained by our own thoughts. Mine focused on Uncle Knut and his many past visits to Ulfhus at Christmas. Sitting by a crackling fire, he'd entertain us with Norse myths and legends between sips of warm *gløgg*, a spicy drink with almonds and raisins floating on its surface, a drink that had Viking roots. Uncle Knut always spoke in a rumbling, rasping tone that seemed just right for such heroic tales. Spellbound, I'd be transported into that other world and I never wanted his stories to end.

Pressing shut my eyes, I said prayers for Father and imagined Mother safe in Sweden or wherever she'd ended up. I wondered how she was coping without us.

The collapse of our shelter came as an unpleasant awakening. The snow on top of me tried to crush me but I fought it, digging furiously with my hands while choking. I managed to forge a hole and that gave me air. Then I thrust a hand up and felt Olaf grasp it. He pulled me from my grave.

'The fire must have partially melted it,' he shouted. 'Made it unstable.'

I gathered my wits. 'What now?'

'It's six o'clock. We might as well set off. No point trying to rebuild it.'

That made sense. As the wind and snow hammered us, we dug out our belongings and readied ourselves. Storms on the Hardanger can pass through quickly or hang around for days. This one had the inclination to loiter awhile and maximize our grief. Looking around, I could see virtually nothing other than a misty, frenetic swirling of large snowflakes. Visibility was less than fifteen feet.

'Olaf, get out your rope. I think it might be a good idea if we tie ourselves together so we don't get separated. What do you think?'

My brother waved his agreement. Unravelling his climbing rope, he fed and tied one end around his waist, the other end around me. The sense of safety I gained far outweighed the annoyance of repeated tugging as Olaf proved once again that his pace on skis outshone my lesser skill. I felt sorry for him. I was slowing him down like a ball and chain tied to his ankles. But as we leaned into the blizzard's full wrath, the confidence in his stride reassured me that he knew where he was going, that his small compass guided him like the Pole Star. I had absolutely no idea where we were.

The Hardanger's terrain was starkly different from Norway's coastal fringes. Most think of our country as being a hysterical, jagged coastline with tall, craggy mountains surrounding deep fjords; an imposing and breathtaking vista that's full of wonderment. And it was true, of course. Few, however, realized that this fortress-like beginning guarded places like the Hardanger. Here, on Europe's largest mountain plateau, the lines were drawn more horizontal than vertical. It was undulating, sweeping and endless. For eyes used to peaks, ridges, walls of granite and shadowy valleys, it might seem featureless, but it had its own kind of detail. We skied up gentle slopes and down the other side and occasionally found ourselves on surfaces truly flat. That meant just a foot or two of snow and as much again of ice separated us from the freezing waters of one of the many lakes. And on the lakes you had to be certain that the ice was of a depth that would support you. If not, you'd become fish food.

My muscles ached hellishly. My skis and boots felt heavy. Snow coated my anorak and had forced its way into every tiny little crease and gap in my clothing. I had to keep wiping my goggles. I'd lost all feeling in my nose and my lips had cracked in several places. I worried about frost-bite, about exposure, about hypothermia, and about death.

The rope went slack.

Olaf had stopped and I saw him leaning heavily on his poles.

'You OK?'

He looked round at me and then back towards the ground.

'What's the matter?'

He pulled off his goggles. 'I'm a bit dizzy,' he shouted. 'Feeling a bit sick. Probably been pushing too hard.'

'How far have we got to go?'

He scanned the wall of white and pointed ahead. 'Due east. Can't be more than a mile.'

'We're almost there?' I felt a surge of elation.

'Almost. Let me rest a moment. I'll be fine.'

We stood for a while, continually battered by the blizzard. Snow settled on our skis and quickly covered them. My brother did not seem to be getting better. His head remained low and I could see his discomfort exceeded my own. 'Come on,' I encouraged. 'Only a mile. Think about it: a warm hut, a fire, dry clothes, a hot drink and some food. What more could a man ask for?' I slapped him hard on his back as if he were an obstinate mountain mule. My cajoling had little effect.

We could not stop for long. The weather would defeat us. I gazed in the direction my brother had pointed and decided there was only one thing for it. I seized his compass, held it true and saw he'd pointed south-southeast. In his maelstrom of exhaustion, he'd pointed the wrong damn way! I knew fatigue and dis-orientation could be our worst enemy. We might end up walking in circles on a path to death. I checked again which way was east and stiffened my resolve. Drawing up the slack in the rope, I tried to forge ahead but Olaf's weight anchored me to the spot. I seized the rope and gave it a hard yank, then another, and another, until I felt it slacken. Thank God. He'd summoned the will and the energy for that final push and managed to place one ski in front of the other. I dug my poles in, leaned forward to take the strain and gritted my teeth. God, it was hard, harder than anything I'd ever done. Every tortured step had me gasping for breath and shooting pains struck down my back and legs. But, ever so slowly, we moved forwards, one ski length at a time.

Surely we had to be getting near to the Johanssens' hut, I thought. I stared into the blizzard and imagined that the outline of the hut would suddenly appear miraculously and we would be saved. But I saw nothing and began to fret. What if I'd drifted off course? What if Olaf had got it all wrong? What if we were miles from shelter? I knew the answers to all these questions but feared to dwell on such an awful fate. If true, we'd lie in this place, buried until the spring thaw. Only then might hunters come across our rotting remains.

Something was wrong! The rope had tightened and I couldn't move forward. I turned round and slid back. My brother lay in the snow.

'Olaf!' I shook him. 'Olaf. Get up. Come on, get up!' He did not move. I knelt down and wiped the snow from his face. His cheeks were red and sore, his lips a little bluish, but, thank God, he still breathed. I lifted his goggles. His eyes were closed. Perhaps he's just fainted, I thought. After all, we'd eaten little and he was a large man with a hearty appetite. I prayed that was it and nothing more serious. He stirred and his eyelids flickered open a crack.

'Can you hear me?' I shouted.

He nodded.

'Can you get up?'

'Need to rest a while, Marek,' he croaked.

I didn't like the tone of his voice. It sounded weak, feeble and resigned. 'No, Olaf. *Get up*. We're almost there. Just another few minutes.'

He fainted again.

No way could I lift him or carry him. No way! I slumped onto the snow in despair. We were done for. This was the end. I felt certain of it. A vision of our last trip to the Hardanger filled my head. We'd been two young hunters at one with nature, at home in the wilderness. How different this was. I looked at my brother and began to sob at how our lives had turned in such a short time from the optimistic, reckless joys of youth into pure horror.

Then a change came over me. It felt as if it came from deep within, somewhere dark, untapped and primeval. And it was strong, determined and all-consuming. Damn it, I thought, this is not going to be how it ends. This is not where our last breaths shall be breathed. I looked directly skywards, into the greyish flurry of snowflakes intent on gently smothering us, and shouted to the gods, to Odin, to Thor, and begged for their strength. I took off Olaf's skis and then my own. I slid them beneath him and tied them to his legs. Made for cross-country treks, they're long, and I thought I could fashion enough of a sledge to drag my brother to safety. I checked the knots and then stomped through the snow, passing the other end of the rope over my shoulder and tying it around my waist. I took up the slack, gripped the rope fist over fist, and leaned forward. I dug my boots into the snow to get maximum grip and then I pulled. And I screamed and I yelled and I gritted my teeth until I began to edge ahead. I took a step, then another, and slowly we moved. The rope ate into my shoulder and my boots slithered and slipped. My back shouted in pain and I felt as if my lungs were about to burst. But one step followed another and I kept on yelling and screaming. I had not known such pain before, yet I would not let it defeat me. I would not let it defeat *us*. I dragged Olaf fifty yards, then a hundred, then two hundred, up slopes and down the other side, always trying to steer a straight course. In agony, my heart pounded as if it were about to explode and I felt sweat pour down my neck inside my anorak hood. Just a little further, I shouted to myself. Another hundred yards, maybe two, that's all.

My vision began to blur. My legs began to fail. I slumped to my knees but kept moving forwards, sinking into the snow. Nausea and giddiness made my head spin and I kept swallowing though my mouth was dry. With one final cry, I collapsed.

Chapter Nine

I can think of fewer more frightening things than waking to see a fearsome bearded stranger staring into your face.

Gingerly I lifted myself onto my elbows. My head swam and I felt slightly sick.

'Here, take a sip of this,' he said, pressing a bowl to my lips.

Whatever it was, it tasted bland and thick. But it was warm. I guessed it was some sort of vegetable soup, probably potato. I swallowed and rested my head back down. Looking up, I saw the angled slats of a pine roof. 'Where am I?'

'You're safe.'

Something pinged in my brain. 'And Olaf, where's Olaf?' I shouted, bolting upright.

'Don't fret, he's over by the stove.'

I saw my brother huddled on a stool by the warmth, a grey blanket wrapped around his shoulders. He sneezed, turned and raised a feeble hand to greet me. God, his face! I shall never forget it. The ravages of snow, wind and crippling temperatures had burned his skin and made him barely recognizable. There were blisters too. *Frostbite!*

The man settled down on a stool next to me. He spoke quietly. 'Now, Marek, tell me your story and leave nothing out. Why are you here? What happened?'

'Who are you?' I asked.

'Jorgen Peterson,' he replied. 'Born in Tromsø and hope to return there one day. We've met before, young man. Don't you remember?'

I peered into his face. There was something familiar about him. And his voice, his accent – from the far north – did trigger some deep memory inside my head, but I just couldn't place it. I shook my head.

'Our paths crossed a few months ago. You were returning from a hunting trip.'

It clicked. Now I remembered. He was the man leading the British commandos. He got up and poured some coffee. 'Here, drink it slowly, it's hot. Now, tell me everything.'

Dare I? Was it safe? I looked to Olaf and he nodded. So I began our tale from when we last met. I spoke of Father's arrest on our return, the evil of Wold's deeds and our revenge. And, while doing so, I thought it odd that Olaf had not already told him. Only as I got to our escape from Kinsarvik did I consider the fact that Jorgen might be testing me, checking my story against my brother's. If it was identical, I supposed he would believe us. But should our tales diverge then he'd doubt every- thing. That might prove fatal. I finished my saga declaring my brother and me to be Jøssings. He laughed and slapped my shoulder.

We had made it to the Johanssens' hut – or rather we'd got here by some means or other. At first I couldn't be absolutely sure it was their hut because a lot had changed since I last visited. And there were rucksacks and bags everywhere, and clothing hung to dry along lines stretched from wall to wall. A pair of trousers billowed and a woman emerged from behind them. I guessed her to be in her mid twenties, pretty but not startlingly so, her shoulder-length hair thin and blonde but not sculpted in any particular fashion. She introduced herself as Ingrid, offering no second name. I thought it rude to ask.

She clutched a small bowl, a cloth and a sharp knife. She settled down beside me and smiled. I tried smiling back but as the corners of my mouth headed towards my ears, my face screamed. She winced. Oh God, I thought, is it worse than Olaf's?

'What are you going to do?' I shouted. Unfortunately I already knew the horrible answer to my question and so slipped down under my blanket, only for Ingrid to tear it from me.

'It's best if I remove the worst of it,' she said matter-of-factly. She unfolded her cloth and placed the bowl next to where I lay. I shook uncontrollably. Lighting a paraffin lamp, she held the knife in the flame, twisting and turning the blade until it turned black. She then peered closely at my face with a disconcerting level of concern.

'Is it bad?' My voice trembled.

'Seen worse. Now hold still. This is going to hurt.'

She could have fibbed just to make me feel better, but as she cut away the small lumps of dead skin on my cheeks and neck, I was grateful for her warning as the operation proved excruciating enough to make my limbs thrash around involuntarily, much to her annoyance. But she was quickly done, dabbing the affected areas, her soft touch accompanied by soothing words. She then set about Olaf similarly. Jorgen dusted some sort of powder over my wounds, saying only that it helped prevent infection. It stung like hell and made tears stream down my cheeks.

'How long have we been here? How did we get here?' I asked.

'Harald Larsson and Leif Brekke found you while out on patrol. You were only a few hundred yards away but heading in the wrong direction. Had you kept going you would've reached Oslo eventually, maybe in twenty years!' He laughed. 'You've been here a day, that's all.'

About to ask what these strangers were doing in the Johanssens' hut, I remembered what my brother had said to me all that time ago – if they're Norwegians or MILORG, don't ask questions. I wasn't sure if the restriction still applied, but for now I decided it was best not to tempt fate.

Jorgen settled back down onto his stool. A large and robust man, he looked to be in his late forties. He'd lost weight; his heavy sweater appeared a size too big, as if he'd borrowed it from a friend. His wavy golden hair had been left to grow into a scruffy winter coat and his natural oils made it gleam; I guessed it hadn't been washed or cut since I last saw him.

I peered around the hut looking for a stash of painted machine guns but saw only a few rifles. Gingerly I rose from my mattress of deerskins, cursed my stiffness and went to join my brother by the stove. He didn't look very happy to be alive.

'We made it!' I said, trying to sound upbeat.

'Huh. Only thanks to Jorgen's men. And that was a stroke of good fortune.' He lifted his snivelling head and looked at me. 'I've been a fool, Marek. I should never have let you get involved. I damn well nearly got us both killed. I'm sorry.'

'Wouldn't have missed it for the world,' I lied.

'It's not over yet, Marek. Not by a long way.'

'I know, but let's count our blessings and say our prayers for Mother and Father.'

He nodded. 'But I failed,' he added. 'Failed you and myself. I really believed I could make it here. I was so wrong.'

'You nearly made it. God, you brought us all the way from Kinsarvik to within a few hundred yards. And in some of the worst weather I've ever seen.'

He grunted.

'Hell, I only managed to drag you a few hundred yards and that was in the wrong bloody direction!'

We laughed. I think I'd managed to crack his spell of wallowing self-pity.

The door to the hut crashed open and four men filed in, pulling hoods and goggles from their faces. They lifted from their shoulders straps attached to machine guns. Snow slid from their anoraks and quickly melted into puddles on the floor. Their conversation was in English and I struggled to translate. We'd studied the language at school, of course, and I'd been ranked about middle of my class in terms of aptitude. Middle in any class, in any subject, fell woefully short of Father's expectations and so he'd tutored me outside of school until I'd been sick of hearing his voice. How strange. What I'd give to hear him again now. Anyway, the product of his nurturing endeavour was to raise my competence to the point where I could listen to English wireless stations and keep up with most of the Allied propaganda. As far as I could tell, the men were discussing some sort of problem with a transmitter.

Jorgen introduced Olaf and me to Harald Larsson and Leif Brekke, men in their twenties and hailing from Kristiansand in the south. They seemed delighted that we were well and accepted our profuse thanks with quiet modesty. We owed them our lives and I wanted them to know our gratitude, so I shook each of their hands until my arm ached.

The other two men were British. Major Tim Fletcher had the typical air of the officer about him, quite stiff and starched in manner, seemingly out of place in our squalid surroundings. He reminded me of my history teacher, Mindur Naerog, a man who'd long forgotten the simple mechanics of a smile. Sergeant Eddie Turner, however, looked to me like the sort of man who'd fit in anywhere: easy going, unruffled; a man who could turn his hand to everything from frying eggs to single-handedly overrunning a well-defended German position. He had forearms the size of tree trunks and a profusion of dark hair that even an elk would be envious of. I thought that, of the two, I was going to get along with Eddie much better.

A little larger than the Borsobu, the hut felt like a crowded train carriage with the eight of us huddled inside together with all our kit. But we each found our own little space and settled in time for a hot meal of stew, boiled potatoes and *lefse*. Yes, my favourite bread! I wondered if I'd died and gone to heaven. Sadly Ingrid could not conjure up any cinnamon sugar but there was a thin spread of unsalted butter. The taste was magical on my tongue and I hurried down my allotted share, much to the amusement of our British guests.

'Have you been here since we last met?' I asked Jorgen.

'Off and on,' he replied. 'We move from hut to hut. That way we stay one step ahead.'

'Been spotted by any reconnaissance aircraft?'

He shook his head. 'We move only during darkness. Of course, they may have spotted our tracks but the weather's been bad and on our side. Within a few hours fresh snow covers our paths.'

'I heard about the raid on the fuel dump at Skånevik and thought of you.'

My brother flashed me an angry scowl. Jorgen just laughed. 'A mighty fine firework display to warm the hearts of all Jøssings. One of many.'

Ingrid lifted a kettle from the stove and made coffee. I thought it odd for a women to be part of all this. My gaze followed her around the hut. Jorgen tapped me on my forearm. 'Her husband was in the Resistance. One of the first to join up.'

I nodded appreciatively and only then realized Jorgen had used the past tense. 'Captured?' I ventured to whisper.

She heard me. 'Captured, questioned and *shot*!'

Her words hung in the air. Nobody spoke or swallowed. It felt abrupt, like being unexpectedly cut off on the telephone. I didn't know what to say. She began handing out the mugs. 'Sorry, but there's no sugar.'

She had clearly taken up where her husband had left off. You could almost sense the bloodlust in her. She possessed such a cold matter-of-factness in the way she spoke that I took it to mean she placed little value on her own life. She had become merely a device for inflicting revenge on those who'd snatched from her all that she held dear. And the fact that she had made it into the heart of the Hardanger indicated she had both the strength and the skill to match the men she travelled with. Something about her – I think it lay in the darkness of her eyes – made me realize she would not think twice about pulling a trigger, plunging a dagger, or detonating a bomb. Ordinary though she looked, there was really very little that was 'ordinary' about her.

Harald Larsson set to work waxing his skis. 'What do you two intend doing now?'

I looked at Olaf. 'We had planned to hole up here for a while,' he said, glancing around the hut. 'I can see that's not going to prove possible. So maybe once we've got our breath back, we'll bid you farewell and make for my father's hut, the Borsobu.' He turned to Jorgen. 'You remember, I showed you on the map.'

Jorgen nodded.

'And then what?' asked Harald. 'Do you know someone who'll hide you?'

'No.'

'Will you try for Sweden?'

'I don't know.'

'Do you know where to get false documents?'

My brother shook his head.

'You boys are in one hell of a mess!'

Leif Brekke snorted mockingly. 'Jorgen, they clearly haven't thought things through.'

'There wasn't time,' my brother replied angrily. 'Things didn't go to plan. We had to act fast.'

'They're a bloody liability,' Leif added, locking eyes with Olaf. 'And we've got enough problems already. They should leave first thing tomorrow.'

Jorgen said nothing and simply continued cleaning his rifle.

'That's enough, Leif,' snapped Ingrid. 'Sending them out there in their present state would be like a death sentence. How would you like it if the tables were turned?'

He shrugged. 'I'd take my chances. Look, this is serious. We don't have the luxury of being charitable. Our mission is too important.'

Harald Larsson rose from his stool and thrust his hands into his trouser pockets. 'You're both right,' he interrupted. 'So I suggest we decide nothing for now. Anyway, until the others arrive there's hardly a rush to do or decide anything.'

Others? Mission? God, I desperately wanted to ask what he meant but thought it was probably unwise. I supposed our circumstances were already precarious enough: if we learned too much, it might narrow their options. If we knew too much, would they risk letting us go?

'Harald's right. We do nothing for now,' said Jorgen decisively.

I felt glad the big man was in charge. I knew we would not survive a trek to the Borsobu. Not yet, anyway.

Chapter Ten

To my delight, Tim Fletcher spoke passable Norwegian. He said he'd studied at Oslo University for a couple of years before the war. An engineer, he specialized in ship construction and I made him promise to teach me a little about the subject. Eddie Turner, though less proficient in our tricky language, understood simple sentences if spoken slowly and clearly, and he seemed keen to improve. He was a stonemason by trade, which I supposed explained his weathered hands and powerful build. It surprised me that he formed part of such a small, tight-knit team. I thought he might prove a liability until Jorgen explained to me that Eddie knew things about handling explosives and detonators that made him rather special.

Every evening at nine o'clock Fletcher headed off from the hut alone. No one questioned this apparently odd habit of his, for he went whatever the weather. And he'd be gone for an hour or more so I knew it had to involve something other than his bodily functions – unless, that is, he had a serious medical problem. Piecing together snippets of conversation, I quickly deduced that his forays were to transmit and receive messages, the radio equipment hidden some way from the hut.

On his return, his comrades eyed him expectantly, as if important news was awaited. Usually he just shrugged and set about unzipping his sleeping bag. After three days my curiosity got the better of me and I quizzed Olaf about it while we sat quietly in a corner of the hut.

'He has to contact England once a day. That's what Jorgen told me. At precisely the same time.'

The idea that someone out here in the vast nothingness of the Hardanger was communicating directly with England seemed unreal. How could any signal reach so far? It fascinated me.

'They use Morse code, of course, and he's the one who knows the correct codes and call signs.'

I'd read about Morse code, but had no idea how someone could listen to a crackling hiss and a barrage of long and short bleeps and from it decipher a meaningful message. I guess it took training and practice and an attuned ear. I decided there and then that I'd ask Fletcher to teach me the rudiments if he had a spare hour or two. 'What if he falls sick?' I asked. 'What would happen? Would Eddie take over?'

My brother had no idea.

'It would become Jorgen's task,' said Ingrid. Despite our whispers, she'd heard every word. I reckoned only wolves had keener hearing. 'But that might prove difficult,' she added.

'You mean he doesn't know Morse properly?'

'No, it's subtler than that,' she said. 'Every radio operator has his or her own style. Perhaps it's the exact length of their dots and dashes or the gap between each, or their rhythm. Whatever, the receiver gets used to the sender's technique, like you get used to someone's voice. Each is unique. So, if Jorgen took over, he'd need to inform them of what had happened to Fletcher to prevent them becoming suspicious.'

'And they *would* be suspicious,' said Harald. I thought he was asleep but he'd been listening in too. 'They'd send some questions to which only Jorgen would know the answers. If he responded correctly, everything would be fine. But should he get it wrong, just one simple mistake even, and those in London would assume our group had been compromised.'

'Then what?'

'No more transmissions. No more supply drops. No more anything. We'd be on our own!'

Occasional breaks in the bad weather lasted for only a few hours. So we remained in the hut most of the time, getting on top of one another, irritating each other with our own peculiar habits. With Harald it was picking his toenails, with Leif breaking wind, and with my brother his incessant sniffing. Jorgen muttered incoherently at times and sang old Norwegian songs rather tunelessly, often forgetting the words mid verse. Fletcher and Eddie seemed able to cope in captivity but fidgeted endlessly. Ingrid behaved like a saint. I did my bit, of course, complaining about everything from the rationing of toilet paper – pages torn from a Russian novel – to everyone's refusal to tell me more about what exactly it was they were waiting for.

We spent the days playing with an old pack of cards and reading the few Norwegian books the Johanssens had deposited during summer vacations. Eddie taught me a game called poker but he taught me so badly that within a couple of days he reckoned I owed him a million kroner. Jokingly he said he'd give me time to come up with the cash, although no way would he accept German Reichsmarks. Meanwhile Harald and Leif fashioned a chess set of sorts from a square of cardboard and various small objects, including buttons, cutlery and bullets. Olaf joined them in a tournament lasting a full day and a half. Naturally he won and was awarded the first Hardanger Challenge Chess Trophy, exquisitely forged from two empty tins and a velvet-smooth antler. And every night at precisely nine o'clock Fletcher donned his anorak and left the hut, returning at ten without news.

On the fifth day our boredom was rudely interrupted. We became gripped with excitement and fervour at the distant whine of an aircraft. Jorgen peered cautiously out of the hut's one small window and, squinting, nervously tracked the aircraft's path over the plateau. Luckily it flew at high altitude. It posed no risk. We settled back down and speculated as to its mission. We continued with our card game, and by dinner that evening I owed Eddie three million kroner, my watch, my skis and my entire collection of manuals. Harald had watched us play. 'I think I've got the hang of this poker game, Marek,' he said. 'Want me to win back all you owe Eddie?'

'You're nuts. He'll take you for all you've got, and more,' I replied. He winked at me. I guessed that he had some sort of plan and that it probably involved cheating. Harald was like that. So I made way for Kristiansand's newest cardsharp.

He cracked his knuckles, shuffled and cut the deck. Eddie grinned and dealt out the cards. It did not take long for Harald to be indebted to Eddie to the tune of eight million kroner. Whatever Harald's plan was, it hadn't worked. And it seemed that Harald was not a good loser.

'You're cheating!' he spat.

'Don't be stupid.'

'You're dealing from the bottom of the deck.'

'No I'm not. Here, you deal, if it bothers you that much.'

'Too late. All debts are void.' He swiped the cards from the small table with a single sweep of his left hand. Eddie merely shrugged and bent down to pick them up. Harald shoved him off his chair and the two of them wrestled in a heap on the floor. Olaf and I tried to prise them apart with little success. It took a loud bark of an order from Fletcher to end the brawl.

That night Olaf whispered to me his fears. 'The hut's becoming gripped by a bad case of cabin fever,' he said. 'Men and women just aren't meant to be cooped up like this.' Dropping his voice even lower, he added, 'It often leads to unbalanced minds and irrational, violent behaviour.'

As far as we could tell, our new friends had been together for many weeks and they'd got to know each other rather too closely and intimately for their own good. The hut had begun to reek with anxiety as well as with our unpleasant body odour. Everyone had grown fractious. I think the catalyst was their worry about the arrival of 'the others', whoever 'the others' were. They wouldn't tell me. And I began to fear what the future held for Olaf and me, as our strength had returned and our faces were healing well. Was it time for us to leave? I did not dare ask.

Worse still, our food supplies had begun running short. I realized they were largely dependent on the British RAF and its parachute drops in order to keep going. With the bad weather, no drops had been made for several weeks. And I knew that our presence drained them of precious resources and aggravated their predicament. Harald and Leif had already begun to treat us a little less kindly – especially Harald – as if we were a burden, and I thought the situation could only deteriorate. And although it troubles me to say it, there was a rather unpleasant side to Harald. I feared he'd become unstable. I discussed the problem with Olaf during a short foray outside for some fresh snow for the pot.

'In a few days we're going to be in serious trouble,' I began. 'And I think Harald's slowly going nuts.'

'You're right and I've been thinking,' he replied. 'We're a pretty tough crowd but I figure that only Jorgen is really like us. I mean, he's from up north. He's a hunter and outdoorsman like we are. He's lived in places like this and survived. Leif and Harald can ski and shoot straight but they're not hunters. I mean, they're from Kristiansand, for God's sake. They're all bloody fishermen! And as for Fletcher and Eddie, well, they're tough soldiers but they've never lived in a place this remote. A food drop would ease things but I don't figure there's much chance of that.'

'What should we do?'

'Killing a deer would provide food for a week,' he suggested.

'Dare we? I mean how? How do we get out of here during the day without them stopping us? You know the rules – only if Jorgen gives the nod. And I doubt he will, the way he worries about our being discovered.'

'We'll leave early. Creep out while they're still asleep. Our tracks will soon get covered. And with any luck we'll be back before they start to worry. We'll leave a note, of course.'

'Of course.'

Our plan was set. And the next morning we slipped from our beds, quietly pulled on our sweaters and anoraks and gently lifted our skis and Olaf's rifle from where they leaned against the wall. The door creaked but we woke no one.

It was still dark outside; the storm had largely blown

itself out and the sky was clear and starlit. Just a stiff icy breeze battered our faces. I could make out a wide flat expanse of snow immediately below the hut. It was a small lake in which the Johanssens loved to fish during summer vacations. Now it was simply several feet of ice and snow. Beyond, the whiteness swept gloriously upwards in a gentle slope towards rocky outcrops; nothing looked too high, too steep or too intimidating. In fact, I felt elated just to have escaped the fuggy confines of our prison and relished the freedom to take to my skis. I breathed the clean air deep into my lungs.

'Which way?'

My brother examined his compass, looked to the horizon and pointed west. 'The reindeer generally migrate clockwise around the Hardanger. I recall Mr Johanssen saying they could often be found in the next valley. He said it's on one of their main migratory routes.'

'The next valley it is then.'

We slid down the slope, forged across the frozen lake and quickly reached a ridge that allowed a grand view into the next valley. We stopped and crouched down.

'Can't see anything,' I said. 'Still too dark.'

'Patience, Marek. Remember what Father taught us. Stay downwind, well hidden, and move slowly. And most of all, be patient.'

We settled down onto our haunches and kept our eyes peeled. Eventually dawn crept above the horizon and delivered a fabulously clear pale light, casting long needle-like shadows from even the smallest rock. My mind drifted to other things.

'Who do you think it is they're waiting for?' I asked.

'Don't know exactly,' my brother replied. 'I overheard Ingrid and Jorgen talking last night, after Fletcher radioed London. Jorgen said something about men arriving by bus.'

'By *bus*? You must've misheard.'

'That's what he said. He figured that if the RAF couldn't parachute them in, then they'd have to come by bus.'

'That's crazy. From where?'

'No idea.'

'And what's going to happen when they get here?'

He shrugged. 'Whatever it is, I think it's something pretty big, pretty important.'

'Like what?'

'Who knows?'

'Can we take part?'

'Don't be stupid, Marek.' My brother rolled his eyes. 'I reckon whatever it is they're planning is special. Think about it. Eddie's an expert in explosives and Fletcher's an engineer. And if more men are coming from England, I reckon they'll be experts too.'

'Really?'

'Yes.'

We sat in silence for a while. But a question gnawed and chewed away at me. 'I still don't see how they can get from England to here by bus!'

My brother grew irritable. 'Well, I don't know, Marek. I'm just telling you what I overheard. I might have got it all wrong.'

'I expect so.'

He scowled at me.

'What's that?' I pointed to what I thought looked like two tiny dots in the distance, at least four hundred yards away. 'Can you see them?'

'See what?' My brother rubbed his eyes and squinted.

'Just below that outcrop of rock, the one that's sort of W-shaped. Right over there.'

'I see it.'

'You think they're reindeer?'

'What, just the two of them? Doubt it. Normally they stick together. I'd expect to see a dozen or more. Let's watch and see if they come nearer.'

The dots did indeed come closer. And as they did so, it became obvious they weren't deer. They were skiers!

My heart drummed and I began to wish we'd not gone hunting and therefore had not seen them at all. 'What should we do? Go back and tell the others? Do you think it's the men they've been waiting for?'

'Don't think so,' my brother replied, shaking his head slowly. 'They're coming from the wrong direction.' He turned round and looked towards our hut. Then looked back towards the skiers. I could see him calculating whether we had enough time to reach safety and raise the alarm before they caught us up. The skiers moved quickly with long strides.

'Lie down, Marek,' he barked.

'What?'

He grabbed my arm and yanked me off balance so I fell. 'Keep still.'

'What's the matter?'

'*They're Germans!*'

'What? Out here? Can't be.'

'Look carefully. See their headgear. See those rifles. They're German all right.'

'What do we do now?'

Olaf chewed his lip thoughtfully. 'See if they pass by. They might simply go on up the valley.'

'And if they don't?'

Shielding his eyes, he stared in the direction the skiers had come from. 'I can't see any others.'

'And if they don't?' I repeated.

'Then we'll have to deal with them ourselves. If we race back to the hut, we'll arrive only seconds ahead of them.'

'What do you mean, deal with them?'

Olaf loaded his rifle.

'You're crazy.'

'Shush, I'm trying to concentrate.' He rested his rifle on the snow and tucked the butt into his shoulder. Staring through the sight, he flicked off the safety catch and toyed with the trigger. The skiers were now just a hundred yards or so from us. They were indeed German and one of them carried a radio on his back, the long aerial rising vertically from it and bending and whipping in the wind. And they were heading towards our valley and our hut.

My brother squeezed the trigger.

His shot rang out across the plateau. The soldiers slid to an abrupt stop and knelt down.

Olaf had missed! Hastily he fumbled in his pocket for a second bullet and reloaded. The soldiers looked around frantically and drew their weapons. The radio operator slipped off his rucksack. I guessed he was about to share their tricky situation with the rest of the German army who, I had little doubt, would come running to their rescue.

'Aim for the radio operator,' I shouted.

My brother did but failed miserably to strike his target. He peered at his rifle in disgust. 'How did I miss?' He set about adjusting the sight.

The soldiers figured out roughly the direction Olaf's shot had come from and, focusing their attention on our ridge, returned fire. I don't think they were absolutely sure where we lay because their shots struck snow a good thirty yards to our left. My brother loaded, fired and reloaded and fired again, and with each miss I grew more afraid.

'Get the damn radio operator!' I cried, knowing that should he send his message we would be responsible for compromising Jorgen and his men. I saw the other soldier lift something to his face. *Binoculars*. And he'd spotted us, because his next shot came much too close for comfort. I drew Father's revolver from my pocket and fired off several wildly hopeful shots. I wasn't even sure the bullets reached that far.

Disaster struck. My brother's rifle jammed.

'Jesus, we're going to have to make a run for it, Marek.'

Although I was racked with fright, a puff of snow a yard from my right ear suggested it was best not to argue with him. I pushed myself back behind the ridge and seized my ski poles.

Short bursts of frenzied machine-gun fire filled the air and I saw the radio operator slump forward. The other soldier managed to fire one more shot before he too got peppered. I looked to my right, from where the frantic volley of bullets had originated, and from further along the ridge Eddie appeared and slid down towards them, his machine gun poised. He arrived beside the bodies and turned each of them over. He waved to us, beckoning us to join him. When we did, he said little as he searched beneath their anoraks and pockets. The radio crackled. I could hear a German voice. A shiver went down my spine.

Eddie stood back and riddled the device with bullets. 'We must bury them,' he said matter-of-factly. 'And quickly too.' He set about gouging a trench in the snow with the stock of his machine gun. I wanted to point out to him that the effort would prove wasted as foxes or other beasts would undo our good work. But I said nothing and instead dug with my gloved hands.

Returning to the hut, I fully expected us to be yelled

at for breaking the rules, for placing everyone in jeopardy. Luckily they had more urgent matters to attend to and largely ignored us. Jorgen paced the hut, back and forth, just like a polar bear I'd once seen in Bergen's zoo; a bear fraught with anxiety.

'We must move on,' he declared. 'Where's the map?' He looked towards Ingrid. 'Start packing. I figure it'll only be a couple of hours before more soldiers arrive.'

Eddie examined my brother's jammed rifle and grimaced. 'About as much use as a fart in a storm,' he said. 'Pity, 'cos it's a fine weapon.'

Olaf shoulders sagged. 'Can it be repaired?' he asked.

Eddie sniffed and handed it back to him. 'Probably, but I reckon it'll need the skills of a master gunsmith. If it were mine, I'd keep hold of it. At least for now.'

It took just minutes for everyone to pack while Jorgen and Ingrid pored over a map drawn on silk cloth.

Listening in, I realized they had arrived on the Hardanger via a route south of Odda, passing by the twin waterfalls of Låtefoss and Skardfoss and close to the Buer glacier. For some reason I couldn't work out, they did not want to return that way. Their attention focused on another part of the map, a part of the Hardanger Olaf and I knew well – the route to Kinsarvik. And Jorgen's finger traced a path to the small village of Jondal on the coast of the Hardangerfjord. He tapped the map thoughtfully. 'There,' he said. 'Jondal, that's where we'll head for. Fletcher, radio London and insist they bring forward the rendezvous to tomorrow night, at midnight. Let's pray they can make it.'

'We know the route like the back of our hands,' said Olaf. 'We can act as your guides.'

Jorgen divided his stare between Ingrid and us. She nodded.

'Bad idea,' said Leif. 'They come from Ulfhus, Jorgen. If they're spotted by someone, it's curtains for them and us. We can't take the risk. And they're not trained like we are.'

Jorgen weighed up his comments and came to a decision.

'They can guide us to the outskirts of Kinsarvik. After that they're on their own.'

I didn't like the bit about being on our own. Still, for now the important thing was to get as far away from the hut as possible, as quickly as possible. And I braced myself for an arduous trip, expecting everyone around me to be faster, more proficient skiers than me. Of course, that proved to be the case, although their heavy rucksacks thankfully slowed them a little. Compared with the journey to the hut, our return was a joy. Fine, clear weather, crisp snow and good light – all the ingredients for perfect skiing. Equally the last sort of conditions Jorgen wanted. Our situation had forced us to travel by day rather than by night. The Hardanger offered little cover. However, good fortune seemed to accompany our journey for we saw no one all day.

We set up camp well after dusk, and Leif and Harald

were ordered to carry out the first watch. They trudged off irritably, carrying their weapons to positions thirty yards or so to either side of our campfire. I helped Ingrid prepare a meal while my brother spoke with Jorgen and our British friends.

'I'm sorry that we broke the rules,' I said.

She scooped some snow into a cooking pot and sat it on the fire. 'That's behind us now.'

'It's just that we thought we owed you for your fine hospitality. We'd deprived you of precious food and thought we could replenish your supplies with a deer or two. We've hunted them up here before and so thought we knew what we were doing.'

'You weren't to know there'd be a German patrol.'

'No. In fact I've never heard of them venturing so far onto the Hardanger.'

She studied me. 'That's worrying Jorgen too.' She returned her attention to the cooking pot, and began stirring the stew. In the fire's glow her blonde hair turned golden, reminding me of summer and fields of swaying corn.

'Do you think they were looking for you?'

'I don't know.' She appeared thoughtful.

'Perhaps they were looking for Olaf and me.'

'Maybe.'

'My brother said he overheard talk of men arriving by bus.'

She said nothing but merely continued to feed scraps of food into the pot.

'I told him he must have misheard because men can hardly arrive from England by bus. Without drowning, I mean.'

A smile fell on her lips. I think she found me amusing, but quickly her mirth evaporated and she sighed wearily. 'Men have drowned,' she said, her expression pained.

'What?'

Despite the shock in my voice, she chose not to expand on her most curious remark.

'Marek, what's the best way from Kinsarvik to Jondal?' shouted my brother.

'Via the ferry,' I replied.

'No, you idiot! Assuming the ferry's out of the question.'

I slid round the fire to where Jorgen and Fletcher were studying their map, my brother peering over their shoulders. 'You have to use the ferry,' I added. 'The way by road would take ages.'

Jondal lay on the western side of the Folgefonn mountains, a wedge of peaks bordered by the Sørfjord to the east and the Hardangerfjord to the north and west. There were just two ways of getting there, by water and by the coastal road that wound all the way around the Sørfjord. The ferry was by far the quickest way.

Jorgen rubbed his chin. 'Far too far by road,' he declared.

'See, Olaf, told you!'

'But I want to avoid the Kvanndal ferry,' Jorgen

added. 'Too many people. Too many soldiers. One problem with any of our papers or a suspicious look and we'd all be in trouble.' He glanced towards Fletcher and Eddie.

I guessed Jorgen remained unconvinced that our British friends could pass themselves off as Norwegians. I thought Fletcher might convince Fritz OK but not a real Norwegian. Eddie stood no chance. He didn't even look vaguely Norwegian and his accent when trying to speak our language sounded like someone talking into an empty tin.

'You'll have to steal a boat then,' I said. 'There are plenty to choose from.'

Fletcher nodded thoughtfully.

'Why Jondal?' I asked. 'Why head for there?'

'We tried planning for every eventuality,' he replied. 'Before we came, we agreed several alternative rendez-vous points with London. In case things went wrong. Jondal's the closest, that's all. So, God willing, that's where we'll find our men and supplies.'

His readiness to share their secrets surprised me. For days we'd been wedged shoulder to shoulder in the confines of the hut and not once had anyone seemed willing to share any information with us. I thought he'd made an error, put off guard by our familiarity.

'Will they come by bus?' I asked, testing the water.

Jorgen flashed me a look of surprise and then frowned deeply. 'You know about the Shetland Bus?'

'*Shetland* Bus?' I shook my head. He looked as confused as I was.

'We overheard someone mention something about a bus,' said Olaf. 'That's all.'

Jorgen visibly relaxed.

We ate supper more or less in silence. Afterwards I settled down as comfortably as I could and Ingrid kindly gave me a blanket as an extra barrier against the snow. My brother remained close to the fire and to Jorgen. I listened as they discussed the type of boat they intended to 'borrow' from some poor unsuspecting local, and although my brother insisted it would be safe to sail all the way to Jondal, I thought it might be better to land some distance from the village and then walk. The Germans patrolled the fjords day and night, and boats were frequently stopped and searched. In the Sørfjord they might be relatively safe, as the narrow stretch of water lies well inland. However, once you pass through its entrance you're in the Hardangerfjord and that's a major waterway. At its westerly end only a few islands and narrow passages separate you from the sea.

At nine o'clock Fletcher put on the headphones of his radio set and began tapping his Morse code. In the hut he'd shown me the rudiments and we'd spent some time at opposite ends tapping simple messages to each other on the bottom of empty tin mugs. I sat transfixed as he wired up the terminals, tapped, paused, and then tapped and paused again. And he maintained such concentration that I think a grenade could have gone off in his trouser pocket and he'd not have noticed it at all. When he finished, he carefully packed everything away and knelt down next to Jorgen.

'They left Lunna Voe on schedule,' he said. 'So we're still on for tomorrow midnight.'

'Good,' replied Jorgen.

'Lunna Voe, where's that?' I asked.

'Shetland Isles, off the coast of Scotland,' Fletcher told me. 'Nearest landfall to Norway. In fact, only one hundred and eighty miles from Bergen.'

'And the weather?' asked Jorgen.

'They predict a pretty rough crossing, maybe force eight or nine.'

'Poor blighters. I bet they'll wish they'd stayed tucked up in their nice, cosy beds,' said Eddie. He laughed maliciously.

'And their captain's unhappy about having to venture across the inner lead and into the fjords. But those are his orders so I guess he'll carry them out.'

I understood the captain's concerns. Crossing the open sea was perilous enough. But then having to navigate the narrow channels and fjords between the islands separating the sea from the inner lead would be doubly hazardous: the German navy patrolled these sheltered stretches, and the army had set up lookout posts on just about every rocky outcrop.

By now I'd guessed that the Shetland Bus was a regular boat service between the British Isles and Norway, a ferry service for the Resistance Movement and for forays by British commandos. 'What sort of boats do they use?' I asked.

Jorgen looked up. 'It varies. Always Norwegian fishing vessels, of course, but different sizes. It all depends.'

'That's enough,' snapped Ingrid. She glared at him sternly.

I think he had already shared too much. After all, we knew where they were heading – Jondal – that they were planning something big, and we knew about the Shetland Bus. As I settled back down, I wondered if the likes of Herr Stretter would be able to extract such detail from me using the Gestapo's various methods of persuasion. I conjured up an alternative story for him that would leak from my lips as he turned the thumb-screws or yanked off my nails. I'd squeal that they used false names, that two of them were Dutch and that they intended to assassinate Mr Quisling by running him over in a bus. I wondered if Herr Stretter would buy it. I supposed he'd have me shot, whatever.

It also occurred to me that a difficult decision awaited Jorgen when we got to Kinsarvik. He'd said that we'd part company on the outskirts of town. Was that wise? If we got caught, we might jeopardize their mission. In truth, I had no idea what Olaf and I would do if abandoned to our own devices. Would we dare return to Ulfhus? I think not. In which case, our only alternative would be to head towards Sweden, dodging all the checkpoints, and figure something out along the way.

Chapter Eleven

Nothing much had changed in Kinsarvik. As dusk fell, we crouched by the edge of the forest and studied people going about their hectic business. Jorgen had not rushed off the plateau nor hurried down the Husedalen valley, saying he preferred to take it steady and reach town only once the light had begun to fade. And I took heart that he seemed impressed by our knowledge of the terrain.

My suggestion that they needed to 'borrow' a boat had seemed so utterly logical and straightforward when I'd spoken it. However, the reality of a busy town cast a shadow over the idea. The very idea of sneaking aboard, weighing anchor and starting up the engine without attracting attention now seemed crazy. And yet the Sørfjord was so enticingly narrow. It felt like you could reach out and touch the opposite shore. In summer you'd think you could cross it by swimming fewer than a hundred strokes. But even then the water could steal your breath and sap the very life from you. And the tidal currents would be overwhelming. Such a simple crossing suddenly seemed impossible.

We slipped back into deeper cover.

'We'll split up,' Jorgen announced. 'Leif and Harald, I

want you to reconnoitre the shore north of town. See if there are any small rowing craft. Anything bigger and it'll draw too much attention. And work out where's best to depart from. Meet us back here in two hours.'

They checked and synchronized their watches. Fletcher and Eddie settled down for the wait as Leif and Harald shed their rucksacks and then strolled off nonchalantly towards town, hands in pockets. I reckoned the confidence in their steps would convince any German that they were simply on their way to a bar for a drink.

Ingrid combed her fingers through her hair. 'How do I look?' she asked. Jorgen studied her a moment and then nodded approvingly. She took my hand and squeezed it tightly. 'Good luck, Marek. May God be with you.' She did likewise with Olaf. Then, as soon as Harald and Leif disappeared from view, she headed off in the same direction.

'Where's she going?' I asked.

'We have friends in Kinsarvik,' Jorgen replied. 'She's going to make contact and find out what the Germans are up to.'

The Germans frequently added to their long list of restrictions and rules with sudden changes. They might close a road to civilian traffic, designate a stretch of fjord a no-go zone, establish new roadblocks or introduce new permits or other documents. All done, of course, in an attempt to stay one step ahead of the Resistance, to flush them out into the open or catch them out.

Jorgen stared after her and I saw concern written

across his face. I knew he was fond of her and feared for her safety. I looked at my brother enquiringly. Was this it? Were we about to say our goodbyes?

'I suppose we must go,' said my brother.

'It's for the best,' Jorgen replied.

I strongly disagreed but said nothing, accepting our fate. I shook hands with Fletcher and Eddie and wished them good hunting. They smiled at me.

'Give them hell,' said Olaf, grasping Fletcher's hand tightly.

'If you choose to go to Odda and make it there safely, there's a café opposite the church,' said Jorgen. 'An elderly woman and her son run it. Speak to the son of your predicament and he may be able to assist you with getting to Sweden. His name's Gustaf.'

'Thanks,' said Olaf.

I felt strangely tearful at our separating. Though few situations could be more dangerous than hanging out with men like Jorgen, I'd felt safe and comfortable in their midst. Striking out alone filled me with dread. But we had no choice.

Walking from the cover of the trees seemed as daunting as taking to the stage in front of a packed theatre for the first time. The sense of nakedness and vulnerability made me nauseous and my legs turned to mush. My brother abandoned his rifle in the bushes and led the way.

'That's Father's prized hunting rifle,' I said. 'Eddie thought it could be mended.'

'Father won't need it where he is now. Anyway, I reckon it's jammed beyond repair. I'll save up and buy him a new one.'

We trudged towards a side street. 'So it's to Odda and then to Sweden, is it?'

He shrugged. 'Got any better ideas?'

In truth, I hadn't. Our future still seemed blank, just like an empty exercise book on the first day of a new school term. 'Do you want to risk going home?'

He looked at me. I saw in his eyes the same desire, the same yearning as burned within me to see all those familiar things we'd grown up with: the kitchen table that held so many memories of family meals and conversations, the warm fire, the slow tick of the mantel clock. 'We could get a change of clothes,' I added encouragingly. 'And have a wash. I'm starting to smell a bit rank.'

'Too dangerous.'

'You could call in on Agnete or Lars.'

'That really is out of the question!' My brother eyed me piercingly.

Not wishing to be recognized, I tightened the cord of my anorak hood. 'Isn't there someone we know in Kinsarvik that we can trust?'

He shook his head.

How awful, I thought. Before the war he'd skied and sailed in friendly competition against the young men of Kinsarvik and other local villages, as had I. And Mother and Father had grown friendly with other parents and we had eaten at their tables, and they at ours. Yet all that stopped when the Germans came. And when neighbour began to doubt neighbour, when us Norwegians separated like curds and whey into Jøssings and Quislings, no longer were such fragile friendships valued. Quite the opposite. But rarely was it obvious where people's allegiances had finally settled. Families grew suspicious of each other, fearing that a word mis-construed or a comment out of turn would find its way to the ears of the authorities. It had the effect of narrowing our spheres of contact to few beyond our immediate family and village. I quickly learned all about the real meaning of trust and the difference between real friends and mere acquaintances. War did that. It clarified things.

We turned a corner and halted in our tracks, un-certain which way to tread. With it being closing time for local businesses, people had spilled onto the street, some walking home, others loitering in wait for their bus. And mingling in the throng was a smattering of German uniforms. After the bleakness of the Hardanger and the company of just a few, the crowds pounded my senses, a cacophony of voices, a blur of motion and con-fusion. Olaf spun round and pressed his nose against a shop window. 'Turn round, Marek. Now!'

I did and pressed my nose against the glass too. 'What?'

'Agnete!'

'What?'

'Across the street. She's just come out of that bakery. She's wearing that light coat and purple bobble hat of hers.'

'What's she doing here?'

'How the hell should I know?'

'What now?'

'Shut up and let me think.'

I kept my nose pressed against the glass. A be-spectacled face from inside the ironmonger's peered at me curiously, his lips twisting up at the corners as his brow creased. 'We can't stay here. We look ridiculous,' I said. I turned round slowly and scanned the street. Agnete walked quickly towards a bus stop and joined the queue waiting for the bus to Odda. It stopped at all the villages along the Sørfjord, including Ulfhus.

'I'm going to talk to her,' my brother announced.

'You're mad,' I fretted.

'Wait here.' He set off, crossing the street with a definite spring in his step.

What the hell was I supposed to do now? The idiot! What if she screamed with fright? What if the Germans were watching her? I wanted to run after him, to grab hold of him, to restrain him, to hammer some sense into him. I was too late. He hopped onto the pavement and joined the queue immediately behind her. I held my breath. He tapped her on her shoulder. She turned and gaped.

Thank God. She hid her shock and surprise well. They chatted a moment and then left the queue and headed further down the street, turning sharply right and dipping into a narrow side street. I followed, keeping a sensible distance. When I turned the corner, I saw them kissing in a tight embrace in an unlit doorway. Knowing when little brother wasn't wanted, I turned my back on them.

About five minutes later I caught sight of Harald and Leif strolling up the road that led down to the Kvanndal ferry pier and the shore of the fjord. They didn't see me. I realized that we'd not said our goodbyes and wondered if I'd get the chance, although I doubted they'd welcome seeing me again so soon. Instead of heading straight back to the woods, they disappeared into a bar. It seemed like a reckless move but I understood their thirst. My brother and Agnete still clasped each other tightly. They looked like Siamese twins I'd seen pictures of in one of Olaf's textbooks. And if my memory served me right, separation was well nigh impossible.

A Mercedes, preceded by two motorbikes, screamed up the main street and screeched to a halt outside a small guesthouse. Passers-by stopped to gawp. I crept to the corner, leaned against the wall and watched. Several soldiers bearing weapons loitered around the door as if waiting for something to happen. The bike riders dismounted and gripped their machine guns at the ready. The back door of the Mercedes swung open and out stepped Herr Stretter of the Gestapo.

Just the sight of him set off the panic sirens in my

head. 'Olaf!' I whispered loudly. 'Olaf!' He ignored me. I ran to him and yanked his arm.

'What?' he growled angrily.

'*Gestapo.*'

'Don't be stupid.'

'Really! It's Herr Stretter. The man I met in Odda.'

He broke free from Agnete and ran to the corner.

'Marek. Glad to see you're OK. I've been so worried.' She kissed me and then hugged me. She smelled sweet and I felt her moist cheek press against my own.

Olaf came running back. 'They've got Ingrid!'

Disaster! My mind flew into turmoil.

'They must have been watching the house she went into. *Damn!*' He clawed the back of his head. 'We've got to get out of here and fast.' He took Agnete's hands. 'You too. Get home quickly. And remember you never saw us. Say nothing to anyone.' He kissed her again. 'Go on. Go.'

Tears streamed down her cheeks and she looked frightened. She refused to let go. He prised himself free.

'Go, Agnete. *Please,*' he begged.

Her face bleeding emotion, she ran into the street and clambered aboard a waiting bus. As it set off, she looked out of the window, a handkerchief hiding all but her eyes. About to offer us a wave, she appeared to change her mind, instead simply pressing her fingers against the partially misted window.

'Come, Marek, we've got to run.'

'Wait – Harald and Leif went into that bar across the road. They're sitting ducks.'

'The idiots,' my brother hissed. He looked sharply left then right.

'We've got to warn them.'

He cursed. 'You head back to Jorgen and tell him what's happening. I'll go to the bar.'

'No, I'm coming with you.'

'You're too young, Marek. You'll draw attention to us. Now, shut up and do as you're told.'

I did my best to hurry back to the edge of town without making it obvious I was running away from something. I ignored all around me and deliberately looked down so as not to make eye contact with anyone who might see my inner angst and grow suspicious of me. Once close to the woods, I slowed and looked back to make sure I wasn't being followed. Satisfied I was alone, I dived into the bushes. 'Jorgen?' I whispered. 'Eddie? Where are you? There's a problem.'

Nothing! They appeared to have gone. Oh God, what was I going to do? I spun round on my heels and peered into the darkness. 'Jorgen?'

A hand clasped around my mouth from behind me and I was dragged to the ground. Lips pressed to my ear and a voice whispered to me, 'Be quiet, Marek. The woods are crawling with Germans.'

Chapter Twelve

Fletcher released his grip and led me into undergrowth where Jorgen and Eddie crouched. I whispered that the Gestapo had seized Ingrid and that Olaf had gone to warn Leif and Harald.

My companions remained remarkably calm. I presumed that we'd wait until the danger had passed or until the beams of torches waved by German patrols faded before we dared break cover. But Jorgen had other ideas. Breathtaking in its audacity, his decision to simply get up and head into town set me all aquiver. I thought it was a joke, and one in bad taste at that, but I quickly realized he was being serious.

Leaving our rucksacks well hidden, we strolled casually out of the woods. 'Remember, Marek, act normal, as if you have nothing to hide,' said Jorgen drily. 'And every time we pass someone in uniform, do not be afraid to look him in the eye.'

I was wobbling like a jelly in an earthquake; my guts tightened and I was sure my limbs looked unco-ordinated as I felt I had little control over them. This had to be either a stroke of genius or pure madness, I thought. I wasn't sure which. We walked in pairs, me and Jorgen behind Eddie and Fletcher. Jorgen adjusted his pace to maintain a good ten yards between us and the two Brits. Reaching the main street, I saw that Stretter's car and the motorbikes had gone, although guards remained outside the guesthouse where Ingrid had been arrested. On both sides of the street I saw soldiers stopping people and inspecting their papers. Now I was sure – *pure madness*.

The secret to success appeared to lie in timing our walk so that we passed soldiers while they were in the midst of their checks on others. At first it worked splendidly and we seemed destined to succeed in running this Nazi gauntlet. Then Fletcher and Eddie stopped and turned to look at us. I don't think they knew which way to proceed. For the first time Eddie appeared fretful.

'Marek,' said Jorgen. 'Lead us to the north side of town and the shore.'

We strode past our colleagues without acknowledging them. All the while I kept my eyes peeled for signs of Olaf, Leif and Harald and, failing to spot them, imagined them demolishing shot after shot of *aquavit* in order to temper their frayed nerves. I could have done with a glass myself! Passing the ironmonger's shop and then the bar, I glanced through the window but could not see them. Where the hell were they?

We were close to the church now. I could see its spire piercing the black night sky ahead of us. 'Jorgen, I know of a shed behind the church. We could hide there.'

'No, Marek. We must get to the shore and find a boat. Kinsarvik is too dangerous a place to loiter.'

I wondered whether Olaf had had the same idea as me. Had he sloped off to the woods behind the church, leading Leif and Harald to his den?

Glancing behind, my heart tripped. I saw that Fletcher and Eddie had bumped into a patrol. A huge lump formed in my throat. Jorgen and I stopped dead in the street and I sensed him dithering. He moved, as if about to cross the road, abandoning them.

The two German soldiers appeared to be having trouble making themselves understood to Eddie and Fletcher. I grabbed Jorgen's arm. 'Do they have papers?'

'Yes.'

'False identities?'

'Yes.'

'What names? Quickly!'

'Fletcher's is Ivar Gjertson. He's down as an engineer from Horten near Oslo. Eddie is Edvard Grieg, as in the composer. His papers describe him simply as a construction worker. He's from Molde in the north.'

'Right. Wait here,' I said. I couldn't believe what I was about to do. I strode purposefully towards them. My heart thumped and pumped beneath my anorak, and inside my gloves my hands sweated. Arriving, I totally ignored the two Germans, who appeared increasingly suspicious. I grabbed Fletcher's arm. 'Uncle Ivar! There you are. Where were you? We've missed our bus. There won't be another for an hour. Mother will be angry.'

Fletcher looked dumbfounded a moment but then said, 'Sorry. I was in that bookshop.' He pointed across

167

the street. 'Lost track of time completely.' He smiled at me.

I glared at the two Germans. 'Well? Are you done inconveniencing us?'

The soldiers were both men in their early twenties. I reckoned each probably had at least one rather annoying little brother back home in the Fatherland, a little bratty brother full of himself, loud and rude.

'Papers,' snarled one of the soldiers.

I thrust my identity card indignantly into his hand and swore at him. I shoved my hands into my pockets and scuffed my boots in the snow at my feet. I yawned excessively and did a little jig as if I were freezing. The soldier took a cursory glance at my card and handed it back to me. Meanwhile the other soldier continued studying Eddie's fake documents.

'You're in construction. Where are you working?'

Eddie stared back blankly. I realized he'd not understood the German's poor Norwegian.

'Where are you working?' the soldier repeated.

'Edvard's here to do work on the church,' I said. 'He's a stonemason. You'll have to shout at him if you want him to answer.'

'Why?'

'His hearing's bad. Got hit on the head. With a hammer! Years ago.'

The soldier peered into Eddie's face.

'And he's from Molde, up north. They speak differently up there.'

I could see the soldier remained unsure about him. *'Und Ihr Norwegisch ist Scheisse!'* I added.

The other soldier burst out laughing. 'Come, Heinrich, let's move on.'

Once the soldiers had wandered off, Jorgen caught up with us. 'That was too close for comfort,' said Fletcher. 'If it hadn't been for Marek's quick thinking, we'd now be experiencing the hospitality of the Wehrmacht.'

'What did you say to them, Marek?' asked Jorgen.

'And why did he laugh?' asked Eddie.

'Told him you'd got hit on the head with a hammer. Oh, and I told Fritz that his Norwegian was *shit*. It seemed to do the trick.' I grinned. I thought I'd just gone up a notch or two in the estimation of my British friends.

But then Fletcher recounted to Eddie everything I'd said and pointed towards the church. 'Just the one weakness to your story, Marek,' he said. 'What would a stonemason be doing fixing up a wooden church?'

I shuddered and thanked God that Fritz had proven marginally more stupid than me.

We proceeded towards the shore of the fjord. Mewing gulls and the sharpness of salt filled the air. Soldiers were checking everyone queuing for the next ferry. Jorgen had clearly been right to discount that route for their journey – far too risky, I thought. Some way from the bustle of the queue I saw my brother sitting on a bench reading a newspaper by lamplight, his eyes peering cautiously above the pages. I left the others and went to join him.

'Where are Leif and Harald?'

'Arrested.'

'What?'

'Bloody fools chose to drink in a bar frequented by soldiers. When I arrived, they were already arguing with a lieutenant over something or other. I suppose they thought being brash provided a good cover. Unfortunately the lieutenant decided to inconvenience them.'

'God, what a nightmare.' I buried my head in my hands and rubbed some life back into my numbed cheeks. 'What now?' In truth, I was tired of running. I yearned for somewhere warm and safe. My brother offered no reply. 'It was good to see Agnete. She looked well,' I said.

He nodded slowly, as if only half listening.

'Does she know anything about Mother from Doctor Haskveld?'

He shook his head.

'Are they still after us? I mean, did they figure out it was us that shot Wold?'

'She didn't say.'

'Did she say anything?' I asked, irritated at my brother's lack of responsiveness. Then I recalled their embrace and figured words had been a low priority.

He folded his paper and shoved his hands deep into his anorak pockets. 'They've moved Father to a camp in the north,' he said.

My ears pricked up. 'North? Where exactly?'

'Don't know.'

'Why?'

He shrugged. 'She said she'll try to find out. Plans to go to Odda next week with Lars. Said they'll camp out at Gestapo headquarters until either the Gestapo tell them or arrest them!'

'Rather them than me,' I replied, picturing Stretter's crooked lips.

Winter in the north was always dark and brutal. Agnete's news carried little hope, as I knew that life in a labour camp there could be akin to a death sentence. I wanted to scream at the injustice, to lash out with clenched fists at every grey uniform. I wanted to do *something*. Instead I simply sat and imagined my courage to have no equal.

Jorgen joined us on the bench and I told him of Harald and Leif's misfortune. He stiffened as if in pain. 'What are you going to do now?' I asked.

His face remained completely expressionless and I couldn't read or judge the processes and thoughts going on inside his head. I had little doubt that his next few decisions would drive his destiny, maybe ours too. If only we could speak with the goddesses Urd, Verdande or Skuld; if only one of them would guide us with their wisdom or send us a sign from the fortress Åsgard. I thought again of Father and wished I had a weapon like Mjollnir, Thor's great hammer. If I possessed such a perfect instrument, I could surely rid our country of evil and free my compatriots.

My brother sparked up a cigarette. He saw my horror. 'Don't worry, it's not an English cigarette, Marek.'

Fletcher and Eddie hung over some railings and stared out across the fjord. I wondered what they were thinking. These soldiers had come a long way, waited patiently for their moment of action and glory, and now everything was falling apart. Mulling over our predicament, I had a question for Jorgen. 'I know you can't tell us about the mission that's brought Eddie and Fletcher this far, but I suppose it's pretty important.'

'Yes, Marek. It's important. We've been planning it for months. A lot of men and women of the Resistance have already risked much just to get us this far.'

'That's what I figured. So I suppose it's vital you get to Jondal despite the fact that Ingrid, Leif and Harald have been arrested.'

'It's too late to stop the Shetland Bus,' he replied. 'They'll be arriving tonight. We have to make the rendezvous.'

It was a horrible question but I had to ask it. 'What if they talk?'

'They won't.'

He sounded so certain but I thought he was somewhat naïve. The Gestapo had a vivid imagination when it came to loosening tongues. Few could sustain silence or spin a credible yarn for more than a day or two. They would surely break eventually.

'Leif and Harald actually know very little,' he said. 'They have nothing really worth telling.'

'And Ingrid?' I knew she was close to Jorgen. I suspected that she knew the plan.

'They'll not break her,' he said emphatically.

'You sure?'

He pulled up the sleeve of his anorak and twisted round the cuff of his shirt. 'See that slight bulge?'

I peered closely. Something small appeared to be hidden inside his cuff.

'Cyanide pill. She has one too. And she'll swallow it given a moment's opportunity. I expect she's already dead.'

He'd floored me. I couldn't believe it. Stunned, I was speechless. Olaf bowed his head and closed his eyes tightly, as if stricken by a shooting pain. I supposed he was praying for her and I did the same. When I'd finished, I managed to say only, 'God, I hate this war.'

Jorgen sat bolt upright and took a deep, fortifying breath. 'She'll be at peace at last.' He sighed. 'She'll be where she yearned to be – with her husband once again. And for ever this time.'

The ferry had docked, unloaded and begun filling with vehicles and pedestrians keen on getting home. I watched everyone board under the eagle eyes of the soldiers. An army truck also boarded. As far as I could see, the truck appeared empty apart from the driver. He slid from his cab and wandered towards the edge of the deck, where he lit a cigarette and stood smoking while staring out across the fjord. I recognized him and an idea germinated inside my skull. I turned to Jorgen. 'Do you want to cross now? Go by ferry, I mean. Quickly, I need your answer.'

'Too dangerous.' He shook his head.

'I think I know a way. It'll be fine.'

He looked at me disbelievingly.

'What the hell are you on about, Marek?' growled my brother.

I pointed to the driver of the truck. 'Recognize him? I figure he owes us.'

My brother peered and then howled. 'Stroke of genius, Marek. You think you can convince him?'

'I think I might.'

To a bewildered Jorgen I explained in haste the kernel of my rather bold plan. And moments later I found myself striding purposefully towards the ferry.

'Hartwig!' I shouted. *It's definitely him*, I thought. I'd never seen anyone else risking such a ridiculous moustache. 'Hartwig Lauder.'

He looked in my direction and I waved. In the gloom I don't think he recognized me but I'd got his attention and he made his way towards the end of the ferry. I pushed past a guard and went to greet him. I smiled broadly and held out a welcoming hand. He peered at me in puzzlement.

'You remember, Hartwig. You drove us into Odda. Months ago. My father's French car. You tried to buy it from my brother. Three hundred Reichsmarks was your best offer.' I smiled again; my best friendly smile.

His confusion melted into a grin. 'Yes, yes, I remember.'

'Listen, can I ask a favour? Damn car's proving just like a temperamental woman, stubborn as hell. She broke down on the way to Kinsarvik. We desperately need to get to Jondal. If you're going that way, we'd appreciate a lift. It's just my brother and me and a few family friends. Please!'

'Only if we can continue our negotiations.'

'OK, but Father won't accept anything less than a thousand Reichsmarks.'

Hartwig laughed. 'He's mad.'

I turned and waved to the others. Olaf ran to the ticket office and emerged just in time to join Jorgen and the others seconds before their turn to board. They all looked apprehensive. Too apprehensive, I thought. One slip and my plan would be in tatters. And it was my plan. I had to make it work.

'Come, Hartwig,' I said, grabbing his arm. 'Come and say hello to Olaf.' I led him towards the back of the line. At the sight of me dragging a German towards him, Eddie appeared terrified. I winked at him though, and his brow softened. He saw I had a plan. Like the best magicians, I was relying on distracting my audience to make the trick work. Unwittingly, Hartwig was the distraction. I barged into the queue just as my brother was about to hand over his ticket and identity papers. 'Olaf, say hello to Hartwig.'

'Great to see you again,' my brother enthused. He seized and then shook Hartwig's hand at length. The sentries appeared surprised. I grabbed the moment. Snatching the wad of tickets from my brother, I thrust them into the hands of the sentries.

'They're for all of us,' I said, gesturing towards Jorgen, Eddie and Fletcher. The soldiers stared at us all for one horrible minute, during which I think my heart stopped, and then waved us through. Heading aboard, I blew a huge sigh of relief, one strong enough to fill the sails of a tall ship. 'Don't look back,' I whispered to Eddie. My brother led the way, talking loudly at Hartwig, who looked bemused by it all.

'Wait!'

The voice came from behind us. I froze. I dared not look round. This was it. We were all going to die. I'd failed.

'Come back.'

I swallowed hard and turned round, ready to face my worst nightmare. One of the sentries stepped forward. 'Here, you forgot your tickets,' he said. He tore the wad in two and handed one half back to me.

'Thanks,' I said. I tried to stop my hand from trembling but it was beyond my control.

The sentry grunted, turned away and finished dealing with the last of the passengers. How close was that? I thought. It was all I could do not to faint.

Chapter Thirteen

The crossing to Utne took just twenty minutes. Jorgen, Eddie and Fletcher kept to themselves, remaining huddled over the railings at the stern of the ferry. Olaf and I held Hartwig's attention as best we could. Keeping up the pretence drained me. My heart just wouldn't stop thumping. Now and again Hartwig glanced towards Jorgen. Did he suspect? I broke out in a cold sweat.

As we arrived, Olaf and the others climbed into the back of the truck. I hauled myself into the cab next to Hartwig. He slammed his door, started up the diesel engine and tapped the accelerator impatiently while waiting our turn to disembark.

'Are you going to Jondal too?' I asked.

'All the way to Hessvik.'

Although I'd never been there, I knew Hessvik to be a small village situated at the end of the road, several miles beyond Jondal. 'Why Hessvik, for God's sake? There's nothing there.'

He snorted in agreement. 'Orders. Always stupid bloody orders.' He laughed. 'The few dozen soldiers stationed there have been reassigned. They're wanted for a *razzia* up to the Hardanger.'

'The Hardanger!'

'Yes. My job to fetch them. Poor souls. Someone with too many medals has decided that men of the Resistance are hiding in that godforsaken wilderness. Personally I think that if anyone can survive up there in winter, they deserve to be left alone.'

'Are you going?'

'No. I'd rather break a leg.'

'Is that why Kinsarvik's crawling with soldiers?'

'Uh-huh. Apparently they've apprehended a few suspects already. And tomorrow several hundred troops will begin the climb to the plateau.' He looked at me. 'If they're up there, we'll find them. Better say an extra few prayers tonight for your fellow countrymen.' My eyes met his stare. Had we been rumbled? I just couldn't tell. I looked away and said a quick prayer.

The road to Jondal proved bumpy and the truck's suspension unforgiving. I thought of Olaf and the others cursing in the back each time their spines were jarred. Hartwig lit a cigarette and slid his window open a fraction. 'So, what about that car then? You said it had broken down.'

'Yes. Problems with the carburettor. The jets keep getting blocked. I've lost count of the number of times I've taken it apart and cleaned it out.'

'You've done that?'

'Yes. I love machines, engines especially.'

He nodded approvingly. 'Probably muck in the fuel tank. My offer of three hundred still stands.'

I laughed. 'Father's in love with Josephine. He'd

want a lot more than that to part company with her.'

'*Josephine*. I like the name. What does your father do?'

'He teaches.'

'And your brother?'

'Well, he got a place at the university in Oslo to study medicine but he's deferred it a year or two. Mother needs help at home.'

Reaching a steep incline, Hartwig changed down a gear and then another, revving hard. 'How did you get on in Odda? You said you were going to the police station.'

'Oh, OK.' I tried not to sound too reticent but I think he detected the failing tone of my voice. Luckily he didn't press me on the matter. In any event I changed the subject and quickly wished I'd kept my mouth shut. 'Do you know Hans Tauber?'

'Tauber? Tauber?' he repeated. 'No. Why?'

Oh God, how stupid of me. All I'd wanted to do was keep the polite conversation ticking over, to fill the silence. I wasn't thinking straight. My simple question would surely remind him that we were from Ulfhus and – my brain began to scream – he would recall what happened to Wold! I figured every German in Norway had probably heard about it. *And* that the prime suspects, the Olsen brothers, were still at large. Surely we were done for. I'd just jeopardized everything. I began breathing heavily and felt my lips tremble. *Keep calm, Marek*, I told myself. *Act innocent. Be brave.* I decided I'd already dug a hole deep enough to bury us all. There was only one thing for it. I had to carry on the conversation as if it were innocent and trivial. I had to be convincing. It was the only way.

'He was stationed in our village until a few weeks ago,' I replied. 'Then he suddenly left. I was just wondering how he was getting on.'

He threw me a puzzled glance and my heart skipped a beat. Obviously my interest in his compatriot surprised him. Damn! 'He seemed a good man,' I added. 'I mean, compared with some.'

His eyebrows climbed his forehead and the ends of his moustache twitched.

'You knew him well?' he asked.

'Not that well. He'd been a teacher before the war. I think he missed his family and the old life a great deal.'

He snorted loudly. 'We all miss the old life.' He flicked his cigarette out of the window and slid it shut. 'I often ask myself what the hell we are doing here.'

'We often ask the same question,' I replied.

He roared. 'You're an unusual one, Marek. It is Marek, isn't it?'

'Yes.' My voice faltered. I felt sick. I braced myself for the worst.

'Still, it's good that at least a few can see beyond our uniforms. Underneath, we're just like everyone else. And we want an end to the war as much as you. I think people forget that we're not here by choice. They forget that we did not ask to wear this uniform or to carry guns. Most of all, though, they forget that the very idea of shooting a fellow human being is abhorrent to many of us.'

'But not all,' I replied.

Pursing his lips, he nodded thoughtfully. 'True. But there are bad eggs in every basket. At least with us, the most rotten are clearly visible.'

'You mean the SS and Gestapo?'

'Uh-huh.'

'Like Herr Stretter.'

'You've met him?'

'Once. And hopefully never again.'

He laughed. I stared at him, desperately trying to figure out what he was thinking. He appeared relaxed, not like a man about to take on a truckload of Resistance fighters. It dawned on me that there were five of us and only one of him. If he was going to apprehend us, he should have done it on the ferry, where other soldiers were present. Now we had the upper hand. Yet he didn't look scared. Maybe he just hadn't put two and two together.

We did not speak for a while. I stared out of the windscreen and focused on the way ahead, lit by the truck's headlamps. Few vehicles appeared to have used the road, as the snow lay largely undisturbed. As well as the noise of the diesel engine, I listened to the incessant crunching of snow beneath the tyres. And I felt bloody confused. I liked Hartwig. How stupid was that? *He's the damn enemy*, I kept thinking. *I should hate him. I should want to see him dead*. But I didn't. Sitting beside him, I felt he could become a good friend if it wasn't for the little matter of war getting in the way. Did he feel the same? My mind was in a quandary: it had once all seemed so simple. I had believed that only two types of men existed. On the one hand there were us Jøssings, and we were pitted against the combined forces of the Germans and Quislings as if in the midst of a heroic battle of good versus evil. Yet the distinction had become blurred. Hartwig's words circled in my head. *Underneath, we're just like everyone else,* he'd said. Was he really just an ordinary man, a decent fellow far from home? A question occurred to me.

'Have you ever shot a man?' I asked. Deep down I hoped he had killed many. It would provide the ideal excuse to hate him. Clarity would be restored.

He shook his head. 'And hope I never have to,' he replied.

Blast!

'Who's with your brother in the back?' he asked.

'Uncle Peterson, Uncle Ivar and his good friend, Edvard. He's from Molde in the north.'

'And why the urgency to get to Jondal?'

Anticipating this question, I had already put some thought into my answer. 'My grandfather is unwell. Not expected to last. We just hope we can get there in time to say our goodbyes.'

'I'm sorry,' he replied. 'I understand. I wish I'd been home when my mother died. There was so much I wanted to say. So much that was left unsaid.' He peered through the windscreen intensely. 'We're almost there. Where shall I drop you?'

'Anywhere will do. Thanks.'

We drove a little further and then he pulled over. I reached for the door handle but paused and offered him my hand. 'Thank you, Hartwig. You have no idea how important this is to us. We shall be eternally grateful.' And so will all of Norway, I thought.

We shook hands and he smiled. 'No problem. Listen, I'm barracked in Odda. If you have difficulties getting spare parts for Josephine, let me know. I'll see if I can lay my hands on them.'

I climbed out. 'Thanks, I'll do that.'

'Tell your father I'll go to four hundred. Discuss it with him. Tell him it's the best possible price. He'd be daft not to accept.'

'What price love?' I shouted, slamming the door shut.

Hartwig leaned across and slid open the window. 'Take care, Marek. These are dangerous times.'

Olaf and the others arrived at my shoulder and I glanced round. With his eyes firmly fixed on Hartwig, Jorgen delved deep into his jacket pocket. I guessed what he was thinking: *We can't let Hartwig go in case he reports us*. He had to die. And that struck me as wrong. I reached out and seized Jorgen's arm. He glared at me. I shook my head. 'It's OK,' I said quietly.

Hartwig drove off, leaving us at the side of the road. Olaf rubbed his spine and stretched his arms above his head. Jorgen scanned around to get his bearings.

We had made it this far but had lost more than just Ingrid, Leif and Harald. Our skis, rucksacks, radio and automatic weapons remained hidden in the woods close to Kinsarvik. That left just four revolvers between us. I gave mine to Olaf. Jondal spread out before us, smoke drifting up from chimneys and lights glowing from the half-dozen or so houses. A few wet snowflakes ghosted around us. I could hear nothing except the lapping of water on the shores of the fjord. The flint–grey surface reflected the moonlight like a giant oil slick. 'Which way?' I asked.

Jorgen stuck a thumb over his shoulder. 'The rendezvous point is a quarter-mile beyond Jondal.' He peered at his watch. 'We have plenty of time. But—' He paused and rubbed his chin.

'What?' asked Olaf.

'The coastline's rugged. I just hope we can find the right inlet or else we'll be waiting for ever.'

We trudged through Jondal and beyond, the road narrowing to little more than a track. I could see the sole set of tyre marks left by Hartwig's truck. Eddie counted his steps under his breath, saying he reckoned it to be the best method for estimating our distance travelled. I persuaded him to try counting in Norwegian. '*En, to, tre, fire, fem, seks, sju, åtte, ni, ti* . . .' Somewhere around thirty-five he came over all tongue-tied and gave up, reverting to his native English. As we walked, we passed many potential rendezvous points. The fjord seemed to offer infinite possibilities for clandestine meetings. We stopped and inspected every craggy inlet, dismissing each in turn as too small, too inaccessible, or too close to Jondal. I began to wonder if we'd missed the place. Jorgen's map lacked the detail needed to find a precise set of co-ordinates. It had become a case of guesswork and intuition and we each had different ideas. When Eddie said he'd paced out well over a quarter of a mile and refused to trudge any further, Jorgen's anxiety boiled over and he kicked a large stone into the fjord. It bounced and skimmed, ripping the silken surface. That was the first time I'd seen any real emotion from him but thought it had more to do with Ingrid than our predicament.

As we retraced our steps, Fletcher stopped without warning and disappeared through a narrow gap between some spiky shrubs burdened by snow. He reappeared a moment later with a hopeful expression and said, 'Jorgen, take a look. There's a narrow path that leads down. The inlet is wide enough for a boat to turn and there's a flat shelf of rock just above the waterline. It's the best we've seen.'

Jorgen took a look and called out for us to join him. 'Better pray we've got this right. If not we're in big trouble,' he declared. 'Find somewhere as comfortable as you can. We're in for a long wait.'

Huddled in a shallow crevice in the granite rock rising from the fjord, I shivered from the biting cold. Each gust of the north wind grazed my cheeks. Fletcher and Eddie settled to my left and gazed out across the water. I admired their patience and lack of complaint. Jorgen kept vigil crouched on a small outcrop some fifty feet above us and to our left. My brother spent time counting and recounting the bullets in Father's revolver. Every second felt like a minute, every minute an hour. I kept looking at my watch but the hands seemed reluctant to move. And my hunger and thirst made my throat and belly feel strangely sore, as if I had succumbed to a sudden illness. Eddie saw me rubbing my guts and reached into his pocket. He drew out a small bar of chocolate, unravelled the foil and snapped off a chunk. He pressed it into my hand. I greedily shoved it into my mouth and let it melt on my tongue. It tasted fantastic, smooth and rich, as if a hundred pints of milk had been distilled into one mouthful of heaven.

'How many men are coming to join us?' I asked.

Fletcher pressed his back against the rock and cracked his knuckles. 'I'm not sure.'

'Experts, I presume.'

Having placed his hands behind his head to fashion a sort of pillow, he looked at me and nodded.

My brother settled down next to Fletcher and lit a cigarette. No sooner had he taken his first puff than Fletcher snatched it from his lips and threw it into the fjord's dark depths. 'What did you do that for?' he complained.

'Bad for your health.'

Eddie sniggered loudly.

★ ★ ★

At about eleven-thirty I heard the rumble of engines. Fletcher rose to his feet and we all looked up towards Jorgen. I sensed anticipation but knew something that they evidently did not. Norwegian fishing vessels did not sound like that. When not under sail they moved under the power of their single-cylinder semi-diesel engines. I had the manuals at home to prove it. And the most obvious thing about these engines was their sound. I'd recognize their *tonk-tonk-tonk* anywhere. This was not a *tonk-tonk-tonk*, rather a continuous burbling.

'It's a German E-boat!' I shouted.

Jorgen waved to us and crouched lower.

'Get down,' I whispered loudly.

Sure enough, the German patrol boat slid into view. Lying about a hundred yards offshore, it silhouetted beautifully against the distant, pale indigo-grey mountains, and I figured she was managing about eight knots heading due west. A powerful searchlight on her foredeck burst on and lit the shore. I trembled. We pressed back into the crevice and squeezed together like tinned beans. We remained perfectly still as the beam passed by. Thankfully, it did not linger or return for a second look. The burbling note of the boat's engine gradually faded. Only once it had gone did we dare flinch a muscle.

'You were right, Marek,' declared Eddie.

I explained my reasoning and he seemed duly impressed.

'There's not much Marek doesn't know about

engines,' said Olaf. 'He was born with a bloody spanner in his mouth.'

With silence returned we settled back down. At just before midnight we heard a vehicle whine and grumble its way along the road above and behind us. I figured it was probably Hartwig returning with his men. I told the others about the planned *razzia* up on the Hardanger and we all let out huge sighs of relief. And then we laughed at the Germans chasing their tails and wasting precious time and resources looking in all the wrong places. But we did not laugh much or for long as we knew they had Ingrid, Leif and Harald. Somehow it made me feel all the more determined that we should succeed. I thought of Father and wondered how he was bearing up. Where had they taken him? As far north as the Arctic Circle? Were polar bears his new neighbours? I prayed that if he knew what we had done and what we were in the midst of, he'd approve and maybe even feel a little proud of us. I tried to think of a plan to get him released. But my mind went blank and then filled with the torture of frustration. Gripped with the ache of despair, I thought of Mother. I still pictured her in Sweden, safe but helpless. Of course, I had no idea where she was. Oddly, though, I had no doubt that she was OK.

I tried passing the time much as I had in the Johanssens' hut. I asked Eddie and Fletcher about their lives and families back home but got little information out of them. In fact, I realized I knew very little about them and had begun to doubt what I did know. I figured that if we were apprehended, they knew my brother and I would be the first to crack under interrogation. After all, we weren't soldiers or hardened Resistance fighters. We were just two young men from a small village up to their necks in the mire. It would be safer for us to know nothing. Were Eddie and Fletcher who they said they were? Was Jorgen really Jorgen Peterson from Tromsø? In a way I hoped they weren't, especially Jorgen. That way, if I were caught, nothing from my lips would jeopardize any family he might still have in Norway.

Olaf heard it first, a slow, solemn, distant *tonk-tonk-hic-cup-tonk*. It grew louder.

Eventually the vessel crept round a headland to the west and changed course towards us. Jorgen flashed a small torch in its direction; two flashes in quick succession followed by three slow and then one final quick one. He repeated it every few seconds. I remembered what Fletcher had taught me about Morse code in the Johanssens' hut and tried deciphering it: *I . . . O . . . E*. It meant nothing. I guessed it was just some kind of prearranged signal. Eventually, he got a reply. I studied the flashes: *S . . . O . . . L . . . A*. Jorgen leaped to his feet and climbed down to join us.

The sight of her closing in on the shore was familiar, as most Norwegian fishing boats look alike, their twin masts piercing the sky, their high bows making them seem proud as they cut through the swell. Then there are the large wheelhouses and the tall exhaust pipes.

I reckoned she was a true Hardanger cutter, quick through the water. And she was big. The larger the vessel, the higher the status of her captain. I figured he had to be a true mariner and not some weekend fisherman.

The engine cut out, and as she drifted towards shore, she turned, her stern swinging round. Dressed in black, a lone figure on deck peered towards us. He clutched a machine gun at the ready.

'Right,' said Jorgen. 'Quickly now, get down to that ledge. We'll board her from there.'

I looked at my brother. What did he mean, *board her*?

Chapter Fourteen

The boat drifted towards the ledge. A narrow plank was pushed out from the deck to produce a precarious bridge. Jorgen crossed first, then Eddie, followed by Olaf, and then it was my turn. The boat bobbed and twisted and the plank slipped back and forth. I held my breath and hurried across, praying my balance would hold. Fletcher followed. Once we were all aboard, the crewman hauled the plank back. 'Welcome to the *Sola*,' he said. 'I'm Thomas Loedder. Better get yourselves inside. The captain's keen to get the hell out of here.'

I heard a splutter, clunk and clatter, and then the deafening beat of the engine. The air seemed to vibrate and a plume of choking black diesel fumes spat from the exhaust pipe. She surged forward. We were underway.

Following Jorgen into the wheelhouse, I felt my brain buzzing with unanswered questions. Not least, what on earth were we doing on the boat? I had assumed men and supplies were being set down at Jondal. After all, no one had said otherwise.

'Better get your men below,' rumbled a deep, reverberating voice. 'We've got a long voyage ahead of us.'

The voice belonged to a short, plump, elderly man clad in the thickest, roughest black sweater and with the whitest hair and beard I'd ever seen. A large, flat nose like that of a particularly unsuccessful boxer completed what I considered to be an unfortunate face. He gripped the wheel tightly, as if fighting a strong undertow. A briar appeared permanently stuck to his bottom lip, and the room reeked of sweet tobacco, stale armpits and cod. Ruddy faced, he cursed and added, 'Well, get a bloody move on. This isn't a bloody pleasure trip.'

Eddie and Fletcher dutifully headed below. Olaf and I loitered beside Jorgen. The captain took one look at me and shook his head. 'Bloody madness,' he muttered.

Captain Kurt Torvic was a man of few words, and of those he did utter, about half would make Mother blush. He spoke slowly, his words like punctuations between silences. And he possessed a hacking cough, spells of which produced copious green phlegm, which he spat out of a small side window propped open with a rusty screwdriver. He did this with such precision and regularity I deduced it had to be a chronic condition. Jorgen explained to him about our trip from the plateau and apologized that he had had to come so far up the fjords. The captain merely grunted in reply.

The *Sola* had a shabby, lived-in feel to her. Varnished wood panels had begun to peel, and faded family photographs nailed haphazardly to walls occupied prime positions around the windows. The deck seemed damp and tacky underfoot.

A gaunt, skinny crewman with odd, staring eyes clambered up from below bearing grubby mugs of hot coffee and a plate of rather stale bread topped with pickled herring. It slid down a treat. He introduced himself as Peter Lomberg from Bergen and took over from Kurt at the helm.

'Suppose you want to see my charts,' said Kurt to Jorgen. He nodded and they squeezed into a small alcove filled with a narrow bench and table and pored over Kurt's planned route. Olaf and I headed below.

I estimated the *Sola* to be about eighteen foot in the beam and about sixty foot from bow to stern. Below deck a doorway led into the forecastle and, peering in, I saw bunks for six men. It looked as untidy as my bedroom at home, clothes strewn about, bedding all twisted and dishevelled. Only one bunk appeared occupied and from beneath a striped blanket came a whistling snore. As the boat rocked in the swell, two empty spirit bottles rolled back and forth on the floor as if playing a game of tag.

Inspecting the rest of the boat, I saw that a small cabin lay aft containing just two bunks. The large hold lay amidships and from it the stench of fish proved overpowering. An access hatch had been opened and I witnessed Eddie climbing in.

'What are you doing?' I asked, having clasped a hand firmly over my nose.

I received no reply but heard Eddie grunt with considerable effort as he hauled himself on top of the huge, slippery, silvery mound of fish. Unable to stand, he knelt and began digging his hands into the catch like a madman searching for treasure. His knees gradually sank into the mass of cod and slushy ice, and the sloshing and slopping sounds made me queasy.

Eventually he seized something and yanked it purposefully. His hand emerged from the gloop clutching a waterproof bag about the size of a holdall. Delighted at his success, he began unfastening the straps. Having peered inside, he looked up towards Fletcher. 'The detonators!' he said gleefully. 'Just the right type too.' He dug deeper inside the bag. 'Ah, and some time pencils. Different delays as well. Splendid!' He waved a handful of the slender devices in the air.

'Good. Better bury them again. In case a German patrol intercepts us and decides to come aboard,' said Fletcher.

Eddie carefully resealed the bag and pressed it deep into the mound of fish. He crawled back towards the hatch.

Making my way along the narrow corridor, swaying from side to side, I saw Olaf leaning against a bulkhead and looking rather confused. 'What's the matter?'

'Where is everyone?'

A good point, I thought. I had only seen Kurt, Thomas Loedder, Peter Lomberg and the person slumbering in the forecastle. Four – hardly an army! Fletcher pushed past us and Olaf and I looked to him for answers. He shrugged.

Returning to the wheelhouse, we squeezed onto benches around a small fixed table. Kurt had finished briefing Jorgen and stood puffing on his pipe while Jorgen pored over the charts intensely, as if he were trying to memorize them all.

'Where are the men you were supposed to rendezvous with?' my brother asked.

Jorgen looked up. 'Kurt put them ashore before entering the fjords. Said it was too dangerous to bring them any further. The Germans have stepped up the patrols. Seems they suspect something. Something big! They're getting nervous and clamping down.'

'Our gear is still aboard,' observed Eddie.

Kurt grunted. 'Didn't have time to offload.'

'What are we carrying?' asked Jorgen.

'A lot of explosives,' replied Kurt nervously. 'And about a ton of small arms and ammunition. Enough to get us all shot.'

Eddie grinned. 'Splendid!'

'Our plan's had to be fine-tuned,' said Jorgen. 'We're heading to rendezvous with the others. The delay unfortunately places us behind schedule but London has been informed.'

'Where are we going?' I asked.

'North,' growled Kurt unhelpfully. I realized that was as much detail as I was going to get. And again I saw him stare at me, his eyes narrowing thoughtfully. I think he wondered what the hell someone so young was doing caught up in all this. And I think he disapproved.

Out came the *aquavit* and we all settled down to get to know one another. Fletcher peered around the cabin and ran his fingers over the wood panelling. I reckoned he was casting his expert eye over the boat's construction. 'This is all softwood,' he remarked in considerable surprise.

'Just her stem is hardwood,' replied Kurt between puffs. 'She has a double frame and her outer planking is three inches thick. Her inner skin is as thick again and the two are fastened with trenails.'

'Trenails! Jesus, you mean wooden pegs hold this crate together? Thought those went out of fashion with the Armada.'

Put out by Fletcher's sharp remark, Kurt bit hard on the stem of his pipe, as if resisting the urge to spit a venomous reply. Instead he leaned forward and jabbed a finger at him. 'She got us here, didn't she?'

'How was the crossing?' asked Jorgen. 'The weather reports sounded dire.'

Kurt settled back. 'Bit choppy.'

Standing at the helm, Peter Lomberg laughed loudly. 'Forty-foot swell. Tossed us about a bit.'

I tried to imagine such a sea and contemplated the awfulness of a relentless surging and dipping of the boat. I knew I'd be seasick. In fact, I felt sick just thinking about it.

'One or two waves nearly had us,' Peter added.

Kurt grimaced and nodded. For a moment he looked lost in thought. I think he was reliving each terrifying moment. 'Spoke a few prayers, we did,' he said under his breath. 'I prayed her over every crest!'

The voyage from Lunna Voe had taken over a day. Kurt cursed that his bonus of ten English pounds for the trip had hardly seemed adequate compensation for all the grief. I reckoned our captain was a difficult man to please.

'How many trips have you made?' I asked.

'Too many,' he grumbled. 'Three already this winter.'

'They only risk the crossing once the days have shortened enough to offer the cover of darkness,' said Jorgen.

'To avoid being spotted by aircraft?' asked Olaf.

Kurt nodded. 'They don't patrol more than fifty miles out to sea. And we make sure that we have our nets out. We do everything possible to make it look as if we're simply doing what the boat was designed for – *fishing*.' He laughed, his mirth collapsing into a hacking cough. He wiped the spittle from his beard and tapped the ash from his briar.

'That explains the hold full of cod,' I said.

'Aye, a bloody waste too,' he replied. 'It'll be off by the time we get back to Shetland. Have to dump it at sea. Still, it conceals the supplies well enough.' With his thumb he tamped fresh tobacco into the bowl of his pipe and sniffed.

Fletcher excused himself from the table and headed below. The boat carried one of the latest transceivers among its stash and he wanted to try it out. He said London would appreciate an update. He couldn't believe that the boffins there had managed to compress all the components into a case weighing just nine pounds. That, he declared, was less than a third of the weight of the last radio sets they'd sent across.

'One of the few benefits of war, Marek,' he said. I knew what he meant. War focused the mind, encouraged ingenuity, driving invention and discovery at a breathless pace. All in order to give one side the edge over the other.

The *aquavit* and tiredness had begun to make my head spin and swim. And the plumes of smoke from Kurt's pipe stung my eyes and made them water. Added to that, I couldn't stop yawning.

My brother quizzed Eddie about what he'd found hidden in the hold. 'What exactly are those time pencils?' he asked.

Eddie tried to explain but his Norwegian wasn't up to the task. Jorgen helped him out. 'They're delaying devices,' he said. 'Quite ingenious, actually. The small tubes are hollow and contain a spring that's compressed and held in place with a wire. When it's released, a striker attached to one end of the spring hits a percussion cap and that sets off a fuse or detonator fixed into the end. The delaying part is the clever bit. Behind the spring is a small glass ampoule of acid. Turning a screw in the end of the pencil breaks the ampoule and the solution comes into contact with the wire. It gradually eats it away. When the wire breaks, the device goes off.'

My brother frowned. 'Eddie said something about different delays.'

Jorgen nodded. 'Different concentrations of acid. The stronger the solution, the quicker it eats through the wire. They're colour coded so we know which is which. The black ones have a ten-minute delay, the red ones thirty.'

'The delay is only approximate, of course,' said Eddie. 'They haven't fine-tuned them but they work well enough. They should come in handy.'

My eyelids had grown heavy and my neck weak, my head drifting down until my chin rested against my anorak. The voices around me became muffled and strangely comforting.

'Best use the bunks aft,' said Kurt. 'Looks like you lads need some shut-eye.'

I awoke to distant shouting. Rubbing my eyes free of grainy sleep, I lifted myself onto my elbows and listened. Kurt sounded furious about something. And then I realized the engine had stopped. Olaf remained buried under a blanket, snoring loudly.

Making my way past the hold, I saw Kurt standing in the doorway to the forecastle, venomously berating one of his crew. He shook with rage. Jorgen appeared and threw me an anxious glance.

'Why have we stopped?' I asked.

'Problems.'

I'd hoped for a more complete explanation. 'What sort of problems?'

Irritated by my presence as if I were an itch that

wouldn't go away, Jorgen snapped, 'Never you mind, Marek. We'll get it sorted.'

Realizing that my loitering wasn't appreciated, I headed up into the wheelhouse. Eddie and Fletcher were on deck and peering into the darkness. Peter gripped the helm and spun the wheel first left and then right as the boat pitched and yawed with a mind of its own. Oh God, I thought, the engine's broken down!

'Need a hand getting the sails up?'

Peter nodded gratefully so I headed out onto deck, where Thomas Loedder was desperately hauling on a rope to lift and unfurl the mainsail. I seized the rope and helped pull on it. The canvas billowed and snapped out of reach but we managed to control it amid shouts of encouragement. And we succeeded not a moment too soon as Eddie spotted steep treacherous cliffs looming out of the gloom. Peter spun the wheel. The boat heaved heavily to port, leaning at what I thought was an impossible angle, its timbers creaking and groaning, and then she straightened and slowly regained her composure.

Returning to the wheelhouse, I realized Kurt's fury had been directed towards the crewman I'd seen sleeping in the forecastle the previous night. Thor Gossen had finally been roused from his drunken stupor and, clad in just a filthy vest and equally horrid pants, he stood scratching himself in front of us all. A big man of six foot with a barrel girth, he was the hairiest person I had ever seen. From every inch of skin, from every follicle, sprouted thick black hairs, yet his skin shone as though he sweated pure grease. And he stank worse than the fish. On learning that Thor Gossen was the *Sola*'s sole mechanic and engineer, Jorgen despaired, as Thor looked incapable of standing up straight, let alone fixing anything. We began filling the beast with strong black coffee.

After extensive deliberation involving much pipe-chewing, Kurt arrived at his decision. We would drop anchor somewhere and try to fix the engine. He didn't relish attempting to navigate northwards through the inner lead under sail alone. But stopping presented its own difficulties as we would be sitting ducks and bound to attract the attention of any patrolling E-boats.

While I'd slept we'd made good progress against the tide and had almost reached the mouth of the Hardangerfjord. Before us lay islands and the open sea, and the water had become choppy. Kurt took over the helm and guided the boat into a sheltered inlet, dropped anchor and threatened Thor with much physical discomfort should he not immediately begin his task. The beast obliged but without enthusiasm.

The engine lay beneath the wheelhouse. Thor squeezed through a hatch into the cramped space lit by a single naked bulb. From beneath our feet echoed a string of curses and hammering followed by more cursing. As time passed, our captain grew increasingly apprehensive. 'Not good being so far south,' he muttered. 'Normally we sail to the Lofoten Islands. It stays dark there at this time of year.' He gazed fretfully out of the window and towards the pale light of a winter's dawn.

We were a long way from Lofoten. The string of islands lay much further north, beyond Trondheim. They're closer to Narvik and Tromsø. *Tromsø!* I looked at Jorgen and wondered if he dreamed of home. I suspected he too would rather be there than here.

Thor called out for the engine to be started. Peter obliged. The result was a loud clattering noise, some painful grinding sounds and then a broken series of *tonks* interspersed with hiccups. There were more hiccups than *tonks*. She still sounded poorly. Thor yelled something unrepeatable and hammered the engine's casing with a hefty spanner. Trying to be helpful, Fletcher knelt down and offered words of encouragement through the hatch. The beast reacted rather unkindly by throwing down his tools, climbing out of the engine room and storming off back to his bunk. He growled that he needed some time to think.

Olaf took me to one side and whispered in my ear, 'Can you do anything, Marek? Do you have any ideas?'

In truth, I didn't. Naturally I desperately wanted to help out but Kurt seemed to be in the midst of an anxiety attack, pacing back and forth, cursing at his misfortune as if the gods had turned against him. Not a good time, I thought, to bombard him with technical questions that only served to remind him of our predicament. I went on deck for some fresh air and spotted Thomas close to the bow.

'Do you know what's wrong with the engine?'

He shook his head.

'What exactly happened? I mean, did it suddenly cut out? Overheat? What?'

He leaned heavily on a railing and continued to shake his head. 'We've had problems ever since leaving Lunna Voe. During the storm we kept the engine running, but every now and again it would miss a beat. Been getting much worse too.'

I scratched my head and tried to figure out what might cause such a fault.

'The problem's worse in heavy seas. As soon as we get into a swell the damn thing starts faltering.'

Heavy seas? That sounded odd to me.

'Trouble is, Thor's drunk most of the time. When sober he's a fine engineer but mostly he's pretty useless.'

My brain buzzed. I felt like a doctor trying to make a tricky life-or-death diagnosis based on an unusual cluster of symptoms. The engine did not appear to be overheating, nor had Thor spotted any obvious leaks. And then there was the weird intermittency. It had worsened during the storm. I reckoned something had to be interfering with the fuel supply. I thought of the forty-foot swell and it gave me an idea. 'Do you think Kurt would mind if I took a look?'

'Why don't you ask him?'

Returning to the wheelhouse, I did, and our captain merely threw up his hands. Evidently he seemed willing to clutch at any straw, however short.

I removed my anorak and sweater and eased myself down into the hot fug of the engine compartment. Perspiration formed on my brow and dripped from my nose. The air stank of grease and diesel and everything felt slimy to the touch. Olaf poked his head through the hatch. 'What do you think?'

'Probably a kink in the fuel line.' I hunted down the right piece of tubing and traced its path back to a bulkhead. Damn! It looked fine. 'It's not that,' I shouted.

'Then what?' my brother asked.

I racked my brain. I could think of only one other possibility – a blockage. Maybe in the storm some sediment or lump of corrosion had been disturbed in the fuel tank and found its way into the fuel line. I worked my way back to where the line met the engine. The rubberized tubing was connected to the pump by a tight screw clip and I reached into Thor's tool tray for a screwdriver to loosen it. While concentrating on the job, I heard a kerfuffle above me and Olaf disappeared from view. I took little notice of the shouts and thumping footsteps, wanting instead to make sure I didn't get drenched in diesel the moment the fuel line came free. That proved wishful thinking because, without warning, the end popped off the pump and snaked through the air, spraying thick, slimy, stinking diesel everywhere. I snatched the end and twisted it to stop the flow. Looking at the mess, I saw the glistening culprit and shouted, 'Eureka!' The fragment of metal shone like a jewel. It looked big enough to block the line every time the boat pitched. I reckoned I'd be hailed a hero and maybe, just maybe, Captain Kurt Torvic would be glad I'd come along after all. I slid the tubing back on and tightened the clip. With a filthy rag I cleaned the spillage as best I could but realized plenty of it had covered me. My blackened skin felt horridly sticky and began to itch.

Clutching the offending piece of metal triumphantly, I hauled myself out of the compartment and called out, 'Think I've fixed it. Shard got stuck in the fuel pipe.' I turned, looked up and saw a German sailor staring down at me.

Chapter Fifteen

Hustled out onto the foredeck, rifle butts nudging into our backs, we were made to form an orderly line while soldiers checked our papers and searched the boat. The *Sola* had become an ant's nest crawling with uniforms and guns. Luckily Kurt bore the brunt of the questioning. I knew just one *Frage* aimed at Eddie and we'd be done for, as I doubted he'd be able to reply convincingly. I began shaking uncontrollably from my knees up and it wasn't due to the cold.

The German E-boat lay thirty yards off to our starboard side, its deck a hive of activity. It resembled a huge grey killer whale. Fletcher and Eddie stood quietly while Olaf chain-smoked. I think we all looked rather nervous, except for Kurt. He simply appeared annoyed at the inconvenience of it all. Huffing and puffing, he shifted his weight from foot to foot. Gnawing angrily on his briar, he looked as if he might actually bite right through its stem. An officer clutching a large file scrutinized Kurt's papers closely and at length.

'What's he doing?' I whispered to Peter, who stood close to my left shoulder.

'Checking the register of fishing boats. Making sure the *Sola* is listed as out of Bergen.'

'And is she?'

He lowered his voice. 'Yes. But this isn't the *Sola*!'

'What?' I threw him a look of abject panic and felt my guts sink despairingly. He grinned and told me not to worry. Not to worry! Who was he kidding?

The search of the boat took an age and I fully expected Fritz to discover the stash in the hold. They quizzed Kurt about why he had stopped and he explained about the engine trouble. An officer ordered him to start her up and he obliged. Loud spluttering quickly turned to a healthy, rhythmic *tonk* and both Kurt and Thor stared at me loose-jawed. The German officer frowned. I think he suspected Kurt had fibbed. Knowing that might prove disastrous, I stepped forward, presented the offending shard of metal and offered a complete technical explanation. The officer strode up to me and shoved his face so close to mine I could smell the menthol on his breath. I wasn't about to let Herr Kapitän put me off my stride so I ignored him and continued my story. He listened and eventually began casting his cold leaden gaze over my filthy appearance, disdainfully taking a step back when my odour proved too much. Thank the gods, I think he believed me! He strutted off and bawled orders to his men.

As we stood obediently, the freezing air first numbed my skin and then began to burn it. Each gust of wind bit into me. My teeth began to chatter and I hugged myself against the cold. Complaining aloud drew no response from the guards, who simply held their heartless gaze upon us. They seemed inhuman.

Men appeared from below deck surprisingly empty handed. Kurt's papers were returned and the boarding party duly departed back to the E-boat amid much gesticulating that I took to mean we'd better not be here when they returned on the next tide. Olaf and I headed below. My brother wrapped me in three blankets and rubbed life back into my blue fingers. Peter handed me a mug containing *aquavit* and coffee in equal measures. It warmed my throat and belly as if I were being cooked from within. I could hardly believe that we'd got away with it, but we had.

'How?' I asked, no sooner than the E-boat had set a course eastwards.

Kurt sucked on his briar and chuckled. 'Papers were in order, all stamped and up to date. Official stamps for every port we're supposed to have stopped at. Damn fine forgeries. Bloody marvellous!'

I received no thanks for my efforts from either Kurt or Thor. The others seemed duly impressed though, so I wallowed in their gratitude. I think Kurt's heart had faltered when the *Sola* started up, not just from surprise but also from fear that Fritz would think his story was a lie. And as for Thor, his pride had been wounded and he sought solace in a bottle of *aquavit*. He returned to his bunk without a word.

Talking to Peter, I appreciated the sophistication of the Shetland Bus. As little as possible got left to chance.

At Lunna Voe they had a copy of the shipping register too. For each trip they chose a name that coincided with a similar type of boat registered as close as possible to their planned destination. The name got painted on the side and the correct paperwork forged. So, unless Fritz happened upon the real *Sola* at about the same time, all would appear in order – the right boat in the right location. As for the stash, well, Fritz hadn't wanted to get his hands dirty. After all, the hold was supposed to contain cod or herring and that's exactly what they saw. *Alles in Ordnung!* as the enemy says when everything's just as it should be.

Passing through the narrow Langenuen channel, we headed north past Osøyro, then past Bergen and into the Hjeltefjord. For two days we made good headway and took shifts at keeping watch. With daylight being such a brief visitor, I soon realized just how huge a challenge Kurt and his men regularly undertook in the name of a free Norway. All beacons and lighthouses had been extinguished by Fritz and so navigation proved highly hazardous. We had to watch out for other boats, friendly and not so friendly, and what Kurt called skerries. I worked out they were rocky outcrops poking from the water. And every time we passed an observation post or gun battery ashore, a shiver sped down my spine and made me tingle.

In truth, I hated the journey because it gave me time to think, and I felt increasingly homesick despite knowing that back in Ulfhus lay an empty house. I longed to speak with Mother and Father and desperately wanted to be reunited as a family. I wanted my old life back, my small world restored, for everything to be OK.

'It's a dream, an impossible dream,' Olaf told me whenever I moaned to him, which was often. The lack of hope in his tone made tears well up and his words felt like sharp daggers being driven into my heart. I refused to believe him. He was hurting too, of course, but dared not let it show. I think he feared displaying weakness in front of the others.

That evening Jorgen summoned Olaf and me to the wheelhouse. We sat on one side of the chart table, he and Fletcher on the other.

'I've been wondering what to do with you two,' Jorgen began. 'Because of your father's arrest, your revenge attack and your mother's escape, I suppose you are fugitives with no home to go to.'

'We're doing fine,' replied Olaf defensively.

Fletcher nodded. 'Indeed, you have proven quite resourceful and not without courage.'

'As I see it, there are just three possibilities,' Jorgen continued. 'One, we put you ashore and let you fend for yourselves. I'm sure you'd do OK for a while but there's clearly no future in that path. Agreed?'

I looked to Olaf but we didn't need to say anything to one another. Jorgen spoke the truth and we knew it, despite our bravado. We nodded in unison.

'Good. Secondly, we could use our contacts to get you new documents and identities and let members of the Resistance guide you to safety, a neutral territory – Sweden perhaps.'

This sounded much more promising and I was all for nodding again when Olaf enquired, 'And the third option?'

'Losing Harald, Leif and Ingrid all in one go has left us rather short-handed. We could do with an extra pair of hands.' Jorgen gazed directly into my brother's eyes. 'So, Olaf, if you want to join us, to take up where your father left off, we'd be happy to have you aboard.'

I detected fire in my brother's eyes, the flames of delight, excitement and anticipation. 'What about me?' I blurted, perhaps rather too indignantly.

Fletcher grinned. 'What did I say, Jorgen? Told you Marek would be put out.'

'How old are you?' snapped Jorgen.

'Fourteen. Why?'

'Exactly!' he replied. He sat back, as if it were all so obvious. But it wasn't obvious to *me*.

'You're a brave lad, Marek, but you're too young. We couldn't have it on our consciences to place you in mortal danger. We simply couldn't.' He shrugged apologetically.

Olaf did not spring to my defence and I could have kicked him for his lack of brotherly camaraderie. I glared at him open-mouthed. 'He's right, Marek,' was all he said.

My blood began to boil. 'Who was it that helped you get rid of Wold?' I shouted. Then I looked towards

Jorgen. 'And who was it that got you across the Sørfjord in time for the rendezvous? Who was it that fixed the damn engine?' I stuck my jaw out defiantly.

Jorgen and Fletcher squirmed in discomfort like landed eels but offered no defence.

'The lad's got a point,' puffed Kurt. Keeping a firm grasp on the helm, he turned and raised a bushy white eyebrow. 'Figure you already owe him a great debt of gratitude. As do I.'

Kurt had to be the last person I expected to lend me his support. Jorgen shook his head though, remaining unconvinced. 'He's too young. It wouldn't be right. What if we get captured? Think about it.'

Kurt grimaced, leaned sideways and spat a lump of phlegm out of the window. 'Your decision,' he muttered.

I wasn't finished. 'This is my country as much as yours,' I growled. 'You have no right to tell me I cannot defend it. I'm as much a Jøssing as any of you and can make up my own mind.'

'He could be useful, Jorgen.' Eddie had draped himself in the doorway and I realized I'd found another ally. 'He can get away with things we can't. Remember how he helped us when challenged by the patrol in Kinsarvik. The Germans didn't suspect him. It's his youth that's his strength.'

I nodded vigorously in agreement. Jorgen clasped his head in his hands and then rubbed his cheeks until they were pink.

'I'm in,' declared Olaf, 'but Marek comes too.

Anyway, Mother and Father would never forgive me for abandoning him. So it's both of us or neither of us.'

'I'll look after young Marek,' said Eddie. 'And I'm sure he'll look after me!' He grinned.

Jorgen threw up his hands. 'Very well – seems I'm outvoted. Can't say I'm happy but I'll take you both on. Welcome to the Resistance!'

We all shook hands. I suddenly felt taller, more powerful and rather special. Jorgen set about briefing us on key aspects of their mission – or rather *our* mission.

'Convoys in the North Sea and Atlantic are still suffering huge losses. The main reason being that Fritz hunts them down and torpedoes them with his fleet of U-boats. And these submarines hide in the fjords out of reach of the Allied bombers and navy. It's time to deal them a hefty blow.'

'You intend blowing up some U-boats?' My brother sounded disbelieving.

Eddie grinned. 'Not exactly.'

'The Germans have constructed a new submarine base in the Orkfjord, west of Trondheim,' said Jorgen. 'Naturally it's heavily defended and would require an army to break in. And we don't have an army. So we have to be subtle.'

I couldn't think what he meant. 'Subtle?'

'Yes. "Disruptive" would be a better description.'

Fletcher explained. 'The thing with submarines,' he began, 'is that their value lies in staying submerged for long periods. There they can stalk their prey almost undetected. But they can only do this because they have a large bank of accumulators on board. These accumulators provide power for propulsion and every-thing else underwater. Without them, a U–boat has to stay on the surface and use its diesel engine.'

'What exactly are these accumulators?' my brother asked.

'Rechargeable batteries, Olaf,' I replied. 'Fancy not knowing that!' His lack of knowledge of all things mechanical and electrical was embarrassing. I wanted to disown him.

'They constructed the new base on the fjord to speed up the servicing of the U–boats between sorties,' said Fletcher. 'There's a new railway line for bringing in supplies. We intend to disrupt it. That's where Eddie's unique skills come into play. And intelligence reports have picked up on the fact that a shipment of replace-ment accumulators is due in soon.'

'So, by sabotaging the railway line you'll stop the delivery,' I said, leaping one step ahead.

'Not exactly – that's not our plan. We're going to let the delivery arrive and *then* sabotage the railway line,' said Fletcher.

This sounded rather stupid to me, rather back to front. 'Why not *before* they arrive?'

'We want the delivery to go ahead and we want them to fit the new accumulators.'

Failing miserably to hide my confusion, I scratched my head.

Fletcher laughed at me. 'Marek looks as dumb-founded as the enemy will be,' he said. 'You see, Marek, they'll fit the accumulators but they won't work properly.'

'Why?'

'Because we intend ruining them.'

'How?'

'With some pills.'

'Pills?'

'Yes, small pills containing platinum. When dropped into the acid cells of the accumulators, they dissolve. When the crew try to charge the new accumulators, the electrodes inside get covered with a black deposit. It gradually ruins them. *Permanently.*'

The look on Fletcher's face was one of sheer delight.

'But how are we going to get the pills into the accumulators?' my brother asked.

'We know the train will stop at Ork station before reaching the base,' Fletcher replied. 'We will have about half an hour to get aboard and complete the job.'

'Won't the train be heavily guarded?'

'Possibly, but we've arranged a little diversion.'

'Diversion?' I asked.

'Yes. We're going to target the fuel and ammunition dumps.'

I thought through their plan and then recognized its merits. 'I get it,' I shouted. 'They'll sail off from the fjord while trying to charge up the new accumulators. By the time they realize there's a big problem they'll be in open water, unable to submerge, sitting ducks for the RAF and Royal Navy. They'll shoot and bomb them to pieces!'

'That's the general idea,' said Fletcher. 'But even if they figure it out before then, it'll disable them for weeks, maybe months. And blowing up the railway line will make it all the harder for them to deliver new supplies. It'll save dozens of merchant ships and maybe thousands of sailors' lives. A rather cunning plan, I believe.'

That night I settled into my bunk and imagined the plan unfolding. I could almost hear the cursing of the U-boat captains as the full horror of their demise grew clear to them, stuck on the surface, their lookouts fretfully scanning the leaden sky for the first wave of bombers, men peering at the horizon for the silhouettes of distant destroyers. My brother tossed and turned in his bunk. 'You OK?'

'Yes, Marek. Can't sleep, that's all. Can't get comfortable.'

'Wondering where Father is?'

'Uh-huh. And Mother.'

'Do you think we'll win the war?'

He turned and looked at me. 'We have to win!'

I wanted to ask whether we'd live to see it but decided not to. I hated tempting fate. The *Sola*'s engine beat a constant rhythm and she rocked gently, comfortingly, from side to side. I thought I could hear the bilge water slopping back and forth beneath me. I wondered just how many Norwegians were like us. How many were willing to sacrifice everything? I hoped it was many, even though our country possessed a tiny population. I thought of Stretter, of old Tauber and of Hartwig. 'Olaf, do you think all Germans are bad?'

'What the hell are you on about now, Marek? They're the enemy, for God's sake!'

'Yes, but take Hartwig, for example. He's just like you and me, an ordinary man who'd rather be at home with his family. He didn't ask to be given a rifle or be sent to a foreign land.'

'But he's here and he's not welcome,' my brother replied.

'Not by choice,' I added.

'What difference does that make?' he snorted. 'He'd shoot us if ordered to do so.'

'Would he? He said he'd never shot a man and hoped he'd never have to.'

My brother sighed wearily. 'Wouldn't you say the same? But if you saw Hartwig pointing his rifle at Father, wouldn't you shoot him first?'

'That's not fair.'

'War's not fair, Marek. Life's not fair. Now go to sleep.' He switched off the light and I stared into the darkness. Trying to figure the world out, I supposed that war always resulted from someone coming up with a particularly bad idea, like wanting to possess more power. And the tragic irony was that such bad ideas had to be carried out by ordinary people, people without a choice. It struck me that true evil probably lurked in only a few men but its effect was felt across borders, continents even. I wondered what would happen if someone assassinated Adolf Hitler. Would the snow-like blanket of oppression melt like a spring thaw? Would darkness and cold be replaced by light and warmth? I thought it would. But, as history had taught us, I knew the next winter would never be far away.

After another day at sea we'd motored and sailed so far north that dawn turned to dusk without the sun appearing at all. In the clear night sky the northern lights provided quite a show, a breathtaking and inexplicable wonder of shimmering arcs of green and yellow. I spent hours staring at them, mesmerized.

Meanwhile Eddie and Fletcher braved the stench of the hold, searching deep into the gloop of slimy cod for specific bags and boxes that contained the tools of their demolition trade. They wanted to make sure everything was present and correct before going ashore. Kurt, having kept to the deep waters in the middle of the channels and fjords, finally spun the helm to starboard and headed towards the rendezvous point. The *Sola* buzzed with activity and even Thor roused himself from his bunk to lend a hand readying the boat. Peter stood on lookout for trouble and for the signal from those waiting ashore. In the darkness I couldn't fathom how Kurt knew where the hell he was heading. To me, the shore simply appeared like a thick grey pencil line against a grey sea and graphite cliffs. Yet he didn't falter, hesitate, or even scratch his beard. He simply guided his boat with small adjustments of the helm while puffing on his pipe, gobbing phlegm and barking orders.

Suddenly torchlight flashed from the distant shore: five quick bursts followed by one short. Peter replied, spelling out the *Sola*'s name. We'd arrived!

Chapter Sixteen

It took over an hour to unload all the supplies from the ship's hold amid much whispering, grunting and treading on toes. We'd met half a dozen fellow Jøssings, armed to the teeth, and they'd helped us lug the explosives, detonators, weapons and ammunition ashore, up a steep, slippery slope and into a waiting trailer hitched to a tractor. Then it was time to say our farewells to Kurt and his men. This involved much hand shaking, back slapping and hugging, but few words. Except, that is, to confirm that one week from now the Shetland Bus would return to pick men up. It would sail to precisely the same place on the fjord, arriving at midnight.

'I'll wait an hour and not a minute more,' said Kurt, twice. Fletcher and Eddie both nodded.

It began to snow and I shrugged off the thick wet flakes that tangled, danced and spun in every direction. Suddenly Kurt and the *Sola*, or whatever she was really called, had gone, vanishing into the night. Only the fading *tonk-tonk-tonk* of her engine told us she was heading back south. The fjord, the shore, the whole world suddenly seemed eerily silent and abandoned. Still possessing my sea legs, I walked woozily, as if the earth wouldn't keep still beneath me.

Our welcoming party appeared keen not to loiter. As we moved off, the flurry turned into a blizzard that stung our eyes. The tractor spluttered into life and slid and bounced along a rocky track. We followed behind on foot. Nobody said a word.

The land struck me as a desolate wasteland. Little grew here; a world of white slopes pocked with fang-like rocks and scree, of bluish ice, of pale indigo mountains, of fjords and whispering rivers. On we trod along the frayed edge of land. Our destination, a remote farmhouse, lay a mile from where we'd landed. Pressed against the mountainside as if cowering from nature, the timber building creaked under a thick smooth layer of snow covering a steeply pitched roof. Icicles dangling from the overhanging eaves glowed white like shark's teeth. Beneath lay dark shadows and drawn curtains. A steady plume of smoke lifted from the chimney, twisting and spiralling to the heavens. It looked a desolate place where desperate men might hide. Undaunted, our escort headed straight for the door and hammered on it.

Once inside, I found my foreboding began to melt. A spacious living room dominated by a roaring fire in a massive stone hearth confronted us, and the burning logs crackled and spat a welcome. Having felt only the cold of winter for so long, I'd almost forgotten the joy of radiant heat against my face. Tearing off my gloves, I settled down close to the hearth and thawed, rubbing life back into my numb fingers as blood returned to my cheeks.

I learned that the farmhouse belonged to one Alfred Straum and his wife, Lotti. They made us feel right at home, presenting a veritable banquet of *fiskeboller* – fish balls in a white sauce – dried elk, salted lamb ribs and boiled potatoes, all washed down with copious weak beer brewed illicitly in an outhouse. With food being so scarce, I guessed our feast had dubious origins.

Of the half-dozen men who had met the boat, only two stayed to eat, the others making off into the night with the bulk of the small arms and ammunition we offloaded. They hid the explosives and detonators in the barn. One of the Resistance fighters, Jan Straum, bore a close resemblance to his father, Alfred, possessing the same hook nose and rather unsettling, deep-set, jet-black eyes that seemed to drill into my head whenever our stares met. Built like a cross between an elk and a rugged Nordland hunter, he struck me as pretty damn intimidating: clearly a man with one mission in life – to kill Germans – and I suspected he'd prove very efficient.

The other man was British – well, Scottish, to be exact, and the distinction seemed important to him. He introduced himself as Angus Fraser and spoke good Norwegian, though every word was flavoured with a rich Highland accent, rendering him barely understandable. He too was thickset and looked a real brute. I quickly realized he knew Eddie well and they spent plenty of time catching up with one another.

I found myself sitting next to Jan. 'Did you arrive by the Shetland Bus?' I asked.

'Yes. Spent the last six months in England.'

'Where?'

'No idea.'

My confusion made him laugh. 'You see, Marek, it's all very secret, top secret. They drove us from place to place without us ever knowing where we were. They trained us in everything from forgery to sabotage, from acting the innocent to unarmed combat. They taught us how to survive amid the enemy while causing him maximum inconvenience.' He laughed again.

I learned that the *Sola* had dropped off Jan and Angus near Bergen before Kurt and his crew came looking for us. They'd made their own way home by train, a journey fraught with danger and near misses, and had arrived just hours before us. The other men I'd seen were all local, all now in Jan's employ.

Jan belched loudly. 'Now they've trained me and sent me home, my job is to lead the Resistance in and around Ork,' he said matter-of-factly.

His mother, Lotti, delivered freshly brewed coffee to the table and squeezed his shoulder lovingly. She said nothing but smiled thinly, a smile borne of pride and fear in equal measure. I decided both she and Alfred had to be as courageous as the rest of us. After all, they risked the firing squad merely by allowing us to set foot in their house.

'When we're done here, will you go back to England?' I asked.

Jan drained his beer in a series of gulps, slammed his

mug down and shook his head. Seizing a chunk of *lefse* and dipping it into his bowl of potato broth, he pointed it towards Fletcher, Angus and Eddie. 'They'll be heading home on the next Shetland Bus. My job is here. This is where I was born and this is where I shall die.' He sniffed and popped the soaked *lefse* into his mouth. Chewing loudly, his mouth still full, he added, 'You look a bit young to be caught up in all this, Marek.'

I described our adventure so far. 'Bloody hell,' he replied in English, having almost choked. 'So, you're an old hand at all this already.'

I nodded proudly. Looking round the table, I thought of our mission. Although Jorgen had been in overall charge, I wondered whether that was about to change now we were in Jan's back yard. Fletcher knew about boats and accumulators and stuff like that, and Eddie explosives. Olaf and I were spare pairs of hands. I wondered about Angus's role and found myself staring at him across the table. Jan nudged me in the ribs. 'They're like chalk and cheese,' he said.

'Like what?'

'Chalk and cheese. When it comes to handling explosives, Eddie's an artist, a surgeon with a delicate touch and an eye for precision. Angus, on the other hand, prefers a more robust approach. He's our "hell raiser".'

'Hell raiser?'

'Yes. They complement each other nicely.' He grabbed another mug of beer and sprang to his feet. 'Gentlemen, your attention. I would like to welcome you all to our humble home and hope you've enjoyed the gracious hospitality of Mother and Father. You have no idea what it took to get hold of those *pinnekjøtt*.'

'Finest damn lamb ribs I've tasted,' belched Jorgen, holding up a chewed bone.

'Anyway, we all know what we're here for. Let us pray for success and hope we may return our fine British friends back home safely. Norway owes them, and all like them, much gratitude. *Skål!*'

We all rose to our feet. '*Skål!*'

I suppose I had expected us to get on with our mission the very next morning. That wasn't the plan. In fact, four days passed by without any of us leaving the safety of the Straums' farmhouse, except Jan, who disappeared from time to time for clandestine meetings with his men. Much of the wait proved frustrating but wasn't a complete washout. From Eddie and Angus I learned much about explosives and, more importantly, how to set them. From our discussions on board the *Sola* the time pencils were already familiar to me. The Imber switches, however, were completely new.

Our gear had been stored in a concealed section of a large barn a few yards from the farmhouse. There I listened to Eddie and Angus discussing the optimal method for disrupting the railway line.

'How many Imbers have we got?' asked Angus.

'Four,' Eddie replied, having searched through all the bags and boxes.

'What's an Imber switch?' I asked.

'Here, catch.'

Eddie threw me one. The metal object was small, about three inches by two, and contained a telescopic rod that when fully extended protruded about six inches. I examined it closely. 'How does this work?'

'Think of a railway line,' said Eddie. 'The rails sit on sleepers and the sleepers on heavy ballast.' He seized the switch from my grasp. 'The main bit is buried in the ballast directly underneath the rail.' He held it at arm's length and then pulled out the rod part way. 'The rod is raised until it touches the underside of the rail. Like so.'

Angus joined in. 'When the train trundles past, the rail bends under its weight. That depresses the rod and activates the switch.' He grinned. '*Bang!*' he added for good measure.

'But there's a problem,' said Eddie.

'What problem?' I asked.

'We want to be sure that it's a train carrying munitions that sets it off. That way we'll cause quite a firestorm.'

Jan entered the barn. He'd overheard our conversation. 'It's important, Marek. Get the wrong train and we might be killing hundreds of Norwegians. That must not happen. Not under any circumstances.'

To avoid such a catastrophe, I supposed it might be better to lie in wait and set the explosives off manually once the train had been identified. My suggestion got shot down rather quickly.

'Impossible,' said Eddie. 'We're laying the explosives in the middle of a tunnel and a damn long one at that.'

He explained that the switches could be adjusted using a tiny ratchet system to count up to eight trains. So the charges could be laid well ahead of the arrival of the intended iron victim, provided we knew the timetable and could therefore count forward to the right train.

'Have you got the timetable?' It seemed the obvious question.

'The Germans keep altering it,' said Jan. 'Every week or so.'

'Then how will you know when the delivery of the accumulators arrives?'

'At the last minute, Marek. That's why we have to be ready to move at a moment's notice. Hence all the preparation.'

'This isn't going to be easy, is it?' I said.

Patience was not my strong point. I tended to get bored rather too easily. And confined to the farmhouse, I soon grew melancholic and prone to prolonged bouts of moaning. And it wasn't just Olaf who found me bloody irritating.

'You weren't like this in the Johanssens' hut,' he complained. 'It was the others who got gripped by cabin fever.'

'I just hate all this waiting. Feels like we've been running and hiding too long.'

'You're getting on everyone's nerves.'

'They're getting on mine too. Guess we're all even!'

'Don't be stupid.'

'I miss home, Olaf.'

'Me too. And I keep feeling that instead of being caught up in this mess, I ought to be trying to get Father freed. I can't get his face out of my head. I keep thinking that his only hope, all that's keeping him going, is the belief that we're doing everything to secure his release. And the truth? We've done *nothing*. If he knew, he'd despair.'

My brother's face appeared crimped with anguish. And I felt it too. 'But Agnete said she would do what they could. Lars and her, that is.'

'It's not enough, Marek.'

'I know but there's no choice, is there? We have our own problems.'

He gritted and ground his teeth. 'Yes, Marek. But once this mission's over, I'm going to look for him and I shan't stop until I find him.'

'We'll do it together,' I said. 'I promise.'

We sat silently a while.

'Remember what Doctor Haskveld said?' my brother asked.

I racked my brain. He told us we were stupid for killing Wold. I remembered that much.

'He said that if we sent him a message, he'd get it to Mother.'

My eyes lit up. 'You mean . . . ?'

'Why not? If we're clever, we can let him know we're OK without alerting the censors.'

'Really? Can we write to him? Can we do it now?'

We spent the whole evening trying to fashion a letter to Dr Haskveld that would defeat the deviousness of even the most clever censor, for we knew most mail got read by the authorities en route. We went through many drafts. But the very act of penning such a note cheered us up no end.

'Done, I think,' said Olaf finally. 'Secret is to keep it simple.'

'Read it out.' I lay on my back and closed my eyes, trying to picture the look on Dr Haskveld's face as he read between the lines.

Olaf cleared his throat. '*Dear Doctor Haskveld, we trust you are well. We are writing to express our gratitude for your assistance and your sound advice. Had we not taken it, we believe our health would have seriously deteriorated by now. However, thanks to you and many other kind souls, we now find ourselves in a healthier environment and the outlook for us is much improved. Indeed, we have been fortunate enough to settle into gainful employment of a sort we feel you would approve of. We should be grateful if you would convey our regards to mutual friends. Best wishes, M and O Bettergard.*'

'You think he'll remember Mother's maiden name?'

'Of course he will. Known her since she was born.'

'Good. Do you think Jan or Jorgen will mind if we travel into town to post it?'

'I've been wondering the same thing. We'd better ask, I suppose.'

Jan's initial reaction was predictably cool. Jorgen said nothing. I think he was keen to let Jan decide. I had a sweetener up my sleeve. 'Is there any reconnaissance we can do for you in town? We could find out the latest changes to the train timetable. Perhaps we could deliver messages to other members of the Resistance.'

Jan paced the living room, arms half folded, chin resting in a cupped hand. 'All right, you can post your letter. But you don't know your way around town and I don't want you drawing attention to yourselves. I'll come too. I need to see someone at Café Fransk anyway. We'll go tomorrow morning.'

It took more than an hour's skiing to reach Ork, a small town west of Trondheim. Along the way Jan did his best to point out the key landmarks on the fjords and mountain slopes, but in the darkness few things really registered. We kept well away from the roads, and much of the landscape seemed as bleak as the Hardanger, the snow crisp and virgin, with just the occasional tracks of a hare or fox ruining the otherwise perfect blanket. But whereas the Hardanger was largely flat, this part of Norway was anything but. And I quickly began to run out of steam, my brother and Jan pushing on ahead in friendly competition. My cries were ignored as my calves screamed in pain. The skis I'd been lent had poor edges and needed waxing. I wished we'd not had to abandon our own outside Kinsarvik. 'Olaf! Jan!' They were a good hundred yards ahead. 'Damn you!'

I caught them up on the outskirts of town. They'd already removed their skis and were finishing a cigarette by the time my gasping, bent frame slid to a halt.

'You OK?' asked Jan. He took my coughs and spluttering as a yes. 'Great. Get those skis off. We'll walk to Café Fransk via the *postkontor*. There's usually a guard or two on duty there but I know the postmaster. I'll buy your stamp for you.' He slung his skis over his shoulder and headed along the road.

Ork nestled along the shore of the fjord. As far as I could tell, war and occupation had led to an expansion of the ancient Viking settlement to a bustling community of predominantly grey uniforms. Everywhere I looked Germans seemed to outnumber Norwegians and I can't say it cheered me particularly. And, still on the outskirts of town, I couldn't help but notice rows of wooden huts set distinctly separate from the town itself. I wouldn't have noticed them at all in the darkness had they not been well lit and surrounded by what looked like a tall wire fence.

My brother had struck up quite a friendship with Jan and they chatted freely while ignoring me completely. I had to shout to gain Jan's attention. 'What's that over there? Why the huts? And the fencing?'

Jan stopped in his tracks and spun round. 'Shush! Not so loud, Marek. It's a labour camp. There's about two hundred Norwegians held there. Numbers are increasing by the week.'

'Why here?'

'They needed labour to build the base and the railway. We think they've got plans to expand this area even further. Rumours suggest that within the month there may be as many as four hundred, perhaps more.' He pointed towards it. 'The soldiers are barracked right next door. I think that's deliberate and for more than just security. The Allies won't try to bomb the area knowing they have a fifty-fifty chance of killing civilians. Clever bastards, aren't they?'

'Who exactly is in the labour camp?'

He grabbed my arm and shook it. 'Men like you and me, Marek,' he snapped. 'Good Norwegians. Now come on. We've got business to attend to.'

I could not help but stare at the huts. Under the arc lights I could see soldiers patrolling the perimeter and I heard the yaps of hungry dogs. What a miserable god-forsaken place. It reminded me of Uncle Knut's description of the ancient underworld, Niflheim, that sombre world of the dead that was coated in hoarfrost and guarded by the monstrous dog, Garm. I shivered.

'Wait here. I'll post your letter.' Jan disappeared into the *postkontor*, a large brick building midway along what appeared to be Ork's main street.

'Olaf?'

'What, Marek?'

'I've been thinking. That camp . . .'

'What about it?'

'Don't suppose that's where they sent Father, is it?'

He shrugged. Jan reappeared. 'All done. Now, to Café Fransk.'

'Jan, are there any other camps near here?'

He thought a moment and then shook his head. 'There's one in Trondheim. Pretty big by all accounts. Can't think of any others. Except those nearer Narvik. Why?'

I explained the possibility that Father might have been sent here. Jan looked shocked. 'Are you sure?'

'Agnete said they'd moved men from the camp near Oslo to a camp further north. It must be a possibility even if it's a remote one.'

'We have contacts,' he replied. 'I'll get someone to look into it. Seems our trip into town may prove particularly worthwhile after all. But' – he hesitated – 'don't get your hopes up. And anyway, even if he were here, I wouldn't consider that good news. Not good at all. Conditions are pretty awful by all accounts. I think few will ever leave the camp in anything other than a wooden box!'

God, what a terrible thought. I hoped Jan was prone to exaggeration. Deep down, I was worried that he spoke the truth. Wandering through town, I realized why Fritz had chosen the place for his new submarine base. The Orkfjord was narrow, and judging by the steepness and breathtaking height of the towering mountains looming over us on both sides, the place appeared well protected by nature. A bombing raid would be tricky if not impossible. And the sheerness of the cliffs indicated that although the fjord was barely two hundred yards wide, it was probably deep right up to the shoreline, perfect for hiding U-boats. 'Where's the base?' I whispered to Jan.

'About two miles on the other side of town. It's a no-go area. Venture too close and they'll shoot you. They won't shout a warning either.'

'And the railway line?'

'They've laid tracks from the station and built a new tunnel. In fact, apart from one narrow road it's the only other way to get to the base by land. The mountains are too steep.'

We walked about a hundred yards down the street and had lost sight of the fjord's shoreline by the time we reached Café Fransk. Inside, a warm smoky fug greeted us, along with a dozen round tables, several occupied by Germans. 'Sit down over there by the window. I'll fetch some beers and coffee,' said Jan.

I had never felt so on show, so exposed. Suspicious German eyes bore down on us from all directions and, had I been a few years younger, I think I might have wet myself. Trying to ignore them, I turned and gazed through the window. Of course, I couldn't really see much, although a streetlamp cast light onto the faces of men and women walking past. It was a brief glimpse of the people of Ork, the misted glass making them all appear ghost-like. Jan took his time at the bar, eventually returning clutching a tray. He and Olaf had beer, while I had to settle for a rather bitter coffee I suspected contained more ground chicory root than coffee bean. A splash of *aquavit* would have eased it down.

'Everything OK?' asked Olaf.

Jan smacked his lips and nodded. 'Seems things are beginning to come together,' he replied. He clapped and rubbed his hands. 'I'll tell you more later.'

'And you asked about Father?' I said.

'Yes, Marek. Someone will try to find out if he's here.'

At last I felt we were actually trying to do something. What if he were here? My heart whirled. I imagined his surprise, the renewed hope breaking out on his face. I pictured the moment of his freedom and willed it to happen.

We sat for about ten minutes, mostly in silence. The Germans seemed a lively crowd, with bursts of laughter erupting from a different table every few seconds. I hated the place. I yearned to burn it down, to blow it up, with all of them locked inside. How dared they drink and be merry in our country while they imprisoned our people in a camp within spitting distance of where they sat? So strong was my anger it gave me bellyache. I rubbed at the anguished cramp but it did little good. Jan and my brother whispered as they sipped the froth off their beers. I resumed peering out of the window.

It came as quite a shock. In fact, I dropped my cup and blinked. Surely not?

Unfortunately the clatter of china on the table startled everyone. I became the centre of attention.

'Christ, Marek, what the hell's the matter?' blurted my brother angrily. He reached out and settled the gyrating cup back onto its saucer and then reached into his pocket for a handkerchief to mop up the spill. He looked around the café fearfully. 'Sorry, my brother's always dropping things. He's fine. Ignore us.'

I kept on blinking. It had been so fast, so brief. But it certainly looked like him. I turned to my brother and whispered, 'I think I just saw Harald!'

'Don't be daft, Marek. That's impossible.'

I needed to know for sure. 'I'll be back in a minute.' I screeched back my chair and headed out onto the street. The chill of the ice wind smacked me repeatedly in the face and I had to blink moistness from my eyes. But amid the throng on the pavement I saw the back of a man who looked remarkably like Harald. He paused, turned and made across the street. Lamplight caught his face. It *was* Harald! Those small, greedy eyes were unmistakable. Olaf and Jan arrived at my shoulder. 'You're nuts, Marek. And drawing attention to us like that! Could've got us into big trouble.'

'Shut up! It's him. Look, see for yourself.'

My brother squinted and then gawped. 'But how?'

'Let's catch him up,' I said and, without waiting for a reply, headed off. 'Harald!'

I wish I could say he looked pleased to see me. Alas, whether it was the shock or something else, he appeared stunned. And when Olaf arrived on my heels the look turned to one of utter bewilderment. 'Marek? Olaf? What on earth—?' He broke off mid sentence and looked around, as if fearing more surprises.

'What are you doing here?' I asked.

'And where's Leif?' barked my brother expectantly.

'Leif's dead!' Harald whispered in an alarmed tone.

Jorgen had spoken to Jan about Harald, Leif and Ingrid in depth so he quickly understood the enormity of our surprise. 'Quick,' he said. 'We shouldn't loiter here. It's only a matter of time before the Germans will show an unhealthy interest in us. We must retrieve our skis and get out of here.'

Back at the farmhouse Jorgen stood by the roaring hearth and, with hands in pockets, listened intently and grimly to Harald's story. We all did.

'The Wehrmacht questioned us briefly in Kinsarvik,' Harald began. 'Then came the orders for us to be moved to Gestapo headquarters in Odda. We knew that was bad news. We left Kinsarvik at about ten o'clock.'

'Did you see Ingrid?' asked Jorgen.

'No. Why?'

'The Gestapo arrested her at the guesthouse.'

He wilted. 'Oh God. What a disaster!'

'So what happened to you?'

'We were about five miles from Kinsarvik when I realized that just one motorcycle and sidecar was providing an escort behind us. In the car there was only the driver and one other soldier in the front passenger seat. I only had to look across at Leif for my thoughts to be understood. Although my hands were bound, I managed to loosen the bindings, reach forward and grab the driver around the throat. Leif did the same to the other guard. We forced the car off the road and made our escape into the woods. They fired into the darkness at us but we zigzagged between the trees and I really believed we had dodged their bullets. But then they got lucky. I thought Leif had just stumbled and fallen but when I tried to help him to his feet I felt the warm blood oozing from the wound in his back. I put his arm over my shoulder and we carried on. Eventually, though, he just went limp on me.'

I could have heard a pin drop. No one spoke for what seemed like an age. Then Harald downed his beer in one, slammed his glass down and added, 'So, no word about Ingrid then?'

Jorgen shook his head. I saw Eddie staring at Harald in a most peculiar way, his eyes hawk-like, somewhat disbelieving. I thought back to the Johanssens' hut, when Harald had accused Eddie of cheating at poker, and the ensuing brawl. I supposed no love was lost between them. Perhaps Eddie wished it had been Leif who'd survived the ordeal. Struck by Eddie's questioning gaze, I started thinking too. How had Harald reached Ork? Jan had the same question and put it to him.

'Got help from our fellow Jøssings,' he replied. 'Used the network to get forged papers and travel passes. Got here mostly by train and ferry. Arrived yesterday. I was planning on making contact with the owner of Café Fransk this evening. I thought about trying last night but the café was crawling with Germans.'

We settled down to eat, Lotti and Alfred once again excelling in their hospitality. But something had changed. Everyone seemed subdued, the atmosphere tense. It reminded me of the oppressive prelude to a summer's thunderstorm. Jorgen appeared especially quiet and reflective. Several times I noticed him scrutinizing Harald across the table and fiddling with the stem of his wine glass. I wished I could read people's minds.

Jan helped himself to a double serving of meatballs and then paused to make an announcement. 'We're on for tomorrow night, gentlemen. The train carrying the accumulators arrives at Ork station at eight o'clock. So let us enjoy this last dinner together and toast to our success.'

Raising our glasses, we chinked them together across the table and then drank them dry. I locked eyes with Olaf. He thumped down his glass and wiped the back of his hand across his mouth. 'Well, Marek,' he said brashly. 'We've come far and made many new friends along the way. And tomorrow we get to work, doing our bit.' He looked round the table at all the faces full of expectation. 'We won't let you down. I promise.'

'We both promise,' I said.

Chapter Seventeen

Unable to sleep, I got out of bed and peered through the bedroom window. I had hoped to be distracted from my troubled thoughts by a display of the northern lights, but cloud obscured my view of the heavens. Outside, the darkness was complete and unbroken.

'Get some sleep, Marek.'

'Can't,' I replied to my brother's semi-conscious mumbling.

'You frightened?'

'It's not that.'

'Then what?'

In my head I had played out the mission a dozen times. There was a lot that could go wrong, I'd realized. But that wasn't what troubled me most. It was the thought that we might succeed! I tried explaining this to Olaf.

'What *are* you on about, Marek?'

'If we succeed, there will be reprisals, won't there?'

'Probably.'

'Fritz might take it out on the men in the labour camp. And what if Father *is* there? I can't bear to think about it.'

'Then don't.'

'Can't help it, Olaf.'

He cursed and threw back his quilt cover. Rubbing his eyes, he yawned and twisted himself upright. 'Look, if we disable those U-boats, thousands of sailors' lives will be saved. That's the big picture, Marek. Anyway, we don't know if Father's here. We don't even know for sure that Fritz will take revenge on those in the camp. If they think the sabotage was undertaken by British commandos, then there won't be any reprisals. So stop worrying.' He lay back down and pulled his quilt up around his ears.

My brother's logic did little to quell my fears. In my head I'd imagined another mission, one in which Jan and his men, the weapons and explosives delivered by the *Sola* were put to another use – to deliver freedom to the hundreds of men held at the camp.

'That's wishful thinking,' said Olaf after I'd vividly described how Jan's small group of Resistance fighters had become an army once the camp had been liberated. Of course, I believed that several hundred of us could defeat the Germans and drive them from our shores. According to Olaf, I was nuts.

A fretful-looking Lotti Straum roused us early the next morning. We were summoned downstairs, and blearily I pulled on my trousers and tucked in my shirt. In the living room Jan took centre stage and went over the plan one final time. We were all to ski into Ork, Fletcher and Jorgen heading for a safe house close to the station, where they'd await the arrival of the train carrying the accumulators. Angus, together with Jan and his men, would hole up in a barn just outside town. Their job was to create the diversion, which took the form of setting light to fuel and ammunition dumps close to the barracks; a demonstration of Angus's hell raising! I hoped that the result would not harm those in the nearby labour camp. Eddie's job – disruption of the railway line and tunnel – was scheduled for the following evening, and I thought he was especially courageous for not complaining about the delay. I would have. Surely, I thought, Fritz would be on full alert after the fuel dump went up. It could only make his job doubly difficult. He said nothing so I raised the point on his behalf.

'Our primary target is to get the pills into the accumulators,' Jan explained. 'The railway tunnel is secondary. But we need the diversion tonight to draw the troops away from the station. Of course, if tomorrow Eddie judges his mission impossible, then we'll abandon it. Don't worry, Marek, we've thought it through.'

Harald seemed happy to link up with Jan and his men for the diversion. I glanced at Olaf impatiently as Jan had not yet mentioned our names. My brother said nothing. 'What about us?' I cried.

'Ah, our secret weapons,' said Jan. 'We've got a special job for you.'

'Really! What?'

'We want you to go to Café Fransk and drink coffee.'

I couldn't help scowling indignantly. 'You want us to do *what*?'

'Drink coffee. Olaf, have a beer if you like.' He smiled so broadly his teeth showed.

'Is this a joke?'

'No, far from it. The Wehrmacht officers use the café. When all hell breaks loose, we need to know how they react. We want you to listen out carefully. Then go to the safe house and await our return.'

'Is that it?' I said. In truth, I felt rather disappointed. I had hoped for a more heroic, central role in proceedings, maybe setting off a couple of bombs or throwing a few grenades. Sipping bitter coffee in the company of the enemy didn't fire my enthusiasm.

Jorgen gripped my arm. 'Just do as you're told, Marek. Jan gives the orders here.'

Angus had a glint in his eye as he cut several lengths of Bickford fuse, each about two foot long. He saw me watching him and paused. 'Sometimes the old methods are the best. Do you want to give me a hand?'

I needed no further offer or encouragement.

'Here, cut some more fuse.'

I picked up the coil of string-like twisted hemp. Gunpowder had been wound into its core and the whole thing waterproofed. 'How fast does this burn?' I asked.

'About half an inch a second. So, once lit, best not to hang around.'

I did the maths. A two-foot fuse would burn for forty-eight seconds. Not long to make your escape. 'What are you going to use these for?'

'Our diversion. I've also filched one of Eddie's time pencils.'

'And the explosives?'

'Mainly plastic but I've also prepared some incendiaries. Do you want to see?'

Silly question but I nodded anyway. He showed me a stack of small containers.

'They're pocket incendiaries, Marek. Filled with petroleum gel. They burn for about four minutes. Not much use on their own but if placed in a fuel or ammunition dump, the results can be quite pleasing.' He grinned.

'What exactly do you have in mind?'

He showed me a hand-drawn map of Ork. 'Here,' he said, his chubby index finger tapping where rows of little rectangles had been drawn.

'But that's the labour camp!'

He frowned and then peered intensely at the map. 'You're right, Marek.' He laughed. 'I meant the barracks next door.' He slid his finger an inch to the right. Relief swept through me. 'The fuel depot's at the back. And the ammunition dump is further along the railway. Personally I think they're pretty stupid to place them so close together but I guess the mountainside restricts where they can build. I'm grateful to them.'

He resumed fixing the fuse wires into the explosives. With his back to me, I felt the sudden urge to do something I'd never done before – a little thieving. There they were, a huge pile of pocket incendiaries. Surely they'd not miss a couple. After all, they might come in handy. I pilfered two, slipping one into each of my anorak pockets. Guilt-ridden, I fully expected to be caught and punished but either no one noticed or no one cared. I crept out of the barn and made my way back to the house.

Olaf stood on the porch staring into the bleak darkness of mid morning. 'Don't know how anybody can live so far north,' he grumbled to me as I arrived. 'Imagine it. Dark for months on end. It would drive me mad.' He flicked his cigarette butt into the snow and peered at me. 'What's the matter, Marek?'

'Nothing.'

'Come on. I know that look. You're up to something?'

'*No,*' I replied. Trust my brother to detect my guilt. I tried fobbing him off. 'It's just that, well, there's a lot that could go wrong tonight.'

'Like what?'

'I don't know.'

'Sounds like nerves to me.'

I scrunched my face up at him and changed the subject. 'Can I have Father's revolver back?'

'No.'

'Why not?'

'Best you're not armed, Marek. Just in case they stop and search you.'

It seemed a poor excuse but I didn't pursue the matter. The incendiaries suddenly felt twice as heavy in my pockets and the slight bulges seemed blatant. I decided I needed to hide them in the inner lining of my anorak and so headed inside to ask Mrs Straum for a needle and thread.

We trekked into Ork skiing in single file, each pre-occupied by his own thoughts, a mix of trepidation, excitement and images of loved ones in whose names and freedom lay the justification for our planned deeds. About two miles from town, amid the feeble cover of a copse of thin, twisted birches, we paused, wished each other good hunting and then split into our respective teams. Jan headed slightly north with Angus and Harald to meet up with the other local Resistance fighters. Fletcher and Jorgen set off ahead of Olaf and me. We held back with Eddie for about five minutes and then followed. We had agreed to accompany Eddie to the safe house and then make the short trip to Café Fransk at around seven o'clock. We had all synchronized our watches. It was four thirty-two precisely.

It is hard to describe my feelings as we trudged into town, our skis draped across our shoulders. Looking and acting entirely normal was essential, yet I felt as if we stuck out, glowing red with danger, in the eyes of every grey uniform. And each time we squeezed past boots and rifles cluttering the pavement I spoke aloud to my brother of trivial nonsense, of gripes and obstinacy, so that Fritz would merely see us as a family returning home, a family with an annoying brat. I figured no soldier would want to be bothered with stopping someone as irritating as me. It seemed to work a treat.

Jorgen and Fletcher were already at the safe house when we arrived. A frail blanket-clad elderly woman, her skin grey with chronic sickness and scabby scalp visible through thin white hair, waved us across the threshold with a gnarled, arthritic hand and pointed up a steep staircase towards the attic with her stick. She was Jan's grandmother, Hilda Straum, and was doing her bit despite her infirmity. In the cramped attic Jorgen crouched beside a tiny dust- and cobweb-laden window and eyed the streets below.

Being within spitting distance of the station, the safe house offered an outstanding vantage point for watching the coming and goings of trains. Although we could not see the tracks, the billowing smoke from the locomotives proved clearly visible as ghost-like plumes in the crisp, frozen air. And their steamy whistles of departure reached our ears.

'Whereabouts on the train will the accumulators be?' Olaf asked.

'In the last carriage,' Fletcher replied. 'Intelligence reports indicate that the rest of the shipment is just a mix of usual supplies for the U-boats: food, clothing, post from home, that sort of thing. We're hoping it won't be heavily guarded.'

'And if it is?' I asked.

'We'll deal with it,' Jorgen replied grimly.

'What, just the two of you?'

'Marek's got a point,' said Eddie. 'I should go with you just in case.'

'No,' Jorgen snapped. 'Jan is in charge of the mission here. He's given his orders. His decision's final.'

I saw Fletcher and Eddie communicate by eye and expression alone and could tell they vehemently disagreed. Fletcher attempted to persuade Jorgen. Their whispered debate grew heated, as neither appeared willing to back down. The tension between them finally cracked when we detected creaking footsteps on the stairs. Embraced by silence, we all stared at the attic door. Eddie quietly drew a knife and slipped into the shadows of the eaves. Jorgen and Olaf reached for their revolvers. I held my breath. The door handle turned.

Chapter Eighteen

Hilda Straum stood in the doorway clutching a tray of coffee. She did not bat an eyelid at the revolvers pointing at her and merely snorted disapprovingly when Eddie and his gleaming blade appeared from behind the door. Without a word she settled the tray down, rubbed her wet nose vigorously, then drew tight the blanket around her neck and shuffled back down the stairs.

From his rucksack Fletcher extracted a tin. He popped it open and tipped out its contents onto a handkerchief. The small white pills looked unremarkable. I guessed there were about forty. He started dividing them into two piles, delivering one to Jorgen in a cupped hand and wrapping up the other inside his handkerchief, taking care to tie its corners together tightly. Jorgen did likewise before tucking the small package into his trouser pocket.

'Will those little pills really destroy the accumulators?' I asked. 'They look so harmless.'

'Yes, Marek. They dissolve quickly. And each can contaminate up to fifty litres of acid. More than enough.'

I found it hard to comprehend. A small pill was all it took to force those huge grey metal whales to the surface, fully exposed to the sight of bomber command

and the massive guns of the Royal Navy. And all we had to do was drop them into their rechargeable batteries. So simple! So difficult. I still couldn't see how Fletcher and Jorgen were going to get aboard the train undetected. There would be soldiers everywhere.

By six-thirty I'd also begun to worry about what awaited Olaf and me at Café Fransk. And I felt guilty about worrying, as it seemed much less dangerous than any of the others' tasks.

'Time to get ready,' declared Fletcher. From his rucksack he took out a uniform. A *German* uniform. Jorgen did likewise.

'What the devil . . . ?' My brother's square jaw unhinged and wobbled. 'Where did you get those from?'

'Some raid or other,' Jorgen replied. 'How do I look?' He smartened his collar, clacked his heels and saluted. '*Heil Hitler!*' He practised strutting back and forth with exaggerated goose steps, turning sharply on his heels.

'Not bad,' said Olaf. 'Just one problem. Those boots are a giveaway. Norwegian snow boots aren't exactly standard issue to a Wehrmacht officer.'

'Correct,' Jorgen replied, raising a finger. 'Our leather boots are downstairs.' He grinned and saluted again.

I must say he looked pretty smart. I thought back to the vision of Jorgen I'd awoken to in the Johanssens' hut, that frightening bearded face, and now realized why he'd shaved the moment he got to the Straums' farmhouse. Fletcher appeared most convincing. The stiffness that set him apart from most Norwegians now served him in good stead. Like most German officers, he stood tall and confident and possessed that all-important air of authority, his nostrils flared as if a bad smell hung around him. They looked magnificent. No mere private or lieutenant would dare challenge them climbing on board the train. A hopeless plan suddenly seemed simple.

Eddie pulled on a heavy raincoat and practised hiding a machine gun beneath the fabric. 'I'll loiter on the platform. I'll buy a paper or something. If something goes wrong, I'll cross the tracks and come to your aid.'

I knew he was a fearless soldier but it seemed like a ridiculous idea. 'You don't look Norwegian, Eddie,' I pointed out. 'Dressed like that you'll stick out like a snowman in summer. If they stop and question you, you'll be done for. There must be somewhere else you can hide.'

'Marek's right, Eddie,' said Jorgen. 'It really is best that you wait here. And that's an order!'

Eddie shrugged and settled back down. He didn't seem particularly bothered now one way or the other. I supposed that was normal for a soldier used to taking orders. He knew well enough he'd see his fair share of the action eventually.

Olaf peered at his watch. 'Time to head for Café Fransk, Marek. You ready?'

'Uh-huh.' I pulled on my anorak and felt the weight of the two incendiaries I'd sewn into the inside lining, one on each side, just beneath my armpits. I wondered if I'd really done the right thing pilfering them.

We all wished each other a pleasant evening and shook hands. Superstition forbade us from wishing each other good luck. Then Olaf and I descended the stairs and headed for the front door. Hilda lay in wait for us, popping out from an alcove and scaring us witless. She shook her cane at us and spat, 'Give them hell!' Nice gesture, I thought.

The safe house lay just five minutes' walk from the café. Approaching Ork's main street, I heard a curious noise. It sounded like hundreds of boots treading on snow and ice. My immediate thought was that soldiers were heading back to the barracks but I quickly dismissed the theory, as the stomping lacked the rhythm of a disciplined march. We paused on the corner and looked back towards the station. I drew a deep breath and grabbed my brother's arm.

'Oh my God,' Olaf whispered, his breath freezing in front of his lips.

I estimated a hundred of them, maybe more. Men shuffling along in rows of four, all clad in heavily soiled winter coats, their weary and sickly pale faces lit by the glow of the streetlights and reflections from the snow. They looked ghoulish. Most stooped forward, staring forlornly at the ground in front of them. Flanked on either side by soldiers, they made painfully slow progress along the street. The spectacle reminded me of a funeral procession. Curiously, most other people ignored them.

'What's going on?'

'Don't know,' my brother replied. 'Probably men

returning to the camp after a day's work at the base. Jesus, they look defeated, don't they? As though their very souls have been stolen.'

I nodded as a fury brewed inside me. I wanted to run and bundle the soldiers to the ground, to thump and pummel them into submission. I wanted to shout to the captives to run for their lives, to make a bid for freedom. But I doubted they'd run far before collapsing with exhaustion. I saw an elderly man stumble. A soldier bellowed at him to get to his feet. The frail man's comrades paused and hauled him upright. The soldier encouraged them forward with his rifle butt.

I found myself rooted to the spot, all thoughts of Café Fransk gone from my head. Instead I stared at each face in turn, searching for a glimpse of Father. I so desperately wanted to see him again, however briefly, that half of me did not stop to think of the horror he'd be suffering should he be one of them. The other half of me prayed that I'd be disappointed. After all, such was their obvious misery, no decent man could wish his family to be counted among them. 'Can you see him?'

'No, Marek. Look, we're late already. We'd better get to the café.'

'I want to see them all pass. I want to be sure Father's not with them.'

Olaf took my arm and dragged me along the pavement. 'We've got a job to do.'

★   ★   ★

Inside Café Fransk light, cheery music filled the air along with smoke and laughter. Most tables were occupied, about one-third by Germans. We headed for the bar, and my eyes met those of a pretty girl pouring a glass of brandy. Her lips formed the briefest of smiles and when she'd finished pouring, she turned to place the bottle back on a shelf. She did so while whispering to a man beside her and he turned to look at us. He had a kind face with warm eyes and a bushy moustache about the size of a mouse.

'Sit at the table underneath the stairs,' he said, pointing. 'I'll bring you some coffee. Everything OK?'

Olaf nodded.

'Good. As you can see, we're pretty busy.' He reached beneath the bar and produced a couple of large books. He leaned forward and whispered, 'In case anyone asks, you're my nephews. Make it look as if you're studying these textbooks. Call me Uncle Heimar.' He smiled.

Neither textbook captured my interest but I thumbed through a few pages anyway. I had never been particularly interested in Egyptology. In truth, I kept getting distracted every time the waitress breezed past our table clutching a tray. Her dark curls bounced and her figure struck me as perfect.

'Stop dribbling, Marek,' said my brother. He thumped me playfully on the shoulder.

'I'm not!'

'Yes you were. I saw you.'

The waitress danced past us and flashed a smile and a sparkling eye towards my brother. *Damn him!* I turned my attention back to the textbook and pretended to read. Olaf took up where I had left off. His leering sickened me.

'What would Agnete say?' I asked pointedly. He shrugged guiltily.

At the nearest table to us, four Germans gambled at cards. It looked as if they were playing poker and I thought of Eddie. He'd crush them with one eye closed, I reckoned. As I sipped my horrid, bitter coffee, I instinctively kept peering at my watch between bouts of nervous thrumming of my fingers on the table. Jan had promised to begin the hell-raising diversion at precisely seven forty-five so that by the time the train carrying the accumulators arrived at about eight, the mayhem would be in full swing.

At seven thirty-five 'Uncle Heimar' reappeared from a back room and came over to our table. Resting his hands on the backs of our chairs, he leaned forward and whispered to us. From his tone, I instantly knew something was wrong. 'Close those books and follow me out the back,' he said gravely. 'There's someone here you should talk to.'

'But it's almost time,' I said. 'We're supposed to—'

He interrupted me. 'Forget that. It's important.' He led the way through a door, down a narrow passage and into a small, dimly lit back room. It was furnished simply, with two armchairs surrounding a small fireplace. In one of the chairs sat a woman with her back to the door. As we entered, she twisted round.

'Ingrid!' I blurted. 'Jesus! We thought you were dead.'

'Shush, Marek,' said Uncle Heimar. 'Keep your voice down.'

She got up and I ran to hug her. 'Thank God, you're alive. Jorgen will jump for joy.'

She pushed me away. 'Get a firm hold of yourself, Marek. We have precious little time.'

'What's the matter?' my brother asked.

'The Germans know of our plan.'

I gasped. 'What?'

'How?' asked Olaf.

'Never mind that now,' she replied. 'We have to warn everyone.'

My mind spun wildly out of control. What could we do? It was almost time. I bit my lip and looked to Olaf for answers. He rubbed his neck anxiously. 'It's too late,' I wailed.

My brother paced the room in search of inspiration. 'Do they know about the safe house?'

'I don't know,' she replied. 'We should assume they do.'

'Jesus!' He clenched his fist. 'We've got less than five minutes.'

Uncle Heimar slumped down into a chair and nervously lit a cigarette, his hands trembling. 'I wish you'd arrived earlier, Ingrid. We might've been able to avoid all this mess.'

'It's not been easy getting here,' she snapped.

'Marek,' said my brother. 'Get back and warn Eddie. See if, between you, you can do anything to help Jorgen and Fletcher.'

'I'll come with you,' said Ingrid.

'OK,' I replied. 'What about you, Olaf?'

'I'll see if I can get a warning to Jan, but I'm sure we're too late.' He took out his revolver and checked that all the chambers were full.

'Don't do anything stupid,' I said.

'As if . . .'

Ingrid and I hurried along the street as best we could without drawing attention to ourselves. Our running walk soon rendered me breathless. 'Jorgen showed me his cyanide pill,' I said between puffs. 'We thought you'd taken yours.'

'Came close, Marek. But those bastards didn't have anything on me. So I stuck it out and let them shout questions at me until they gave themselves headaches.'

'Did they torture you?'

'Nothing I couldn't handle. I don't think they ever realized who I am. My false documents checked out, you see. In the end they let me go. But for a day or two they had me followed so I kept a low profile. When I was ready, I gave them the slip.'

'Bloody hell! But how do you know we've been compromised?'

'When I heard that the Gestapo had shot Leif but not

Harald, I became suspicious, especially when they released Harald without charge.'

'What? That's not quite the story Harald told us.'

She stopped and turned to face me. 'So he *is* here then! Figured as much. The intelligence reports were right. I'm sure he spun a convincing yarn, Marek. He must have cut a deal with them. His life and liberty in return for information.'

'The bastard.'

'Don't be too quick to judge, Marek. Faced with a firing squad and the promise that your whole family will be arrested and tortured, most human beings would understandably seize any offer, however treacherous.'

'I wouldn't.'

She looked at me disbelievingly.

'There's the safe house.' I pointed. 'Eddie should still be in the attic.'

We arrived at the door and I hammered on it. It seemed an age before we heard the sliding of bolts and rattling of chains. The door creaked open a fraction and Jan's grandmother's small, wizened face peered out from within. I leaned heavily on the door, pushed it open and pressed past the old women without a word. I raced up the stairs. 'Eddie?' I whispered loudly. 'Eddie?'

He met me halfway, clutching a machine gun. The look of horror on his face told me he'd guessed our mission had been compromised. Between gasps, I blurted the gist of the unfolding nightmare and watched his shoulders wither. Then he caught sight of Ingrid and his scowl turned to delight. He brushed past me and seized her in a tight but brief embrace, planting a kiss on her cheek. 'I'll grab my things,' he said, hurrying back up to the attic.

Clutching his rucksack containing the explosives and Imber switches, he reappeared at the top of the stairs.

'Best leave those behind,' said Ingrid, eyeing his stash. 'It'll draw too much attention.'

Reluctantly he set his rucksack down but refused to let go of his machine gun, which he slid beneath his coat. We left the safe house via the back door and crept along a narrow alleyway in single file. Our boots crunched on the snow, and with every step I felt sure the noise would give us away. Curiously I found breathing difficult, my chest oddly tight, my throat dry and sore, my head throbbing to the point where I could barely think straight. We reached the end of the alleyway and crouched down. 'What now?' I asked.

My watch glowed seven-fifty and there was no sign of the diversion. Had Fritz intercepted Jan and his men? I hardly dared dwell on the idea. Several army trucks were parked outside the station's entrance. Soldiers milled about on every street corner. Others had gathered in front of the main thoroughfare leading onto the platforms. 'We'll never get past them,' I fretted.

'Come on,' said Eddie. 'We'll try to get through further up the road, towards the goods yard.'

Wire-mesh fencing about eight feet tall and topped off with spirals of rusting barbed wire separated us from the railway tracks. But the mesh had been poorly maintained, the steel posts were loose in their footings, and Eddie's sheer brawn proved sufficient to pull and bend the wire back enough to create a gap to crawl through. Arc lights bathed the area with cones of a mysterious pale white light. We rolled under and lay flat in the snow.

'What now?' asked Ingrid. She pulled a revolver from her pocket and held it with intent.

'Let's hope Jorgen and Fletcher made it as far as the fork in the line and to where the train should stop. It's on the other side of the yard.' Eddie lifted a finger in the general direction and I saw the full extent of the difficulty facing us. Several lines had to be crossed in open, lit ground. Then there was the small matter of negotiating our way past the sheds. They were bound to be guarded, probably with dogs – dogs which would sniff out our presence long before we were spotted. I swallowed hard and felt my heart drumming violently. Eddie cursed.

'What's the matter?' I dared to ask.

'Where's that damn diversion?'

Our worst fears had been delivered. Ingrid was right about Harald's treachery, I realized. Jan and his men had failed. There would be none of Angus's hell raising that night – or any other night, come to that. It felt a crushing blow.

Eddie stiffened and rose to his knees. 'Guess it's now or never,' he declared. 'Wait until I get across and signal for you to follow.' With that, he was gone. Like a fox, he sped across the lines, keeping low and zigzagging until he reached a stack of oil drums. He dived behind them. Moments later he popped up and waved the all clear.

I froze. I couldn't believe it. I couldn't move. Struck with utter trepidation, I didn't want to risk taking even one step. 'Coward!' rang inside my head, the word repeating itself, thrashing me on the inside. I wanted to roll up into a ball, a tiny ball, an invisible ball. I wanted the ground to swallow me up. I wanted to be whisked away to safety. I didn't want to die!

'I'll go next,' said Ingrid softly. She rested a hand on my shoulder. Her touch snapped me from my giddy maelstrom.

'No. I'll go,' I said. The words, though from my lips, felt like someone else's. Being afraid was natural, I kept telling myself; to be expected, to be *overcome*. I drew a deep breath and saw Eddie still waving frantically. Blindly I ran, a crouching run that kept me stooped low and rat-like. I scurried and scrambled, slipped and slithered, and reached the oil drums breathless. I flung myself into the shadows. Lying on my back, I forced huge gulps of air into my lungs and thanked the gods for watching my back.

Eddie waved to Ingrid. 'Come on,' he hissed. 'Quickly.'

Voices! Shouts! German voices! Dogs! Jesus, a patrol had emerged from the goods yard. Eddie dropped his wave and remained perfectly still. 'Stay back, Ingrid. Not now. For God's sake, not now,' he muttered quietly under his breath.

We were helpless. All we could do was watch Ingrid readying herself for a fateful dash. I willed her to see the patrol. Eddie tightened his grip on his machine gun and released the safety catch.

'Got a revolver?' I whispered.

Without a word or look, he dipped into his anorak pocket, his hand emerging with a gun that found its way into my clutch. I gripped it tightly and pointed it at the soldiers strutting not thirty yards from us. I watched them down the barrel and decided I'd shoot the taller of the two men first. Glancing back to where we'd penetrated the fence, I saw Ingrid had gone.

'Where is she?'

'She saw them just in time. Just made it back through the fence.'

'Shall we wait for her?'

'No. Once the patrol's out of sight, we have to move on. There's not much time.'

The two minutes we sat in silence felt like a lifetime. And my thoughts turned to Harald and his treachery. How many were going to suffer due to his actions? How many good Norwegians were going to die? I hated Harald and promised to myself that, should I ever see him again, I would deliver revenge on behalf of my fellow Jøssings. I would show no mercy. None whatsoever!

Quietly we slipped round the outside of the large

goods shed, hugging the corrugated walls and black shadows, our guns poised. As we edged towards a corner, I became aware of a prolonged hissing amid German voices.

Eddie knelt down behind another stack of oil drums and waved me to his shoulder. 'There she is,' he said. 'She's arrived early.'

I took a quick peek and saw the train. Its three wagons and steaming locomotive stood stationary like a sleeping monster. The smell of smoke, oil and grease filled the misty air. I peeked at the dragon again. Beside each of the wagons guards stood to attention, their rifles resting neatly on their shoulders. They stared straight ahead like lifeless statues and I wondered if it might be possible to slip between them undetected. It was a fool-hardy thought.

'Do you think Jorgen and Fletcher are inside the wagon?' I asked.

'Dunno.'

'Will they be able to escape?'

'Shush, Marek.'

'Sorry. It's just that—'

'For God's sake, shut up for once, Marek.'

'Right. Sorry.' Eddie had sounded anxious and I guessed he was thinking what I was thinking – the train was early and it was unlikely that Jorgen and Fletcher had managed to get aboard yet. All we could do was wait.

My German is far from fluent but I possess a good ear

and keen memory for voices. As I crouched, rubbing my aching shins, a familiar tone drifted out from inside the shed. I tried placing it and translated as best I could. It appeared that soldiers were waiting inside for something to transpire and the owner of the voice was growing impatient at the delay. Then it clicked. My brain matched voice to face and an image of Herr Stretter of the Gestapo flashed before my eyes. I shuddered. Surely I had to be wrong. What on earth was Herr Stretter doing here? But I kept listening and my certainty grew. I reached forward and tapped Eddie's shoulder.

'What is it now?' he hissed.

'The Gestapo are here!'

'What? You're crazy. Your imagination is running away with you.'

'No, Eddie, I recognize a voice. Honestly.'

'If you're right, then they really have laid a perfect trap. Jesus, I hope you're wrong.'

But I knew Eddie's hopes would be dashed.

'There they are,' he said.

I peered past him, and some forty yards behind the train I saw Fletcher and Jorgen walking side by side, confident in their military stride. I felt a fizz, and sparks erupted inside my belly as I held my breath. *Come on*, I willed. *Just another twenty yards, just another ten, you're almost there. You're going to make it. My God, you're actually going to make it.* I gripped Eddie's arm tightly.

'Halt!' A shrill whistle blew. '*Halt!*'

Within seconds the air filled with shouts, stomping

boots and the hideous yelping of dogs. Soldiers rushed to surround Fletcher and Jorgen, some being dragged by slavering Alsatians straining at their leashes. Startled, Fletcher broke away first and began running towards us, Jorgen quickly on his heels. Two men against a dozen or more. I raised my pistol and aimed it at a soldier who'd swung his rifle off his shoulder, sunk to his knees and started taking aim.

Eddie's left hand grabbed my wrist and pulled my arm down. 'No, Marek, that's suicide.'

'But, we have to—'

'No!'

I knew that what I was about to witness would trouble my soul until the day I die. First Fletcher then Jorgen raced past me, not twenty feet from where I crouched. I saw fear glistening in Jorgen's wild eyes and I think he caught a glimpse of me because I detected a brief hesitation in his stride. But he did not come towards us; he did not betray our presence. Instead he kept on running beside the tracks. Reaching into his pocket, he seized his handkerchief and flung it away to his left.

A single shot rang out and Jorgen dropped like a dead bird onto the tracks. Fletcher kept on running. A burst of machine-gun fire ripped at the ground behind him, gaining on him until it caught him up. He stumbled and staggered, spun on his heels and fell. Troops rushed past us in pursuit. Dogs, let off their leashes, raced up the tracks.

Tears welled up but I could not look away. The horror transfixed me. I thought I saw Fletcher trying to crawl forward but couldn't be sure. The dogs reached him first and seized his arms and legs, tugging and tearing at him. Soldiers surrounded him and pointed their rifles at his pitiful, defenceless body lying across the rails. Herr Stretter strode past me, his long black leather coat flapping. His thin lips barely hid his delight. On reaching Fletcher, he drew a pistol from beneath his coat, aimed with a steady hand and fired a single shot into the brave Englishman's head.

About to explode inside, my jaw clenched so tightly it hurt, I found myself hissing hateful spittle from behind my teeth. I wanted to kill every German within a thousand miles. I wanted to tear off Herr Stretter's limbs and feed him to the dogs. So this was the full horror of war and what it did to people. Now I was at war, and now I would fight to the bitter end. Like the final battle between the gods and giants, between men and monsters, this was my Ragnarok, this was my plain of Vigrid. And here all evil would be destroyed and, I prayed, a better world would be born from the ashes. I rose to my feet and stood tall.

Chapter Nineteen

Eddie's arms wrapped around me, his grip so tight it forced the air from my lungs. He dragged me to the ground. 'Be still, Marek,' he breathed into my ear. 'For God's sake, be still.'

I realized I was shaking.

'We cannot undo what has been done.'

His words did nothing to dampen my fury and despair. 'I want Stretter,' I hissed.

'I know,' he whispered. 'But we came here with a job to do. That outweighs everything. And we must not fail.'

'But we have failed,' I blurted.

'Shush. Keep to a whisper. There's still one chance left.'

'What?' My mind banged with confusion. 'What chance?'

He loosened his grip on me. 'Did you see Jorgen throw his handkerchief?'

'Yes.'

'I figure he saw us and discarded his platinum pills. Even in his panic he saw an opportunity. If we can locate them once things have quietened down, the mission will rest on our shoulders.'

I sat up and wiped tears from my eyes. 'You mean we'll have to get aboard the train?'

'Yes.'

'Impossible!'

'You might be right, but we have to try. If only Jan and Angus had succeeded with their diversion. If only I'd ignored Ingrid and brought my rucksack.'

I gathered my wits. Meanwhile soldiers dragged Fletcher and Jorgen's bodies away, led by Herr Stretter, who, no doubt, was keen to inform his superiors of their successful operation. Eddie began planning the best way to approach the train, which appeared temporarily unguarded.

'Would a couple of incendiaries help?' I asked.

'Shush, Marek, I'm trying to think. This isn't the time for idle chatter.'

I felt beneath my jacket and slid my fingers between the loose stitches under my left armpit. I tugged and tore the lining from its seam and gripped the incendiary. Removing it, I nudged Eddie. 'Here, take this. Thought it might come in handy.'

Instinctively he seized it and it took a few moments for him to register what now lay in his hand. 'Bloody hell, Marek, where did that come from?'

'Ask no questions and I'll tell no lies.' I produced the second incendiary like a magician's finale. 'Sorry, that's it. Just the two. Are they enough?'

'Let's hope so.' He peered about again and huffed. Then, inspired, he gently tapped the oil drum closest to him. 'Aha!' He tapped several others and then reached up and unscrewed the caps on all of them. 'Listen carefully, Marek. Here's the plan. When I say go, try to find Jorgen's handkerchief and let's hope it stayed tied up with all the pills intact. I'm going to tip over one of these oil drums and let it spill. One incendiary should be enough. I'll give you a couple of minutes and then ignite it. It'll burn the oil and cause quite a blaze, not to mention plenty of smoke. That'll keep them busy for a while.'

I nodded and peered into the gloom where Jorgen had despatched his knotted handkerchief. Beside the railway lines lay conical mounds covered with snow. They looked like miniature mountains. I suspected they were stockpiles of coal. A white hanky would have stood out against the black lumps and, if it had been summertime, my search would have been simple. The white blanket, however, made my quest a hundred times harder.

'On the count of three, Marek. One, two . . . *three*.'

I broke cover and scrambled into the darkness. Reaching the mounds, I slithered on my belly like a lizard, groping, hoping to touch the softness of cotton. I climbed by pushing with my boots, all the time feeling about me frantically. Nothing! Had Jorgen thrown it over the top of the mounds? Had it travelled that far? Reaching the peak, I slid like a toboggan down the other side. Pushing snow first one way then the other with outstretched fingers, as if I were swimming the breaststroke, I feared that my blind search was doomed to failure. Then . . . there it was! My hand closed around the soft bundle and I drew it to within inches of my face. I could feel the pills inside, hard as dried peas. I wanted to cry out at my success but instead rolled over and began to climb up the slope.

Someone grabbed hold of my left leg. I twisted round and duly received a poke in the stomach from a rifle barrel. I looked up and in the grey dimness saw the face of a young German soldier bearing down on me. He peered quizzically for a moment and then said, '*Was machst du hier?*'

Oddly I think he was more scared than me. His rifle trembled and his expression struck me as fearful. Though it was difficult to tell, owing to his grey uniform and helmet, I guessed he was barely older than me because his cheeks bore the acne of adolescence and smoothness of one who didn't yet need to shave more than once a fortnight. '*Wie heißt du?*' He prodded me again and it hurt.

'Marek Olsen,' I replied, rubbing my bruised belly. I seized a lump of coal and held it up. 'Sorry. I just wanted a few pieces. Just a small fire to keep warm.'

His Norwegian appeared non-existent so I racked my brain for the right words in German. '*Kohle,*' I said, thrusting the lump towards him again. '*Für Feuer. Verstehen Sie?*' Surely, I thought, he must know that people were always trying to pilfer a few lumps of coal in order to stay warm.

He tutted and shook his head. '*Kinder, dumme Kinder!*'

There followed an awkward silence during which I think he considered whether or not to shoot me. Curiously, he did not strike me as the type eager to fill us Norwegians with lead. Then, to my surprise, he burst out laughing and smiled broadly. 'Go home.'

I stared at him in disbelief. Had I heard right? He lowered and then gestured his rifle to one side. 'Go on, go home. Now. Quickly.'

I leaped to my feet and smiled back at him. About to scarper, I heard quick steps from the shadows behind him and his expression suddenly changed. His smile vanished and his eyes bulged like a startled rabbit's. His head jerked forward and blood spurted from his mouth. He fell beside me and in his place I saw Eddie clutching his knife, the blade dripping.

'Found the pills?'

I couldn't speak so nodded instead. I looked down. The young soldier lay beside me, his final breath a hideous bubbling of red froth on his lips.

'Splendid!' Eddie grabbed my arm. 'Come on, we'll head for the far side of the train.'

Like scurrying rodents, we kept close to the walls of the shed and, timing our dash perfectly, made it undetected across the railway lines some yards behind the train. Sliding down an embankment, we lay on our stomachs. Eddie lifted his head and peered across to the oil drums.

271

'She's starting to glow,' he enthused. 'Any minute now. Come on, my beauty, give us a show.'

Without warning an oil drum exploded, the casing rising a good thirty feet into the air amid a blinding flash. Burning oil sprayed in all directions, settling on the ground as tongues of fire that crackled and spat acrid plumes of smoke.

'Now, Marek!' He hauled himself over the top of the embankment, turned and caught hold of my anorak, and together we ran to the last of the three wagons. Another drum detonated. I did not stop to look at the unfolding havoc, but out of the corner of my eye I saw figures and long shadows scurrying in all directions amid yells of consternation and surprise.

Eddie wrenched the lever locking the sliding door to the wagon and, using his full weight, managed to open it a couple of feet. He stooped and cupped his hands. 'I'll give you a leg up. Quickly now.' I put my left boot onto his clasped fingers, grabbed a handrail and pulled myself up and into the wagon. Eddie followed and slid the door shut.

Inside, darkness enveloped us. However wide I opened my eyes, I could see nothing but black. Eddie sparked a lighter and held up the flickering torch. The wagon appeared full of crates of different shapes and sizes, all bearing swastikas and eagles of the Third Reich. There were stencilled numbers too, and German text on every wooden panel.

'Which ones?' I asked.

'No idea. We'll have to check them all.'

That, I thought, would take hours. 'These accumulators, how big are they?'

He shrugged.

'Damn. Here, hold the lighter still. I'll try this one.' I gripped the top of a crate measuring about two foot by three foot and used the barrel of my revolver to prise the lid along one edge. Beneath lay straw and I slipped a hand inside. I felt something smooth, curved and cold to the touch, cylindrical and about four inches in diameter. I seized it and pulled and heard the chink of glass on glass. 'Bottles, I think.'

'Blast, probably the finest vintage French champagne,' Eddie cursed. 'Let's try another one, a bigger crate this time. Like one of those over there.' He pointed to the far end of the wagon. We pressed along a narrow gap. Something caught my eye.

'Shine your light on this,' I said. The words ACHTUNG! KONZENTRIERTE SÄURE glowed – DANGER: CONCENTRATED ACID. My heart leaped. 'I think they're here. In these crates.' I started levering the lid with my pistol.

'Careful, Marek, we must leave no trace. Don't damage the crates. Ease the lid up. Here, hold the lighter, I'll do it.'

We changed places. Eddie's lighter felt white-hot and I didn't know how long I'd be able to hold it. He used the metal butt of his machine gun to gently prise off the lid. Inside lay large gunmetal-grey blocks. I was right.

These were the accumulators. 'Hand me the pills,' he said.

While I reached into my pocket and then untied the knotted hanky with one hand aided by my teeth, he removed the tops to each of the acid cells. Then, carefully, he dropped a pill into each cavity. Fumes of concentrated acid rose and burned my nose and throat. I suppressed the urge to cough and splutter. He replaced the tops and then gently lowered the crate's lid, using his weapon to sink the nails as far as they'd go. 'Right, let's find the next crate.'

The lighter began to falter, its flame growing feeble, flickering and spitting, just as we closed the fourth crate. I had half a dozen platinum pills left and, judging from the remaining crates, we had contaminated only about half the shipment of accumulators. All the while I had been aware of voices outside and had feared the sound of the wagon door being slid open and our discovery.

The lighter died. 'That's it,' he said. 'We've done what we can.'

A sudden, heavy jolt of the wagon threw me unceremoniously to the floor, bruising my elbow. 'What's happening?'

Before Eddie could reply we began to move slowly forward amid loud, straining grunts of the locomotive. Hissing and clunks of metal against metal accompanied our gradual acceleration. Eddie headed for the wagon door. He waited a couple of minutes and then slid it open a fraction and pressed an eye to the gap. 'We'll be out of the station soon,' he said.

'Then what?' I fretted. 'How do we get off? There's only about half a mile of track before the tunnel!'

'We'll jump.' He said it so calmly, so matter-of-factly.

'Jump?' A lump filled my throat. 'You're kidding, right?'

'Only way, Marek.'

The train gained speed rapidly. I took a turn at peering out, and everything beside the tracks – poles, fences, rocks and bushes – flew past in an increasing and frightening blur. The lump in my throat would not go away. Eddie pushed me aside and slid the door open a foot. A wall of icy air rushed in. Poking his head out, he looked both ways. 'I can see the tunnel. It's about two hundred yards away. Get ready.'

How? I thought. How do you get ready for such a crazy act? I slipped back from the door. I had no wish to smash my head against rock, to splinter a bone, to get wrapped around a telegraph pole. 'I can't do it,' I cried. 'I'm scared.'

He hauled the door open another foot. 'No time to be scared, Marek.' He seized my arm and pushed me to the brink. I felt nature's frozen breath cut across my face.

'No!' I cried. I tried reaching out to grasp something.

He shoved me firmly in my back. 'Remember to roll,' he shouted as I started to fall.

Flying through the air, I felt strangely free and

unburdened. Time seemed to slow down. I truly thought I was about to die and expected to see my life flash before my eyes. Instead I hit the snowdrift punishingly hard, driving the air from my lungs. 'Roll, Marek, roll,' screamed Eddie's voice inside me. I tried, but slid more than turned, a dense bush finally halting my journey with a loud snap and flurry of snow. I lay for a moment and blinked. Was that snapping sound the bush or me? I wondered. I felt for my legs and checked both were present and correct and then warily touched my face. I still had both ears and my nose remained in its proper position between my eyes, pointing forwards. Damn it, I'd survived! The thrill caused me to scream with joy and then I laughed and laughed, a loud laugh of invincibility.

I rose slowly to my knees and glanced around. I saw the train snaking its way into the tunnel. 'Eddie?' I couldn't see him. Was he still on the train? Was he lying dead in the snow?

Something moved about fifty yards away. A hand poked out from the drift and waved. I hurried through white powder up to my waist and found Eddie gingerly rising to his feet. 'You OK?'

He nodded but could not hide a pained expression, and I saw him clutch his left arm rather cautiously. 'Is it broken?'

'Don't think so. Just twisted, I reckon.'

'What now?'

He winced and dropped down to one knee. 'Head

back to town and see what's happening. If Harald has betrayed us, then we need to determine whether his treachery is complete.' He looked up at me. 'The safe house may no longer be *safe*!' He coughed. 'And Café Fransk may have been raided.'

I thought of Herr Stretter and imagined that he must be thinking Christmas had come early. Then I thought of Olaf and wondered what on earth had happened to him. I feared he too might have been captured as he crept towards the fuel and ammunition dumps. 'I suppose it all depends how much Harald knew and how much he told the Gestapo,' I replied.

Using his machine gun as a crutch, Eddie forced himself up, letting out an anguished cry.

'You sure nothing's broken?' I asked.

He ignored me. 'You may have a point, Marek. Jorgen only told us the bare bones of the plan in advance. He kept the details back as they were Jan's responsibility.'

'And since Harald arrived here,' I said, 'he's not been out of our sight.'

'That's true. But he knew about the contact at the café, didn't he? Remember? He said that he'd intended making contact but didn't because the place was full of Germans.'

'That's right. Damn you, Harald,' I spat. I thought of Jorgen and Fletcher and a dizzying wave of emotion rocked me. I thought of Ingrid and her despair.

'Come on. Keep your eyes peeled, Marek. I'd appreciate a hand.'

I wrapped his good arm round my shoulder and bore a little of his weight. We kicked our way out of the drift and headed off at right angles to the railway line. The lights of Ork glowed like an oasis in a desert of black but we skirted them, fearing to enter the town on the main road as we expected checkpoints to be well manned. Instead we trudged in the direction of the mountains that hung menacingly over the fjord, a collection of craggy peaks and broader, barrel-like sweeps of unfriendly terrain topped by a leaden, dark, featureless sky. The lower slopes comprised a rug of bluish white pocked with jutting fangs of rock. We darted as best we could from one granite tooth to the next. The higher we climbed, the more the wind blustered and howled, seizing up grains of powder snow and pelting them into our faces, stinging and scratching.

Eddie struggled, each burst of activity causing him to yelp and groan and pant desperately like a dog. Despite his denials, I suspected his arm was indeed broken, or at best fractured. Either he didn't want to worry me unduly or didn't want to contemplate the days of agony ahead. After all, our present predicament seemed bad enough. A serious injury complicated things. I recalled a favourite phrase Uncle Knut used whenever Olaf or I proved stubborn or stupid. He'd look glum, shake his head and mutter, 'Even the wisest men can behave like idiots in the name of some great cause.' Never a truer word spoken, I thought.

We took shelter in a bleak, rocky crevice. 'Need to

rest a while, Marek,' Eddie puffed. Settling down heavily, he nursed his arm like a sick babe. I stared down towards Ork and could make out the labour camp and barracks. The area remained tranquil and undisturbed. I wondered what it might have looked like if Angus had succeeded. I pictured the fires of hell.

'Marek?'

'Yes, Eddie.'

'You did a grand job tonight. Thanks. Couldn't have done it without you.'

'Yes you could have.'

'No. Doubt if I'd even have got to the train.'

I possessed mixed feelings. Naturally I felt proud that we'd dealt Fritz a blow that might cost him some U-boats and possibly save thousands of merchant seamen risking the North Atlantic crossing. Yet they were distant things, intangible, almost unreal. What was real, to me at least, was the loss of two men I had grown to know a little and like a lot, two good men, one a Jøssing, the other a brave British commando. They seemed of far greater importance to me. I sat for a while and pondered what the hell the future held for my brother and me, not to mention everyone else.

When I eventually turned to check on Eddie, I saw perspiration on his brow and noticed he'd begun to shiver rather worryingly. He needed a doctor and I remembered that we'd passed Ork's small hospital during our earlier trip to the post office with Jan. I had to get Eddie there somehow and, from the look of him, without delay.

'Time we moved on,' I urged. 'Come on. Or we'll freeze to death out here.' I judged the temperature to be minus ten or thereabouts, with a chill factor that would quickly sap our energy. 'We need to get someone to look at that arm.'

He shook his head. 'Too dangerous.'

We could have argued the point but I decided that would be wasted effort. Instead I helped him to his feet and we hobbled down towards the lights of Ork. Avoiding the roads made our trek all the more arduous as the snow lay deep and crisp. I knew we were leaving clear tracks but somehow it didn't seem important. We moved painfully slowly, Eddie as reluctant as a lame horse. Oh, how I wished we had our skis so we could glide. But they were neatly stacked inside the safe house.

Reaching town, we paused for a moment and I peered around to get my bearings. It was ten o'clock and I felt unsure whether that would prove an advantage. Much later and the streets would be deserted and our presence would draw attention. Yet it was early enough for the bars and restaurants to be busy and Fritz was undoubtedly still on high alert. Eddie leaned against a wall, bent double in agony. I grabbed his machine gun and hid it in snow under a bush. 'Come on,' I encouraged. 'This way.'

'Where are we going?' he mumbled deliriously.

'Somewhere safe,' I replied, seizing his good arm again.

Keeping to quiet back streets, we headed in the general direction of the hospital. Avoiding everyone proved impossible, but thankfully we crossed paths with only a few local men and women. Of course, they eyed us with concern but I had a plan to allay their fears. Only one paused to ask if we were OK, an elderly Norwegian with stale breath. 'What's the matter? He looks in a bad way,' he said.

I laughed and thanked him. 'Too many beers,' I said. 'He slipped on the ice. Mother will be angry. Again!' The old man chuckled, shook his head and went on his way.

Ork hospital appeared quiet. In the waiting area sat an elderly woman coughing fitfully, a man slumped across a bench – I figured he was either drunk, asleep or dead – and a younger man in his twenties with his left leg in plaster. In the corner sat a German guard, his rifle resting against the wall. He looked up as we entered but quickly returned his attention to a colourful magazine. The sharp smell of disinfectant itched my nose.

I sat Eddie down and went to the reception desk, peering past it and through an open door, as nobody appeared to be on duty. 'Hello!' Eventually a set of double doors banged open and a young doctor breezed in, his hands pressed deep into the pockets of his white coat, his stethoscope dangling untidily from his neck. Tall, with short curly brown hair and dark-rimmed glasses, he looked the studious type.

He spotted Eddie and then me. 'I'm Doctor Ingavar Klose. What's the problem?'

'Broken arm, I think,' I replied, gesturing towards Eddie. 'Fell over.' I threw a glance at the guard but thankfully he took no interest in us. Though I think the doctor spotted my nervousness.

He gently prised Eddie's good hand from its protective hold and began feeling up and down his injured arm. Eddie let out a bloodcurdling yell that set the doctor back on his heels and even roused the man sleeping two rows back. The guard looked up and stared.

'Right,' said the doctor, 'better see to that right away. Come through to my office and we'll organize an X-ray.'

He hurried us through the double doors, down a corridor and into a room decked out with treatment couch, desk, a sink, several chairs and a wall cabinet full of bottles and vials. From a drawer he removed a glass syringe, screwed a needle into its end and reached for a bottle of clear liquid. 'Something to dull the pain,' he said. 'Then we'll get that jacket off and have a proper look.'

The morphine worked quickly and the creases in Eddie's brow soon unfolded. Between us we managed to slip his jacket off but needed to cut away his sweater with surgical scissors. The doctor began unfastening Eddie's shirt but suddenly stopped, the blood draining from his face. A fearful clutch gripped my belly. Something was wrong. Then I realized. The doctor had spotted Eddie's dog tags. He turned and looked at me angrily. 'Why the hell did you risk bringing him here?'

I stuttered something about needing urgent help but the doctor turned away and paced his office, rubbing the back of his neck and tearing at his brown locks. 'Madness,' he muttered. 'Jesus.'

I reached into my anorak pocket and placed my hand around the handle of my revolver. 'Will you hand us over to Fritz?' I asked. Or, I thought, will I have to shoot you?

Chapter Twenty

Having thought for a moment, Dr Klose reached forward and seized Eddie's dog tags, ripping them from around his neck. 'I think it's best if I look after these for now,' he said. 'I'll see to the X-ray myself.' He put the dog tags into his pocket and rubbed his chin. 'We'll need a name,' he added. 'For the paperwork.'

'Edvard Grieg,' I said.

He laughed. 'The Germans won't believe that for a minute.'

I rifled through Eddie's anorak pockets and found his false identity. 'There's proof,' I said.

Shaking his head, the doctor reached for some forms and began filling them in. Eddie started to mumble incoherently in English. 'Be quiet, Eddie,' I told him. 'If you can't say it in Norwegian, then don't say it at all.' He looked up at me and grunted.

'Of course, he can't stay here for long,' said Dr Klose. 'Too many soldiers milling about.' He pointed to the window. 'We treat some men from the labour camp here. Those who need surgery or are too sick to be treated in the camp's makeshift infirmary. And they're closely guarded day and night.'

I went to the window and peered beyond the drawn

blinds. Outside the back of the hospital lay several long timber huts, a single lamp glowing over each doorway, a single guard standing by each set of wooden steps. Fearing being spotted, I dipped back behind the slats.

'Right,' said Dr Klose. 'Let's do the X-ray now. The machine's next door. Wait here,' he said to me, 'and touch nothing.' He helped Eddie to his feet and guided him to the door, all the while humming a melody from Grieg's *Peer Gynt*.

Alone, I sat on a chair and reflected on the day. So many things had gone dreadfully wrong, I thought. At least the mission had been a partial success. But what about Olaf? And where was Ingrid? I realized only Eddie and I actually knew that the mission had been carried out. Though gripped by a sudden sense of urgency that others needed to be informed, I decided to wait for the good doctor's full diagnosis before making my next move. I felt wearier than I could ever recall, exhaustion tugging at my aching muscles, rendering my eyelids as heavy as granite boulders. But sleep had to wait.

I killed time wandering around the room, peering into the drugs cabinet, toying with a strange medical device comprising various lengths of rubber tubing, and studying the charts pinned to the walls. I kept glancing towards the window. Eventually I could not resist and peeked between the slats towards the huts. Inside lay many Norwegians who were suffering terribly, I realized. Could Father be among them? I took heart in the knowledge that at least they were receiving medical attention. Stories back home about the labour camps spoke of men with open wounds left to fester, of deep infections left untreated, of men treated worse than wolves. I was glad that had proven an exaggeration.

The door clicked and I spun round. Dr Klose, clutching the X-ray film in one hand, led Eddie back in. 'All done,' he said. 'Just a fracture of the radius. Pretty nasty but it'll heal quite quickly, I think. I'll use a splint and bandage and give you some painkillers to take with you.'

'How many men are there in the huts?' I asked.

He stopped and looked thoughtful. I think he was doing the mental arithmetic. 'About two dozen,' he said finally. 'No, make that thirty.'

'Do you have a list of names?'

'Why?'

'There's a possibility my father might have been moved to this camp.'

He stopped abruptly and stared at me. 'Really? What name?'

About to say, I hesitated. If I told him my name, Dr Klose would know who I was and could therefore betray me, even if only under duress. 'The list,' I repeated.

He pointed to his desk. 'Top drawer on the right.'

I turned the small key and slid open the drawer. Inside lay a clipboard with a wad of papers attached. I seized it and scanned the first form. *'Nils Haglund, male,*

46 years old, appendicitis.' I flipped to the next page. '*Harald Torsen, male, 28, pneumonia.'* I flipped page after page, my eyes dancing from form to form.

I gasped. There it was! '*Bernd Olsen, male, aged 47, TB.'*

'What's TB?' I asked.

'Tuberculosis.'

'Oh, right.' I'd heard about tuberculosis from Olaf. He liked trying to teach me stuff he'd read about. I wished I'd paid more attention to him. But, if my vague memory was correct, TB was a damn nasty lung infection. So nasty, in fact, it killed many.

'Afraid we see a lot of cases. Tricky to treat,' Dr Klose added.

I hurriedly scanned the rest of the form and tried to read the doctor's notes but the handwriting was a dreadful scrawl. As far as I could make out, Father had begun to improve, was eating better and gaining strength. I wondered in which hut he lay and tried to decipher the form. I compared the numbers in the right-hand top corner to those on other pages. Most specified Hut A or Hut B or C, followed by what looked like a bed number. Father's, however, merely stated '2.09'. It got me thinking – a room number? In the main hospital?

'Here, give me a hand,' said the doctor. 'Hold this splint in place so I can wind the bandage around it.'

I tried to hold the slender wooden splint steady while minimizing Eddie's visible discomfort. Dr Klose started unravelling a long, wide bandage.

'Thanks,' I said. 'I'll always remember your help.' He

did not smile or reply. 'Those men with TB,' I added. 'I suppose they're kept separate from the others?'

He glanced up. 'Yes. How did you know that?'

'My brother wants to become a doctor,' I said, thinking quickly. 'I recall he said something about TB being contagious. But only if you breathe in their coughs.'

'That's right. When we have spare rooms, we move them into the main hospital. The Germans don't like it, of course, but often we don't tell them until after we've done it.'

I guessed '2.09' meant room nine on the second floor. 'Does that mean Fritz has to guard each room?'

He shook his head. 'They're not going anywhere, so the guards don't usually bother.'

The urge to see Father overwhelmed me. The fiercest storm, the heaviest barrage, a whole German division wasn't going to stop me. 'I need the toilet,' I said.

'Along the corridor and to the right.'

Out of the room in a flash, I looked both ways and spotted a stairwell at the end of the corridor. I ran and scaled the steps three at a time. Reaching the second floor, I hurried past each door, pausing only to read the small numbers: '2.05 . . . 2.06 . . . 2.07 . . . 2.08 . . . 2.09!' I ground to a halt and listened. The corridor lay silent. I took a deep breath and gripped the door handle. Feeling sick with anticipation, I turned it and pushed the door open an inch. The room lay in darkness. I slipped in, closed the door and leaned against it.

Slowly my eyes adjusted and I could make out a bed;

I could hear the deep rasping breath of someone asleep. I stepped closer. 'Father?' I whispered. 'Father? It's Marek.'

I heard him stir but he simply turned over and resumed the rhythmical breath of distant dreams. Placing a hand on his shoulder, I shook him gently. 'Wake up, Father, it's Marek.'

Reaching down, I felt the cord of a bedside lamp. I traced its path to a switch and flicked it on. It came as quite a shock. Father looked different from how I remembered him. Thinner in the face, almost gaunt, his skin was grey rather than glowing, and rough stubble covered his hollow cheeks and scraggy neck. He opened a watery eye a fraction and blinked away the pain of the brightness. Then he frowned and rose up abruptly onto his elbows, coughing and spluttering. 'Marek.' He shook his head. 'A dream?'

'No, Father, it's really me.'

He looked left then right. 'Olaf?'

'He's here in Ork too.'

'But . . . but how?'

'Never mind that now. How are you?'

He did not answer. I think he truly believed it was all a cruel dream. 'And Emma?' he asked.

Of course, I did not know the real answer but said simply, 'Mother's safe.'

A rare glint of cheer settled on his lips. He lay back down and twisted his head to look at me. 'Give me your hand, Marek. It's great to see you. I had lost all hope of ever seeing you again.'

A solitary tear ran down his cheek and his thin, chapped and blistered lips quivered. I had not seen Father cry before, not ever. It upset me to see him as a weak shadow of the man I knew. I choked. Always a tower of strength, a pillar supporting us, he had radiated energy, which I had absorbed as I grew up. Now I knew it was me that had to provide the strength. 'I can't stay long, Father.'

'Don't go.' He tightened his grip.

'I must. But I shall return. I promise. And soon too.'

His brow creased in anguish.

'Be ready to leave here,' I said. 'I'm coming back to rescue you.' I know it was rash to say such a thing, perhaps cruel to offer words of hope, but right then I truly believed that we would all leave Ork together, or not at all.

'No, Marek, that's impossible. Nowhere is safe.' He shook his head despairingly. 'You mustn't risk all on some foolhardy plan. I couldn't bear to see you captured. I know what they can do to a man. Anyway, where would we go? We can't hide from them for ever.'

'We'll go to England,' I said decisively. 'It's safe there.' I thought of the Shetland Bus, of Captain Torvic, and believed he'd grant us safe passage. The only obstacle was getting to the rendezvous point.

Father managed a sour laugh. 'England! And how do you propose we get there?'

'By bus, Father, by bus.'

Again his brow furrowed.

'Don't worry, it'll all become clear in due course,' I said confidently. 'Now get some sleep. I've got to go. Pray for us all, Father. Pray hard. I'll return tomorrow.' I leaned forward and kissed him on his forehead and briefly I detected the familiar warm musky odour of his sweat, which reminded me of home. I prised myself free from his tight clasp.

'Marek?'

'Yes, Father.'

'Listen to me carefully. Get away from here. As far as you can. To England, if that's really possible. Don't come back. Promise me!'

'Shush, now. Sleep, Father, and say nothing to anyone of my visit.' I switched off the lamp and retreated to the door.

'Get lost or something?' said Dr Klose sharply. He eyed me suspiciously.

'Yes. Matter of fact, I did.'

Eddie had regained his senses and appeared keen to leave.

I shook the doctor's hand energetically to show my appreciation. 'You're a true Jøssing, Doctor Klose,' I declared. 'Norway's proud of you.'

He smiled. 'How old are you?'

'Fourteen. Why?'

'Remarkable.'

'What is?' I asked indignantly.

'Nothing. Listen, good luck to you both. Glad I could

be of assistance. But I'd rather we never set eyes on each other again. Understand?'

'Yes.'

'Right. Better go via the side exit. That way you'll avoid old Wolfgang in reception. He can be an awkward old goat when it suits him.'

'Side entrance it is then,' I said. 'Oh, better give Eddie back his dog tags.'

The doctor dipped into his pocket and handed the identity discs and chain back to Eddie. 'I've given him some pills,' he said. 'He should take no more than ten a day. Keep the splint on for a fortnight or until you can get to another doctor.' He reached for the door handle. 'Do us all a favour and avoid getting caught! Good luck.' He smiled patriotically.

We walked the streets slowly. 'How's your arm?'

'A little better,' replied Eddie, inspecting the neat knots of the bandage.

'I think the safe house is a better option than the café. Harald knew the Resistance could be contacted at Café Fransk, so we should assume Fritz knows it as well.'

'Agreed, young Marek. Lead the way.'

Midnight approached as we dipped into the alleyway to the rear of Jan's grandmother's house. A weak glow from an upstairs window suggested someone was home.

'Wait here, Eddie. Let me check the place out.' I drew my revolver, skulked through the shadows and pressed hard up against the wall beside the back door. Listening,

I thought I detected faint voices. Or was it just the wind? I reached out and turned the handle but found the door bolted from within. I tapped gently, and then a little harder, and peered up at the window. The curtains did not move. Stepping back, I crouched, cupped my hand into the snow and squeezed a handful to fashion a small ball. I threw it at the window. It thumped nicely against the pane of glass, leaving a wet, circular mark. The lamp dimmed, the curtain twitched and a figure peered out. I waved.

I don't know who I realistically expected to have found sanctuary at the safe house but, having begun the day among quite a gathering of brave men and women, to find only Olaf, Ingrid, old Hilda Straum and the pretty girl from Café Fransk inside saddened me. We all hugged and kissed but for the first five minutes said little. Like a wake, the atmosphere proved sombre. The young girl, I discovered, was called Katerina, or Kate for short. She was Uncle Heimar's sole daughter. She plied Eddie and me with steaming hot coffee, freshly brewed.

Eddie, straddling a chair, spoke quietly to Ingrid in one corner, his good elbow resting wearily on the straight wooden back. Ingrid had seen what had happened to Fletcher and Jorgen and, as always, displayed no emotion. I knew she had to be hurting inside, just as I was, just as we all were. Before me stands one tough lady, I thought. I overheard Eddie debrief her on the success of our mission, our escape, his injury and trip to the hospital. Kate informed us that the café hadn't been raided but Uncle Heimar had left shortly after we had. He'd gone to warn the families of the other Resistance fighters.

Seizing Olaf's attention, I withdrew with him to the hallway. My brother appeared more miserable than words can describe and he sat at the bottom of the stairs, his shoulders hunched. 'They were waiting for Jan and his men,' he spat. 'Pounced on them before they got anywhere near the blasted barracks and dumps.'

'What happened? I didn't hear any shooting.'

'No, soldiers were all over them. By the time I got there, Jan had surrendered. Must say, he didn't appear very happy. In fact, if looks could kill, the Wehrmacht would have been decimated by his stare alone.'

'And Harald?'

'They took him too. But if what Ingrid said about his treachery is true, then I suppose Harald might live to see the first sunrise of spring.'

'Damn. There's no justice, is there? Never did like him.'

'Neither did I. So, Marek, sounds as if you've had quite an adventure.'

I lowered my voice. 'That's not the half of it. I saw Father!' Of course, I'd been bursting to tell Olaf from the moment I saw him, but when Eddie and I first stepped into the house, it didn't seem quite the right moment.

My brother gawped at me in a way I hadn't seen since the winter of 1938, when at my first attempt I'd plucked a four-pound fish from a hole in the ice during a hunting trip to the Borsobu. His expression screamed 'impossible' at me. I grinned.

'Honestly! I was *this* close. I spoke to him too. He's in a room on the second floor of the hospital.'

My brother struggled to take it all in. 'Whoa, Marek, start from the beginning.'

I did, and told him all that had happened.

'TB,' he repeated. 'He's lucky to be alive.'

'The best bit of all,' I added, 'is that Fritz doesn't bother to guard the few patients actually inside the main hospital.'

My brother did not react.

'Don't you see?' I said.

'See what?'

'We can get him out. We can rescue him!'

'How?'

From memory I drew a plan of the main hospital building on a scrap of paper, marking the approximate locations of Father's room, the stairwells, Dr Klose's office and the waiting room, including the position of the guard's chair. 'His name's Wolfgang,' I said and, recalling what the doctor had told me about him, added, 'And he can be as awkward as a goat!'

My brother studied my artwork closely and questioned me at length on various details, most of which I couldn't answer. He sighed heavily. 'This is all madness, Marek. We can't go walking in there, seize a patient and walk back out again, and not expect to encounter trouble. Anyway, if Father has TB he's in the best place possible.'

I couldn't believe my ears – best place possible! I scowled at him. 'You want to leave Father there? You're joking, surely? You saw those men from the camp. They have no future except in wooden boxes.' My voice had risen sharply and, with the door to the parlour open, everyone paused and stared at me. I felt the angry burn of my flushed cheeks. 'I'm going to rescue him and that's that. I promised.'

'Calm down, Marek. Of course I want to free Father, you idiot. It's just that we need a sensible plan, a plan that stands some sort of chance. It's been a long day. Let's sleep on it. I'll see what I can come up with.'

That night I lay on a smelly mattress covered with two heavy, itchy blankets, and stared at the ceiling, counting the cobwebs and imagining the cracks in the plaster to be a hundred interconnecting rivers in some far-off land, like a map I'd once seen of the Amazon basin. All I could really think about, though, all I could see before my eyes, was Father's face. I had made a promise to him and recalled the many times he'd told me, in his stern, fatherly way, earnest and grave in tone, that a man's word was his bond and that to break it was to be no man at all. I felt resolute. I would remain true to my word. I swore an oath to myself.

My brother snored annoyingly, except during brief bouts of fidgeting, which rattled the iron frame of the bed and made the elderly springs squeak beneath us. A plan. I needed a plan. How to get Father to the rendezvous with the *Sola*. Was Father well enough to ski? Would we have to carry or drag him? I realized I should have quizzed him about his well-being and strength. The distance we had to cover from Ork to the rendezvous was some miles across difficult terrain – unless we risked the road skirting the fjord's shoreline. The road, I decided, had to be our last resort, as Fritz patrolled it. Unless—

A flickering at the window caught my eye. I pulled back the blankets and crept towards the curtains, lifting one up an inch to peek outside. The room faced north and, the sky having cleared, the heavens now treated me to a display of sweeping and shimmering arcs of light, brighter than I'd ever seen before. Enthralled, I gazed and lost myself in their play. I remembered that night Olaf and I had lain in our house of Norwegian ice on the Hardanger, recounting the story of Ragnarok, and how I had explained to him that from utter destruction came renewed hope. Hope! As my focus drifted across the heavens, a thought occurred to me. The contents of Eddie's rucksack, if employed properly, could turn Ork into a firestorm, could make men think the end of the world had arrived. I imagined Ork ablaze and wondered if it could be used to cloak an audacious escape. A plan began assembling in my mind.

Chapter Twenty-one

At breakfast the next morning Eddie swallowed five painkillers and declined all offers of bread and dried meat. I sensed what he was thinking. He longed to be on his way home, back to England. Jan's grandmother clucked about us, pouring coffee and muttering under her breath that life in Ork wasn't what it used to be. Ingrid appeared thoughtful.

'Well?' I said to my brother.

'Well what?' He stuffed an oversized wedge of *lefse* into his mouth and frowned.

'You've slept on it. So have you got a plan?'

He shook his head. Ingrid peered at us enquiringly, so I explained.

'Marek,' she said softly, 'I understand what you're saying, but think about it. The Resistance has been decimated, the streets are crawling with troops, and I don't think the Gestapo have finished here yet! And there's the small matter of Jan and his men. Trying to help them has to be our first priority.'

She had a point and I knew it. However rational her words, though, I was not for turning. 'I promised Father I'd rescue him, and I'm a man of my word.'

Reaching out, she squeezed my arm. 'I know. I

understand. Really. But sometimes we have to accept that not all things are possible.' She smiled at me, a smile full of shared pain and anguish. 'Maybe in a while,' she added. 'Maybe in a few months when everything's quietened down. When we've regrouped.'

'No!' I cried obstinately. 'You can help Jan yourself. I'm going to help Father and that's that!' I screeched back my chair, stormed out of the room and hammered up the stairs. Flinging myself onto my mattress, I sobbed.

Olaf followed me upstairs. 'Go away!' I cried.

He refused, settling beside me instead. 'I want to rescue Father as much as you, Marek. But Ingrid's right,' he said.

'Go away!' I shouted again, burying my face in the blanket.

'Listen, this is no time to be foolhardy. There's no sense in getting ourselves captured. If Father's as sick as I think he is, then he'd not make it. He wouldn't have the strength to ski or walk more than a few hundred yards.'

God, how I just wanted to be left alone! I didn't want to hear any of this reasoning, this common sense. I just wanted to rescue Father. That's all. Was that too much to ask?

Half an hour later, when I'd shed about as many tears as I possessed, Eddie arrived and leaned against the doorway. 'The situation's looking pretty bleak, lads. Word is, the Germans are holding Jan and the others at the police station. The Gestapo have taken over the place. And they've doubled the patrols in town.'

I lifted my head from the blanket. 'That bastard Stretter,' I hissed.

Eddie loitered. 'Ingrid's gone to radio England. She needs to send news of our success.'

'Success!' my brother snorted. 'Jesus, I'd hate to see what you consider failure.'

'We got the pills into the accumulators, didn't we?' I protested.

'Yes, but the enemy was lying in wait for Jorgen and Fletcher. That means they knew our objective was the train. I expect they figured out that our target was those accumulator things.'

My guts sank. Fritz knew *everything*.

'Don't be so pessimistic, Olaf,' said Eddie. 'They intercepted Jorgen and Fletcher *before* they got to the train and they didn't check the wagon before it reached the tunnel. We know that because we were inside the damn thing. I figure they hadn't banked on Marek and me. I do believe we got away with it.'

I stared at his bandaged arm. 'Have you abandoned attacking the railway line?'

'Yes. No way can I get in and out of that tunnel and lay the charges one-armed. Still, our main objective was met, and that's the important thing. Must say, I'm looking forward to reaching the Shetland Bus tonight and getting the hell out of here.'

'It's still coming?' said Olaf in surprise.

'Suppose so,' said Eddie. 'Ingrid will check with London.'

'Surely Jan or one of the others will reveal everything about it when the Gestapo interrogate them?'

'Life's full of risks, Olaf.' Eddie settled on the end of the bed. 'Marek, about your father—'

'I don't want to talk about him any more,' I snapped. 'I know what you're going to say. *It's too dangerous. It's stupid to even think about it.*'

'Actually, that wasn't what I had in mind.'

'Then what?'

'Well . . .' He hesitated. 'I was just wondering if you had any sort of plan figured out?'

I turned over and sat upright. 'Of course I've got a plan.'

He smirked. 'Now, why did I never doubt that for a minute? So, fill me in.'

Olaf shook his head. 'For God's sake, don't encourage him.'

Eddie held up a restraining hand. 'Shush. Before dismissing it, let's at least hear Marek out.'

I began describing the idea that had germinated in my head during a restless night of tossing and turning. 'Your explosives, Eddie, they're the key to my plan. If we could create enough mayhem, then we can get Father out of town under the Germans' noses.'

'How?' said Olaf disbelievingly. 'Father won't be able to walk far. Are you going to carry him?'

'Won't need to,' I replied. 'Thought we could borrow an ambulance.'

He roared with laughter. 'Are you sure you didn't crack your head when you jumped out of that train?'

I scowled and pictured giving him a bloody nose.

'Anyway,' he added, 'you think we can just walk up and steal an ambulance?'

I displayed my best 'remember who you're talking to' look. 'I know how to bypass the ignition,' I said, raising my eyebrows.

'Oh, right,' he replied, his voice still dripping with sarcasm. 'Well, supposing you could do it, do you really think we could just drive out of town?'

'Actually, yes!' I replied. 'To be honest, though, there is a major weakness to my plan. Just the one.'

'And what's that then?'

'Well, with Eddie's arm busted, unfortunately that leaves just you to drive the ambulance, Olaf.'

'Ha, very funny.'

Eddie's face began to shine. 'I like it,' he said.

'What? Are you nuts too?' bellowed my brother.

'Think about it, Olaf,' he said. 'Imagine fires and explosions, people running wildly in every direction, soldiers unsure what the hell's hit the town. What could be more natural than an ambulance hurrying through the streets with its bell ringing? If I were a German, it would be the last vehicle I'd stop.' He looked at me approvingly. 'Well done, Marek.'

My pulse raced. Eddie had fire in his eyes. Was it

really possible? Could we persuade Ingrid? *Ingrid!* She had only Jan and the others on her mind. I raised the problem.

'Leave her to me,' said Eddie. 'Ever heard of killing two birds with one stone?'

Ingrid returned shortly after midday. 'London sends its thanks for what we achieved,' she said wearily. Turning to Eddie, she added, 'And the *Sola* will make the rendezvous as planned tonight at midnight. Same place as you arrived.'

Eddie had just begun to gently broach the subject of our plan when Uncle Heimar slipped in through the back door, stomped loose snow from his boots and cursed. He then tore off his anorak, grumbling like an angry polar bear, and threw it across the room.

Jan's grandmother, Hilda, raised a shaking hand to her lips. 'What's wrong, Heimar?'

He settled down at the table and began scratching at the thin veneer with a grubby nail. 'Bad news. Word is that the Gestapo intends to make an example of all those captured last night.'

She wilted at the knees and reached out to steady herself by grasping the edge of a pine dresser. My brother offered her a supportive hand. The obvious question, I thought, was what exactly 'an example' meant? When nobody asked it, I assumed it meant the worst.

'How much time have we got?' asked Ingrid.

Uncle Heimar raised his arms and shrugged. 'A day, maybe two.'

Eddie now spoke of my idea, at least in part. 'So, if we can liberate Jan and the others,' he concluded, 'there's the chance that we can get them all to the rendezvous point.' He had talked of my firestorm, of my requisitioning of an ambulance, and thought it might be possible to raid the police station, as surprise would be on our side. He had not, however, spoken of Father. I stared at him expectantly. He cast me a glance but did not add to his explanation.

Uncle Heimar thrummed his fingers nervously on the tabletop and then started twisting and tugging the ends of his moustache. 'I doubt if there are more than half a dozen fit and able men and women willing to risk so much,' he said. 'All the most committed are already inside the damn police station!'

'We have to try,' implored Ingrid. He reluctantly nodded in agreement.

We pored over a map of Ork, Eddie keen to see how best to employ the contents of his rucksack. The fuel and ammunition dumps appeared obvious targets but could not be attacked easily with so few of us. So, gradually, our attention drifted towards the town itself. My brother chewed a nail and offered a suggestion. 'I figure our best chance is to create a diversion that isn't obviously an act of sabotage.' Everyone looked at him in puzzlement.

'Like what?' asked Ingrid.

'Well,' he said, 'for example, why not set fire to some

buildings in town? Preferably where there's the risk of it spreading. In fact, the bigger the blaze the better.' He pointed at the map. 'That church is built of wood. And it's right in the centre of town.'

The house of God!

'Sacrilege,' muttered Hilda Straum.

I detected a gasp of incredulity at what my brother had proposed and I fully expected his idea to be dismissed out of hand. And I think it would have been had not Uncle Heimar said something I thought to be quite profound. 'A church can easily be replaced,' he said, 'but not a family, not Norwegian souls.'

I think the recognition of her grandson's plight forced Hilda to swallow any further protest. Naturally we sought an alternative target, but sadly nothing leaped out at us from the map. Our eyes kept returning to the church. The church it had to be.

'The incendiaries will work best,' said Eddie.

'I'll help you lay them,' Heimar added.

Kate had remained in the background as we plotted and she looked increasingly ill at ease. 'What's the matter?' I asked.

'If we succeed in freeing the men at the police station, there will be reprisals,' she said. 'I fear for us all. Remember what happened last year in Telavåg? They sent everyone to the camps and then torched the town. And men died. All for killing a couple of Germans. It doesn't bear thinking about.' Her eyes glistened.

What a dilemma. She was right, of course. Hilda

rubbed Kate's shoulder comfortingly but said nothing. I looked first at Uncle Heimar and then at Ingrid, expecting one of them to lay before us the justification, the solution to that most awful of equations. The truth left me feeling hollow. Neither way could we win. Do nothing and Jan and his fellow Jøssings would face execution. Liberate them and an equally horrid fate might befall the good people of Ork. The enormity crushed me and I had to sit down, glum-faced. Any sense that we were trying to do something brave or heroic vanished from me. It boiled down to a simple fact. We were deciding who would live and who would die – or, at the very least, who would suffer most at Fritz's hands. And what crippled me inside, what knotted my guts and made me feel sick, was that all these people were Norwegians, my fellow countrymen, most undoubtedly Jøssings. I realized this most difficult of equations had no satisfactory solution. Yet, most tellingly, no one spoke up against the plan. We had made our judgement and I wondered if our souls would be damned.

Hilda, though physically frail, appeared to have a full set of marbles. 'You do realize,' she said, 'that Jan won't leave these shores? He returned from England to fight the occupation and lead the Resistance.'

I recalled what Jan had said to me that first night we'd met at the farmhouse: that indeed he intended to stay whatever his fate, and I decided that Hilda knew her grandson well.

'They'll head for the mountains,' she added. 'They know how to survive where most men would fail.'

Uncle Heimar stood up. 'I'll round up as many as I can,' he said. 'And I'll ask them to bring extra pairs of skis, spare clothing and supplies. If you're right, Hilda, then Jan and his men will need them. We'll assemble here tonight.' He turned to Eddie. 'What time?'

'Six o'clock,' Eddie replied. 'Let's aim to set the diversion for seven, which means the raid on the police station can probably be carried out about eight. That should leave enough time for the rest of us to get to the rendezvous at midnight.'

Uncle Heimar's face bore a determined look as he pulled on his anorak and gloves. 'In the meantime,' said Ingrid, just as he was about to leave, 'we'll finalize our plan for the police station.'

The back door to the safe house clicked shut and Ingrid bolted it after Heimar. I tugged at Eddie's arm. 'What about Father?'

'One thing at a time, Marek.' He poured some coffee and settled down next to my brother at the table. He looked at him. 'This is important, Olaf. Do you think Marek stands a chance? Can we really steal an ambulance?'

My brother hesitated a moment, a moment in which he clawed at his blond locks, picked between his teeth and gazed at me. I felt as if I were undergoing some sort of examination. 'A chance, yes,' he replied. 'I can't say more than that. Luck will need to be on our side.'

'That's good enough for me,' declared Eddie. 'Ingrid, what about you? Are you coming to Lunna Voe with us?'

'No, Eddie. My place is here. I'll lead the raid on the police station with Heimar. You just concentrate on getting to that boat.'

Eddie nodded first to Olaf and then to me. 'Just us then.'

'And Father!' I added.

'And your father,' he replied. 'Our success will lie in our timing. We must leave town at the height of the confusion, not a moment before and not a moment after.'

Giddy with anticipation, I already pictured myself on the *Sola*, sailing towards the craggy shores and skerries of Shetland.

'I think it's a good idea to do some reconnaissance,' said Olaf. 'We should make sure we know exactly where they park the ambulances and whether any guards are sited nearby. Come on, Marek, wipe that silly grin off your face, we've got serious work to do. And there's not much time.'

Chapter Twenty-two

'I wonder what England's like?' said my brother.

'Don't know,' I replied. 'At least it doesn't stay dark for months on end, not even as far north as the Shetlands. Although that's Scotland, of course.'

'I like it already, Marek. And I've come to a decision. I'm going to get them to train me, like Jan. You know, in all that secret stuff. Then I'm going to take the first bus home and kick Fritz's arse all the way back to Bavaria.' He sparked up a cigarette and sucked on the tip defiantly.

'Me too,' I declared. I braced myself, expecting him to shoot me down, to say I was too young, that the authorities would never entertain such a request. I knew it was true, of course, and it hurt inside. But he did not destroy my dream or laugh at me; instead he handed me his cigarette so I could take a puff of sweet tobacco. I felt taller and imagined that the British authorities might just make an exception in my case. After all, I already had some experience!

We scuffed along the streets, heading for the hospital. For the first time I noticed some shopkeepers had made an effort to bring festive Christmas cheer to our oppressed country: improvised decorations, home-made paper chains and old tinsel hung in the windows. The occasional candle glowed from within. Yet such rare treats could not hold my attention for long. Nor could the many troops mingling with us natives. I found myself drawn to gazing skywards. It had begun to snow, and heavily too. The ice wind from the north flexed its grip, blustering down the street in waves that shoved my back and bit deep into my skin. I tightened my anorak hood around my face.

'Blizzard's setting in,' I moaned. 'Quite a storm. Hope the road stays open, otherwise we're in big trouble.'

'Better make sure we take our skis, just in case, then,' Olaf replied.

Skulking in the shadows of a narrow alleyway opposite the hospital, we watched the comings and goings for a while. When not in use, the ambulances were parked down one side of the main building. Luckily, as far as we could tell, the area appeared unguarded.

'Splendid,' I said in English, having caught Eddie's favourite word like a cold. 'They're close to the side entrance. I reckon I can get one started without drawing attention.'

My brother's teeth chattered noisily. 'I hope you're right, Marek. Come on, I'm freezing my manhood off out here. Let's get back.'

Approaching Café Fransk, I saw no lights from within. I wondered if it had been wise for Uncle Heimar to shut the place while he went about organizing men for the evening's raid. Surely Fritz would be suspicious. In the midst of fretting about it, I spotted Kate heading our way.

'Just going to open up,' she said. 'Want a coffee or beer?'

My brother required no further encouragement, the sparkle in her eyes merely hastening his step as he followed her inside. She poured two beers.

'Here's to us all,' said my brother, raising his glass high into the air. 'To brave men and women who've sacrificed so much in the name of freedom. May tonight bring us success. *Skål!*'

'*Skål!*' We banged our glasses together.

I settled at a table as Kate began readying the place for opening. I gazed through the window at the towns-folk milling past, their faces lit by ghostly lamplight, while my brother's eyes followed Kate around the café. I think he was going all soft and mushy over her. I can always tell when that happens because he fixes a stare with an unsettling, lost-looking, lustful glaze to his blue eyes. About to berate him for such impure thoughts at Agnete's expense, I refrained because I didn't really blame him. In fact, I forgave him. After all, I realized that within a single day our fate would be determined. Either we'd be well on our way to safe shores, or dead! I could see no middle ground. Capture didn't bear thinking about. No, I decided, I'd rather be dead. Slowly the con-sequences of failure dawned and drained me of all confidence. My simple plan had become a sheer cliff face, an impossible climb. I had a bad feeling and couldn't shake it off. 'Olaf?'

'What, Marek?'

'Are you scared of dying?'

'What the hell are you on about? Don't think about such things.'

'Can't help it.'

He peered into my face with surprise. 'Think about all we've been through in the last few months. It's a strange time to start worrying about dying.'

'I know, but are you scared?'

'Of course I'm scared. If I said I wasn't, I'd be lying. But,' he said, leaning forward and jabbing a finger hard into my sweater, 'it's irrelevant! We can only try our best and hope it's enough. So swallow your fear and lock it away, somewhere deep inside, somewhere it won't trouble you.'

I swallowed hard but my fear lodged in my throat and wouldn't budge. I gulped my beer, hoping to dislodge it.

Later, when stepping outside, I took several deep breaths of clear Norwegian air, knowing they might be among my last. 'Olaf?'

'What now?'

'Do you think Doctor Haskveld will get our letter soon?'

'Expect so.'

'I wonder how Mother is.'

'I've been thinking about her too.' He stopped and grabbed my arm. 'I've just had an idea. There's a public telephone in the *postkontor*. I'm going to try and call him.'

Back in Ulfhus, apart from the Germans, only half a dozen people owned telephones. Dr Haskveld was one of them. We had not dared contact him in this way before because we knew that few conversations were private. Usually either Fritz or the operator listened in and made notes. But now I figured we had nothing to lose. To know Mother was safe would make the difficult times easier to bear.

'Best not draw too much attention to ourselves, Marek. You head back to the safe house. I'll go and make the call.'

'But I want to listen in.'

'Do as you're told, Marek. And no arguing for once.'

I felt lightness in my stride as I headed back to the house. Entering through the back door, I was greeted with caution by half a dozen unfamiliar faces. Uncle Heimar had gathered his volunteers and Ingrid appeared to be in the midst of briefing them. Against a wall rested dozens of skis, rucksacks and weapons. 'Where's Eddie?'

'He's upstairs preparing his Imber switches,' said Uncle Heimar.

I found him crouched in the attic. 'What are you doing?'

'Small addition to our plan, Marek. Heimar and one of his nephews will see to the incendiaries at the church. He asked me if I might add to the confusion by derailing a train as it enters the station.'

'But your arm!'

'I'll manage.'

'But we've got to escape. You heard Ingrid. She said we had to focus on getting to the rendezvous.'

'I know, but I figure they've got their work cut out. The more Germans tied up with our diversions the better. You do realize Ingrid and Heimar's chances are fifty-fifty at best?'

To be honest, I hadn't realized. In fact, concerned only with rescuing Father, I hadn't bothered to think through the rest of the plan. I saw Eddie had made up his mind. 'I'll help you,' I offered. 'We'll both help you. Anyway, we must stick together this evening.'

He glanced up. 'Thanks. Where is Olaf anyway?'

I explained and then set to work holding the package of explosives steady while Eddie connected an Imber switch. 'I remember what you told me about how this works,' I said. 'Raise the telescopic rod until it touches the underside of the rail. Listen – when we get to the railway, just point to where you want it laid, and leave the rest to me.'

About half an hour later my brother returned. I ran over to him expectantly. 'Olaf, what did Doctor Haskveld say? Is Mother all right? Where is she?'

'Calm down, Marek. Couldn't get through. Tried several times too. And the operator was sure she'd found the right number. She said it was often a problem, especially if the weather's bad.'

What a letdown. I felt as deflated as a popped balloon

and was intent on having a good sulk. Olaf looked pretty fed up too. Wanting to be alone, I slipped quietly into a back room and sat in darkness. Would I ever find out whether she was safe? I thought of my words to Father. 'Mother's safe,' I'd said. Those few precious words had stoked his dwindling life force like kindling on the dying embers of a fire. But was it true? He wouldn't forgive me for lying.

'There you are, Marek.' Eddie ruffled my hair with his one functioning hand. 'Come on, time to go. Collect up your things. By the way, I got one of the volunteers to give your skis an extra waxing for good measure, just in case. Let's hope we won't need them. And I've put those extra clothes into my rucksack like you asked.'

I looked at my watch – six-thirty. I'd been sitting alone in the darkness for an hour. It had felt like five minutes. Downstairs the air buzzed and crackled with activity and trepidation. Uncle Heimar and his nephew had already gone to lay the incendiaries at the church. Ingrid marshalled her troops, a rather motley-looking bunch, quietly running over the plan again and again until all were certain of their roles. Following Eddie, I picked up my skis and headed towards the door, stopping to thank and say farewell to old Hilda Straum. Eddie, meanwhile, seized Ingrid in a tight, lingering clasp. He whispered something to her, his lips pressed to her ear. She hugged Olaf and then it was my turn. As I drew close to her, I saw the birth of tears in the corners.

of her eyes. Those were the first tears I'd seen from her. Despite them, she smiled at me, a smile that came naturally and filled her face.

'Take care, young Marek,' she said quietly, straightening the collar of my anorak. 'Rely on those wits of yours – they've served you well. One day I feel sure we'll meet again, and I think we'll have many mighty good stories to share by the light of a fire.'

'Good hunting,' I said, my voice an emotional, uncontrollable tremble. As she broke free, I had one final question on my lips. 'What will you do with Harald when you find him?'

'That's not up to me,' she replied. 'But unless he's got a damn good reason for his betrayal, I think he can expect the ultimate penalty. It will be Jan's decision.'

As Eddie led the way out, I reckoned Harald's days were indeed numbered: Jan had never struck me as being particularly merciful.

Heading down the street, I turned and took one last look back at the safe house. I promised myself that one day, when the war was won and the people of Norway were free, I'd return.

Chapter Twenty-three

Damn it! I thought positioning the Imber switch would be the easy bit. But digging a hole beneath the rail proved harder than I had expected. I couldn't see a blasted thing.

'Deeper, Marek. Come on, hurry up. God, you're slower than an arthritic snail.'

My brother's impatience was not helping matters. We had both crawled from the cover of bushes and slithered on our bellies the twenty feet or so until we reached the precise place Eddie had pointed to. The shiny surface of the rail glistened. Beneath it, I dug furiously with my gloved hands to fashion a hole large enough to hide the taped-up lump of plastic explosive attached to the Imber.

'Here, let me try.' Olaf pushed me to one side and set about finishing the job. He pressed the explosives into the hole. 'That'll have to do.'

I scratched some stones back to hide our work. 'Shall I set the Imber now?'

'Yes! For God's sake, get on with it, Marek.'

I positioned the Imber switch directly under the track and pulled up the telescopic rod until it touched the underside of the rail. I double-checked its positioning and made sure it was firmly in place. 'Done!'

'You sure?'

'Of course.'

Hastily we retreated back to the bushes where Eddie was hiding. 'Well done, lads. Now let's get the hell out of here.'

The blizzard showed no let-up, the frenzied swirling of flakes reducing visibility to a few yards even in the best-lit streets of town. Few others trod the pavements in such awful weather. I thought that was just as well because the fronts of our anoraks were filthy from all our crawling about and might attract unwelcome attention. Strangely I did not feel the biting cold. Instead I felt oddly euphoric, light-headed and invincible. My skis felt weightless on my shoulders and I had a spring in my step. We had just completed the first part of the night's mission. The next train into Ork was in for one hell of a big surprise. Eddie had adjusted the Imber to detonate immediately when a locomotive rolled over it. And we'd positioned it just a few hundred yards from the station.

'Do you think it'll be a shipment of munitions?' I asked. I imagined the destructive consequences of such good fortune.

'Let's hope so,' said Eddie.

'And not a train carrying Norwegians,' I added.

'This is war,' spat Olaf. 'Any bloody train will do!'

My brother appeared not to share my crisis of conscience. In fact, he bore the look of someone raging inside, his jaw protruding unnaturally far and his teeth grinding. Not wishing to experience his wrath first hand, I decided it best not to ask what was nagging him. We marched through town, along empty, desolate streets. Beyond the rooftops I saw rising smoke. Tapping Eddie on the shoulder, I said, 'Look, it's begun. That must be the church.' We quickened our pace.

A tall figure suddenly stepped out of the shadows of a doorway. 'Halt! Papers.' We froze. The wretched soldier looked chilled to the bone and keen to relieve the boredom of a routine patrol. His eyes narrowed. 'Papers!' he bawled again angrily and twice as loudly. I reached into my pocket. While we fumbled for our identity cards, I saw him peer at our grubby anoraks with more than a hint of suspicion.

'What's in the rucksack?' he barked at Eddie.

'Just clothes,' I replied. I did my little act of petulance, shivering, cursing and stomping my feet. Unfortunately on this occasion Fritz seemed unimpressed and remained intent on inconveniencing us. Eddie had put some clothes I'd found for Father into his rucksack – a pair of trousers, a warm sweater and a windproof jacket. I figured Father might be rather glad of them. But mixed in with these innocent items Eddie had a couple of time pencils and enough plastic to demolish a small house or blow Fritz's tin helmet all the way to Finland.

'Let me see,' the soldier snorted, beckoning with an outstretched hand.

Slowly Eddie slid his rucksack from his shoulders. I cast Olaf a fretful glance. His face paled to the colour of chalk and his eyes bored hatefully into the soldier. Eddie held out his rucksack with his one good arm. Fritz barked, 'Open it!'

Eddie rested the rucksack precariously on a raised knee and began loosening the straps. My brain whirling in overdrive, I reached into my anorak pocket and felt the cold handle of my revolver. I gripped it tightly and waited for the moment when the soldier discovered our stash. I told myself I'd have to shoot him. There was no other way. I'd have to pull the trigger. I wondered if I'd actually be able to do it, and somehow doubted it. Maybe I could shoot him in the foot. Maybe just threatening him would be enough. Perhaps Eddie would think of something. My brother appeared frozen to the spot. I wanted to yell at him to do something. Rivulets of sweat trickled down my neck like the start of the spring thaw. Eddie remained perfectly calm.

'The church!' cried Olaf suddenly. He grabbed the soldier and yanked him round to face the opposite way. He pointed. 'The bloody church is on fire. Look!'

We all looked. What a distraction! Uncle Heimar and his nephew had done us proud. The sky glowed orange and, as we watched in awe, we saw the first flickering flames lick the outside of the tall spire.

'Quick,' shouted my brother. 'Get help.' He gave the soldier an encouraging shove.

The soldier looked bewildered. My brother grabbed his arm again and shook him violently. 'Go on. Get help.' The soldier tore himself free and nervously took a step back. He reached for the rifle strapped across his shoulder. Without hesitation, my brother lunged forward, grabbed hold of him and pressed him back into the shadowy recess of the doorway. I heard a scuffle, a muffled cry and brief groan. It all happened in the blink of an eye. Then Olaf backed away. The soldier slid down to the ground, his limbs and head limp. My brother put his bloodied hunting knife back into his pocket. I couldn't speak or breathe. I saw only hatred in Olaf's eyes, hatred in its purest form, cold as ice diamonds and without remorse. Who was this standing before me? Could it really be the same brother as the one I thought I knew, the one who'd wanted to study medicine and dedicate his life to helping his fellow man? It felt odd, as if I didn't quite recognize him, as if he were some stranger.

'Well done,' said Eddie coolly, like one soldier to another. He slapped my brother's back. 'Come on, best not hang around.'

As the church's timbers crackled and spat, men, women and children emerged from houses screaming and shouting, and soldiers ran in all directions. Panic had arrived and settled in the town of Ork. We fought our way through the growing mêlée, first Olaf then Eddie breaking into a slithering, unsteady jog on the icy pavements. I soon became breathless trying to keep up and, on reaching the hospital, had to bend double and gasp while clawing at a tight stitch in my side.

'Hear that?' cried Olaf.

I had. The hooting whistle sounded distant but I knew the panic around us would soon be raised to a whole new hideous level. And when the explosion came a minute later, it lit the sky and flung burning debris into the streets like a storm of meteors. The locomotive had been blown into a million pieces. People milled around in utter bewilderment while soldiers yelled, their faces lit with fear.

'Splendid,' said Eddie. 'Let's not waste time. You two get inside the hospital and fetch your father. I'll wait outside and keep an eye on the ambulances.'

We hurried across the street and headed for the hospital's side entrance. I could feel blood pulsing around my body and my mouth felt parched. Eddie slipped into the shadows between two of the ambulances. 'Right,' said Olaf, 'let's do this as quickly as we can. And pray nobody spots us. Lead the way, Marek.'

I ran to the side door and punched it open. 'Up these stairs,' I said, pointing. We scaled them three at a time, our feet hammering heavily on the stone steps, our climb echoing to the top of the stairwell. 'Along here, fourth or fifth door on the right.'

Skidding to a halt upon reaching room 2.09, I burst in and switched on the light. 'Father, it's Marek. Get up.' I ran and tore back the blankets. 'Wake up, Father.'

Olaf stepped towards the bed cautiously. I think he found seeing Father rather shocking, just as I had the previous night. Disorientated, Father blinked and squinted at me. 'Marek?' he croaked sleepily.

322

'Yes, it's me. And Olaf's here this time. Look.' I pointed towards the end of the bed and Father turned his head.

'Olaf! My God. I didn't dare believe—'

'There's no time to chat, Father. Here, put these clothes on. Quickly. Olaf and I will help you.'

We managed to dress Father's feeble frame as he mumbled questions that we ignored. We got him to stand up and only then realized how weak he was. The TB had sucked the strength from him. 'You'll have to help him, Olaf. Put his arm round your shoulder.'

Two thumps in quick succession, each sounding like distant thunder, preceded the pops and cracks of gunfire. 'They've begun the attack,' I said. 'We must hurry.'

We made it to the bottom of the stairs and had just turned towards the exit when a voice shouted, 'What the hell do you think you're doing?' I turned and saw Dr Klose standing outside his office doorway, hands on hips, stethoscope draped like an asp around his neck. He strode purposefully towards us. 'You!' he bellowed. 'I thought I said I never wanted to set eyes on you again.' He shook his head at me, glanced at Olaf and settled his gaze on Father. 'You can't just walk in here . . .' he added, pausing in his stride. He bit his lip and nodded as if he suddenly understood everything. 'Ah! Your father, I suppose.'

'Yes,' I replied.

'Well, you can't take him out of here. He's too sick. I simply won't allow it.'

'We haven't got time to debate the matter,' said my brother.

'I'll summon the guards,' threatened the doctor.

My brother took his revolver from his pocket and pointed it towards Dr Klose. The doctor stood his ground. My brother raised the stakes by cocking the hammer. Still he did not yield.

'Wait!' I shouted. 'This is madness. Don't shoot, Olaf, he's a Jøssing.' I ran in between them. 'Listen, Doctor, we're taking him somewhere safe, somewhere a long, long way away. It's best if you just turn round and walk away. Forget you ever saw us. Please.'

He regarded me sternly.

'Please!' I pleaded. 'My brother will shoot you if he has to,' I added, including for good measure an over-dramatic emphasis on the 'will'. 'But that's not what any of us wants. And anyway, the people of Ork are going to need you. Hear those shots? The war has come to this town and the wounded will be arriving shortly.'

Dr Klose absorbed my words. I think I detected the precise moment he connected what I'd said with the cracks and pops drifting in from outside, because his expression suddenly changed. 'Oh, dear God,' he said through a clenched jaw. He turned and ran quickly the opposite way, towards the hospital's main entrance, where the injured would arrive.

Outside, Olaf helped Father and Eddie into the back

of an ambulance and loaded up our skis while I crept to the front, slipped open the driver's door just enough, and wedged myself between the driver's seat and the steering wheel. I ran my fingers under the dashboard in search of the wires. My brother climbed into the passenger seat. 'Need a hand?'

'Here, hold this torch while I strip the wires.' I passed him a small torch I'd liberated from a drawer in the safe house.

I know what I'm doing, I kept telling myself. *Cut the wires, strip off the insulation, touch together the right pair and the engine will spring miraculously into life.* The theory was crystal clear in my mind, just as if I had the manual in front of my eyes. My haste got the better of me, however, and I was all fingers and thumbs.

My brother did little to settle my nerves. 'Get a move on, Marek,' he hissed. 'The Germans will be here any minute. We're running out of time.'

'Shut up. I'm going as fast as I can!'

I caught the last of the wires between my finger and the blade of my knife and pulled to strip off the insulation. 'Hold that damn torch still, will you?' I complained. 'I can't see what I'm doing.'

'I am holding it still, you elk.'

'No you're not.'

'Yes I am. See, as steady as a rock.'

A partition between the front seats and the rear of the ambulance slid open and Eddie's head poked through. 'Just concentrate on the job. You can argue about it later.'

I brought the bare ends of the two copper wires together. They sparked, fizzed and crackled, and the starter motor turned. She spluttered into life. I pressed a hand onto the accelerator and revved her. Olaf squeezed across into the driver's seat and I ran round the front and hauled myself into the passenger's side. My brother settled his hands on the steering wheel to get the feel of her, then switched on the headlights and selected first gear. 'Ready?' he shouted.

'Ready,' I cried.

'England, here we come!' he yelled, and we lurched forwards.

Eddie reappeared. 'Find the switch for the bell. Let everyone know we're in a hurry.'

My brother's driving showed no signs of improvement and I wondered just how much grinding the gears could withstand. He swung us round a corner and we belted up Ork's main street, our bell clanging frantically to clear the way. 'Straight ahead,' I said. 'At the end we turn left towards the shore and then take the last road heading west. It's the one that hugs the fjord.'

'I know that, you idiot. Just shut up. I'm trying to concentrate.'

He needed to as well because the road proved slippery and braking didn't seem to have much effect. We caught glimpses of the church and saw men trying to douse the blaze but they were being beaten back by the sheer intensity of the heat, stabbing spear-like flames and falling timbers, each glowing red hot and spewing sparks and embers. Luckily our route did not take us too close to the police station. But I could hear the gunfire and it sounded fierce. I prayed for Ingrid and Heimar, asking that they'd liberate Jan and make their escape to the safety of the mountains, and that having done so they'd deliver justice to Harald.

Eddie lodged himself in the gap behind the front seats. 'How's Father?' I asked.

'He's fine. I've put an extra blanket around him.'

My brother accelerated hard and cursed the vehicle's lumpy handling. I peered through the windscreen at the mayhem gripping Ork and couldn't help but marvel at my plan unfolding like a perfect dream. Eddie was right, I thought. An ambulance was unlikely to get stopped at a time like this. Glancing at my watch — eight-thirty — I saw that we also had plenty of time to get to the rendezvous. I berated myself for ever doubting that we could do it. *Of course we can!* I shouted inside. *We're the Resistance. This is what we do!*

Through the swirl of wet flakes I saw a figure standing in the middle of the road waving frantically at us. My brother slammed his foot on the brake pedal and we skidded. Instantly I recognized the black leather coat and puny frame. 'Jesus, it's Herr Stretter of the Gestapo,' I cried.

'What?'

'It's him! Don't stop, Olaf.'

'Damn right.' He thumped his foot back down on the accelerator.

I observed a moment's hesitation in Herr Stretter and then a look of alarm as it dawned on him that we had no intention of stopping – quite the contrary, in fact. He leaped towards the pavement.

'What are you doing, Olaf?' I shouted. My brother had spun the steering wheel to the left to maintain a perfect heading to run the horrid little Nazi down. 'Are you crazy?'

With a thump, the ambulance lurched and bounced, rocked and pitched wildly. We had not struck Olaf's intended target, but had unfortunately become acquainted with a raised kerbstone. The ambulance spun a full quarter turn and stopped. My brother crunched the gears and hit the accelerator again. We slid and squirmed as the tyres searched for grip, the coarse engine howling at full revs. I heard a shot and the ping of its ricochet. Fearing another, I sank low into my seat. The engine's vibration shook my bones. The tyres whined on the ice. I thought we'd met our end. But just as the idea of capture took hold of my wits, we began to make headway and then accelerated quickly. I slid open the side window and risked peering out. Looking back along the street, I saw Herr Stretter pointing at us and barking orders to nearby soldiers.

'What the hell did you do that for?' I cried.

'I saw an opportunity,' replied my brother.

'Idiot! We should have just concentrated on getting out of here. He might have recognized me.'

'So what?'

Eddie reappeared from the back of the ambulance looking a little shaken. 'I expect we'll have company,' he said. 'Better put your foot down, Olaf.'

No way could we outrun them, I thought. I imagined an entire division of the Wehrmacht bearing down on us, closing in and surrounding us, our lives ending abruptly the moment the ambulance was drilled by a thousand bullets. I shivered and rubbed my belly. I was chilled to the bone and my guts hurt as if pricked by the ice needles of an unwelcome hoarfrost. 'What can we do, Eddie? I'm scared.'

'Just keep going. I'll think of something.' He disappeared into the back of the ambulance again.

I removed my revolver from my pocket. I didn't know what I was going to do with it, but I just felt better having it in my grasp. We tore down the street towards the shore of the fjord, directly into the full force of the blizzard, the huge white flakes smacking into the windscreen and settling. I didn't know how Olaf could tell where the road ended and the pavement began. In fact, I could hardly see more than twenty yards ahead.

'Slow down!' I shouted. 'We mustn't pass the turning.'

'Shut up,' he bellowed. 'I know what I'm doing.'

To give credit where it's due, he did somehow figure out where the turning was and we cornered sharply onto the narrow road hugging the fjord. Within minutes Ork lay behind us.

'That's much better,' said my brother.

'What is?'

'No one's been this way for a while. Snow's undisturbed. Makes driving easier. Is Fritz behind us?'

I knew the answer to that question without even taking a look. Of course they were in pursuit. Eddie reappeared behind my left shoulder.

'Marek, take hold of this,' he said, dropping something heavy into my lap.

I seized it and recognized it – a time pencil, attached to a lump of plastic explosive. 'What's this for?'

'Screw in the end of the pencil. Quickly now. I'm doing the same with the other one.'

Fumbling with it, I located the end containing the threaded screw. I tried turning it but it proved stiff. Tearing off my gloves, I tried again.

'Make sure it goes all the way in, Marek.'

The screw proved stubborn but eventually yielded. It suddenly seemed very loose. 'Eddie, I think I've broken it. It's turning too easily.'

'No, that's fine. The screw loosens once the ampoule breaks inside. Just keep on turning it until it stops. That way it won't leak. Then give it a little shake for good luck.'

I did as ordered and an awful thought struck me. 'Eddie?'

'Yes, Marek?'

'We've just activated these, haven't we?'

'Yes.'

'Couldn't they go off at any time?'

'The pencils have a ten-minute delay, so don't worry.'

I glanced at my watch and made an extremely care-ful note of the time – eight forty-seven and thirty seconds. And then I remembered the conversation on our first night aboard the *Sola*. Eddie had admitted that the delays were only approximate! I desperately wanted to chuck the device out of the window. 'Eddie, what now? I'm kind of nervous.'

'Just hold on tightly and don't drop it. Olaf, keep your eyes peeled for a bridge. I think I remember seeing one on Jan's map. Stop when you get to it.'

The road snaked along the shoreline of the fjord, rising and falling as it twisted and turned to match the complex contours of the rock. One moment I could see through the blizzard to the black expanse of water, the next just granite either side of us. The water reappeared and then it vanished again. Jan had told us about the winding road but it was unfamiliar territory. So when we came to a short wooden bridge dripping with icicles and saw beyond it that the road forked, none of us knew for sure which way was best. Once across the bridge, Olaf braked and we skidded to a stop.

'Right,' said Eddie, 'hand me those explosives.'

I gladly obliged.

'Be back in a minute.' He tumbled out of the ambulance and ran onto the bridge, stopping halfway across to plant explosives on either side.

'Right, Olaf, get a move on,' he shouted as he clambered back in.

We snaked forward, accelerating fast and, as the fork

drew nearer, I sensed uncertainty in my brother. 'Go right!' I cried.

'No, left is better!' he shouted. He spun the steering wheel but it was too late. The ambulance appeared to have a mind of its own and refused to respond. I shut my eyes and screamed.

Chapter Twenty-four

I suppose it could have turned out worse. The ambulance ploughed into a snowdrift, lifting slightly on impact. I was thrown forward and my nose smacked the windscreen. I heard a crack, felt sudden agonizing pain like I'd never felt before and, falling back into my seat, tasted the sharp silver of blood in my mouth. The engine stalled and, slowly, we began sinking into the drift.

'Jesus!' cried Eddie. 'What the hell—? You both OK?'

Olaf sat motionless, staring straight ahead. I think he was in shock. Neither of us replied to Eddie.

'Try reversing!' he shouted. My brother didn't react. 'Come on, hurry up.'

I thumped Olaf's shoulder to snap him from his trance. He turned, glared at me and then thumped me back, and pretty hard too. Then he pressed his eyes shut, sighed heavily and said, in a remarkably calm tone, 'OK, how do I get this thing running again?'

Eddie climbed out of the back and kicked his way through the snow to the front of the ambulance. Leaning his good shoulder against the bonnet, he tried pushing. I reached down for the wires, fumbling for them in the darkness.

'It's no good, she's stuck fast,' barked Eddie.

'Everybody out. We'll have to ski the rest of the way. Let's just hope your father can make it.'

I dug a handkerchief from my pocket and pressed it against my nose to stem the flow of blood. I wiped the tears of pain from my eyes with my forearm. Olaf unloaded the skis and helped Father.

Although we could not see our pursuers, we could hear them. Motorcycle engines rumbled menacingly in the night air and they were closing in on us, revving and growling like a pack of starving wolves. I hurriedly fixed my boots to the bindings of my skis and ignored my throbbing face. Father shivered and looked somewhat bewildered. I couldn't see him lasting long in the blizzard, as each gust of the ice wind stole a little of his feeble strength. What had I done? I had dreamed up this crazy plan. *Me!* No one else. That earlier feeling I'd had, that premonition of doom, now resurfaced and grabbed me by the scruff of my neck and shook me to the core.

Eddie scanned the terrain. I don't know what he hoped to see but the blizzard meant he saw very little. Olaf took Father by the arm. 'I'll ski beside Father to make sure he's OK,' he shouted. 'If we go left' – he hesitated and scowled at me – 'if we go *left*, I think the road takes us to Jan's parents' farmhouse. We can hole up there until nearer midnight. There's no way Father can stay out in this weather.'

'Agreed,' Eddie shouted. 'You all go ahead. I'll follow and keep an eye out.'

Our progress proved painfully slow. For once I wasn't

the weakest link. Eddie, not the finest skier in the world, had difficulty with just one usable arm and one ski pole. But he fought to make headway with purpose and infinite determination. His soldiering skills and strength stood him in good stead. Seeing him, I thought of Tyr, the god of war, son of Odin, the bravest of the gods, a god who sacrificed one hand so that the evil giant Fenris Wolf could be bound to a rock and subdued.

My brother had to drag Father like a dead weight. We headed along the left fork, the road quickly rising up the mountainside. All the while the wolves were gaining on us. I could see the sparkle of their eyes through the blizzard as they snaked along the road below us. They weren't far behind. My brother paused for breath. I slid back and stopped at his side. 'Need a hand?'

Father's head hung low and he coughed and spluttered, his frothy spittle dripping from his bottom lip. He did not stand straight and tall like the man I'd known all my life in Ulfhus. He looked bent and broken. 'Take his left arm,' my brother panted. 'I think we're close to a ridge. After that the going will get easier. It should be downhill all the way to the farmhouse. Least, that's how I remember Jan describing the road when we skied into Ork the first time.'

I looked at my watch – eight fifty-nine. More than ten minutes had passed. 'Eddie, something's wrong with those time pencils. They should have gone off by now.'

He shrugged. 'Might be the cold. The wire inside might take a little longer than usual to dissolve.'

I hoped he was right.

We reached what seemed like the crest of the hill and paused to take stock. The ice wind howled and jostled us, the hoods of our anoraks flapping about our faces, the snow stinging our eyes. My brother pointed a ski pole into the darkness and said, 'Quickest way is across country. I reckon a mile shorter than by road. Are you all up to it?'

'Are you sure of the way?' I asked. My brother raised a fist. 'All right, I believe you! Across country it is then.'

Eddie's plastic detonated with two sharp cracks in quick succession, each preceded by a bright white flash. We all gazed back down the hill. The bridge lay out of sight so we just had to hope the explosives had done enough and that Fritz had got stuck on the wrong side.

'Come on,' said Olaf. 'Father's on his last legs.'

We broke off from the road and headed in the direction Olaf had pointed. The snow lay three feet deep, four in places, dry and powdery, and our skis sank every time we slowed. I noticed Eddie grimacing in discomfort. 'You OK?' I called out.

He nodded. 'Banged my arm when we crashed.'

Father collapsed in a heap. Olaf tugged at his jacket, desperate to lift him. 'Is he conscious?' I shouted, dropping to my knees. I cleared snow from his face and rubbed his cheeks. 'Father, get up. It's not far now. Come on, get up.' I grabbed hold of his sleeve and pulled but simply fell onto my backside. Together, Olaf and I eventually dragged him to his feet and divided his weight across our shoulders once again. Step by step we pressed on into the full wrath of the biting ice wind, the tips of our skis frequently crossing and causing us to stumble. We were like a drunken chorus line. 'This is going to take years!' I shouted.

'We have no choice,' barked Olaf. 'I don't think it's far to the farmhouse. Just think of warm *lefse*, a roaring fire and hot coffee.'

'Heaven!'

By ten o'clock I'd lost all feeling in my face, my arms and legs and I didn't know how I was able to keep sliding one ski in front of the other. On the bright side, my nose had stopped bleeding. I tried to breathe deeply and slowly to prevent my usual fatigue but kept swallowing snowflakes, which made me cough and splutter. Now and again Eddie dropped back a way to determine if Fritz was on our tail, each time returning with good news. 'No sign of them,' he'd shout. I figured blowing the bridge had halted their advance.

Thankfully the blizzard waned and the terrain's undulations softened. As visibility improved, I saw that we were midway across a relatively flat area of ground bordered by the fjord to my right and mountains to my left. It seemed vaguely familiar. 'Where's the farmhouse?' I shouted.

'Over there,' replied my brother. He swung a ski pole in the general direction of the mountains.

Squinting, I could see only black and grey, a mix of granite and shadows. 'Where exactly?'

'There!'

I took his word for it and we altered course. Father's breathing had grown increasingly laboured, each rasping gasp adding to my worry. I knew he was close to the end of his tether. But he did not complain. In fact, he said nothing. He'd placed his life in our hands, so it was up to us now.

The first time I'd set eyes on the Straums' farmhouse, I thought it was a foreboding place. Maybe it had something to do with the way it hid against the mountainside, most secretively. And its shabby timbers and dripping icicles the length of a man's arm added to its air of desolation. As we approached, I had the same reaction. But then I recalled stepping inside and being greeted by the warmth of a roaring fire and equally generous warmth of the Straums' limitless hospitality. The memory fortified me. I thought it odd, though, that no lights glowed from within.

We slid past the barn and headed for the main farmhouse. Eddie paused. 'I think there might still be some weapons and ammunition hidden in the barn. I'd feel better in possession of something a little more robust than my pistol.'

'I'll go and look,' said Olaf. 'You all get into the house and thaw out.' He removed Father's arm from round his shoulder and I bore Father's full weight until Eddie offered us his good side.

I hammered on the front door of the farmhouse with my fist but got no reply so hammered again. Still no reply. I looked at my watch – half ten – and briefly supposed that the Straums had retired for the night. That would explain the lack of lamplight. About to shout out and knock for a third time, I heard a noise behind me. Assuming it was Olaf, I turned to say something to him.

'Mr Olsen!'

I gasped and my legs instantly turned to jelly. I blinked in disbelief.

'Well, well, well, I must say this is quite a surprise. And young Marek Olsen too. It is Marek, isn't it?' Herr Stretter stood ten yards from us, his nine-millimetre automatic Luger pistol held in a steady hand. He grinned, his razor-thin lips twisting with what I guessed had to be evil thoughts and wicked intent. 'You can knock as loudly and for as long as you like, young man,' he said. 'There's nobody home. We arrested the Straums this morning, along with several others in the valley.'

I spat at him but he just laughed. I scanned around and saw only one other soldier, about ten feet to Stretter's left, his machine gun poised. Surely there had to be others, I thought. But where were they? I wondered if Eddie's time pencils and plastic explosives had dealt with the motorcycles. Or perhaps, with the road forking, they'd split up. The possibility that we faced only Herr Stretter and his sidekick circled inside my head; if only I could think of something, and quickly too.

'I remember our little chat in Odda,' he added. 'You struck me as troublesome even then. I had a suspicion that one day our paths would cross again.'

Father looked at me curiously.

'How did you know we'd come here?' I spat.

'When you headed out of town in this direction, I put two and two together,' he replied. 'We know Jan Straum leads the Resistance here, so I figured his parents' farm would be your obvious destination. I presume you intended to hole up here or make off into the mountains.'

He looked so damn smug; it irritated the pants off me. But I laughed to myself because he hadn't guessed everything. He didn't appear to know about the Shetland Bus and our planned rendezvous. It seemed Harald had not compromised that part of the operation. And evidently Jan had not yet succumbed to interrogation. Herr Stretter began pacing back and forth, his stride commanding and victorious. 'You Norwegians can be quite tiresome at times. Did you really think you could successfully raid our new submarine base?'

The base! That had never been the plan. I caught Eddie's eye and he winked. I felt a flush of bravado. OK, so we'd been captured and our futures looked both short and bleak. But – and it was a very big but – we *had* succeeded in our mission. They didn't know about the accumulators and the platinum pills. Their U-boats would become sitting ducks and our merchant navy would breathe a huge sigh of relief in the North Atlantic. I felt proud. Part of me wanted to taunt the evil little man, to point out our success, to dispel his air of supremacy. Of course, I remained tight-lipped.

'I suppose you were responsible for the mayhem in town this evening too,' he said, casually inspecting his gloves.

Spotting his over-confidence, I slipped my free hand towards my anorak pocket in search of my revolver.

'I wouldn't do that if I were you,' he snapped.

Hastily my hand retreated.

'The people of Ork will not thank you for your efforts. Not when we drag them from their beds, torch their houses and send the men to the labour camps.' He looked up at me and grinned. 'Well, I can't spend all evening chatting like this, much as I'd like to. I think it's time you joined your comrades back at the police station.'

The police station. I wondered how the raid had gone. Would we arrive in defeat or would Stretter be confronted with an empty jail? Father straightened up. He leaned back heavily against the front door and fixed his watery stare on Stretter. 'Let the boy go,' he said. 'He's only fourteen, for God's sake. Do what you will with me. Just let him go.'

Stretter roared and slapped his thigh mockingly. Shaking his head, he tutted loudly and then said sharply, 'You Norwegians need teaching a harsh lesson. The boy will act as a deterrent to others!'

I gulped and hoped for a miracle. The consequences of Harald's treachery had now become very, very personal. I wanted to know what had led him to betray us. 'What sort of deal did you cut with Harald?'

I shouted. 'What cowardly threats did you use to make him reveal our plan?'

Stretter looked puzzled. 'Harald? Harald who?'

'Come on, at least tell us that.'

He remained puzzled and it confused me. He gestured his pistol towards Father. 'Surely you realize,' he said, 'that we first learned of the raid from your father?'

'Liar,' I shouted.

'No, really. He proved most helpful to us. Isn't that right, Mr Olsen?'

I flashed Father a glance. His eyes looked sad, a deep hollow sadness that told me it was true. I stepped away.

'Tell me it's all lies!' I shouted. He did not reply. 'Please, Father, tell me it's a lie.' Even as I repeated my request, my voice faltered as a wave of emotion rolled through me. I felt unsteady.

'I'm sorry, Marek,' he whispered. 'It's true.'

'What?' I yelled. I wanted to punch and kick him. I wanted to strike him hard for every Jøssing who'd suffered because of his weakness. I thought of Jorgen, of Fletcher, of Leif, of Jan and his men, the good people of Ork and Harald. *Harald!* Ingrid had been mistaken. Harald *was* a Jøssing after all. It flashed into my mind that even if the raid in town succeeded, then a great injustice would follow, as Harald would find it difficult to prove his innocence, especially to men convinced of his guilt. 'Do you realize what you've done?' I screamed.

Father's head dipped forward and he stared at the

ground. 'I did it for your mother,' he whispered, his voice broken with emotion. 'And for you as well.'

'What?'

He looked up at me. 'Please, try to understand. When they told me they'd arrested Emma close to the border with Sweden, I despaired. They said that unless I revealed what I knew, she'd be shot, a fate destined for me too. And Stretter said he'd make sure neither you nor Olaf had a future. What could I do?'

Mother arrested! My brain fizzed and I felt sick. 'Mother!'

Father looked towards Stretter. 'He said that if I co-operated, Emma would be released, that they'd leave you alone and send me to a labour camp rather than a firing squad.'

Stretter had begun to lose patience. 'Enough!' he shouted.

The rifle shot broke the night's quiet and echoed around the fjord like a gathering thunderstorm. The soldier bearing the machine gun spun and fell. Startled, we all looked towards the barn, from where I'd seen a flash. My brother advanced towards us from his hiding place, a rifle firmly held to his shoulder, the barrel pointing at Stretter. 'Drop it!' he yelled.

Stretter froze. 'Drop it now,' my brother repeated. Stretter reluctantly let his Luger slip from his fingers. I shall never forget the look of sheer terror on the bastard's face. My brother continued his advance to within a couple of feet and then, in one swift movement, rotated his rifle so that its butt swung upwards to greet Stretter's chin with an audible crack. Stretter yelped like a kicked dog and toppled over. 'But you didn't release my mother, did you?' my brother hissed, staring down at him hatefully.

On the ground, Stretter writhed in agony, nursing his chin with both hands. It took a moment for me to register what Olaf had said. And when it did, a spark of anguish flew through me like the jolt of an electric shock. 'What do you mean, Olaf?' I cried.

As Stretter tried to drag himself to his knees, my brother planted his right boot in the Gestapo's midriff, knocking him back down. 'He sent her to a camp near Oslo.'

I gawped. 'How on earth do you know that?'

'Doctor Haskveld told me.'

'But I thought you didn't get through on the phone.'

'I lied.'

'Why?'

'Didn't want to worry you.'

I felt in freefall, all twisted inside. I reached for my revolver. I wanted to shoot Stretter.

Eddie grabbed my arm. 'We've got to get a move on,' he said. 'It's almost eleven o'clock. We must get to the rendezvous by midnight or else we're stuck here.'

I lowered my pistol and met my brother's stare. 'Eddie's right,' he said. 'Do you want to kill him or shall I?'

'Kill me and your mother will be executed along

with all the people of Ork,' spat Stretter from a bloodied jaw. 'Give yourselves up. I promise we'll be lenient. I have the authority here. I can make it happen. Whatever you Resistance people do, it won't change things. Norway is our country now. It is part of the Reich.'

My father summoned his strength and staggered forward. On his second unsteady step, he reached out and seized a three-foot icicle the shape of a spear dangling from the overhanging roof. It broke away and he held it like a dagger. 'So,' he spoke softly, 'you think this is your country, do you? You think you've defeated us Norwegians? You think we're all just servants of the Reich, do you? Well, Herr Stretter, I have news for you. Our country is a harsh land in which to survive, and we Norwegians are tough people. We shall never yield. And to prove it, I want you to feel how unforgiving both our land and our people can be. You say Norway's your country. Well then, it's about time you experienced some Norwegian ice!'

He lunged forward and sank the frozen dagger deep into Stretter's chest, falling and lying on him until all signs of life had evaporated.

'But Mother!' I cried, imagining that we'd just signed her death warrant.

Eddie grabbed hold of me. 'Marek,' he said, shaking me. 'We had to kill him. They won't know it was us that did it. They'll have no reason to take revenge on your mother. Now, get a hold of yourself, we have to get to the fjord. We haven't got much time.'

★ ★ ★

As Captain Torvic turned the *Sola* about and motored towards the entrance of the fjord and open water, I made for the bow of the boat and sat alone. I had a very odd feeling inside. I'd imagined reaching this far would have left me elated, wanting to repeatedly punch the air in victory. But instead I felt sick, and it wasn't the swaying of the *Sola*. Mother was in a camp. Father had betrayed his fellow Jøssings. Half of me, the rational half, shouted that he'd had no choice. He'd done it with the best of intentions. The other half of me, however, thought of Fletcher, Leif, Ingrid, Jan and the people of Ork. The price seemed high. And what about Harald? Was he to be mistaken for a traitor? God, how awful, how unfair.

'Next stop Lunna Voe,' said Eddie. He leaned on the rigging next to me and stared across at the mountains. 'You OK?'

I nodded. 'I'm going to miss my country,' I said.

'Don't worry, you'll be back soon enough.' He patted my shoulder. 'Listen, don't rush to judge your father. I think the Gestapo caused him great suffering. In fact, you should feel proud of him. It takes courage to act as a messenger for the Resistance. And he managed to hold out right up until they arrested your mother. In his position, I'd have done the same.' Although his tone seemed convincing, I doubted him. After all, he was a soldier, trained and sworn to sacrifice his life for others.

'We just have to be grateful that he only knew the

bare bones of the plan. At the time of his arrest, messages referred only to Ork and the U-boats being our targets. He didn't know that we were actually after the shipment of accumulators. So, it could have turned out worse. I mean, had he been arrested a few weeks later he might have known all the final details.'

I began to cry and couldn't stop, despite desperately wanting to.

'I'm glad our paths crossed, young Marek. I'll never forget what we've been through, and your countrymen owe you a great debt. Here, I want you to have this.'

He pressed his lighter into my hand. 'It's solid silver. I've had it since I was sixteen. Think of me every time you spark its flame. Think of our mission and of all the merchant ships we've saved from a watery grave.'

'Thanks,' I said. 'I will.' I wished I had a gift to give in return. He ruffled my hair and left me to my thoughts.

'Father's sleeping,' said Olaf. He sat down beside me and gazed towards the mountains. 'One day soon, this land will be ours again. How's your nose?'

'Fine,' I said. 'But my shoulder still hurts from that punch you gave me.'

'Sorry.'

'Don't suppose you've got any of those English cigarettes, have you?'

He grinned. 'I just might have a few left!'

Chapter Twenty-five

Three years later

For my seventeenth birthday Mother and Father promised me that they'd pay for me to travel to Ork. I'm looking forward to it. I've not been back since that eventful night when we caught the Shetland Bus. Now that the Nazis have been defeated once and for all, the people of Norway are enjoying their freedom at last. But it's taking quite a while for everyone to adjust.

Having reached Lunna Voe safely, thanks to the skill of Captain Kurt Torvic and his crew, Father got transferred to a TB clinic just north of Edinburgh, Scotland. There, the doctors prescribed heavy doses of fresh air, which meant all the patients' beds got pushed outside almost whatever the weather. He hated every minute of it. He's fully recovered now, thanks to God and the efforts of all the doctors and nurses.

I'll probably never know for sure just how successful we were in crippling Fritz's fleet of U-boats. Many Allied ships still got sunk and many thousands of sailors drowned. I suppose had we failed it would have turned out worse. Success is relative.

I remained mostly at Lunna Voe until the end of

hostilities, working alongside Captain Torvic and Thor Gossen as assistant engineer on the *Sola*. Actually, her real name was the *Waverider*. I accompanied Kurt on several missions during 1944, mostly to collect and drop men and women off on the Lofoten Islands in Norway's far north. It got a bit hairy at times but nothing I couldn't handle. My brother achieved what he'd set his heart on. Arriving in Shetland, he got himself recruited into SOE, the Special Operations Executive, and in May 1944 returned to Norway in the dead of night to wreak havoc on Fritz in preparation for the Allied invasion of mainland Europe. According to his storytelling, his unit caused untold damage to German morale. Finally he made it to Oslo, and has begun training to be a doctor at the university.

I still keep in touch with Eddie Turner, who miraculously survived the war despite being wounded somewhere in Normandy. I think we'll remain close friends for ever.

The raid on Ork's police station succeeded, and Jan, Ingrid and Uncle Heimar made it into the mountains. The good people of Ork suffered greatly afterwards but have now rebuilt their church twice as big.

A couple of months after I returned to Ulfhus we received the sad news that Ingrid had been killed during a raid outside Trondheim just weeks before Fritz finally capitulated. So I guess we'll never get to share our adventures around a roaring fire, and I'll miss that. Still, as I recall Jorgen saying, she's now where she wanted to be, beside her husband once again. In truth, I knew her only briefly, yet she's left an indelible mark on me.

Jan made it though to the bitter end and he's taken over running the Straums' farm. I'll be staying with him for a few days during my visit to Ork. Thankfully Harald came through it all too, and has returned to Kristiansand to carry on the family fishing business. Some while back I wrote to him and apologized that any of us ever doubted he was a Jøssing. I thought it was important that he knew how I felt. You see, with the end of war, you might think everything would return to normal. That's not the case. We true Norwegians, we Jøssings, revile our countrymen who proved to be collaborators and Quislings. Many were arrested, some imprisoned, others shot. As for the rest, well they're openly despised and shunned in the street. I believe in France they even shaved the heads of those collaborators they caught. We haven't gone that far but feel the same in our hearts. It seems forgiveness is thinly spread and rationed like just about everything else. Time is needed to heal the wounds of our nation because the cuts run as deep as the fjords.

In quiet moments I frequently reflect on how life changed so dramatically, so quickly. War revealed hidden sides to people, some remarkable, some good, and some less so. I often wonder how life would have panned out had Lieutenant Wold not been posted to our village. And I remain confused. The enemy had several faces. When I think of Wold or Herr Stretter, I find it easy to feel hatred. Yet, if I picture others, like Hartwig Lauder for instance, I feel a curious fondness. And I can't help sniggering every time I recall that ridiculous moustache. I told Father about his persistence in wanting to buy Josephine. 'How much? What a cheek!' he'd cry, shaking his head. I knew it – what price love?

In my dreams, however, nightmares bring forth images of Jorgen and Fletcher, and of that young soldier at the station, a soldier barely older than me. All I can see is his bulging eyes and the blood on his lips. It jolts me awake in a cold sweat.

Mother and Father don't speak of the war. I think I can understand. For Mother, her period of internment is something she'd rather forget, though of course she never will. I think she struggled to keep her faith. And Father, well, he has moments of deep depression and often goes off walking in search of solitude. I think the war tore him up inside. I worry about him. He was tortured by the Gestapo and had held firm until that day Herr Stretter informed him that Mother had been captured on the border with Sweden. Both their fates rested in Father's hands. My anger has long since gone. I know he did the right thing in impossible circumstances. He had no real choice, despite the consequences, and they were severe. But it all troubles him still. One day I'll try talking to him about it, when I think he's ready.

Guess what? Lars is getting married! To Agnete! Olaf's been invited but I doubt he'll go to their wedding. He told me he doesn't care but I know when he's lying.

As for me, well, I'm going to finish school and become an engineer. I figure I've demonstrated a reasonable aptitude for the job. But I shan't work in Ulfhus. I may go to Bergen or Kristiansand. You see, during those difficult times I dreamed and prayed that the life I'd known could be restored. But that's impossible, of course. Everyone has changed. The world has changed. I've changed. Life's different now and there's simply no going back. War does that.

Postscript

Norway was strategically important to Germany during the Second World War. Its rugged coastline of mountains and fjords offered ideal hiding places for German naval ships and submarines, the U-boats, with easy access to the North Atlantic and the Allied convoys; Admiral Dönitz's infamous U-boat wolf packs hunted down and sank millions of tons of shipping. The northern port of Narvik was also vital in the supply of Swedish iron ore to Germany's thirsty industrial machinery of war.

Without warning, Germany invaded Norway on 9 April 1940. The small, lightly equipped Norwegian army proved no match for the combined German air, sea and troop assault. The southern and central regions of the country were quickly overrun. Within days the main coastal towns were seized. King Håkon of Norway fled Oslo and took refuge in Britain. With the aid of Allied troops, the most northerly parts of the country hung on for a few months but eventually fell under Nazi control.

Adolf Hitler appointed Joseph Terboven as *Reichskommissar* in charge of running the country. However, as civil unrest grew, a state of emergency was declared. In February 1942 Vidkun Quisling of the fascist Nasjonal Samling Party (the only legal political party under occupation) was appointed by the Nazis as a puppet prime minister. This is the origin of the term 'quisling', meaning a collaborator, a traitor who aids an occupying enemy force. He set about Nazifying the country, forming a state police force modelled on the Gestapo (known as the 'Stapo'), and tried to exert strict control over key aspects of life. There was limited support for him and his party among the population.

The wartime regime was oppressive, although not as harsh as in some other occupied countries. Nevertheless, radios were confiscated and movement restricted. Labour camps were set up and men sent to them. Many in the church, universities, schools and trade unions protested and refused to co-operate. Some resigned from their jobs, including more than twelve thousand teachers, who rejected Quisling's order to join the Nazi Teachers' Union. A thousand were arrested and five hundred sent north by ship to do hard labour at ports inside the Arctic Circle. Simply giving in would have earned them a ticket home. But few did, eventually forcing Quisling to back down. Victorious, the teachers returned home to a heroes' welcome.

Resistance to occupation took many forms, from simple unifying acts of defiance, like wearing lapel pins, to obstruction and direct action. Underground news-papers emerged, numbering about three hundred at their peak. The Germans traced and destroyed many printing presses, arresting and imprisoning those caught.

The MILORG (Military Organization) was formed in 1941 under the control of the High Command in London. Many thousands took part and formed clandestine groups throughout Norway. Intelligence and communication networks grew, as did the Home Front, with men and women forging documents and operating hazardous escape routes to neutral Sweden.

There were many acts of sabotage and commando raids, including the attack on the heavy water Norsk Hydro plant at Vemork (Germany's attempt to make an atomic bomb), made famous in a 1965 Hollywood film and recently re-told in detail by Ray Mears in his book *The Real Heroes of Telemark*.

Life was fraught with danger for those desperate to fight back. Idle chatter, a whisper overheard, a slip of the tongue could all end in tragedy. The destruction of the village of Telavåg, as mentioned in this book, is just one example. A tip-off brought the Gestapo and SS to a small farm near to the village west of Bergen where two agents were hiding out in a barn. In the attack that followed, two Gestapo officers were disarmed and killed by the agents. Retribution was swift. The entire village was razed to the ground and the inhabitants imprisoned. Rising smoke could be seen for miles.

In October 1942 the Gestapo and Stapo attempted to purge the northern part of the country of Resistance fighters. Hundreds were arrested. A number of MILORG leaders were subsequently executed, as were some civilians.

6 June 1944 saw the start of Operation Overlord, the Allied invasion of the Normandy beaches and the beginning of the end of the war. By October the Russians had crossed the Norwegian border far to the north and the Germans were forced to retreat. The Resistance played a vital role in these final months too, with a campaign of railway sabotage effectively disrupting troop movements. The German army surrendered on 7 May 1945. Vidkun Quisling was subsequently arrested and shot, along with a number of other high-ranking traitors. Many collaborators were punished, as happened in many occupied countries after liberation.

Although *Resistance* is a work of fiction and key locations (Ulfhus and Ork) have been created for the purpose of telling this story, inspiration was derived from many real events. The so-called Shetland Bus existed and ran the Nazi gauntlet, with many brave Norwegian fishermen risking all to transport agents and supplies to and from the Shetland Islands under the cover of winter's darkness. Some never made it home. Eventually the slow fishing boats were replaced by much faster naval submarine chasers, the MTBs (Motor Torpedo Boats).

The forerunner of the SAS, the SOE (Special Operations Executive), played an important role in training agents – men and women from both Britain and the occupied countries, including Norway. Many ingenious devices were developed during the war to aid the Resistance effort. As well as radio transmitters, tiny motorcycles, exploding rats and explosives disguised as lumps of coal, there were pocket incendiaries, time pencils and Imber switches. Undoubtedly many of these tools were used, albeit with varying degrees of success. Platinum pills were developed too, for exactly the purpose described in this story – to disable U-boats by striking at their most vulnerable point, their banks of accumulators.